"THE FIRE ESCAPE IS PERFECTLY STURDY, SEE? IT'S HOLDING US BOTH UP JUST FINE."

Savannah lowered her gaze to the platform just for a second before latching back on to his stare.

"You still shouldn't tempt fate."

Her laugh coasted past his cheek on little more than a breathy sigh. "In case you haven't noticed, I'm not really a play-it-safe kind of girl. I'm fearless, remember? I think fate shouldn't tempt me."

Oh, to hell with fate. Cole was going to tempt her, long and hard and right goddamn now.

He slanted his mouth over hers, kissing her in one seamless stroke. Her lips were so much softer than he'd expected, so sweet and seductive at the same time that they were almost like a puzzle he was dying to figure out. Cole uncurled his fingers from their grip at Savannah's shoulder, sliding his palm under the curve of her jaw to cup her chin. Holding her in place, he coaxed her mouth open with a brush of his tongue. But rather than submissively giving in to the kiss, she returned every movement, sweeping her tongue from the hot confines of her own mouth to boldly kiss him back.

FEARLESS

KIMBERLY KINCAID

ZEBRA BOOKS
KENSINGTON PUBLISHING CORP.
http://www.kensingtonbooks.com

ZEBRA BOOKS are published by

Kensington Publishing Corp.
119 West 40th Street
New York, NY 10018

All Kensington titles, imprints and distributed lines are available at special quantity discounts for bulk purchases for sales promotion, premiums, fund-raising, educational or institutional use.

Special book excerpts or customized printings can also be created to fit specific needs. For details, write or phone the office of the Kensington Sales Manager. Attn.: Sales Department. Kensington Publishing Corp., 119 West 40th Street, New York, NY 10018. Phone: 1-800-221-2647.

Zebra and the Z logo Reg. U.S. Pat. & TM Off.

First Printing: August 2016
ISBN-13: 978-1-4201-3775-0
ISBN-10: 1-4201-3775-1

eISBN-13: 978-1-4201-3776-7
eISBN-10: 1-4201-3776-X

10 9 8 7 6 5 4 3 2 1

Printed in the United States of America

To Robin Covington and Avery Flynn,
who have advanced degrees in talking me
off the book ledge
and get my crazy affinity for bunker pants.
There are no finer best friends than you.

ACKNOWLEDGMENTS

I am always astounded by the willingness of others when I utter the words, "So I'm writing this book and I was wondering if you'd help." The following people went above and beyond (and above again, in some cases), and I am so incredibly grateful.

To the men in Atlanta Fire Department's Squad Four—Captain Williams, Lieutenant Nour, Clarke, Jason, Jordan, and Peter—this book just never would've happened without y'all showing me how it's done. Thank you for not laughing (too hard) when I did the obstacle course that I borrowed for this book. To Nicole Carter, for helping me keep my medical facts real, I am so thankful. Any mistakes or liberties taken are mine, but all the expertise belongs to you. To retired firefighter and wicked-awesome guy, Chris Kulak, for lending me your duckling story. I hope I did it justice. (No ducks were harmed in the writing of this novel. I promise!)

To the romance writing community that is full to the brim with amazing, talented, funny-as-hell people, I could never name you all (but you know I'm going to try). Alyssa Alexander, Tracy Brogan, Jennifer McQuiston, Liliana Hart, Bella Andre, Cristin Harber, Pamela Clare, Sara Humphreys, Kate Angell, Carly Phillips, Jill Shalvis, Susan Donovan—you have all touched my writing career with your encouragement and your kindness and your blurbs. Grateful doesn't even begin to cover it.

To Robin Covington and Avery Flynn, thank you for keeping me sane with your never-ending patience, your plot panda sessions, and your unfailing ability to make me laugh when I need it most.

To Reader Girl, Smarty Pants, and Tiny Dancer, I love you bunches. To Mr. K., thank you for hearing me, getting me, and loving me. I do, however, love you more (heh).

And lastly, to every single one of you holding this story in your hands, thank you from the deepest part of my heart. I have the best job in the universe, but I could not write a single word without you wanting to read. I am honored and thrilled to share this book with you.

Chapter One

Cole Everett stared at the string of bright orange flames reaching up from the six-burner cooktop with a whole lot of business as usual filling his chest. Okay, so at least there was an actual fire at this fire call—unlike the last three he and the guys from Station Eight had responded to. But a kitchen flare-up in a hotel restaurant was hardly the high-rise fire they'd expected when they'd hauled balls out of the station, even if the flames *had* spread halfway up a small stretch of the grease-streaked wall behind the cooktop.

Cole blew out a steady exhale, aiming a look at his best friend and fellow firefighter, Alex Donovan. "You want to hit it or should I?"

Donovan dropped a calm, cool, and let-me-see-here glance to the commercial-grade fire extinguisher sitting between their booted feet on the kitchen tiles. "Be my guest, big shot."

A cocky grin bracketed his buddy's mouth, but Cole knew better than to metaphorically whip out his dick for a friendly game of I Can Piss Farther Than You. Screwing with Alex was like stepping in quicksand. The more Cole quipped back, the deeper they both sank, and ninety-nine times out of a hundred, keeping the peace by keeping his cakehole shut was so much easier than the alternative. Plus, knowing how much a non-response would hack Donovan off was worth the price of admission. He'd deal with the good-natured ration of shit the guy was trying to dish up later. Right now, they had a fire to put out. Albeit a small one.

Instead of giving Donovan the friendly *oh fuck you* the guy damn well deserved, Cole turned to Station Eight's rookie, Mike Jones, who stood behind him in the narrow aisle of the galley kitchen. "Okay, Jonesey. Knock this one out so we can go back to the house for lunch, would you? I'm starving."

"Copy that," Jones said, keeping his usual quiet efficiency as he reached down for the fire extinguisher. Pulling the pin and dropping it to the floor with a metallic *clink*, he focused his blue-eyed stare on the cooktop, dispatching the flames in a few minutes' worth of decisive movements. A healthy dose of airborne chemicals stung Cole's nose and lungs from the spot where he stood near the rookie, but it was better than the smoke beginning to clog the kitchen around them. Small-time fires still burned, and putting out the flames was the best part of the job.

Even if Cole had barely broken a sweat over this one.

"All right." He took a step back, shifting his weight from one foot to the other and swaying back and forth so the motion alarm on his pass device wouldn't let out an ear-shredding screech. After delivering an all-is-well update over the radio strapped to the shoulder of his turnout gear, Cole opened his mouth to remind Jones of the standard protocol for making sure the fire stayed out—after all, flare-ups could be a tricky bitch, especially with grease fires—but the guy was two steps ahead of him.

"Someone wants to impress the rest of the class," Donovan said, raising a blond eyebrow to the brim of his helmet as he stepped back to watch Jones secure the scene.

But Cole just laughed. "Right. Because you were a total slack-ass as a rookie." Even now, eight years removed from Fairview's fire academy, Alex jumped into pretty much everything he did with both boots first and all of his questions on the flip side.

Hell if that didn't make the two of them polar freaking opposites in terms of how they grabbed their ambition. But it also made them a kickass team, and had since they'd been recruits at the academy themselves. The only thing Cole knew he could rely on more than a good, solid game plan was that Donovan—or any man at Station Eight, on engine *or* squad—would always have his back.

Even if, for the last year straight, Cole's biggest career wish had been to transition from engine to squad, no matter what it took.

Alex's less than polite snort echoed through the galley of the smoke-hazed kitchen. "You're a good one to talk about ambition, you goddamn overachiever," he said, and hell, Cole should've known better than to think Donovan would let the conversation he'd overheard this morning between him and Lieutenant Crews ride.

"You really want to do this now?" Cole asked, keeping his easygoing smile in place as they both kicked their boots into motion to exit the kitchen.

The return smirk tugging at the corners of Alex's lips marked his intentions loud and clear. "In a word? Fuck yes."

"That's actually two words," Cole pointed out, although he knew the distraction strategy wouldn't save him from the raft of crap Donovan had clearly been holding at bay.

"It's cute that you think you're going to get out of this on a technicality. But no chance in hell am I going to treat you all special once you move over to squad."

Cole metered his breathing to match the precision of his footsteps. *Focus.* "Nobody said anything about me going anywhere."

Alex's snort returned with renewed intensity. "You've had a hard-on for a promotion to squad for the last year, easy, Everett. You've busted your balls on a metric ton of extra training, and your name is headlining the short list. Crews comes to tell you that not only is a spot *finally* opening up—at your home station, no less—but that Cap wants to see you as soon as he gets back from that redistricting meeting at the chief's office, too? Yeah, man. I'm going to be 'doing this'"—Alex paused to sketch air quotes around the words with his gloved fingers and a pop of laughter—"until you come out of Captain Westin's office and confirm that as usual, I'm right, all that ruler-straight planning of yours has finally paid dividends, and your elitist ass is moving to squad."

Despite the highly ingrained superstitious streak that Cole shared with pretty much every other firefighter on the planet, he cracked a grin. "There could be fifty different things Cap might want to talk to me about," he said, but damn it, hope still flared in his chest.

"Uh-huh. And forty-nine of them qualify as bullshit." Alex reached out to palm the handle to the door leading from the restaurant back to the sunbaked pavement where Engine Eight stood in all its bright red, lights-flashing glory. "Squad's been running light ever since Jensen got promoted to lieutenant and moved to Station Twenty-Six last month, and with the redistricting that went through four months ago, they're running way too many calls not to replace him permanently."

"Yeah," Cole said, although his agreement was short-lived. "But I don't exactly have a stunt double. Moving me to squad would leave us down a man on engine."

Alex, being Alex, refused to be swayed. "Funny thing about firefighters is they're always making more. The academy just spit out a fresh batch of candidates last week. And even though Jonesey's still technically at the six-month mark, he's catching his stride. Shit, he's barely a rookie anymore, and anyway, it's not as if Eight has never had two candidates at once."

No arguing the truth there. Hell, he and Alex were walking, talking proof. But still, Cole's ironclad calm stood its ground against the yes-yes-yes trying to build in his gut. "Okay, but just because there's a spot opening up on squad doesn't mean I'm going to be the man to get it."

For as much as Alex joked, squad *was* elite. While fire and rescue was their primary function, Cole couldn't deny that the hazmat response, the water rescue, and the specialized calls like building collapses that squad also handled gave him a giant fucking hard-on. But half the FFD had the same career boner. Plenty of guys were gunning for a chance to prove their mettle on squad, and Cole had already been passed over once for a spot at another house. Granted, the firefighter who'd ended up landing the position instead had more seniority and training at the time, but being passed by had only made Cole work his strategy even harder.

He didn't just want to be a firefighter. Hell, he didn't even want to be elite. He needed to be the best, and that meant landing a spot on the rescue squad.

After all, if there was one thing his old man had taught him decades ago, it was how to prove the hell out of his worth.

"I don't know," Alex said, his cocky tone going uncharacteristically soft as his words yanked Cole back to the here and now of Oak Street. "Call me crazy, but I think your number's up, dude. I've got a really good feeling about this one."

Cole barked out a laugh. He might usually take the easy-does-it route, but this was too good to pass up. "A *feeling*? Seriously, Teflon. Does Zoe keep your nuts in her purse?"

A lightning-fast smile flickered across Alex's face at the mention of his girlfriend's name. Jesus, after only five months, the guy had it so bad, Cole couldn't even enjoy mocking him. Even if Donovan was talking crooked out of his ass right now.

"First of all"—Alex tugged open the side compartment door on Engine Eight, swinging his Halligan bar inside with a metallic *clunk*—"that's pretty rich coming from a guy who's as unlaid as a pile of goddamn bricks. Christ, Everett. The last time you had sex, there was snow on the ground."

Ouch. "I have . . ." Cole counted backward, his argument dying in his throat. When the hell had August rolled around?

"Not. Sorry, brother, but doing the no-pants dance with your hand doesn't count," Donovan said over a smirk. He tossed Cole a bottle of water from one of the storage coolers before swooping in for the kill. "And secondly, just because my gut feeling can't be neatly quantified by one of your elaborate Spock strategies doesn't mean it's not spot-on. I'm telling you. Something major is going down at Eight, and it's going down today."

"Maybe." Cole turned his glance about fifty yards up the street, where it landed on the guys from Station Eight's rescue squad. They *had* been running light ever since Jensen's promotion, with only four regular guys on C-shift and a floater here and there on weekends when they tended to go on more calls. Calls that had gone to nearly time and a half since the city had widened Station Eight's response district last month.

Ah, screw it. For all their smack talk, it wasn't as if Donovan didn't know the score, and all of Cole's planning and preparation did have him logically poised to get the next available placement on squad.

"I just want the spot, you know?" His throat locked over the massive understatement, and he uncapped his water for a long swallow. "Guess I don't want to jinx it."

"I get it," Alex said, his tone backing up the sentiment for just a second before he added, "But it's kind of hard to jinx a sure thing. Just don't forget us common folk over on engine when you transfer over to squad, all fancy and shit."

"Yeah, yeah." Cole opened his mouth to deliver a decidedly *un*-fancy directive when their lieutenant cleared his throat from behind them.

"You two done gossiping over here?" Crews asked, the barely-there lift of his brows the only thing keeping his expression out of dead neutral. For a guy who was six-two and 230 pounds even before he slung on his turnout gear, the man's stealth was actually pretty frightening.

"Yes, sir. As soon as Everett braids my hair, we'll be all set."

Cole shifted his SCBA tank from his shoulders, fixing Alex with a deadpan stare. "Don't be an asshole, Donovan. It's your turn to braid my hair."

Crews shook his head, but hiding the smile hinting at the corners of his mouth was pretty much impossible. "Jesus Christ. It's like kiddie hour over here. You're worse than my daughters. What are you guys, twelve?"

"Great timing, Jonesey," Alex said, tipping his chin as the rookie made his way over to the engine and unstrapped his helmet. "Crews was just talking about you."

Jones grabbed a bottle of water, pouring half of it over his blond head before pausing to down the rest. "We can't all be geriatric like you, Donovan."

"Careful, Jones." Crews wagged one gloved finger at the rookie. "I've got seven years on Teflon, here, and I have no problem taking each and every one of them out on you for the rest of this shift."

"With respect, sir, you'd have to catch me first. And if there's one thing you've taught me, it's how to be slicker than owl snot."

"Yeah, yeah," the lieutenant grumbled, although a smile

threaded through his words. "Get your ass on the rig before I decide I want the workout."

Cole fought the bubble of laughter rising in his chest and lost. But it took a shitload more than a little smack talk to rattle Crews, or any of them, really. Thin-skinned fire-fighters lasted less than ten seconds, and that was before anything even caught on fire.

"By the way," Donovan said, delivering a firm but friendly nudge to Jones's shoulder as they turned toward the engine, "I just turned thirty, dude. I'm in my fucking prime. Once you finish puberty, I'll tell you all about it."

Jones's smile was a flash of white teeth against his soot-smudged face. "Whatever you say, Father Time. Whatever you say."

They all finished the trip to their respective spots in the engine, with Alex and Jonesey climbing into the back step and Crews storing his coat and helmet before sinking into the officer's seat in the front of the vehicle. Cole slid behind the wheel. He'd been driving Engine Eight more often than not for the last year, but man, the operator's spot never got old. He'd miss it when his strategy finally panned out and he moved to squad. Whenever that happened to be.

Damn, he wanted it to be today.

Anticipation swirled with hope to form a potent one-two punch in his veins. Considering how exclusive rescue squads were, Cole had come to terms with the fact that he'd almost certainly have to leave Station Eight in order to be on one. Spots were few and far between across the board, and with an abundance of qualified guys looking to fill them, being choosy about location wasn't really on the options menu. Of all the things he'd had to gut through in the last two years' worth of studying and planning and training, leaving the station he'd called home for the last eight years had been the only thing to make Cole hesitate. The firefighters and paramedics at Eight weren't just his coworkers. Hell, they weren't even *just* his friends.

Every single person who punched the clock at Station Eight was his family. They had his back, all the time, every time.

Which was more than Cole could say about the people he was actually related to.

He stiffened against the well-worn operator's seat, his knuckles going tight over the wheel, and he battened down to extinguish the uncharacteristic spark of emotion pulsing through his rib cage. All this back-and-forth about the open spot on squad was turning his focus into tapioca. Searching for the control he normally wore like his favorite weather-beaten bomber jacket, Cole ordered the facts in his mind.

Crews had made it clear that a position was opening up on squad, and he'd been equally crystal about Captain Westin wanting a one-on-one as soon as he got back from his trip to chief's office. Westin might keep a keen eye on every man at Eight, but like the rest of them, he wasn't exactly an air-your-feelings kind of guy. Every meeting had a purpose. Private meetings all the more. And despite giving it his very best effort, Cole couldn't come up with a single reason Cap would ask for a sit-down with him, save one.

Holy shit. After eight years as a firefighter and over a year of actively training for the rescue squad, Cole was going to get promoted.

Today.

His excitement burst out by way of a smile as he finessed Engine Eight into the far right side of the engine bay. A quick visual tour of the two-story concrete and cinder-block space revealed Captain Westin's city-issued Suburban sitting quietly in its designated spot, and Cole swung a glance at Crews from across the cab of the engine with his pulse hammering.

"Unless you need me to help off-load the rig, I'm going

to go see Cap, as requested." He hung the words between them like a question—it might be his last day on engine, but Crews was still his lieutenant. Scrimping on the respect that went with that definitely wasn't on Cole's agenda, squad or no squad.

Crews acquiesced with a tight nod. "Copy that," he said, waiting for Donovan and Jones to jump down from the back step and start moving through the engine bay before he tacked on, "Hey, Everett?"

"Yeah?" Cole paused, but God, Crews's expression was a wall of stone.

"Take your time."

Cole took a few seconds to let the surprise from the lieutenant's comment bounce through him before he followed the guy's lead and clambered down from his seat in the engine. For a second, he thought about a quick trip to the locker room to trade his sweat-damp T-shirt and bunker pants for something decidedly less worked in, but screw it. Cap might run a tight house, but they were hardly a decorous bunch. He settled for tugging a hand through his hair to straighten what he could and making sure his FFD T-shirt was tucked in before hitting the hallway leading into the station.

The din of voices and various kitchen sounds filtered in from the main room at the heart of the house, but Cole continued down the stretch of gray linoleum he'd mopped just this morning. Aiming his boots into a hard left, he found himself at the end of what everyone at Station Eight referred to as the hall of pictures. Frame after frame of photos and commendations lined the walls on either side, so many that the painted black picture frames were stacked four, sometimes five high. They spanned the two decades that Station Eight had operated from this building, the same two decades that Captain Westin had been at the helm, and a shiver ghosted down Cole's spine as his boots echoed over the floor.

Practice drills. Company barbecues. Active fires. Flash flood rescues. The group shot of everyone in the house slung arm in arm that had been taken not even two months ago in front of the house. The men he worked with every shift, who he knew without question would always have his six.

He was so goddamn grateful not to be leaving this place.

Cole placed a no-nonsense knock on the door at the end of the hallway, sliding a deep inhale all the way into his lungs as Captain Westin waved him in through the glass panel set in the wooden frame.

"Come on in, Everett. Go ahead and close the door."

Cole's pulse joined forces with his breath in a game of tag-team body betrayal at Westin's non-question, but he didn't hesitate to step over the threshold and pull the door shut. Westin waited until Cole had planted his boots on the floor tiles across from his desk before removing his reading glasses to pin Cole with a steely bronze stare.

"I'm sure by now Crews has told you we've been approved by the city to add a permanent position to Squad Eight." Westin delivered the words with the same straightforward tone he used on everything from fire drills to five-alarm blazes, and Cole tried his damndest to return the favor as he answered.

"Yes sir."

"And am I correct to assume that per your active application on the city database, you're still interested in transitioning from engine to squad?"

Adrenaline whisked through Cole's bloodstream in a hot burst. "Yes sir."

"Good," Westin said, the slightest smile edging up at the corners of his mouth before his expression smoothed back to business as usual. "Then let's not dance around the bullshit just so we can call it a party, shall we? I've spoken with Lieutenant Osborne about the position we have open-ing up here at Eight, and we both agree you'd be a good fit."

Cole barely managed to get his "thank you" past all the *holy shit* barging through his chest. Dennis Osborne had been a firefighter for almost as long as Captain Westin, with nearly a decade under his belt as a lieutenant on squad. Getting the salty old man's stamp of approval as rescue squad material was like winning the lottery. Only with steeper odds.

"Don't thank me yet." Westin's lifted blond-gray brows sent a sheen of moisture over Cole's palms, but he'd seen enough guys come and go on both engine and squad to know the drill.

"I understand that making the move to squad will put me back at square one with seniority, Cap." Christ, if anyone could haze a rookie, it was Oz. And Cole's eight years on engine wouldn't count for squat in the face of the eight seconds he currently had on squad. Still . . . "I know I'll have to prove myself."

Westin's rumble of laughter arrived with a three-to-one ratio of irony to humor. "That you will. In more ways than one."

"I'm sorry." Worry peppered Cole's belly full of holes. "I don't follow."

"As much as I'd like to offer you the spot free and clear, Everett, I can't. Not yet, anyway."

Cole's lungs burned for air, and he scraped together every last ounce of his waning calm as he managed a hoarse "Sir?"

Westin gestured to the inches-high stacks of paperwork covering the desk in front of him. "This redistricting might be what prompted the city to approve another permanent spot on squad, but moving you into it—even if you are the best candidate for the job—will leave me down a man on engine. At the end of the day, robbing Peter to pay Paul still has me coming up short. Fortunately, after a bit of convincing, the chief was willing to help us out in that regard."

Just like that, Cole's shock tolerance redlined. "*That's* why you were at the chief's office all morning? To figure out how to get me on squad?"

"Among other reasons, yes." Westin paused, so fast that Cole might've missed it if he hadn't been trained to notice every last detail of his surroundings. "Chief Williams and I also met with Brennan regarding the latest class of recruits who just graduated from the academy."

Cole's head snapped up, but the news allowed him a much-needed exhale. Nick Brennan was not only one of Cole's best friends, but he'd also been a firefighter at Station Eight until a devastating injury had eventually sent his career path back to the academy as an instructor.

"So we're getting a new candidate on engine."

"While I'd prefer to train one candidate at a time, the city's redistricting of our call jurisdiction has clearly provided us with a set of circumstances that defies normal protocol. In plain English, yes. Station Eight is getting a new candidate on engine."

Hope did a slow rebuild in Cole's gut. "To replace me," he clarified.

"To fill your spot, Everett." A hint of humor crinkled the edges of Westin's otherwise by-the-book stare. "Jones will still technically be a candidate until he passes his one-year review, but he's come along nicely over the past six months under Crews's guidance. Since that mentorship isn't broken, I'm not inclined to fix it. But the situation does leave me with another candidate who needs six weeks of orientation training."

Realization hit Cole with all the subtlety of a cartoon anvil to the head. "And you want me to do it before I transition to squad."

Under normal circumstances, the commanding officer for either engine or squad was directly responsible for training his candidate while other firefighters offered assistance as requested. But it was hard enough to keep tabs on one rookie when shit went pear-shaped, let alone two. Crews was a great firefighter—not to mention a tough son of a bitch—but he was only one man. Having three veteran firefighters on engine to balance out the two candidates made sense, at least until the new guy wasn't quite so wet behind the ears.

Westin exhaled, his expression softening by just a hair as he steepled his fingers over his desk and fastened Cole with a stare. "I truly believe you're the best man for this spot on squad, Everett, and I know you want it."

Cole gave a deferential nod, not wanting to interrupt fully but also not wanting to let the sentiment go by without acknowledgment.

The captain continued. "That said, I can't leave engine running light with two rookies just to get you there. Jones is close, and if Crews buckles down on his training, in another six weeks, he'll be all but good to go. Overseeing a new candidate through the orientation period would be an excellent use of the leadership skills you're going to need on squad. The situation isn't ideal. But it *is* the only situation we've got that can get you onto squad and keep this house right. Are you on board?"

Cole didn't even think twice. "I'm not going to deny that I want the spot, Cap, because I really do. But we're supposed to have each other's backs, no matter what. Upending engine for the sake of promoting me to squad isn't right."

He tugged a hand through his hair, letting his palm rest on the back of his neck for a brief second before returning to attention. Okay, so he'd never led a rookie through his first six weeks, but Westin wasn't wrong. Not only was it the decent thing to do for the guys on engine, but it would help Cole prove his worth in front of guys like Oz, who would surely be watching with a keen eye. The training wouldn't be a cakewalk—adjusting to the adrenaline-drenched rigors of fighting fires and the grueling schedule of working in-house were hell on a guy's body and his nerves. Their candidate would have growing pains, no doubt, and Cole would have to guide him through each one. But it was only six weeks. Cole could do this. He *would* do this.

The promotion he'd wanted since he'd been a candidate himself depended on it.

"If you need me to mentor a new candidate through his orientation before I transition to squad, of course I'll do it," Cole said.

Captain Westin let out a rare smile. "Excellent. There is just one more thing you should know—" His gaze caught on something over Cole's shoulder, cutting the response short and coloring his expression with an emotion Cole couldn't quite place. "Well. I suppose there's no time like the present."

Cap lifted his hand in a tight *come in* motion, and Cole turned toward the door. Confusion threaded together with a long, hot pulse of *oh hell yeah* in Cole's veins at the sight of the brunette opening the door and walking her mile-long legs over the threshold. With the brown-and-turquoise cowboy boots on her feet, she had to be just shy of six feet tall. A healthy dusting of freckles dotted her sun-kissed face, her tawny skin the perfect complement for her milk chocolate stare and her darkly fringed lashes. Even in her plain white T-shirt, jeans, and the girl-next-door ponytail cascading down from the back of her head, she was a fucking knockout and a half.

Never mind that Cole had no clue who she was or what she was doing there.

"Sorry to interrupt, Captain," the brunette said, a Southern drawl hugging the words and tripping Cole's switch one notch farther. Even though her apology was sincere, she looked Westin boldly in the eye as she walked right up to his desk to deliver it, her confidence practically busting out of her. "Lieutenant Crews said I should come on back."

"You're not interrupting, Ms. Nelson. In fact, you've got great timing. Cole Everett, meet Savannah Nelson."

"Ms. Nelson," Cole said, and whoa. She packed a helluva handshake for someone so slender.

"Nice to meet you." Savannah let go of his palm and turned back toward Westin, all self-assurance. "Thanks for asking me to come meet everyone during today's shift, Captain. I appreciate the opportunity for a little face time before things get official on Monday."

"Of course." Westin stood, smoothing a hand over his faultlessly ironed uniform shirt. "I'll go round up the rest of the house for introductions. If you've got any immediate questions you need answered before your first shift, you can go ahead and ask Everett now. You two should probably get acquainted anyway."

Realization slammed into Cole like a two-ton wrecking ball, but no way. No fucking way. This couldn't be right. While one of C-shift's two paramedics was a woman, and a pretty tough one at that, the difference in job description wasn't even apples to oranges—it was more like apples to bacon.

Station Eight had never had a female candidate on engine. Hell, female firefighters were so few and far between citywide that they'd never even had a female firefighter fill in for a shift. And now Cole's livelihood depended on making sure their very first one was not only well-trained but well-acclimated to a job that nearly broke both the will and the backs of men twice her size?

As if Cole had spoken the question out loud, Captain Westin split his stare between him and Savannah, pausing for just a breath before hammering the answer all the way home.

"Firefighter Everett will be in charge of your orientation and training for the next six weeks, and you will be glued to his hip as such. Welcome to Station Eight, Ms. Nelson. Let's make a firefighter out of you."

Chapter Two

Savannah inhaled as far as her lungs would allow and channeled all her effort into keeping her pulse from pitching a fit in her veins. Rocking back on the heels of her lucky Tony Lamas, she silently repeated the mantra that had gotten her through her year at the academy along with the twenty-five that had come before it.

Nerves of steel, girl. Be tough.

Not exactly the easiest thing going since the guy standing barely two feet to her right—who was allegedly her lifeline to the job she'd busted her butt to finally land— was eyeballing her as if she had something horrifically contagious.

Savannah breathed out, refusing to lower her gaze. Okay, so her social graces were questionable even in the best of situations, but they were already halfway to awkward. Riding out the silence wasn't going to make things worse. Plus, it gave her a minute to size up the man who'd be in charge of her training for the next six weeks.

Everett topped her by about two inches, which put him at a good six-one. His sandy-brown hair was just tousled enough to suggest he'd been tugging at it recently, and the trepidation in his olive-green eyes corroborated the theory.

The T-shirt/turnout gear combo outlining his frame looked freshly used but not filthy, and okay, that was probably a decent sign. But between the hard set of his otherwise smooth jaw and the leanly corded arms knotted over his chest, he might as well have been advertising his unhappiness with a fifty-foot billboard.

Despite Captain Westin's polite professionalism when they'd met earlier in the chief's office, Savannah had known better than to think everyone at Station Eight would be doing back handsprings at the idea of welcoming a female candidate to engine. She had been one of only three women in her class of over fifty recruits, one of whom had washed out at the nine-week mark, and Captain Westin had admitted she'd be the first one ever at Eight. All three of Savannah's older brothers had warned her she'd likely have a hell of a row to hoe, no matter where she ended up.

She'd been quick to remind them that their Texas-tough father, Battalion Chief Duke Nelson, had taught her every single thing he'd taught *them* when they trained to be firefighters, the same way his daddy had taught him a generation before that. Every single branch on the Nelson family tree was occupied by a firefighter, to the point that calling the job a legacy was the world's most massive understatement. True, she was the only female blood-born Nelson in a sea of uncles, cousins, and brothers. But that had never bothered Savannah a whit.

No chance in hell was she going to do anything other than make her family proud by fulfilling the legacy she'd always wanted, no matter how much this Everett guy tried to stare her down.

Nerves of steel. Nerves of steel. Nerves of . . .

"So how come Lieutenant Crews isn't training me?"

Savannah trapped her tongue between her teeth two seconds too late. She hadn't meant to be so brash right out of the gate, but when it came to fight or flight, her default setting was firmly stuck on duking its way out of sticky situations.

Even if that meant getting her into even hotter water.

"I'm sorry?" Everett asked, his eyes narrowing although his expression didn't budge. But she couldn't un-ask the question, and backing down now would only make her look weak.

Savannah lifted one shoulder in a brief shrug. "That *is* the way training works, isn't it? Commanding officer is in charge of the candidate."

"Under normal circumstances, yes."

Even though Everett's tone was completely neutral, her jitters formed an indignant tangle in her belly. "So my circumstances are *unusual*?"

One light brown brow arched upward. "Clearly."

Savannah stared, unable to rein in her shock or her irritation. "Because I have breasts?"

"Because you're not Station Eight's only candidate."

The reply tagged her in the sternum like a sucker punch, but she managed to work up a soft *oh* in response. "Captain Westin didn't mention anybody else from my class being placed here at Eight."

"That's because our current candidate came up six months ago, in the class before yours. Lieutenant Crews is going to finish his training while I handle yours for the next six weeks," Everett said, lowering his chin to meet her gaze head-on. "Which brings us to our first lesson."

"And that is . . . ?"

"Assumptions are as dangerous as guesswork around here. If you want to know something, ask. And after you ask, make it a point to remember what you learned."

Savannah's cheeks flamed. "I just graduated from the academy at the top of my class. I promise I'm not an idiot."

She'd meant the words as a reassurance, but the muscle

twitching in the strong angle of Everett's jaw signaled that she'd missed her mark.

He said, "I'll lead by example, since it seems you're still not sure how this works. How did you know that?"

Her confusion beat out the unease in her chest, but only by a millimeter. "How did I know what?"

"That the lieutenant usually trains a candidate. That's one of those things you usually learn through experience. Most rookies don't know it before they start. So I'm curious as to how you did," he said, his arms unfolding from their bullet-proof knot over the front of his chest. He hooked his thumbs beneath the thick line of his suspenders, and Jesus, Mary, and all the saints, how was she just noticing the way his T-shirt hugged both his shoulders *and* his biceps?

"Uh," she grunted, and between the unexpected streak of heat sparking between her thighs and the new-job jitters free-flowing through her veins, the truth toppled past her lips without thought. "My older brothers were all trained as firefighters, two back in Texas and one here in Fairview, so they gave me the inside track on what to expect."

"You have a brother in the FFD?"

Everett's brows winged upward at the same time Savannah's gut took a southerly slide, but she'd spilled the intel. Now she had no choice but to back it up.

No matter how much she wanted to button her lip.

"Not anymore. He moved from Station Nineteen to the arson investigation unit about six months ago." Savannah squared her shoulders, ignoring Everett's biceps in favor of looking him in the eye. She had a boyfriend, for Pete's sake! So what if things had been more ho-hum than hot and heavy between them lately. Ogling Everett—no matter how sexy the bulk-to-definition ratio of his upper arms looked—was still unacceptable. He was in charge of her training. Her job. Her *everything*. Plus, if the look on his face right now was any indication, he still hadn't gotten over his obvious disdain for her.

And if she didn't want to be treated differently just because she had lady bits, then she damn well needed to keep those parts of her anatomy in check.

"Brad Nelson is your brother."

The recognition lighting Everett's features made Savannah's belly clench. Damn it, she'd thought she'd be safe now that Brad wasn't technically in-house at Nineteen anymore. She should've known that after the five years he'd spent in the FFD, firefighters from other houses would probably at least recognize his name.

"Yes sir." She straightened into the words without elaborating. The edges of Everett's mouth twitched with the suggestion of a smile, and how about that. He had settings other than *serious* and *completely serious*.

"I appreciate the sentiment," he said, although the hint of amusement that had just played on his lips was already gone. "But I'm not your boss, and I definitely don't outrank you. Everett is fine."

Savannah's slow nod accompanied the steady beat of *well duh* running through her brain. Talk about a rookie mistake. She'd been raised on the pecking order in a firehouse, having watched her father earn his way up the ranks, step by step. Not that she was about to give that little nugget any airtime, but still. "Copy that."

"And there's lesson number two. Your brother's a good firefighter, but your pedigree and your history at the academy don't mean a thing now that you're over the threshold here at Eight. If you know what's good for you, you'll think twice about trotting them out."

Savannah knew—she *knew*—that she should make her mouth form the words "copy that" again so they could drop the subject and move the hell on. After all, she'd meant to swerve around the topic of her family history for this very reason. But come on. Her *pedigree*?

Nope. No way was she leaving that alone.

"I'm not a show puppy," she said, her spine snapping up to its full height.

But Everett's expression simply idled in neutral, his dark green stare cool enough to irritate her even further. "And I didn't call you one. All I'm saying is that if you want the firefighters who work here to respect you, the only way you're going to make that happen is to earn it."

Wait . . . "Are you trying to intimidate me?"

"Not at all. But I'm here to train your ass, not kiss it." He stepped toward her, close enough for her to see the faint smudge of soot on his cheek and feel the warmth of his exhale as he added, "So let me make this perfectly clear. If you want to become a good firefighter, I promise I'll get you there. But you're going to have to work for it, and I do mean every step of the way. If you're not willing to do that, don't even walk through the door on Monday. Are we straight?"

Savannah didn't even hesitate to counter his forward motion with one of her own, cutting the already slight space between them in half. "As an arrow, Everett. But as long as we're making things clear, let me say this. I don't mind hard work, but by the time our six weeks are up, I plan to be a hell of a lot better than just good. In fact, I fully intend to blow your damn mind. So you'd better make sure that's in your plans, too."

Savannah curled her car keys into her palm, tight enough to feel the bite of metal on skin. After her standoff with Everett had ended with Captain Westin's return to his office, the rest of her walk-through at Station Eight had been un-eventful, at least on the surface. But despite the captain's

professional introductions and the polite tour of Station
Eight that Everett, Donovan, and Lieutenant Crews had
taken turns leading, Savannah could feel the shock and
unease that accompanied her presence like thick gray storm
clouds, heavy with impending rain.

The darkest and most impenetrable of which had come
from Everett.

Savannah shrugged to herself, the weight of her duffel
shifting over her shoulder as her Tony Lamas kept time with
the sidewalk leading up to her apartment complex. Brad had
warned her that her orientation would be full of prove-this
and do-that, and Savannah had no beef with either. She
was signing on to fight fires and save lives—it wasn't as
if she'd been expecting a walkover, and what's more, she
fully planned to make good on fulfilling the expectations
that went with the job. A little support from the guy responsible for training her might be nice, but she'd gritted her
way through the academy on her own. She could do this
solo, too.

Even if her nerves *had* gotten a jump on her mouth about
her family's track record on the job for the first and only
time since she'd moved from Texas. God, she was never
going to look at Everett's biceps again.

No matter how ridiculously lickable they'd looked
peeking out of those snug blue T-shirt sleeves.

Blowing out a hard exhale, Savannah singled out the key
to her apartment and slid it into the lock. Her boyfriend
Roger wouldn't be home for another couple of hours—hell,
she wasn't even supposed to have gotten out of the firehouse so early. But she had to admit, a bit of solitude, along
with a cold beer and whatever action movie was next in her
Netflix queue, sounded like a little slice of oh hell yes after
the uber-tense house intro she'd just had.

Stupid perfectly sculpted biceps.

The first sign that Savannah's private life was about to

turn as shitastic as her workday were the four-inch heels and the crimson lace push-up bra strewn across her living room carpet. She'd never met a pair of stilettos she'd gotten along with, and the lingerie in question looked two times too frilly and two sizes too big for her modest bust.

The second sign came by way of an ultra-feminine giggle floating in from down the hall, followed by a husky moan that sounded highly intimate and sickeningly familiar.

No way. No *way*. Things with Roger might not have exactly been all hearts and flowers lately—or okay, ever, because all that sappy stuff pretty much made Savannah want to blow her grits. But come on. Insult and injury couldn't possibly have it out for her this bad.

With her heartbeat kicking into a sprint against her ribs, Savannah slid her keys into the duffel bag on her hip with a quiet *clink*. She lowered her belongings to the floor, balling up both her fists and her courage as she tiptoed toward her bedroom.

Savannah paused, an icy chill running the length of her spine. Actually, it was Roger's bedroom, which she'd thought was simply a technicality they'd take care of at some point after she moved in with him. But the lease on her apartment had been up, and she'd spent as much time here as he'd spent at her place. Moving in with Roger had seemed logical at the time.

That had been three months ago. God, how had she managed to get herself into yet another going-nowhere-fast relationship?

Check that. Her relationship with Roger was about to go somewhere. But she was pretty sure hell didn't count as a luxury destination.

"Ahem." Savannah stood in the open door frame, averting her stare after the first eyeful of the leggy blonde wrapped around her boyfriend. "Hi, honey. I'm home."

"Savannah!" Roger jackknifed up from the mattress,

causing the blonde to scramble beneath the bedsheets with a squeak. "What are you doing here?"

"I live here, you jackass." Or at least, she used to. Humiliation and anger collided in her veins, but neither emotion stopped her from putting her sweat-slicked hands to good use on the dresser drawers.

"I, uh. I know." Roger's face turned the same shade as the tacky unmentionables he'd likely just stripped off his new friend. "I meant . . . I thought you were going to be at the academy until five."

Savannah's snort vibrated up from her chest as she started yanking her belongings from their neatly folded piles. "And I thought I had a boyfriend who wasn't a conniving bastard. Surprise! We were both wrong."

"You never mentioned having a girlfriend. You don't even have a picture of her at the office." The blonde pouted, drawing the tousled bedsheets over her boob job. Damn it, Savannah should've known something was up when Roger had started "working late" a few weeks ago. He was an accountant, for God's sake. Which would be fine if it was April instead of August and the man had an ambitious bone in his body.

None of the above.

"I can explain," Roger said, at the same time Savannah popped off a "no."

"He doesn't have a girlfriend anymore, sweetheart. Believe me. He's all yours."

She shoveled handfuls of tank tops and underwear into the messenger bag she'd snapped up from the floor in the closet, biting back the absolute irony of which drawer she'd randomly yanked open. Oh screw it. She could come back later for the rest of her things. Right now she just needed to get the hell out of there.

Savannah yanked the top flap of the bag into place and turned on her heel, locking her eyes on the door. Roger fumbled awkwardly for the pants he'd discarded in a sloppy heap at the side of the bed, following her out into the living room with a halfhearted apology.

"Savannah, wait."

"Why?" she asked, and the question was more genuine than bitter. But even though she'd spent the better part of six months with Roger, her opposite-sex relationships always fell into the burn bright, then burn out category. She liked him—or at least, she *had*—well enough.

But if there was one thing she'd learned as the only woman in a family brimming over with work-hardened men, it was that she was tough enough to make it on her own.

Even when being on her own stung like a sonofabitch.

Roger cleared his throat, suddenly enraptured by the plush carpet beneath his bare feet. "Look, I know I should've said something." He paused while she glared out a non-verbal *you got that right*, because, hey, as out the door as she was, a girl had her pride. "But you and I haven't really had much of a spark lately, you know? You've been practically married to that sweaty bunker gear, and all you ever talk about are training exercises and firehouse placements. It's kind of tough to be with a woman who has so many rough edges, you know? So things with Tiffani just kind of, ah, happened."

"They just happened," she repeated, resisting the sudden ridiculous urge to smooth a hand over her unkempt ponytail. Yeah, she preferred jeans and boots to skirts and stilettos, and yeah again, her favorite way to unwind was with a beer and a Bruce Lee movie. But that didn't make her worth cheating on.

Wait a second . . . "Have you been with her more than once?"

Guilt flashed through Roger's eyes like a highway road sign signaling a nine-car pileup ahead. "Maybe."

"It's pretty cut-and-dried as far as questions go," Savannah said, her jaw going tight enough to make her molars beg for leniency.

"Then I guess . . . yes."

Her fight-or-flight instinct begged to let him have it, but her wounded pride told her it was past time to cut her losses and just get airborne. "I don't have a shift until Monday morning, so I'll be by tomorrow at ten to pick up the rest of my things. If you're in any way smart, you won't be here."

"You, um, have a place to go?" Roger asked, stuffing his hands into the pockets of his dress pants with a guilty shrug.

Oh hell. She'd been so eager to blaze out the door, she hadn't stopped to think about where she'd blaze *to*. Her brother was pretty much her only local option. While Brad would certainly give her a buttload of (mostly) good-natured grief over this latest crash and burn, he'd never turn her away. Her brother's place was the size of a paperback novel, and his couch felt like a pile of bricks masquerading as furniture, but Savannah wasn't about to complain. While she'd never admit it out loud, she'd missed her father and brothers pretty deeply in the year and a half she'd lived in Fairview. She'd moved for damn good reasons—also something she'd rather be flayed alive than cop to. But despite the ribbing, spending a little time with Brad while she bounced back wouldn't be the worst thing going.

Plus, she needed a landing spot, and she needed it five minutes ago.

Savannah stood as tall as her frame would allow. "How very noble of you to worry about my well-being. Don't worry, I'm sure Brad will be happy to put me up."

Roger stepped into her path at the same time she made a move for the door. "Hold on," he said, his pretty-boy face taking on a noticeable pallor. Savannah answered by way of a withering glare, and Roger stutter-stepped back to give her a wider circle of personal space. "You're not going to tell your brother about, uh . . . this, are you?"

Finally, something that made her lips twitch with a smile. "Which are you more concerned about, Roger? That my older brother and I are extremely close, or that he's an arson investigator on a specialized team that deals in major crimes and dead bodies on a weekly basis?"

Roger's pallor turned decidedly green. "Savannah, I didn't mean to hurt you. Really."

"Well, good. Because you didn't." She breezed past him, scooping up the duffel bag she'd left on the living room floor as she marched a straight line through the cozy foyer.

"Wait! We can keep this just between us, right?" he called out, clearing his throat in a poor effort to cloak the wobble in his voice.

But Savannah barely looked back from the door frame as she beat feet toward the front door and, more importantly, her freedom.

She'd never needed a man before, and she sure as hell wasn't going to start by getting weepy over this sorry excuse for one.

"There's *nothing* between us anymore, Rodge. Have a nice life."

Chapter Three

Cole leaned against one of the brick partitions in front of Station Eight's engine bay, staring out at the Monday-morning sunrise with slivers of unease stuck between every last one of his ribs. The emotion itself was odd enough. Not only was the view beautiful, with the sky painted in deep purples and dusky, light-edged pinks that would soon give way to a gorgeous summer day, but he'd channeled the better part of a decade into making certain his feelings walked the straight and narrow, all the time, every time. The last eight years had shown him enough bad-to-worse scenarios to fill an Olympic-sized swimming pool, yet Cole had always made damn sure to keep himself calm, cool, and on the level for each and every one.

Then again, he'd probably tapped out his lifetime supply of emotions nine years ago when he'd left Harvest Moon. Being forced to choose between farming and firefighting had been gut-twisting enough.

Realizing his old man would choose farming over family? Yeah, that shit had shown Cole exactly how dangerous emotional investments could be. Whatever sap had waxed poetic about how it was better to have loved and lost than never to have loved at all was chock full of horseshit. Not letting your emotions rule you in the first place usually landed you at the same damned endgame anyway, just minus the messy feelings and the busted heart.

Win-fucking-win.

A set of boot treads sounded off on the concrete pathway leading around the firehouse from his left, sending Cole into high alert even though he didn't move a muscle. Shift change wasn't until seven A.M., and although a lot of guys started trickling in around the 6:30 mark, no one ever arrived at six like Cole. Not even Captain Westin. But the footsteps were lighter than average, although their cadence was determined and sure, and his pulse tripped in recognition two seconds before their owner came into view from the side of the building.

He should've figured his pain-in-the-ass rookie would be the exception to every goddamn rule standing, both on the books and off.

In hindsight, giving Savannah a put-up-or-shut-up on Friday had been a risky strategy. But if she expected to be treated with kid gloves, either because she was a woman or because her brother had gone through the ranks at the FFD, Cole needed to know now. Before anyone's time got wasted. Because as badly as he wanted the spot on squad—and *fuck*, he really did—the only thing he wouldn't do to get it was scrimp on another firefighter's training. Of course, if Savannah's response to his ultimatum was anything to go by, Cole was going to need boxing gloves instead of kid gloves.

How the hell was he supposed to push her to be a good firefighter when all she did was ball up her fists and push back?

Cole bent one knee, propping the sole of his foot against the bricks as he took a long draw off the cup of coffee in his palm. "Guess it's a good thing you don't value your sleep. We don't usually get much around here."

Savannah's jump was accompanied by an impressive stream of swear words. "Jesus, Everett! Give a girl a coronary, why don't you?"

His conscience took a slap shot at his gut, but he countered with a matter-of-fact shrug. The guy in him might feel like a bit of a dick for startling her on purpose, but the firefighter in him would've startled Jonesey the exact same way, and for the exact same reason.

If Cole wanted to train Savannah right, he was going to have to forget she was a woman. No matter how sexy she looked with the flush of surprise currently covering her face.

"It's not my fault you're startled," he said, modulating his voice to its most even setting and hoping the tiny, dark part of him that had noticed her blush would take the hint and follow suit.

Savannah huffed her disagreement, crossing her arms over the front of her dark blue FFD hoodie as she shifted her weight from one boot to the other on the concrete. "Okay. I'll play. How is it *my* fault that you scared the crap out of me?"

Damn. The guys were going to eat her alive, and him along with her if she didn't at least take the edge off her attitude. Not to mention she'd learn jack with a side of shit about being a firefighter with that giant chip weighing her shoulder down.

"Because you let me. I might've startled you, but I'm not the one who wasn't paying attention," Cole pointed out, and ah, that made her brown eyes go wide. "You're going to need to put your head on a permanent swivel if you want to get anywhere as a firefighter."

Her hands found the hips of her faded jeans, locking in

nice and tight. "Call me crazy, but I don't see anything around here that's on fire."

"And how would you know if you weren't even aware enough to see me standing right here in front of you?"

Savannah opened her mouth. Closed it. Examined her surroundings in a full three-sixty. And finally, they were getting somewhere.

"I didn't see you standing there, no," she admitted slowly, the heel of her boot scraping softly against the concrete as she turned back to face him from her spot a few paces away. "But I would have noticed something as overtly dangerous as a fire."

Of course Cole should've known better than to think she'd cave completely. He pushed off the bricks, gesturing to the empty street in front of them and the still-sleeping city block beyond. "Immediate danger doesn't always look like you think it will, and a fire isn't the only threat at any given scene. You need to see everything, even if you think it's not significant."

"Just because I didn't see you impersonating a ninja over there doesn't mean I missed *everything*," Savannah said, and ooookay, it was time to take the bloom off this rose once and for all.

"Really. Then what color are the awnings over the windows of the bakery behind you?"

She paused, and he had to give her credit. Her instinct had her trying to dial it up in her mind rather than swinging around to look. "Red," she finally said, lifting her dark brown brows at him in a nonverbal *ha!*

Cole took another sip of coffee, his gut twitching with remorse at how badly he was about to piss her off. His eyes flicked to the awnings across the street, the scalloped edges of all three fluttering in the early-morning breeze. Maybe he should just let her have a tiny victory before she started

what was bound to be a grueling first day. A win might
soften up her sharp edges, at least a little bit.

*You don't need to soften up her edges, jackass. You need
to make a firefighter out of her, and fast. Your spot on squad
depends on it.*

"Guess again."

Savannah swung around, her eyes flashing and her argument clearly at the ready . . . right up until she realized the
red awnings were over a hardware store, not a bakery.

"I got the color right," she said, and Jesus, they were
going to have to do this the hard way, every step of the way.

"It doesn't matter. You still got the details wrong."

Her lips pressed into a hard seal. "Bakery, hardware
store . . . who gives a shit? It's just an *awning*."

Something dark and hot snapped free from deep in his
chest, and he took a step toward her without thinking. "You
really don't get it, do you? That awning could be the closest
fire hydrant, or the only unobstructed exit in a burning
house, or the window that gives you the most direct route to
the spot where a person is trapped. It could be the busted
fire escape that'll trap *you* inside a building, or a million
other things that normal people look right past every day.
But you're not a normal person anymore, Nelson. If you
want to be a firefighter, you need to stop arguing and start
fucking listening."

For a second that coalesced into a minute, the only sounds
Cole could distinguish were his heartbeat slamming in his
ears and the muted *shush* of the occasional car gliding down
Church Street, half a block away. God *damn* it, Savannah
might've needed a little comeuppance, but he knew better
than to let his emotions take ownership of his mouth. Rising
to the call of her tenacity wouldn't get them anywhere good,
and he had to lock that shit up and focus on his strategy if
he wanted her to learn anything.

"The hardware building is two stories," Savannah finally said, her voice softening in tone but not intensity. "Four windows across the second floor, like there's an office above the shop space."

Cole blinked, and holy shit. She challenged every reasonable word he'd offered up, but the minute he blew his stack, she decided to actually hear him?

"Good," he said, because as crazy as her response seemed, hell if he was going to lose the opportunity to actually get somewhere with her other than the end of his rope. "What about the building next to it on the Bravo side?"

Savannah's brow furrowed, but still, she didn't turn. "It's another storefront. Brick, with glass double doors and big display windows facing the street."

At least she was well-versed in how the FFD referred to the four sides of a structure. The military terminology threw off more than a few rookies. "Is it attached to the hardware store?"

"I . . ." Her eyes squeezed shut, the intensity of her thought etched on her pretty face as her lips parted, and a bolt of heat shot all the way through his belly, destination: south.

"I don't know," Savannah admitted. She opened her eyes and angled herself toward the street to uncover the answer, which gave him the perfect opportunity to send a cease-and-desist memo to his dick. Sure, firefighters sometimes broke the no-fraternizing rule with members of the opposite sex in the same house—as a matter of fact, Cole knew not one but three firefighters who'd been involved with female paramedics they worked with every shift. Just because it was frowned upon didn't mean it didn't happen.

But Savannah wasn't just any housemate. She was the housemate he needed to train in order to prove his worth and take his spot on squad.

And that was exactly what he was going to do.

Cole cleared his throat and blanked his emotions, grabbing his game plan by the throat. "The stores are all attached," he said, pointing across the stretch of neatly kept asphalt. "A lot of the buildings downtown are older structures that have been renovated. The storefronts on this street used to be row homes, back when the developed part of the city wasn't quite so big. But then as the downtown area grew, more people wanted to live in the quieter sections of Fairview. So these homes were converted to offices and small businesses, like the hardware store, the dry cleaner, and the real estate office over there on the end."

"Wow." She scanned the storefronts one by one before pivoting on her heel to face him fully again. "You know an awful lot about Fairview. Did you grow up here?"

"No." Ah, hell. That had come out a lot gruffer than he'd intended, although he sure as shit wasn't going to get gabby on the subject, not even to apologize.

But if Savannah noticed the heavy coating of ill-temper he'd slapped over his answer, she either wasn't letting on or didn't care. "So fire obviously spreads faster in buildings like these because they're attached."

Cole embraced the change in subject as if it were a long-lost friend. "Yes, but it's not so much because they share walls, although that doesn't help."

"What could possibly be worse than sharing walls with a burning building?"

"You mean other than sharing attic space *and* your roofline with one?"

Savannah made her understanding known with a soft swear. "I guess I hadn't thought of that. So is there rhyme or reason to noticing this stuff? I mean, I know you said to see everything, but aren't some details more important than others?"

"Some details will serve you better than others, yeah."

"Like exits instead of awning colors?" she asked, a sassy smile forming on her lips.

Touché. "It's still important to see everything. You just need to learn how to filter through what you see so you can call up what you need, when you need it."

"Okay. How do I do that?"

His laugh lasted a solid five seconds before he realized she was as serious as a sledgehammer. "Practice," he said. "It takes most rookies a good couple of months to get the hang of really assessing a scene. For now you can start by taking a closer look at your surroundings wherever you go, both when you're on shift and off."

Savannah lifted a brow, tilting her head at him just enough for the sun to showcase the strands of lighter brown and gold hiding in the darker fall of her ponytail. "Great. So are you going to give me anything I can use *today*, Obi-Wan?"

Cole threw back the last of his coffee, but mostly just to hide his smile. Training her might take everything he had, but he wasn't going to hesitate to get the job done the right way, with calm determination and as little fanfare as possible.

No matter how much she tested his patience or tempted his emotions.

"Sure. Don't be late for roll call. You've got a hell of a first day in front of you, candidate."

Savannah smoothed a hand over the front of the navy-blue uniform pants she'd just tugged into place, making sure the FFD T-shirt that went with them was tucked in just as neatly. As far as she could tell, the locker room was one size fits all just like at the academy, and no way was she going to risk not being ready for roll call for lack of a place to change. Savannah had heard some of the guys move through the main space a few minutes ago, although the row of bathroom stalls where she currently stood was far enough removed from the locker bays and the adjacent shower room that she'd been unable to pick up anything distinct.

She hadn't seen Everett since he'd scared the hell out of her on the sidewalk nearly an hour ago, then irritated the hell out of her by pinning the blame on her alleged weakness rather than his underhanded intentions. In hindsight, his point about being more aware of things was pretty valid, but he didn't have to speak in riddles or make her feel like she didn't have the sense God gave a rock while he was at it. She'd just spent an entire year gutting her way through the academy. She might've missed the damned awning thing, but she wasn't exactly a waste of space.

Unless her brain called up the slow and sexy smile Everett had covered with his cup of coffee just before he'd walked away from her. Because *that* had reduced her to a non-speaking, non-thinking pile of whoa Nelly, even if she was ninety-eight percent certain he hadn't meant for her to see it.

Boy, had she seen it.

Savannah shook her head, grounding herself back in the firehouse locker room as she tightened her belly and blanked out the heat blooming between her hips. Considering recent events with Rat-face Roger, the last thing she needed was a man, even temporarily. Not that she'd choose Everett if she did. He wasn't her boss or anything, but still. Talk about the world's biggest occupational hazard.

Speaking of which . . .

"Nerves of steel," Savannah whispered, mentally tacking on *you idiot* as she reached for the duffel hanging on the hook in front of her and flipped the latch on the bathroom stall. Everett hadn't assigned her a locker on Friday, nor had anyone else, and while there were a handful of empties peppered in between the labeled doors, Savannah knew far better than to assume. For now, her duffel could stay right where it was on her hip. She'd find a place for her things after roll call.

Oh God. After a year's worth of grueling work and a lifetime's worth of wanting the job that went with it, she was about to report for her first roll call.

"Hey! There you are," came a feminine voice from over Savannah's shoulder, and ugh, maybe she *did* need to start working on that awareness thing. Scooping in a deep breath to counteract the jackhammer of her heart against her rib cage, Savannah turned, finding herself face-to-cute-as-a-button-face with the redheaded paramedic she'd met in passing on Friday.

"Hi. Um, Harrison, right?"

The redhead nodded, her smile turning into a full-blown grin as she stuck out her hand to shake Savannah's. "Or Rachel. Take your pick. I'm not choosy."

"Nelson. Savannah," she added, falling into step with Rachel as the paramedic started walking toward the door leading out of the locker room.

"Welcome to Eight, Nelson. I've got to be honest, I'm pretty excited to see another woman join the ranks around here. I'm hoping the added estrogen will help balance out some of the fart jokes and Xbox tournaments that tend to break out when things get really slow."

"You guys have Xbox tournaments?" Savannah's head sprang up in interest, sending Rachel's laughter into a groan.

"Argh, not you, too?"

Savannah bit her lip, but hell. No point in going for anything other than full disclosure now. "I've got three brothers, so . . . yeah, sorry. I'm pretty fluent in video games and action movies."

"Three brothers, huh? Well, you'll definitely fit in around here." Rachel tipped her head at the door leading out to

Station Eight's main living space, tucking back the handful of curls that broke free from the loose knot at her nape. "The firehouse is essentially a big square, with the hallway running the perimeter. The engine bay and locker room are on this side of the building, and Captain Westin's office and sleeping quarters are on the other. The main living area, with the kitchen and the common room, is in the middle, and the bunks are off the back of the house."

Savannah nodded, committing the information to memory. "Thanks. Most of what I saw when I was here on Friday was the captain's office and the engine bay."

"Figures," Rachel said with an amiable eye roll. "I swear those guys on engine would spend half a day showing off every last hose, nozzle, and Halligan bar in the storage compartments, but heaven forbid they show you where to eat or sleep or pee."

"I don't know. I'm kind of here for the hoses and Halligan bars. To be honest, the other stuff seems like it's mostly extra."

Rachel's flame-colored brows winged upward, and Savannah realized the weirdness of her statement too late. But rather than giving Savannah a hard time or distancing herself with an awkward *alrighty then* maneuver, Rachel simply said, "Damn, girl, you really *will* fit in around here. Come on. With any luck, the guys on squad haven't hogged all the coffee."

"Okay." Savannah nodded, a tentative smile on her lips. "Sure."

She followed Rachel into the comfortably noisy common room, a thread of relief uncurling low in her belly as they made their way past the pair of couches by the door and headed for the kitchen area running the length of the far wall. She'd expected a decent amount of friction in her first couple of shifts. Her brothers had made no bones about pointing out that her being female was likely to turn her rookie status into a high-expectations double whammy, and she was certainly no stranger to doubtful expressions and disbelieving stares.

But between the tiny bit of headway she'd made with Everett outside and how honestly welcoming Rachel seemed to be despite Savannah's lack of girly tendencies and social graces, maybe—just maybe—Savannah had misjudged how much her gender would affect her acceptance at Eight.

And then the chatter of conversation and the soft clinking of coffee cups being filled came to a rough halt, and she realized all at once what Everett had meant when he'd told her she was going to have a hell of a first day.

Savannah steeled her spine, following Rachel to the rectangular island-slash-serving counter separating the kitchen, from the rest of the common room. Mimicking the paramedic's casual actions, she grabbed a white ceramic mug from the tray next to the coffeepot and filled it with a quick pour. She was wired enough that the caffeine was probably not her best plan, but she didn't want to call any more attention to herself than absolutely necessary.

The dead silence still pushing against her eardrums was already taking care of that.

On second thought, screw this. She'd never been good at blending into the walls anyway.

"Morning, everybody." Savannah planted her palms over the stainless-steel counter, making sure to face everyone in both the kitchen and the dining area beyond. She waited out the surprise-widened stares that accompanied the continuing quiet, but she was already in for a penny. Might as well go for the whole damn pound. "I know my being here on engine is a bit of a new situation for all of us. I just wanted to say how excited I am to have landed at Eight. I'm glad to be part of the team."

The pin-drop silence lengthened for five seconds, then five more before a rude snort cut through the air, the sound coming from the head of one of the two farmhouse-style tables running parallel to the island. "Then you'd better get comfortable where you're standing."

"I'm sorry?" Savannah asked, adrenaline tightening her chest like a steel tourniquet. The back of her neck prickled hard as C-shift's rescue squad lieutenant, Dennis Osborne, stood to stare her down, but she jammed her boots into the floor tiles and leveled her gaze right back.

Five-ten, maybe five-eleven. More salt than pepper in both his crew cut and the three days' worth of scruff on his jaw. A lean, work-hardened frame with an expression to match.

Stone-gray eyes so full of disapproval that Savannah nearly flinched.

"House rules. The rookie cooks," he said, his gravel-covered voice as unyielding as it was unfriendly. "So from now on, the kitchen is your part on the team, sweetheart."

Instinctively, she turned to her right, where Everett stood at attention by the kitchen counter, flanked by Donovan and Crews. Although he met her eyes, his expression was unreadable—giant shocker there—and after a second, it became clear that she was not just on her own, but on her own in front of the entire house, save the still-absent captain.

Lieutenant Osborne was obviously testing her mettle by throwing down a challenge right out of the gate, and she'd bet dollars to doughnuts he was assigning her KP because she was a woman, not because she was their newest candidate. Savannah opened her mouth, primed and ready to loosen the retort burning a hole in her tongue.

But she bit down on the words just shy of launch. As badly as she wanted to tell the lieutenant exactly where to shove his Cro-Magnon mentality, she also knew that breaking bad with the second-highest-ranking firefighter in the house before her first shift had even started was a recipe for ruin. Just because she knew how to cook, and cook well, didn't mean *he* had to know it. If Osborne wanted to strong-arm her with his gender bias, fine.

Like her daddy always said, it took two to tangle assholes. And while she wasn't about to start her career in the ditch, she wasn't exactly a take-shit kind of girl, either.

"All right." Savannah inhaled all the way to the bottom of her lungs with a sickly sweet smile as she met the dare in Oz's flinty stare. "I'm happy to cook for y'all."

"Good." The corners of his mouth lifted in a hint of sharp-edged satisfaction.

But rather than shrink back or admit defeat, Savannah held his gaze despite the rush of her pulse in her ears.

"After all, they're your taste buds, Lieutenant."

Chapter Four

Cole sat with his ass firmly planted on the bench alongside the dining table in Station Eight, just as he had for the last twenty minutes while Captain Westin had gone through roll call, announcements, and shift assignments.

Christ, he was screwed, and not even in a way that would leave him satisfied and smiling. Of all the people Savannah could've gone toe to toe with, she'd just had to poke back at the one firefighter in the house with the most tenure. Not to mention the most influence, on both engine and squad.

On second thought, *screwed* might not cover this.

Cole shoved himself to his feet, ignoring the side-eye he was getting from Donovan and Oz and pretty much everyone else in the house other than Rachel and Jonesey. Westin had dismissed them, although the captain was unaware of what had transpired between Savannah and Oz thirty seconds before he'd come into the kitchen for roll call, and Cole would be damned if he'd let all the emotions flying around get in the way of doing his job.

"Nelson," he said, jerking his chin at the doors leading out of the common room, and miraculously, she jumped up from her spot next to Rachel to follow him into the hallway. Her duffel bag bounced sloppily against the hip of her dark blue uniform pants, which brought Cole to their first order of business. "I'll assign you a locker so you can store your stuff. The locker room and bathrooms are both unisex, but we rotate with Rachel for the showers. She bunks in at night just like everyone else, and so will you. I'm sure she'd be willing to answer any questions you've got about protocol."

"I appreciate the offer, but I'm not a paramedic. I'm a firefighter. If it's all the same, I'd like to take direction from you."

Cole tamped down the counter-argument brewing in his chest. He was going to train Savannah, no matter what. If she wanted to opt for the hard way, fine by him. She'd learn fast enough to be careful what she wished for.

"Suit yourself," he said, aiming himself toward the locker room and the adjacent engine bay. "Speaking of which, your turnout gear is in the equipment room. We can grab it while we're back here."

"Okay." Savannah's expression brightened, the shot of pure excitement lighting her chocolate-colored eyes tempting Cole to smile. Instead, he pocketed the urge and reached for the locker room door. He might understand her enthusiasm, but he wasn't here to be Savannah's friend. With her track record so far this morning, he really just wanted to get them through the damned shift unscathed.

"Don't get too excited. We usually spend the first hour or so after roll call on housekeeping, both literal and figurative, and today's no exception. You've got your house assignment. You just need your gear ready to go in case we get an early call."

Savannah slipped a palm around the strap of her bag, her knuckles going white over her grip. "You're seriously going to stand by the decision to make me cook."

"Since the person who made that decision outranks the hell out of me, yeah. I sure am. The chain of command isn't optional around here." He stopped at a bank of lockers in the middle row, most of them labeled with Sharpie on masking tape. The one a few doors down from his stood vacant, and he pulled it open with a metallic *squeal*. "I'll grab the tape while you get comfy here in Shangri-La."

Ninety seconds later, Savannah's things were safely stored, but she looked no happier than when he'd left. "You don't think sticking me in the kitchen is a little sexist?"

"No, I don't," Cole said, not just to knock down the idea, but because it was the truth. "Oz wasn't bullshitting you about the house rule. Jones did kitchen duty before you, and before him, when we had no candidate, we rotated. You won't cook every time you're on shift, but for now, your name is on the list next to KP, so that's what you'll do."

She closed the door to her locker, her body language still balking all the way. Cole tugged a strip of masking tape from the roll in his hand and slid it over the flat metal surface, penning her last name in block letters before turning back to meet her stare.

"What about when I'm done cooking breakfast? What do I do then?" Savannah asked, and huh, couldn't say he'd been expecting *that*.

Cole shook off the shock running through his veins. "Why don't we make the theme for today 'one step at a time'?"

"I can handle it, you know. I'm good enough to do this job."

Whether it was the sudden vulnerability threading through her voice or the odd sense of solidarity he felt in her desire to prove herself, Cole couldn't be sure. But something deep and almost forbidden propelled him toward her, close enough to see her dark lashes fan upward in surprise as her chest rose on an intake of breath.

"Don't tell me, Nelson. Show me. Got it?"

She nodded, and the bounce of her ponytail filled the

space between them with the crisp scent of fresh laundry on the line. "Copy that."

"Good. Now let's get moving."

Cole peeled his stare from hers, forcing his boots through the locker room and his suddenly sketchy pulse back into submission. Savannah kept up with him stride for stride the whole way to the equipment room at the back of the engine bay, and at least he wouldn't have to worry about her lagging behind when shit got critical.

"Boots, bunker pants, coat, hood, gloves, and helmet are all standard issue," Cole said, clicking on the light switch to illuminate the tight confines of the equipment room. "When you're not on shift, all of your gear stays in here. When you are, you're going to want to keep it handy in the engine bay."

Savannah's chin popped up, her feet coming to a halt at about three steps into the dimly lit space. "Whoa, that's a smell," she said, gesturing to the soot-laced gear cramming the double-wide wooden storage cubbies lining either side of the narrow room.

He took a deep inhale, recognizing the sharp bite of smoke permeating the air around them as if the scent was an afterthought. "Ah, you get used to it."

Her expression suggested she highly doubted it. "Is there some kind of station-wide code against actually washing your stuff?"

"There are machines right off the common room. You can use 'em as much as you'd like. But no matter how much you wash your gear, after a while, it'll see enough use that the smell of smoke just sticks around."

"So you guys see a lot of fires, then?" She took the box Cole had pulled from the shelf already labeled with her name, and a kid on Christmas morning had nothing on her as she started rooting through its contents.

"You're putting the cart before the horse again, candidate."

"And you're dodging the question, Everett. How am I supposed to learn things if you don't tell me when I ask?"

A quick laugh escaped from his chest before he could check it. "Fine. Yeah, we see our fair share of fires. Along with bunches of other things you'll need to be ready for."

She unearthed the helmet from the bottom of the box, her brows climbing in question. "Such as . . . ?"

"Floods, chemical spills, gas leaks, people trapped in all sorts of places . . . oh, and car wrecks. We get a ton of those," he said, and it didn't escape his notice that the last entry on the list made Savannah's jaw go tight.

She lifted the helmet to the crown of her head, fumbling with the straps around her ears. "Wow. Guess you see a lot of everything, then."

"We," Cole corrected, letting her struggle with the tangled mess for another minute before lifting his hands in a nonverbal offer to help. "You have a problem with car wrecks?"

Savannah leaned forward, waiting until he'd righted the straps and tightened her helmet before shaking her head. "No. I don't have a problem with anything." She brushed her fingers over the straps, as if she were trying to memorize them by feel. "And what do you mean, 'we'?"

Cole shrugged. While he was going to lean on her and lean on her hard so he could take his spot on squad, he'd never been one to fuck with a rookie's head just for the sake of seniority. Especially when it came to Station Eight's golden rule.

"You might be a rookie with a hell of a lot to learn, but you're still part of the house, and we work as a team. *We* see a lot of everything."

"Oh." She blinked. "Okay."

Rather than sticking her response with a cocky comeback—or worse yet, that vulnerable mind-meld thing that had thrown him for a loop a few minutes ago—Savannah simply undid her helmet and grabbed the rest of her gear from the box. He'd moved his own gear to the engine bay just before roll call, so his arms were as empty as hers were full, but he resisted the urge to offer to help on their trip out of the equipment room. When shit caught fire, she'd have to be able to manage her gear on her own just like everyone else. Not that she'd probably let Cole help her, even if *she* was on fire.

And not that her determination and drive weren't one hell of a turn-on.

"Right." He ground to a halt alongside Engine Eight, pulling himself into the boxy confines of the back step. "Most of your gear can stay in here. There's a storage space for your mask and SCBA built into the back of your seat. Where you want the rest is up to you, but most guys keep everything in the engine so they can gear up on the way to a call."

Surprise colored Savannah's face in the shadows of the back step. "You . . ." She paused, then backtracked. "*We* don't gear up before leaving the station?"

"Nope," Cole said, sitting back on his heels to look at her. "It takes too long, and believe me when I tell you, the engine operator will leave your ass here if you lag behind when that all-call goes off."

"Let me guess. You drive, don't you?"

Damn, her intuition really was pretty good. Either that or she spoke fluent sarcasm, which wasn't a bad skill to have around this place. "Very good, candidate. Yes, I usually operate the engine."

He took a minute to show her the best places to store her equipment and to assign her an empty seat in the step, purposely putting her across from Donovan. For all his smartass tendencies, the guy was one of the best firefighters Cole knew. He'd have Savannah's six if she needed help gearing up. Provided she'd actually ask for any.

"Looks like you're set out here," he said, jumping back

down to the concrete floor of the engine bay. Cole braced himself for round two of the breakfast wars—she still clearly didn't want to cook, if the look on her face was any indication.

So it surprised the shit out of him when she stepped back down to the engine bay, squared her shoulders, and turned toward the house without pause.

"Yup. Unless we get an early call, I guess I'll see you at breakfast."

Cole was three compartments into his equipment check on the rig when the echo of footsteps signaled he was about to become a party of two. Sure enough, Alex poked his head around the entrance to the narrow alley between the ambo and the engine, a shit-eating grin spreading over his face.

"Hell of a Monday so far," he said, sauntering over to slap Cole on the shoulder before leaning against the red-and-white side panel next to the open compartment.

"Hell of an understatement." Cole huffed out a laugh, tucking the inventory clipboard under his arm with a little bit of wing and a whole lot of prayer. "Please tell me Nelson is in there cooking breakfast and not trying to start World War Three."

"She's in the kitchen, as assigned. Whether or not you can call it cooking . . ." Donovan held one palm parallel to the floor, angling it side to side in an *eh* motion. "Let's just say she's giving it a shot."

"Wonderful." Cole shut the engine compartment with a metal-on-metal *bang*, dropping his voice to keep their conversation private despite the limited visibility of their surroundings. "Listen, I need a favor. It's kind of a big one."

"I'm always happy to have you owe me, the bigger, the better," Alex said over a grin. "Shoot."

Cole dialed down his breath nice and easy in an effort to set the bar for his pulse. But he couldn't afford for Savannah's knee-jerk reactions to get in the way of him getting her trained. "I put Nelson across from you in the step since I'll probably be in the front whenever we roll out. Can you just keep an eye on her? She's wound pretty tight, and the last thing I need is for her to stroke out from all the adrenaline on her first couple of calls."

"Ooooh, you are gonna owe me big. But you got it, brother." While Donovan's nod of agreement came without hesitation, the rest of his answer arrived after a solid pause. "We do some pretty heavy lifting around here, and not just physically. I know she made it through the academy, but . . . you think she's going to be able to haul her weight now that she's on engine for real?"

"I think hauling her weight is going to be the least of her worries. Especially if she keeps pissing off guys like Oz."

A smile Cole would bet wasn't voluntary lifted one corner of Alex's mouth. "Yeah, she's a little scrappy, huh? I kind of dig that in a rookie, though."

"Sure," Cole said, caught halfway between wanting to laugh and wanting to cry uncle. "You're not the one whose job is riding on getting her trained and not shit-canned."

Before Donovan could work up an appropriately cocky reply, Oz appeared at the front fender of the engine, cutting Cole's conversation with Alex short.

"Everett. A word," the lieutenant rasped, and great, just when Cole thought this morning couldn't get any stickier.

He put a stranglehold on the unease suddenly churning through his gut, giving Donovan a quick "see you later" and making sure his expression was completely noncommittal before crossing the engine bay to the spot where Oz stood. "Hey, Lieutenant. What can I do for you?"

Whoa. On closer inspection, the guy looked a little more

ragged than usual. Or maybe that was the disdain suddenly hardening his features.

Still, Cole couldn't help but tack on, "Is everything okay? You look kind of beat."

Oz lifted a shoulder. "Did a double over the weekend. Filled in over at Four, and we got slammed with calls. Typical Saturday night."

"I hear that," Cole said. Between the car wrecks, the heart attacks, and the drunks, Saturdays usually gave them all a run for their freaking money. "The back-to-back over a weekend is brutal."

"Yeah, but the money ain't." Oz's stare hitched just briefly before turning back to steel. "Anyway, I just had a sit-down with Westin. He told me you're in charge of training our new candidate." His voice curled around the last word like a plume of black smoke, the rock-hard set of his jaw just as nasty.

"I am," Cole agreed, keeping his response neutral despite the shock dominating his chest. Oz might be kind of an old-school firefighter, but Savannah *had* made it through the academy on the same standards as her male classmates. True, that didn't make her a firefighter right off the bat, but she was a hell of a lot closer than most people.

Oz folded his arms over his chest. "You know Tommy Briggs, over at Thirty-Six?"

Cole spun through his mental files until recognition hit. "Lieutenant on truck, right?"

"That's him. He had a female candidate last year. Real piece of work, demanding her own bunk, making a stink about not having enough privacy. Gargantuan pain in the ass."

"Yeah?" Cole tread with extreme caution. Savannah might've flipped the lid off this can of worms by pissing Oz off, but if he could smooth things over from his end, it would go a long way toward problem solved. "I just took

Nelson through the locker room and she didn't seem to mind the idea of bunking in. Maybe Tommy just got unlucky."

"What Tommy got was screwed," Oz flipped back, and while he'd never been a particularly warm and fuzzy guy, his stare was downright glacial beneath the glare of the overhead lights in the engine bay. "See, his female rookie didn't just get prissy about bunking in. She couldn't keep up with drills or hauling gear, either. But when the guys over at Thirty-Six leaned on her, she went crying to the captain about how the training was sexist."

"Just because the training is rigorous doesn't make it sexist," Cole said. Hell, plenty of male rookies had trouble gritting it out. "It's hard for a reason."

"Yeah, well, tell that to the guys at Thirty-Six. Their girl over there ended up falling behind on a search and rescue in a pretty sketchy house fire. Then she panicked when she couldn't find her exit path."

Cole's brows went up, but still, he tread lightly. "Sounds dangerous."

Oz's answer—and the frost-covered frown that accompanied it—wasn't nearly so neutral. "Not just for her. The firefighter who had to go back for her ended up getting banged up real good dragging her ass out. The whole thing turned out to be a complete cluster fuck, all because she couldn't hold her own."

Strategy had Cole keeping his mouth shut, but his pulse pressed louder in his ears as Oz continued. "I'm all for treating people equal, provided they earn equal. But this job ain't for everybody, Everett. With the eight you've put in plus the squad training you've got under your belt, you know that as well as I do. One weak link is dangerous for the entire chain of command."

Oz stepped closer, the shadows beneath his eyes cutting even deeper in the seriousness of his expression. "We lost a good man three years ago. I'm not about to put anyone else in this house at risk. No matter what."

Every last one of Cole's muscles went bowstring tight at both the mention of his fallen friend, Mason Watts, and the implication coming out of Oz's mouth. Discrediting Savannah based on her gender wasn't part of Cole's game plan, but she was still Station Eight's rookie, and she'd gotten off on the wrong foot with the wrong firefighter on top of it. She had a metric ton of worth to prove, and it was Cole's job to get her there. Of course Oz would be watching his every move while he did it to make sure he was rescue squad material.

And of course, Cole intended to deliver.

"I'd never put anyone in this house in harm's way. I'm going to train Nelson the best I know how, Lieutenant. You have my word on that."

Oz broke into a smile, but Cole realized just a second too late that the expression was all teeth.

"She's got a mouth on her. Do yourself a favor and break her early. Then we can get someone in here who can actually pull his weight and move your ass to squad where it belongs."

Chapter Five

Savannah scraped the last two sausage patties from her frying pan, dropping them to the serving plate by the cooktop with an ominous *thunk* before turning toward the island to examine the rest of the meal. Overcooked chunks of scrambled eggs sat lifelessly in the bowl by her elbow, with grits that could stunt-double as waterlogged cement in the one next to it. She'd had to get creative about wrecking the canned biscuits she'd unearthed from the house fridge, but in the end, she'd simply relied on what she knew best.

When in doubt, just turn up the heat. After all, she *was* a firefighter.

"Whoa. Breakfast looks . . . interesting." Rachel skidded to a halt by the coffeepot, her fellow paramedic Tom O'Keefe seconding the affirmation with a wary, wide-eyed stare.

Savannah's gut tightened with the tiniest pang of remorse, but she slapped a smile over her face to cover any hint that might translate to her expression. "Thanks. Everything is ready, if you want to let the guys in the engine bay know."

"Sure," Rachel said, although she sounded anything but. She turned toward the common room door, not so subtly placing her elbow in Tom's ribs in what Savannah would bet was an effort to remove the open-mouthed look from the other paramedic's face.

"Are these . . . grits?" he asked, ladling up a scoopful and watching the pasty-white mess plop gracelessly back into the bowl.

Savannah could barely hide her wince. As a Texas girl, she knew that runny grits skirted the boundaries of sacrilege. But she'd set out to prove a point, and come hell or high tide, she was going to do it.

"They sure are. Go on and help yourself."

"Huh. I had no idea grits could even do that." Tom shook his head, grabbing a plate from the stack at the end of the island. "What the hell. A guy's gotta eat."

Rachel reappeared in the kitchen a minute later, with Donovan and Jones and Crews in tow. They filed around the kitchen island, their expressions turning from caution to outright fear as Savannah presented the serving plate full of torched sausage patties to complete the spread.

"Jesus, Nelson. What'd these eggs ever do to you?" The question came from Donovan, and although his tone held the definite edge of you're-the-rookie shit-giving, he still bit the bullet and grabbed a plate from the stack on the stainless-steel counter.

"I'm not sure these actually count as eggs anymore," Crews speculated, looking over Donovan's shoulder, and even Jones, who was normally head down, eyes forward, nodded in agreement. Too bad for them, Savannah had a master's degree in fortitude, courtesy of her three brothers. This was child's play compared to the jawing that had gone on at the Nelson family dinner table every night for nearly two decades.

Lieutenant Osborne's flat-out stare of disapproval, however, was not.

"You'd better hope you don't fight fires the same way you handle the kitchen, because that's a pretty sorry showing for your first assignment, candidate," he said, making his way across the common room in a handful of precise steps. But rather than adding anything else or reluctantly picking up a plate to serve himself some breakfast, Oz simply stood across from her at the kitchen island, waiting. The obvious disapproval flashing through his stormy gray eyes scrambled Savannah's breath, but she forced herself to hold his stare.

"I would apologize, but to be fair, I did warn you, Lieutenant. It's not my fault you assumed I knew how to cook when you put me on kitchen duty."

Just like that, the disdain in Oz's eyes shifted into something harder and a whole lot less forgiving. But before he could turn the emotion into a response, Everett appeared at the other man's side.

"Lieutenant," he said, waiting for Oz's tight nod of acknowledgment before reaching for a plate and pinning Savannah with the full force of his serious-as-sin gaze. "It seems no one's told Nelson the most important house rule for kitchen duty."

Confusion guided Savannah back a full step on the linoleum, her guard tacked firmly into place. Was Everett on her side or not? "And that is?"

He handed over the plate between his fingers without hesitation. "Whoever cooks is supposed to eat first."

Unease replaced the air in her lungs. "I didn't know that."

"Yeah," O'Keefe admitted from his spot at the table. He gave a sheepish shrug. "Sorry. You said for me to help myself, so I just figured Everett had told you and you didn't want to, uh, try your luck. Otherwise I'd have waited for you to lead the charge."

Everett exchanged a blank glance with Oz, who frowned one last time at the sad excuse for a breakfast on the kitchen island before stalking to the coffeepot instead of fixing himself a plate.

"Well," Everett said. "Now that we've remedied your lack of knowledge, why don't you go ahead and help yourself, Nelson. There are a lot of hours between breakfast and lunch, and you're going to need all the energy you can get. Especially if we get a couple of calls before then."

Well, shit. Of course he had to go and be all logical. Not that she was going to tip her hand. After all, the meal might be a culinary train wreck, and yeah, she might've made it that way on purpose, but it was still edible. She'd wanted to prove a point, not poison anyone.

"Okay," Savannah said, lifting one shoulder for added nonchalance. She placed a lopsided biscuit and some sausage on her plate, waiting as Everett did the same. He upped the ante by scooping up a bunch of scrambled eggs, but they both steered clear of the grits. Savannah might be hard-wired to prove her worth by rising to whatever challenge lay in front of her, but hell, even she had hard limits.

"So, um, what do we do after breakfast?" she asked, grabbing a banana as a failsafe before aiming her boots toward the dining table where Rachel sat across from O'Keefe.

Everett parked himself next to the male paramedic on the long wooden bench seat. "After all the gear checks are done, we'll go over shift assignments. Then you and I will work on some drills."

"Sounds like the academy."

Her observation drew irony-tinged laughter from both Donovan and Jones, but it was Everett who replied. "Do yourself a favor, Nelson. Look forward, not back."

Savannah's spine straightened to its full height. Okay, so she occupied the bottom spot on the totem pole as far as experience went, but come on.

She'd only opened her mouth to defend the experience

she'd worked her ass off to gain over the last twelve months when the shrill sound of the station-wide overhead system cut the response forming hotly on her tongue.

"Ambulance Eight, motor vehicle accident, pedestrian struck. Ninety-six hundred block of Wilson Boulevard. Requesting immediate response."

Savannah's heart clattered against her ribs, her palms going instantly slick as she recalled Everett's words from barely an hour ago.

Oh, and car wrecks. We get a ton of those.

Her throat locked over a hard swallow. *Please, God. Please, not the first call. Please . . .*

As if providence had decided to finally do her a solid, the overhead system fell silent without a request for additional backup from squad or engine, and Savannah exhaled in a *whoosh* of relief.

"Good morning to you too, Fairview. Nothing like a big call right out of the chute," O'Keefe said, pushing back from the breakfast table and taking one last bite of his biscuit before popping his chin at Rachel. "I'll flip you for the driver's seat, Harrison."

Rachel rolled her eyes toward her bright red bangs and followed her partner to the front of the common room. "Not a chance. You drove all of last shift. Your ass is riding shotgun, pretty boy. Take it or leave it."

The pair made their way toward the engine bay, the back and forth of their easygoing banter fading down the open hallway, and Donovan let out a low whistle.

"Man, we just got away with one. Wilson Boulevard is a busy throughway. With rush-hour traffic, I bet that scene looks like a finger painting."

"Pedestrian versus car doesn't usually have a happy ending," Jones agreed, using the edge of his fork to saw through the overcooked sausage patty on his plate. "Hey, isn't that close to where we did that other really nasty MVA last month?"

"Motorcycle versus SUV, where squad had to cut the roof off the vehicle? Or single rider versus oak tree? Because that was messy, too," Donovan said around a mouthful of scrambled eggs.

Crews shook his head. "No, the SUV wreck was over on Delancey, and the tree guy was Michigan Terrace. The one on Wilson was that FUBAR with the glazier's truck, remember? I think the guys on squad are still picking chunks of glass and who knows what else out of the bottom of their boots from that extraction. The driver was pinned in there and bleeding something fierce."

The chorus of *ohhhh*s sounded ominous in its recognition, making Savannah's stomach bank hard left. She'd known that being on the roster at Eight meant she'd have to face hairy situations, but God, these guys might as well be rattling off baseball highlights.

She was tough, no doubt, but would she ever be this indifferent about things like car wrecks? Or fires?

Or worse?

"Not hungry?" Everett asked, dropping his tone a register and flicking his gaze at her untouched breakfast while the other firefighters and guys on squad shifted topics and continued their own conversation at the other end of the table.

"No." Savannah inhaled on a five-count, shaking off her jitters once and for all. "Guess I'm just anxious to get started."

"I wasn't just giving you a hard time when I said you should eat something."

She raised a brow in a silent call of bullshit, and Everett tipped his sandy-brown head in concession.

"Hey, I said *just*. But turnabout is fair play." He kept his voice quiet, but serious. "No one freelances at Eight, on calls or otherwise. You earned a taste of your own Franken-breakfast."

Savannah's shoulders tightened with a fresh shot of re-morse, although she wasn't quite ready to give up the ghost. "Maybe. But didn't you say assumptions are as dangerous as guesswork around here? Oz shouldn't have jumped to conclusions about whether or not I have kitchen skills."

Ah! That got his attention. Everett froze to the bench across from her for a full ten seconds before saying, "It might've been a bad idea for Oz to assume you could cook, but it's an even worse idea for you to alienate the rest of the house to prove your point. If you're going to make it to lunch, you need to realize that none of us fly solo. Ever."

She slid a glance at the firefighters at the far end of the table before dropping her chin. As much as Oz's implication had hacked her off, Everett was right. "Understood."

"Another thing you're going to need to do if you want to make it to lunch is put something in your stomach. Turnabout aside, you pass out on your first day and I can pretty much guarantee you'll end up with a nickname you despise."

Damn it, he had her on all counts. "Fine," Savannah said, flipping her biscuit over to remove the burnt bottom layer before taking a bite. She'd been far too antsy to eat before she'd left this morning—not that her brother's kitchen played host to anything other than ramen noodles, beer, and condiments. Her three-night stint on Brad's torture device-slash-couch had left her both sleepless and sore, so saving the strength she had was probably a smart strategy.

Insult, meet injury.

Savannah ate the rest of her breakfast in silence, taking in the conversations around her. When the other firefight-ers started to disperse to continue with their various house assignments, she pushed up from the table, moving toward the back of the kitchen for cleanup.

Lieutenant Osborne stood with one hip against the countertop, blocking her path just shy of the sink. "I'm out of coffee," he said, sparing a lightning-fast glance at the mug by his elbow before lifting his eyes to spear her with a stare.

Savannah's pride demanded that she not look away, even though her heart hammered beneath her T-shirt. "There should be plenty." She knew because she'd seen Donovan brew a fresh pot not even five minutes ago before he'd gone out to the engine bay.

"Oh, there is. But you *are* on kitchen duty." Oz's implication hung in the air like smoke in a small space, and oh hell no. No way was she going to serve him like a fucking waitress.

But she swung a surreptitious gaze over the common room, discovering that her options amounted to shit and shittier. The only people left in the room were Everett and two guys from squad, and they were far enough away to be well out of earshot of her conversation with Oz. Impulse dared her to tell him to take his coffee and cram it up his ass. But if she gave in—and oh God, how she wanted to give in—everyone would believe the lieutenant when he slanted the story in his direction and made her look insubordinate. Pushing back would only spray paint her with a giant troublemaker-colored bull's-eye.

And judging from the smug ass look covering his weathered face, Oz knew it.

Savannah sucked a breath through her teeth. "Well then. Why don't I get that for you, Lieutenant." She reached for the coffee carafe, willing her fingers not to shake as she filled Oz's mug to the brim.

"That's more like it, sugar."

The carafe in her hand hit the burner with a clatter. "What did you just call me?"

"I didn't call you anything, Nelson. All I said was, pass the sugar."

His hard gray stare sent an icy chill down the length of her spine, triple-dog-daring her to green light the heated response that had shot upward from her chest.

Nerves of steel, girl. Be tough.

Wordlessly, Savannah reached for the yellow sugar canister. She gritted her molars hard enough to make her jaw throb, sliding it over the countertop until it reached the no-man's-land between them.

Oz huffed out a joyless laugh. "Thought so."

But instead of sugaring the coffee she'd just poured, he reached over to dump every last drop down the drain, breaking their stare only to give her his back as he turned on his boot heels and walked out of the kitchen.

Fifteen minutes' worth of dishes did nothing to quell either the anger or the nerves running amok in Savannah's belly. She gave the stainless-steel counter one last swipe with her dish towel, calling her kitchen duty done as she looked at Everett with anticipation thrumming through her veins.

"So are we good to go?" Now that breakfast was finally out of the way, she was dying to actually do something of value.

"Sure." He pushed back from the now-empty table, finding his feet. Her pulse notched higher in excitement as they made their way toward the engine bay, although for someone whose job required speed and precision, Everett seemed to be moving slower than molasses headed uphill in January.

Finally—*finally*—they came to a stop at the open door of Engine Eight, where he planted his feet over the concrete and gestured to the back step. "Go ahead and grab your turnout gear," he said, and it took her all of seven seconds to comply.

"Okay," Savannah said. There had to be a billion different cool drills they could do now that she was officially on engine. Bonus points for active fire or immediate danger. "Now what?"

Everett pulled a stopwatch from his pocket, the muscles in his forearms flexing over the dark blue cotton of his T-shirt as he crossed one arm over his chest and flipped the timer faceup in his opposite palm. "Now we see how long it takes you to gear up."

"I meant after that." She started to laugh, but Everett's head shake made the sound catch in her throat.

"After that, you'll dress down and we'll do it again. That's how gear drills work."

Her grasp on the gear overflowing from her arms tightened in shock. "You want me to practice getting dressed?"

"I want you to do what you're told. Following directives isn't optional, candidate." He paused, releasing an audible breath before adding, "But to clarify, yes. I also want you to practice gearing up. It's not as intuitive as you think. Now go."

The soft *click* of the timer's start button jolted Savannah into motion. She'd geared up plenty at the academy, although they'd never done timed drills. Still, maybe if she just got this over with, they could move on to something good.

She crouched down low to drop her gear to the ground in front of her, snapping her hood from the top of the haphazard pile. A quick yank had it over her head, and she toed off the boots she'd been wearing next. Thank God she'd had the foresight to fit her heavier set of work boots inside the cuffs of her bunker pants when she'd left them in the back of the engine earlier so she could slide them all on at once. Of course, said bunker pants were twisted up with the rest of the gear in the pile, and she cursed as she took precious seconds to untangle everything, then even more precious seconds to tug the bunker pants over her hips and jam her feet into the boots at the bottom. She slapped the Velcro closure into place, her palms rasping beneath the stiff, unbroken-in suspenders gaping loosely over her shoulders.

But Everett's frown told her she had zero time to adjust them, so Savannah reached for her gloves, which were next in the pile. Her coat followed . . . or it *would've* followed if the bright red strap on her right shoulder hadn't flopped to her elbow and immediately gotten caught in the coat sleeve where she'd just put her arm.

"Damn it." A sheen of sweat burst over her brow beneath the hood, her frustration threatening to bubble over. She reached inside her sleeve with her opposite hand to right the suspender over her shoulder, then her coat around her frame. Her breath came in short bursts that she felt as much as heard, wedging itself in her throat as she realized too late that working the zipper on her coat was going to take damn near an act of God with her thick-fingered gloves in place.

With an aggravated huff, she shook the gloves back to the concrete. The zipper closed with a *hiss*, and Savannah moved on to the SCBA tank between her feet. The adrenaline zinging through her bloodstream turned the buckles into advanced rocket science, and after her fourth attempt to get them locked into place, she found success and reached for her helmet. She tightened the straps under her chin, and her lower back muscles—which were already madder than a wet hen from spending the weekend on her brother's couch—screeched in protest as she bent down for her gloves . . . *again*. But they were the last item standing, and Savannah wasn't about to quit so close to being done.

Even if she knew beyond the shadow of a doubt that she was dragging her ass across the finish line.

"Time." Everett's voice echoed off the cinder blocks as he clicked the stopwatch with a flick of his thumb. His olive-green stare raked over her with enough intensity that she could practically feel it on her skin, and she braced herself for his scathing criticism of her performance.

Only it never came.

"All right," he said, resetting the stopwatch. "Dress down and let's do it again."

"That's it? You're not going to yell at me?" The words left a trail of heat on her face. But it wasn't as if added brazen-ness was going to shock him at this stage in the game, and anyway, Savannah couldn't deny wanting to know the answer to her question. Nearly all the training she'd done at the academy had been delivered drill-sergeant style. She'd certainly expected more of the same, or maybe even an added level of emotion, now that she'd taken the next step.

Everett examined her, his expression more unreadable than ever. "Will yelling at you change the fact that your drill time is in the shitter?"

Her stomach dropped even though the criticism was one hundred percent accurate. "No."

"And do you want me to yell at you?"

"No, but—"

"Good," he said, and something about the soft yet serious tone of the interruption made her bite back her argument and listen. "Because it's pretty clear that teaching you how to gear up properly is going to be a full-time job. I'd hate to add one more thing to my To-Do list."

Savannah paused for only a second, her heart still doing the triple lindy with her rib cage beneath the heavy layers of her gear.

But if she wanted to learn the best way to get her equip-ment in order without killing herself in the process, she was going to have to swallow her pride—and her burning curiosity—faster than a double shot of her daddy's Johnnie Walker Blue.

"Okay then." Savannah shucked her turnout gear piece by piece until she stood in front of Everett in nothing more than her uniform and her balls-out determination. "What do I need to do first?"

He met her eyes for just a split second before nodding. "Most of getting geared up quickly is a matter of practice. That and figuring out what works best for you on the fly. But just because you're moving fast doesn't mean everything is chaos. It also has to be right, so you need to find a strategy and stick with it."

He showed her a few tricks for getting her gear on in a more effective order, helping her to adjust her suspenders and suggesting that she go gloves last to avoid fumbling with the straps on both her helmet and her SCBA. He explained everything methodically, showing her the motions with equal precision, and after the fourth time through, her mouth got the best of her already questionable inhibitions.

"Just out of curiosity, do you have any emotions?" Savannah asked, twirling a finger around her face before sliding her newly adjusted suspenders over her shoulders and hefting her coat from the floor of the engine bay. "Or is it one size fits all up there?"

Everett's mouth pressed into a hard line, his eyes not budging from the stopwatch in his grip. "Emotions are dangerous, especially on this job."

God, he was so *serious*. It had to be painful.

But everyone had a tipping point, a hot button, a trigger, and for a split second, Savannah found herself wondering what could possibly rattle Cole Everett.

What would it take to for him to really, thoroughly lose his composure?

Warmth flashed high over her cheeks. "That doesn't

answer the question," she said, dropping her gaze to the gear in front of her.

"Are you trying to be insubordinate? Or does it just come naturally?"

She zipped her coat into place and slid a covert glance over his face. His tone sounded even enough—not that he ever seemed to deviate from neutral territory. But his eyes didn't crinkle, the corners of his lips didn't lift upward in the slightest. Oookay. Guess it was a legitimate question rather than the general sort of teasing she'd gotten from everyone else at breakfast.

"Also not an answer," Savannah pointed out, her muscles squeezing beneath the now-familiar weight of the SCBA tank as she shouldered the thing and got to work on clasping the buckles. "But since you asked, I'm pretty inquisitive by nature. So I guess it comes naturally."

"Why am I not surprised?" Everett tapped the button on the stopwatch, shaking his head slightly before rotating his index finger in the universal sign for *let's do it again*. "And for the record, of course I have emotions." His gaze darkened, although the rest of his expression remained unaltered. "I'm human just like you. But letting your emotions rule your actions will only get you into trouble. You need to check them at the door if you want to hack it around here."

"Yeah, I got that at breakfast," Savannah said, her belly knotting at the memory of the car wreck conversation.

"Well, make it a point to keep getting it. The work isn't going to wait for you to get your shit together."

Everett's pointed glance had her moving despite her frustration, and she pulled at her gloves, piling her gear back to the floor in moves that had become much more fluid over the last half hour. "Does getting dressed and undressed really count as work? Or is it more like a diabolical plot to bore me to death?"

In an instant, Everett was in her personal space, so close that the woodsy scent of his soap filled her lungs on a sharp, surprised inhale. "I'm sorry, candidate. Did you say I'm boring you?"

Oh God. Savannah was suddenly far, *far* from bored. "N-no. I just meant . . ."

She trailed off, her shoulders bumping against the side panel of the engine at Everett's closeness. His chest was barely an inch from hers, their bodies completely lined up from hips to shoulder to mouth. Heat arrowed a direct path to her core, and she hung on to his unyielding stare by the barest of threads.

"No," Savannah said. "You're not boring me."

"Good." His exhale moved past her ear in a warm puff as he dropped his eyes to the bare expanse of her neck, right to the spot where her pulse was currently slamming through her veins.

"Now do yourself a favor and control your emotions instead of letting them control you. Because I don't care if this is the only drill we do for a month, but you *will* learn how to gear up and pull your weight just like everyone else. Do you copy?"

Chapter Six

Four hours after Everett had led her out to the engine bay for gear drills, Savannah's muscles felt as if they'd been massaged by a five-alarm fire. Her ponytail was plastered to the back of her head, having long since been turned into a rat's nest from the repeated on-off-on-off of both her hood and her helmet. Her uniform fared no better, and between the heavy dotting of perspiration running from her temples to her shoulder blades and the inevitable layer of grime from her countless drop-downs over the garage floor, Savannah had no doubt she was a hot mess from head to toe.

Make that an achy, exhausted, halfway to starving hot mess. But the second Everett had thrown down the gauntlet with this gear drill, the unbidden snap of heat in her body had become sheer determination. If he thought she couldn't pull her weight, he was going to be in for the mother of all rude awakenings. No matter *how* hot his body had felt against hers.

"You ready for lunch?" Everett flipped his wrist to check his watch, and Savannah bent at the waist, bracing her palms over her thighs to catch her breath. She'd been so focused on proving herself with the task at hand that she hadn't realized until now that they must've bypassed lunch by at least an hour.

"I don't know," she said, cautious. Just because she thought she'd aced the last handful of drills he'd put her through didn't mean he thought so, too. "Am I?"

Everett turned toward the storage compartment at the back of the engine, grabbing a bottle of water from the small cooler inside and handing it over. "I might be here to train you, but like I said at breakfast, I'm not too interested in testing the threshold of your blood sugar levels. You're no good to me or anyone else on engine if you pass out."

Savannah took three long, greedy swallows before coming up for air, and sweet baby Jesus, water had never tasted so delicious. "Aw, thanks, Everett. You're a peach."

"You're welcome." He gave her a minute to finish her water, then one more to store her gear in the back step of the engine. "Lunch is usually do it yourself around here, depending on who's on calls."

"Yeah, squad and ambo have been busy today, huh?" She flicked a glance at the empty slots in the engine bay as they crossed the space and headed toward the door to the house. The all-call had sounded off twice each for rescue squad and the ambulance since Rachel and O'Keefe had come back from their gruesome accident this morning, but requests for engine assistance had clocked in at a whopping zero. Much to the chagrin of Savannah's overeager nerves.

"A little. But don't worry. We'll haul out soon enough."

She followed Everett into the station, pausing to wash up and right her disheveled uniform as best she could before heading into the center of the house. Although the TV was on in the common room and Donovan and Jones were parked comfortably on the faded brown couch in front of it, the station house seemed eerily quiet without the rest of the group around.

"Wow." Savannah lifted her brows, joining Everett at the

kitchen island. "I guess I never really thought there would be much downtime."

"Sometimes there isn't," he said. "But it's not a bad plan to take a breather when you can. You never know when a shit storm will come down the pike."

He pointed to the loaf of bread and handful of sandwich fixings on the counter in wordless invitation, and Savannah's stomach rumbled despite the simple ingredients.

"Still." She picked up a plate, her shrug feeling tighter than it should. Damned gear drills. "Doesn't being idle feel weird to you? I mean, wouldn't you rather be out on a call than sitting here making sandwiches?"

Although Everett's face remained neutral as always, she could swear she saw the tiniest hitch in his movements as he reached for the container of roast beef in front of him.

"I'm a firefighter, Nelson. I'd rather be out on a call than doing anything. But you learn to take the downtime where you can get it, otherwise you'll fry your motherboard."

"But I thought working hard was part of the deal," she said. After all, she hadn't been expecting a nine-to-five. Been there, done that. Most yawn-worthy year of her life, much to her mama's chagrin. "How else am I going to learn how to do the job other than to *do* it?"

Everett shook his head, muttering something about doing things the hard way instead of giving her an answer, and they spent the next few minutes putting together a pair of sandwiches in silence. While Savannah was tempted to demolish the turkey and Swiss in front of her in about three bites, she forced herself to take the slow road. If she didn't want the sort of nickname that would accompany an episode of light-headedness, she could only imagine how unshakably bad her moniker would be if she tossed her cookies— or in this case, her entire lunch—on day one.

"Okay," Savannah said, finally brushing off her hands after she'd put an apple and a giant scattering of chips on top of the sandwich in her belly. "So what's next on the agenda?"

"You really are unfamiliar with the concept of pacing yourself, aren't you?"

Everett's tone made it impossible to tell if he was teasing her or actually asking. But since her answer wasn't going to change either way, she simply shrugged.

"I'll have plenty of downtime when I leave here. There are two whole days in between shifts," Savannah said, her muscles thrumming with jittery anticipation even as they ached with fatigue. It couldn't really be normal to not have one single call all morning, could it?

She was so caught up in the antsy twist in her gut that she noticed Everett's pointed eye contact with Donovan a full ten seconds too late.

The other firefighter sauntered over to the kitchen island, all swagger. "Speaking of downtime, I was just about to head to the back to grab a sweatshirt. Why don't I get Nelson here settled into a bunk for a breather while I'm at it?"

"That's okay—" Savannah started, but Everett cut her off with a tip of his head.

"You know what, Donovan? That is an excellent idea."

Oh, you've got to be kidding me. "You're sending me to my room to take a nap?"

"We're offering you a rare opportunity," Donovan corrected, breaking into a ridiculously charming smile. "You're going to need a bunk at some point anyway. There's really no time like the present."

She chanced a last-ditch look at Jones, who didn't even bother to hide the fact that he'd muted the TV to listen in. Although he said nothing, her fellow rookie's expression suggested there were far worse things she could be asked to do than downshift for an hour.

Savannah thought back to this morning's kitchen assignment, and okay, point taken. The idea of sitting on her hands when she could be doing something of actual value might not be thrilling, but it wasn't the worst thing that could happen, either. Plus, it wasn't as if she'd be expected to stay in the bunks if something major went down.

Please, God, let something major go down.

"I guess you're right, Donovan," she said in slow concession, although man, the words pinched on the way out. "I am going to need a place to sleep sooner or later. I might as well get comfortable now."

"That's the spirit, rookie." He clapped her on the shoulder, waiting for her to push off from the counter and put her plate in the sink. She frowned at Everett, who deflected with his garden-variety unreadable stare, and Donovan led the way out of the common room. Savannah followed reluctantly, sliding a hand over the ache in her lower back as they headed down the hallway toward the engine bay.

"So the bunks are on the other side of the locker room, right? Off the back of the house?" They were the only part of the place she hadn't seen yet, but it made sense that they'd be more removed from the common area yet still accessible to the engine bay for quick exits.

Alex nodded, breaking into an affable grin. "See? And you thought you wouldn't learn anything by taking a breather."

"Funny," she said, although she couldn't keep her tiny smile at bay.

"I know, right? It's a gift." He lifted his blond brows in an exaggerated waggle, and God, she missed her brothers in Texas. "Anyway, yes. We try to keep the bunks separate so they stay as quiet as possible, but I'm not gonna lie. It's hit or miss during the day. You might as well kiss your circadian rhythms good-bye now."

Even though Brad had given her an identical warning weeks ago, Savannah still nodded. "Good to know."

"Both Crews and Andersen on squad snore like goddamn

lumberjacks, and the beds back here have probably been around since before the turn of the millennium. But otherwise, spending the night in-house really isn't too bad."

The image of her brother's couch popped into her head. "Are you kidding? At least here I have a mattress."

Donovan pulled up halfway over the tiles of the locker room floor, a bark of non-malicious laughter spilling past his smile. "That's a story."

"Oh. Uh." Heat tore across her face. Damn it, damn it, *damn* it, would she ever learn to think first, then speak? Spilling the embarrassing-as-hell details of her breakup with Rat-face Roger was so not on her wish list, especially not to a fellow firefighter who she wanted to take her seriously. "Nah. Not really."

Alex rolled his blue eyes sky-high, giving up a brotherly tsk that felt oddly comforting. "We can work on your absolute lack of a poker face later, because truly, you're going to need one in order to survive. Right now . . ." He paused, flipping his palm up and wiggling his fingers to signal *give it up*. "Come on. Come on! You dangle a nugget like that in front of me and think I'm going to let you off the hook? Spill it, rookie."

"Okay, okay, fine." Savannah laughed, rolling her eyes right back at him. "Let's just say I'm recently and unexpectedly single, and my brother's couch is my only available sleeping option until I can find a new apartment."

"Ouch. Sorry about the breakup," Donovan said, and funny, he actually looked contrite.

"Ah, I'm not." She capped the words with a shrug. Just because she hadn't wanted to cop to her breakup with Roger didn't make her lack of regrets any less true. "He was pretty much a jackass, and to be honest, I'd rather focus on the job right now anyway."

Donovan examined her with a no-bullshit stare before

kicking his boots back into motion toward the door on the far wall by the shower room. "You're pretty ambitious."

"You mean for a woman?" She froze, but he didn't even skip a beat.

"I mean for a candidate. No wonder Westin put you with Everett. I mean, aside from the squad thing."

Surprise erased Savannah's chagrin in one quick stroke. "What squad thing?"

"He didn't tell you?" Donovan dropped his voice, but whether it was to keep his words on the down low or out of habit at entering the bunk room, she couldn't tell. "Everett's moving to squad in six weeks."

Okay, so surprise was now a gargantuan understatement. "When my orientation is done?"

"Yup. We'll do a bit of musical chairs with assignments, but it'll all work out."

His easygoing expression marked the personnel shuffle as no big deal, and other than the initial burst of shock the information had sent through her, Savannah knew that it probably wasn't. Firehouses saw plenty of turnover, and Everett certainly seemed serious enough about the job to be a good fit for the rescue squad.

Donovan shifted gears, gesturing to the room in front of them as he whispered, "Welcome to Station Eight's bunk room. As you can hear, I wasn't kidding about Crews. Or your sleep cycles."

The distinct sound of snoring drifted over the maze of six-foot cinder-block half walls dividing the open space of the sleeping quarters into smaller cubicles, and Savannah stifled a laugh.

"Copy that."

She took in the large, semi-shadowed room, peeking past the threshold to the bunk on her left. It wasn't much to write home about—an eight-by-ten rectangle just big enough to allow for a twin bed with a light fixture built into the headboard, a small storage locker, and an even smaller side table. A dark blue curtain hung from a tension rod spanning the top of the cubicle's entryway, which at least offered a tiny bit of privacy. The row of narrow windows marching a horizontal line over the top of the south wall let in enough daylight to keep things visible, but not so much that catching up on sleep during off hours would be impossible.

Or at least, it wouldn't be if Savannah needed the break. But if resting for a little while would satisfy Everett into teaching her something more exciting than how to put on her turnout gear, then fine. She could play along.

"Okay. Let's see." Donovan kept his tone at a low murmur, scanning the row of cubicles on either side of them. "We loosely assign bunks by squad and engine, just to keep things streamlined when calls come in. Bunks for engine are on the left, so let's put you . . ." He tapped his thumb over his lightly stubbled chin, stepping over to the second curtain in the row. "Here."

"Sure. Great," she said, sending up a silent prayer of thanks that Crews was at the other end of the room. She pulled back the curtain to her cubicle, eyeballing the neatly made bed and the starched, standard issue pillow waiting for her. "I guess I'll see you later."

"You got it, rookie. Have a good break. Just make sure you come running—and I do mean running—if the all-call goes off."

It took every last ounce of Savannah's willpower not to laugh at the irony. "Believe me, Donovan. That all-call goes off, and I'll be the first person in the step."

Cole gripped the basketball between his fingers, dribbling with a methodical *thunk thunk thunk* as he examined both his opponent and his options. Despite the otherworldly amount of trash talk that had been coming out of Donovan's mouth for the last half hour, Cole had taken the smartass two games for two in the makeshift court adjacent to the outside wall of the engine bay, and with one more well-timed shot, he'd make it a bragging rights trifecta.

God knew he had enough steam to blow off. Seven hours into her very first tour, and his candidate was trying to kill him, one sweet moment at a time.

"Come on, dickhead. I don't have all day for you to plot this shit down to the nanosecond." Donovan laughed, his expression pure bravado. But after eight years of friendship, Cole could read the guy like the front page of the Fairview *Sentinel* and pick apart his game with just as much ease.

Shift right toward the weaker side. Fake. Break away on the opening and take the layup for the win.

By the time his neurons had carried the string of commands from his brain to his body, the *clink* of the metallic basket chains had already signaled Cole's victory.

"Damn, Teflon. Are you still falling for that move?" The familiar voice filtered in from the side exit of the engine bay, interrupting Donovan's litany of swear words and Cole's less-than-humble smile. "He's been faking to your weak side since my rookie year."

Cole swiped a forearm over his sweat-laced forehead, his smile morphing to a grin as he turned toward their buddy and former Station Eight housemate, Nick Brennan.

"It's not my fault he always falls for it," Cole argued, passing the ball to Brennan when his friend had crossed enough asphalt to reach the court.

Brennan lifted a black brow toward the brim of his baseball hat, dribbling twice before taking a shot. "Uh-huh. Easy trash talk from Station Eight's newest squad rookie. How's it going now that you're too good for engine, you fucking snob?"

Cole let out a groan, although he couldn't put his back

into it. As one of his closest friends, Brennan could be counted on to deliver a ration of good-natured crap over Cole's impending bump up to the rescue squad. As a former active-duty firefighter who had made squad himself just before a crushing injury forced him into early retirement? The shit-giving was nothing less than a total prerequisite.

Not that Cole couldn't—or wouldn't—return the favor. "The pot and the kettle called. They both said to tell you you're an asshole."

Brennan's laughter combined with Donovan's as the three of them met midcourt. "Yeah, yeah. Congratulations, dude. I know it's what you wanted."

"I do," Cole agreed, although hell if it wasn't the biggest understatement he'd uttered all week. "I take it you talked to Crews."

"And O'Keefe. And Harrison," Brennan said, and Jesus, nothing was sacred in a firehouse. His buddy smoothed a hand over his FFD T-shirt, right over the spot labeled *instructor* on the left upper chest. "And Captain Westin."

Cole's heart knocked against his ribs, and not from the exertion of the one-on-one. "So you knew Nelson would be placed here at Eight and that I'd have to train her in order to move to squad."

As an instructor at the academy, Brennan was sometimes consulted on candidate placements. Since he'd been one of Westin's firefighters for nearly five years before his injury, it made sense that the captain would've at least put Brennan in the loop over specifically which candidate to recruit as Cole's replacement.

Brennan exchanged a nanosecond's worth of a glance with Donovan before nodding. "I knew Nelson would land here once the placement process became final. The rest . . ." He paused, but finally added, "I didn't know for sure, but I had a strong suspicion, yeah. How's she doing so far? I know she can be kind of—"

"An epic pain in the ass?" Cole supplied, and Brennan coughed out a laugh.

"I was going to say headstrong. She's actually not a bad candidate, if you can get her to check her attitude. She definitely wants to be a firefighter, that's for damn sure."

"She is pretty tough," Donovan said, clearly a compliment. "When I took her in to the bunks, she told me her boyfriend broke up with her a couple of days ago. She might as well have been giving me the weather report, and it didn't seem like a cover."

Cole's shock led the way for the upward snap of his chin. "You talked to her about her personal life? What are you, Dr. Phil?"

"Don't hate, Everett. It's not my fault I'm a likable guy. Anyway, yeah. Apparently the ex is a total douche canoe, so she's crashing with her brother. But she blew it off like it was no big deal, said she'd rather focus on the job anyway. I'm telling you, girlfriend's got chops."

Brennan latched on to the segue before Cole could counter that there was such a thing as too much attitude. "What'd you put her through this morning?" his buddy asked.

"Gear drills," Cole said. After Savannah's initial trouble with the straps on her helmet when they'd been sitting in the equipment room, it had seemed like the most logical place to start.

"How'd she do?"

He hesitated, but he wasn't about to downplay the truth, especially since once Savannah had gotten over being pissy, she'd done even better than he'd thought she would. "Pretty good, actually."

Donovan's blue eyes narrowed to a squint in the overhead sunlight. "Yeah? How good?"

Oh screw it. Cole looked from Brennan to Donovan, blowing out a breath. "She came within three seconds of breaking your rookie record."

"Shut the fuck up," Donovan said, all shock and no anger. "The only person who's ever done that is . . ."

Both of his best friends stared at him outright, finishing in unison. "You."

"Yeah," Cole said, biting back an ironic laugh at the fact that Savannah's personal best had clocked in at a near-identical number to his own when he'd been a rookie. "She did great—once I *finally* got her to shut up and listen."

Cole's brain zeroed in on the hitch in Savannah's breath as he'd stepped in close to her, his gut forming a knot at how he'd let his emotions guide him into her personal space not once, but twice today. The laundry-line scent of her skin . . . the hypnotic heat of her body, nearly pressed against his in all the right places . . .

Focus, asshole! He shook the image of her wide, dark brown stare and the curve of her breasts beneath her T-shirt from his mind's eye. "But after she stopped giving me shit, she pretty much killed all the drills I threw at her."

Brennan recovered from his surprise first. "That's good, though. I mean, if Nelson catches on fast, not only will she be an asset to the house, but then you can move to squad, no sweat."

Cole raked a hand through his hair, letting his palm rest on the back of his neck. "In theory, yeah. The problem is, she's too hotheaded to use her ambition to her advantage. All she wants to do when I push her is push back. Plus, she really stepped in it with Oz this morning, and believe me when I tell you, he is none too happy to have her in-house."

He gave them the bullet-point version of his conversation with the lieutenant, complete with Oz's ominous words of parting. After a heartbeat's worth of stunned silence, Donovan stepped back on the asphalt and whistled under his breath.

"Jesus. Nelson really did piss him off, huh?"

Tension rippled down his spine at the understatement,

making Cole choose his words with care. "I think between the concept of having a female candidate and the reality of having *this* female candidate, he's just looking for a reason to drag her in front of Westin."

Which would be detrimental not just to Savannah's spot on engine, but to Cole's spot on squad. While he certainly got Oz's irritation with this morning's kitchen byplay, the reasoning behind Savannah's pushback had made a glimmer of sense once she'd aired it. Still, her screw-you strategy was going to get both of them into boiling-hot water, and while Cole had never minded a little bit of heat, he sure as hell minded getting burned.

"Nelson's just going to have to put her emotions in check—and fast—if she wants to get right with Oz and prove herself around here."

The corners of Brennan's mouth tightened beneath his dark goatee. "Did Westin tell you—"

Cole's brow had just creased at the unease on Brennan's face when the all-too-familiar sound of the station-wide alarm cut his buddy's words short.

"Engine Eight, Squad Eight, Ambulance Eight. Structure fire, ninety-seven hundred Wabash Avenue. Requesting immediate response."

Alex broke into a grin at the same time he and Cole started moving toward the engine bay.

"Guess your rookie's about to get a little trial by fire."

Chapter Seven

Crews, Donovan, Jones . . .

Cole bit out a low curse as his head count came up suspiciously short. Swinging his gaze from the step to the engine bay, he leaned an elbow out the side window of Engine Eight, irritation beating out the adrenaline in his veins two to one.

"Nice of you to join us, Nelson," he called out over the growl of the engine, taking in Savannah's sleep-rumpled ponytail and her half-bleary, mostly shell-shocked expression as she scrambled into the step and yanked the door shut with a heavy *bang*. Cole snapped the headset off the hook in front of him, guiding it into place and giving the traffic signal in front of the house a second's worth of a make-sure glance before steering his way out of the engine bay.

"All right. Let's see what we've got," Crews said into the mic on his headset. Although the lieutenant had been just as asleep as Savannah when the all-call had blared through the overhead two minutes ago, he worked in precise, efficient movements, sitting up straight against the officer's seat beside Cole and clacking his way through the computer system they used to communicate with dispatch.

"Ninety-seven hundred Wabash is on the east side of the

docks, on Industrial Row. Nearest major cross street is Franklin. Looks like either a warehouse or a factory of some kind."

Cole rolled through the map in his mind before matching it against the GPS screen embedded in the dash, using the methodical process to temper the fast-paced thump-*thump* of his heartbeat.

"Copy that," he said, and Donovan echoed the words through the headset from his spot in the step. Between the amount of space and equipment dividing the front of the engine from the back and the wail of the sirens over their heads, hearing each other without assistance was more fantasy than reality, and seeing much of anything over the partition—especially when Cole was also responsible for maneuvering the engine through Fairview's city streets—was even less likely. Although there were enough headsets in the step for each firefighter, usually only one person in the back wore them, communicating with the others as necessary, but as the operator, Cole always wore a set to be sure he'd hear Crews barking out orders and updates.

Case in point. "Listen up, ladies and gentlemen! Dispatch just confirmed two reports of smoke at the scene and it looks like we're going to be first in, so it's time to put your tray tables up and fasten your fucking seat belts. GPS has us seven minutes out. I want each of you ready to put your boots on the ground in five."

This time, Donovan's "copy that" was joined by Savannah's through the headset, sending a hot pulse of energy through Cole's blood. Of course she was ambitious enough to listen in for herself. Even if she'd lagged behind when the all-call had gone off, she'd made no bones about wanting to prove herself, often and well and immediately if not sooner.

Jesus, he was going to have his hands full in T-minus six minutes and counting.

Cole guided the engine over the narrow downtown side

streets, the landscape changing block by block as they got closer to Industrial Row. The buildings grew shabbier and more dilapidated, some with bars on the windows, others with the openings boarded up completely. The clusters of businesses still up and running were of the questionable variety, with pawnshops and convenience stores and seedy-looking bars headlining the pack. Cole smelled the acrid punch of smoke about sixty seconds before he saw the fat gray puffs seething out from the second- and third-story windows of an older warehouse-style building. Damn, the place had to be upward of twenty thousand square feet, with more than half of it actively burning.

Time to make the doughnuts.

"Okay, people," Crews hollered through the headset as he yanked his coat closed and grabbed his gloves. "Squad's right in front of us, and Westin's on the two-way, calling the ball. Let's go."

Cole jumped down from the engine, a blast of heat from the sunbaked street combining with the thick haze of smoke to rush upward and cram inside his lungs. To his left, Donovan's boots hit the pavement, and the guy turned just briefly to place an affable slap over the top of Savannah's helmet before hauling off to follow Crews and Jonesey.

But Savannah didn't move. She stood glued to Wabash Avenue, eyes like dark copper dinner plates as she stared at the flames licking their way up the front of the building. As sleep-startled as she'd looked pulling herself into the step ten minutes ago, her current expression marked her as wide awake, although she didn't seem any less stunned now that they were on scene.

Cole needed to snap her out of it. And *fast*.

"Nelson." He stepped directly into her field of vision, fastening his gaze over hers as he edged close enough for the brims of their helmets to nearly touch. "You're on my hip. Not ahead of me, not up my ass, not ten steps behind. On my hip. Got it?"

She blinked. Reset herself. And just like that, the glimmer was back in her eyes. "Copy that. On your hip," she said with a hard nod.

He exhaled in relief. Turning toward the back of the engine, Cole covered the space in only a few strides, not stopping until he'd reached the spot on the street where Captain Westin stood issuing no-nonsense orders.

"Oz, you and Andersen get up on that roof for a vent," he said, his keen eyes not wavering from the warehouse's roofline. "I want to knock this fire down before it spreads any farther. Crews, you're on the nozzle with Donovan. Jones, fall in to advance the line. According to dispatch, this warehouse is storage only, but keep your eyes open for entrapment just in case. Everett, take Nelson to tap a hydrant and stand by on engine. Get it done."

"Okay," Savannah said, recovering her voice as everyone broke into motion. "So once we get the line open, then what do you and I do?"

Cole inhaled, the scent of soot and smoke clogging his senses and making his eyes water. This warehouse was burning faster than dry kindling in a drought. "What we *don't* do is get ahead of ourselves. Where's the closest hydrant, candidate?"

"Uh." She swung her gaze up and down Wabash Avenue in a panicked search, and hell, they didn't have time for this.

"It's half a block up on your nine." He shouldered the hose from the back of the engine, his muscles going into a full-on burn that didn't stop him from turning to his left and hauling ass over the crumbling sidewalk. Once Nelson got over her momentary stumbling block, she fell in behind him, right on his hip.

"Go ahead," Cole said, jerking his head at the ancient, once-red fire hydrant he'd put eyes on about seven seconds after his boots had met the asphalt. Nelson dropped to the pavement and got to work tapping the hydrant, and miraculously, the freaking thing wasn't stripped. Although her motions were far less smooth than Cole would've liked, Savannah managed to get the water line set without too much of a delay.

"Water's a go," Cole said into the radio on his shoulder, waiting for Captain Westin's "copy that, water is a go" in response before starting back toward Engine Eight.

As soon as their boots stopped moving, Savannah lifted her hands in question. "Now what?"

"Now we stand by, just like Cap said."

"But"—she broke off to aim a pointed look at the warehouse, which was still showing signs of active fire from both the second and third floors—"this fire is huge. Shouldn't we all be inside?"

The adrenaline coursing through his system shot out a steady stream of *yes yes yes*, but still Cole shook his head. *Focus.* "The rest of the guys on squad are heading in while Oz and Andersen vent the roof, and Crews and Donovan and Jones will back them up. Two in, two out."

A spark of hope crossed Nelson's heat-flushed face. "So when two of them come out, we go in."

"Negative," he said, scanning the scene in another systematic sweep. "Your assignment is your assignment, and it doesn't change. Two in, two out means that when two men— or in this case, more—go inside a building, two stay outside at the engine. No exceptions."

"So we just have to *sit* here?"

Cole's molars came together in a hard *clack*. "No. We have to stand by."

The frustration on her face was as plain as the burning building in front of him, but beneath her creased brows and her pinched mouth, Cole could see the gears moving, processing. "In case something goes wrong and they need someone to go in for a rescue?"

Halle-freaking-llujah. "Now you're catching on. So tell me. What do you see?"

"I see a gigantic fire, Everett," she said, and so much for her frustration taking a hike. "What else is there?"

He bit the inside of his cheek until it stung, but damn it, she needed to look past the fire, and the only way she was going to learn how to properly assess a scene was if she was properly taught. "Standing by doesn't mean just sitting on your ass waiting for something to happen, Nelson. Remember that swivel your head is supposed to be on? There's plenty to see if you just look, and you never know if you're going to need the intel. Now try again."

Finally, she lifted her head, the black brim of her helmet shading her eyes as she shifted her gaze from left to right. "A four-story warehouse, detached structure, second and third floors fully involved. Showing flames in six windows on the Alpha side. Three on floor two, three on floor three. Primary point of entry is the front door, which appears unimpeded."

"Good." Cole split his attention between the scene in front of him and the back-and-forth going on over the two-way at his shoulder, his brows lifting slightly in surprise as Nelson paused to mimic his actions. "What else?"

"No reported entrapment, and the police have the street blocked off, so no bystanders are in danger from the fire or falling debris."

Savannah proceeded to run down the details of the scene, pausing along with him to listen to the radio byplay as the guys on engine and squad worked to contain the blaze. Although Cole itched to be in the thick of the fire just as fiercely as she did, she had to learn how to manage both a scene and her nerves from the outside in.

Otherwise the only thing they'd both be managing was a swift trip to the captain's office.

"All right," Westin finally called out over the radio as the last of the flames disappeared and the steady plumes of smoke began to subside. "Nice work, men. Oz, you and Andersen do one last walk-through. I'm none too interested in seeing this place flare up for another go-round. Crews, Donovan, Jones, fall out."

Savannah turned toward him, lips parted. "So that's it?"

"We have to load up all the equipment, and squad will come back at some point to do the official report. But yeah. The fire's out, so that's it."

"But I didn't even do anything," she argued.

Cole's gut twitched. He knew he should take a deep breath, grab his focus with both hands, and calmly remind her that she wasn't even halfway through with her very first shift.

So it surprised the hell out of them both when instead, he scooped up the challenge in her words and threw down one of his own.

"Actually, you had the most important assignment of anyone. But until you figure out why that is, you aren't going to get very far."

By the time Savannah's shift was finally done and she'd dragged herself back over the threshold of her brother's apartment, she was fairly certain collapsing was a foregone conclusion. Whether the cause of her demise would be muscle failure or sheer exhaustion remained a bit of a coin flip, but between the incessant throbbing in her body and the punch-drunk weariness of her brain, there was one thing Savannah did know for sure.

Nothing she'd ever practiced at the academy had come within a country mile of the twenty-four hours she'd just spent at Station Eight. And she hadn't even *done* anything other than cook, run an ungodly number of drills, watch every other person in the house fight the one honest-to-God fire they'd been called to, and get about three hours of broken sleep as they'd hauled out on false alarm after false alarm in the middle of the night.

"Hey! The prodigal daughter returns." Brad looked up from the narrow stretch of countertop that doubled as the breakfast bar separating his kitchenette from the rest of the apartment's teeny-tiny living space. "How was your first shift?"

"Unnnf," Savannah managed, not even bothering to kick off her boots before trudging over to the couch and flopping facedown onto the cushions. Oh *God*, she must be hurting something awful, because not even hellfire and brimstone could drag her from this spot, and the couch was more uncomfortable than ever.

"That sounds about right." Her brother nodded, his brown eyes crinkling just slightly at the edges as he folded up the newspaper he'd been reading in favor of giving her a closer look. "So seriously, are you going to make me drag the details out of you? Because I'd hate to put the screws to you when you're so weak."

Savannah rolled over, mustering just enough energy for her family-famous death glare. "Careful, brother of mine. This dog may be tired, but she'll still bite."

"Atta girl." Brad took the three steps necessary to reach his refrigerator, then six more to deliver the water bottle he'd unearthed to her spot on the couch. "So come on. Before I go to work and leave you here in the castle all day, out with it. How'd it go over at Eight?"

Well, hell. She might as well fork over the details because she knew her brother way better than to think he'd been kidding about putting the screws to her.

"It was . . ." *Physically challenging. Mentally draining.*

Frustrating as shit. "Interesting," she finished, propping herself up on one elbow to crack open her bottle of water.

Brad raised a nearly black eyebrow in his trademark call of bullshit. "What are you, some sort of delicate flower all of a sudden? You just did your first tour as a firefighter, for Chrissake. A little truth, please."

Busted. "Well, seeing as how I didn't get to do anything other than housekeeping and drills, I'm not really sure I'm qualified to comment."

But rather than getting huffy in her defense, her brother just nudged her feet over, parking himself at the end of the couch. "That sounds about right for a brand-new candidate. What drills?"

"Gear *and* equipment," Savannah said, her shoulder muscles thudding at the reminder. When they'd gotten back from their lone fire call, Everett had run her all over the engine bay, finding and hauling and replacing various hoses and equipment from every last compartment of Engine Eight until she'd been ready to scream.

As if mocking her with that whole you-had-the-most-important-assignment thing hadn't been aggravating enough. Okay, so she'd screwed up a tiny bit by actually falling asleep when Everett and Donovan had exiled her to the bunks, and yeah, she'd been disoriented enough to lag behind when the all-call had ripped her awake. But she'd recovered just fine—fine enough to gear up without any help, and fine enough to have been able to at least go into that warehouse and advance the line. Not that her prep had done her any good, since her only purpose on the call had been to stop, drop, and watch. How the hell could that possibly be the most important assignment in the house?

And more importantly, why couldn't she forget the flash of pure intensity that had crossed Everett's face as he'd said it?

"Gear and equipment, huh? No wonder you look like

death on a dinner tray," Brad said, his grin tugging her back to the reality of his fun-sized apartment.

"Aw, thanks, Bradley." She slapped her armor over the sting building in her chest, splaying a hand over her heart in an exaggerated sweep. "You really know how to compliment a girl."

"That is a compliment, SB. Death warmed up means those drills didn't kill you outright like they would most people."

At the mention of her childhood nickname, Savannah groaned. "Don't call me that!"

"What? Savannah Banana?"

"I swear to God, I will find the energy to leave this couch," she threatened, although the smile poking at the edges of her mouth had to be watering down her mean factor something awful.

Her brother held up both hands. "Ah, as much as I live and breathe to torture you, I know better than to kick someone when they're down. Even someone as tough as you."

Brad's pause was just long enough to let her know that the next thing out of his mouth would be a notch up on the serious scale, and when he spoke again, he didn't disappoint. "I've heard they're a pretty tight group over there at Eight. Any issues with you being the new kid in the schoolyard?"

Savannah shifted on the couch cushions, the muscles in her upper body throbbing in protest of her shrug. "I'm their candidate, and the first woman they've ever had on engine. I'd be naïve to think they'd just welcome me into the fold."

"Is that a yes?"

Leave it to her brother to get right to the nitty-gritty. For a second, she considered letting her frustrations fly over Lieutenant Osborne putting her on KP and the coffee-pouring stunt that had gone with it. But having a hissy fit about Oz wouldn't change the guy's sexist opinions, and anyway, he'd steered pretty clear of her for the rest of the shift. She was tough enough to handle it without whining. "It's nothing I can't manage."

Just like that, her brother's smile was back. "I know. Speaking of which, I left the Icy Hot and a shitload of ibuprofen out for you in the bathroom. Oh, and there are two bags of peas in the freezer."

Okay, so she knew she was brain-fried, but now Brad was just talking crazy. "And how exactly is eating two entire bags of peas going to make me feel better?"

"They're not for your belly, smart mouth. They're for your back. Don't you remember Dad's solution when Tyler accidentally popped you in the face during our touch football tourney that one Thanksgiving?"

As spent as she was, Savannah had to give in to the grin forming on her lips. "An ass-whupping?"

Lord, her daddy had been so mad at their brother for that errant elbow he'd thrown trying to get to Brad, who'd been playing QB at the time. The black eye she'd gotten really had been an accident, and she'd taken it like a champ, not even crying in front of the boys. But Tyler had been fourteen, so not only had he had five years on her, but he'd also outweighed her by nearly double at the time. The hit had hurt like hell.

"The cure for your shiner, not for Ty's ass." Brad laughed. "Dad put that bag of frozen succotash on your cheek and it worked like a charm on all that swelling. Sorry to say the grocery store was fresh out of succotash today, but the peas will do the same for your back. Trust me."

Savannah's heart twisted in her rib cage. The double whammy of the family memory and the fact that Brad was clearly looking out for her in his own older-brother way made her throat go tight, and she swallowed twice before saying, "Yeah. Thanks."

"Sure." Brad braced his forearms over the thighs of his

uniform pants, turning so Savannah couldn't escape his dark brown stare. "So are you going to call him?"

She swallowed again, third time being the charm and all. "Maybe at the end of the week, after I have a few shifts under my belt."

Translation: after she got to do something other than wreck breakfast and work standby detail. No way could she call her battalion chief father with the scoop on her job until she had something of substance to say. Something that would make him proud.

Something that would make leaving the Texas hometown she'd loved almost as much as her family itself worth the heartache of uprooting.

"You know he and Mama just want you to be happy," Brad said, nudging her gently.

At least this, Savannah could answer with ease. "I do know. But it's different for me than it was for the three of you. I need to earn it, Brad. On my own."

For a minute that she measured in heartbeats, they sat there in silence, until finally, her brother let out a breath and a nod. "I get it, SB. I really do. But in the same way it was hard for you to make the decision to leave, it's hard for Dad to live with it. Just remember there's a flip side to every penny. Now go on and get some sleep."

Cole lowered the duffel containing yesterday's clothes to the same post-shift resting spot he'd used for the last eight years, his keys ringing out a metallic jangle as they found the kitchen counter. His condo wasn't much to speak of, but it was neat, with plenty of space for him and his stuff—and most importantly, it was close to the firehouse. Station Eight was his real home anyway. Where he ate his meals and laid his head when he wasn't there was really kind of secondary.

Kind of pathetic, jackass. Donovan's right. You need to get laid.

Cole's head snapped up, a bark of laughter barging out of his mouth. Okay, so he was having more of a dry spell than he'd realized. But Fairview wasn't exactly a map dot, and while his job was his number one priority, he also wasn't a fucking monk. He'd remedy his situation soon enough.

But first, he needed a shower and some shut-eye. In that order.

Making his way down the hall toward his bedroom, Cole yanked his shirt over his head and blearily kicked out of his cross-trainers. Usually he could at least sneak in a little sleep during a shift, even on the crazy nights. But every call they'd been hauled out of bed for last night had amounted to squat, and after five false alarms plus the fire he'd stood by on, Cole's normally disciplined adrenaline was just plain strung out from the dicktease of it all.

Of course, it hadn't helped that Donovan had put Savannah in the bunk directly next to Cole's, their beds separated by nothing more than half a wall's worth of cinder blocks. How was he supposed to get any shut-eye with her sighing in her sleep barely six feet away?

Sweet, breathy little sighs . . . soft pink lips on that smart, sexy mouth . . .

Jesus. Cole cranked the shower handle to the On position, chiding himself the entire time the water warmed up. Ditching the rest of his clothes, he stepped into the spray, letting the nearly-too-hot-to-bear water rudely remind him that he had no business thinking of Savannah's sighs, her mouth, or any other part of her.

Too bad his cock had other ideas. Hot ideas. Hard ideas.

Right now ideas.

The ache in his balls grew more insistent, his dick stirring to life in the warm spray of the shower. He should turn the water all the way to cold and get on with getting clean, he knew. But between his pent-up frustrations over work and the wicked reminder of Savannah's soft, sweet exhales, Cole was rock-hard in less than three seconds. Another two had his hand moving between his legs instead of toward the shower handle, and fuuuuuck, the thought of Savannah's mouth made his cock jerk in his palm.

The thought of her naked had him moaning before his fingers had even formed a fist.

Cole closed his eyes, skipping the pleasantries of a slow glide in favor of a hard, steady rhythm. Want rippled up his spine with each pump of his hand, daring him further into forbidden territory. Images flashed—Savannah's dark brown hair spilling over his pillow, her gorgeous face caught up in desire as she stroked his shaft from root to tip. Her naked body, all sexy, strong curves, under his. The sweet, hard beads of her nipples pointing up in invitation, begging for his mouth. The tight, slick heat between her thighs, gripping his cock as he sank into her again and again and again . . .

The base of his spine tingled in warning, his balls drawing up tight to second it. But the thought of Savannah, the fresh-laundry smell of her skin and the sound of her voice curving over his name with that deep-honey drawl, worked his hand even faster. The muscles in his arm ached, his hips thrusting and his cock begging for release, until finally— God *damn,* yes, yes, yes—he came with a shout.

It wasn't until Cole had finished his shower and let his head hit the pillow that he realized he hadn't just called out in release.

He'd come screaming Savannah's name.

Chapter Eight

Savannah did a triple scan of the parking lot next to Station Eight before heading toward the side entrance with her duffel on her shoulder. The sun had barely edged itself toward the horizon, sending just enough smoky purple daylight over Church Street to illuminate the twin rows of stone-and-brick buildings and the quiet ribbon of asphalt dividing them down the middle. The firehouse stood like a silent sentry to her right, the small patch of grass in front neatly kept, the row of windows set into the top of the garage bays dimly lit by the emergency fluorescents beyond.

This time, she saw Everett from thirty paces away.

"You've been early for a whole week now," he said, popping the cuff of his FFD hoodie to glance at the thick black watch circling his wrist. "Four shifts in a row."

"So have you." Okay, so she'd deflected rather than admit that she'd been up since quarter to five with every last one of her nerves doing the up-and-at-'em in her belly. There were a lot worse things she could be than ambitious. "Guess we're both just early risers."

"Or overachievers. I saw you checking out your surroundings just now." His expression betrayed no emotion, but Savannah made up for it with a laugh.

"Careful, Everett. That sounded dangerously like a compliment."

"More like an observation," he corrected, although the corners of his mouth lifted just slightly. "So how are you feeling after Sunday's shift?"

"Fine." Of course, it had taken both days between then and now to get her that way. All those damned drills he'd been putting her through had been murder on her body, and Donovan had been spot-freaking-on about her sleep cycles taking a massive hit. Not that she'd admit it out loud. "It's amazing what sixteen hours of sleep and a bag of frozen peas will do."

Everett nodded, taking a long draw off the coffee mug in his palm. "I usually go for mixed veggies myself."

Savannah's chin jacked up in surprise. "Seriously?"

As if he'd be anything but serious. "Yeah. Just do yourself a favor and don't try to cook with them afterward. Although with your track record in the kitchen, I probably shouldn't be giving you any bright ideas."

The mention of her house assignment and the likelihood of a repeat appointment yet again today squeezed her gut, but she refused to show her irritation, delivering a saucy smile instead. "Still hilarious, I see."

"And you're still determined to be insubordinate."

Savannah paused, heat creeping up the back of her neck. While she'd never claimed to be a yes-girl, she wasn't going to get very far by landing herself in Everett's bad graces before roll call. Again.

"Sorry I'm not all sunshine and roses. Not that I'm ever going to be perky." She paused to grimace, because really, the thought made her teeth hurt. "I guess I'm still a little edgy about being on shift."

By the time she registered the surprise flickering in Everett's stare, it had already disappeared.

"You're really going to need to learn how to leave your

emotions at the door," he said, and Savannah coughed out a laugh that was both humor and irony. She didn't mind the blunt response. After all, the easiest path between two points *was* a straight line. But with her personality, making that theory play nicely with practice was going to be a bitch and a half.

"Thanks. I'll keep that in mind."

Everett looked out at Church Street, his face showing glimmers of an expression she couldn't quite pin down. "I know asking you to check your emotions sounds callous, but the faster you learn to compartmentalize, the easier it'll be for you to adjust."

"I'm not a robot," she said, keeping her tone simple instead of sarcastic, and funny, Everett did the same as he answered her.

"I'm not suggesting you stop *having* emotions in order to become a good firefighter. Hell, Nelson. Your gut is the most important tool you've got, and I meant it when I said every last one of us is human."

Her mind snagged on last week's breakfast conversation. "I don't know. Crews and Donovan and Jones seemed awfully nonchalant talking about all those car wrecks during my first shift."

"And you think that's because they're desensitized? Or they don't care?" Everett asked.

"No." The answer crossed her lips automatically. While her fellow firefighters on engine were certainly tough, none of them had tripped her jackass meter. But still, the detached vibe of the conversation she'd listened in on stuck out in her mind. "I don't know. Maybe you guys have seen enough to be a *little* desensitized."

"Or maybe we've learned to manage the emotions that go with the gig." He pushed off the expanse of bricks dividing the first two engine bays, his shoulders tightening to full attention. "Two of the three accidents those guys were talking about last week involved DOAs."

Sweat formed just beneath Savannah's ponytail even though the early-morning temperature was still far from toasty, and her palms began to shake. *Nope. Don't go there. Do. Not. Go there.* The three calls for car wrecks that they'd been on this week had all been fairly minor. She was going to be *fine*.

"That's awful," she managed, forcing her chin to stay on the level.

His gaze tapered by just a fraction before he slipped into an unreadable nod. "The truth is, this job will show you all sorts of things that should never be seen. But it's part of the territory, so you've got to choose. You can either let the emotions that go with those things fuck with your head, or you can learn how to put them in a box. I highly recommend the latter if you value your sanity."

Savannah dragged a deep breath past the knot in her windpipe, realization gluing her boots to the concrete. "So all that 'no big deal' treatment is essentially just a defense mechanism?"

"That's a bit of a nutshell, but yeah. I suppose it's a pretty good way to explain it."

They stood there for a minute, just taking in the *shush* of the occasional passing car and the perfectly timed flash of the amber caution light in front of the station.

Finally, she said, "I shouldn't have assumed that Crews and Donovan and Jones were just blowing off the seriousness of those calls."

"I guess that's today's first lesson," Everett said, and even though he could've used the opportunity to take her to task for the whole assumptions-are-dangerous thing or make her feel like an idiot jumping to the wrong conclusion, to Savannah's surprise, he gentled his voice instead.

"You never quite get used to the truly horrible stuff. But you do get used to how to react to it."

"Really?" she asked, her doubt guiding the question right out.

But Everett just lifted one corner of his mouth, tossing back the last of his coffee as he turned toward Station Eight's side entrance.

"Sure. How do you think we've all been making it through your breakfasts this week, rookie?"

Cole checked, then double-checked the regulator attached to his mask, carefully storing both in one of Engine Eight's compartments right next to the rest of his gear. Savannah had gotten the hang of going through gear check after only a couple of walk-throughs, although Christ, he wished he could say the same for her ability to pick up some kitchen skills. True, today's breakfast hadn't been nearly as frightening as last week's debacle—seriously, they could've used those grits to spackle drywall—but it had still drawn arched brows and muttered curses from half the guys on squad, including Oz. Cole had to admit, once he'd gotten past the ugly factor of the freakishly lopsided omelet Savannah had slapped over his plate this morning, the damn thing hadn't tasted half-bad.

Oz hadn't even tried a bite before dumping his in the trash.

"Okay," Savannah said, jumping down from the back of the engine and brushing her hands together with a no-nonsense rasp. "My gear is ready, set, and good to go. So what's first on the list of drills today?"

Her Southern accent curled around the words, sending an involuntary bolt of heat through his blood. Why couldn't he have a thing for British chicks? Her girl-next-door vibe was seriously going to kill him . . . if her confidence and the curves beneath her turnout gear didn't do the trick first.

Check that. His dark and devious imagination had already gotten a head start on both of those things the other day in the shower.

Cole straightened, clearing his throat. "Sledgehammer."

He popped the door on the storage compartment in front of him, dragging two yellow-handled sledgehammers from the steel tray. Passing one over to Savannah, he shouldered the second and headed through the open garage door to Station Eight's tiny front yard.

"We use Halligan bars way more than sledgehammers, don't we?" Savannah tipped her head at the sledge in her hand. Judging by her grip on the thing and the words that had just gone with it, he'd picked a winner with this drill.

"You pretty comfortable with your irons?" Cole asked. She wasn't wrong about the Halligan bar being the usual go-to for most firefighters, and knowing Brennan, Savannah had probably drilled the hell out of both her Halligan bar and her ax at the academy.

She squinted hard against the already blazing sunlight beating down from above. "I can hold my own."

"That would be why we're working with the sledge-hammer instead."

"So you picked something you knew I wouldn't be good at on purpose?" Savannah slid her free hand to her hip in a gesture that read *seriously?* At least he wouldn't have any trouble getting her to rise to the challenge.

"Yeah." Cole stopped just shy of the old tractor tire he and Donovan had dragged out to the double-wide cement walkway just before breakfast, turning to lift a brow at her. "Starting with the hard stuff makes everything else easier as you go. Plus, how else are you going to *get* good if you don't practice?"

Her silence was answer enough, so he jumped right in to

explain the drill. "We'll start out with some basic overhand swings." He gestured to the tire, which was already broken in and battle scarred from all the drills that had come before this one. "Go ahead and give it a shot."

"Okay." Savannah jammed her feet into the concrete, her body strung tight enough to snap as she white-knuckled her sledgehammer and used the momentum of her arms to hurl herself into the swing. The dull *thwack* of the sledge-hammer hitting the tire was immediately followed by a pained grunt-and-grimace combination that Cole had been expecting, but winced at nonetheless.

"The reverb hurts like a sonofabitch, especially when you go at it with just your upper body."

Savannah's grimace became a glare. "You couldn't have told me that before I took the swing?"

"Not if I wanted to give you a really good incentive not to swing the wrong way." Cole angled his frame toward the tire, keeping his own sledgehammer nice and fluid in his grip. "The sledge isn't so much about brute force as it is control. You want to stay loose and put yourself into the swing from the ground up. Like this."

Planting his boots, he firmed up his muscles from shoulders to hips, sliding a deep breath into his lungs before releasing his energy and his air on a tight swing.

Savannah blinked, her face already flushed from the heat that promised to turn today into a scorcher. "Oh," she murmured, a strange expression crossing her face as she blinked twice more, then nodded. "Right. Control. Got it."

Her next handful of swings backed up her affirmation, and Cole had to admit, despite her penchant for acting on pure impulse, he could've been stuck with a lot worse in the motivation department. They worked through drills on both sides—you never knew when logistics would screw you into not being able to use your dominant hand—then switched to low swings and a few other grips and methods before even Cole was silently screaming for a break.

"That'll wake you up in the morning, huh?" Savannah asked, but the way her breath sawed in and out made the words a gigantic understatement. Lowering the head of her sledgehammer to the concrete, Savannah slid a palm over her opposite shoulder, a streak of pain crossing her face and sending a pang of something odd through Cole's gut.

"You okay?"

"Oh." She paused in a moment of clear indecision before saying, "Yeah, I'm good. My shoulder is just a little sore. I must've slept funny."

Ah. In hindsight, that made sense. "Donovan mentioned that you're crashing on your brother's couch. I don't guess that's too comfortable."

"Donovan told you that?"

Cole registered the shock parting her lips and lifting her dark brown brows a beat too late, and damn it. *Damn it.* His brain-to-mouth filter was normally right up there with death and taxes as far as reliability went, but somehow, Savannah kept blowing his composure. "Sorry. I should've told you nothing's sacred around here once you say it out loud. Especially if you say it to Donovan."

He hadn't meant to let his knowledge of her personal details slip. Sure, everyone at Eight was more like family than just a bunch of coworkers, but still. Her relationship status—or lack thereof—was none of Cole's business.

What kind of moron would break up with a woman like Savannah and leave her stranded on her brother's couch?

Her surprise coalesced into a shrug. "It's not really that big a deal. The couch is more painful than the breakup. I don't think my back will ever be the same."

"So you're really not upset about the actual breakup?"

For a second, Cole wished for the nosy words back. But Savannah didn't seem uncomfortable, and anyway, talking about each other's personal lives to some extent or another was pretty common fare around the house. She *was* part of the group.

"Well, I might have been a tiny bit upset at the time," she said, letting out a soft laugh. "I mean, he did cheat on me with the living embodiment of a Barbie doll. But it seems kind of stupid to get torqued up over someone who would treat me like that, so . . . no. I guess I'm not that upset now."

"The guy sounds like a dick. No offense," Cole tacked on, but if anything, Savannah's smile grew bigger.

"None taken. He is a dick. I'm better off solo."

"That's pretty pragmatic for someone who normally staples her emotions to her sleeve." Cole gestured to the tractor tire in front of them with a question on his face, not at all shocked when she hefted her sledgehammer with a nod. Squaring off with the tire, Savannah took a few low swings before responding.

"I only get emotional about the important stuff, Everett. The job is a big deal to me. Everything else is extra." She continued for a full minute, adjusting her grip on the sledge and hitting the tire with a methodical *thunk thunk thunk*. "So can I ask who Mason Watts is?"

Cole's heart tripped against his ribs. "Sorry?"

"Mason Watts." Savannah lowered her sledgehammer in favor of pointing to the helmet hanging directly over Station Eight's middle garage bay. Over the helmet stood a boldly lettered plaque reading: *In memory of Mason Watts. Firefighter, brother, friend.*

Jesus, Cole missed him.

"Mason was a firefighter here on engine. He came up in the class after me." The facts felt stiff in his mouth, like gum that had been chewed two hours too long. But the alternative would rip into a wound Cole worked too hard to keep under wraps, so he blanked his expression and stuck with the nuts and bolts. "He died in an apartment fire three years ago when the floor of the building collapsed."

"Oh my God." Savannah froze, her spine at perfect attention. "I'm sorry. I shouldn't have—"

"No." The word flew past Cole's lips before he realized he was going to say it. "If you're going to be a firefighter here, you should know who Mason was."

"You two were close," she said, and even though every last one of his anti-emotion instincts shrieked at him to jam a sock in it and have her finish the drill, he nodded.

"We were best friends. Me and Mason and Donovan and Brennan."

Her sledge hit the concrete with a heavy *thump*. "Instructor Brennan?"

"Yeah. He was on engine here before he became an instructor." Cole kept the details of Brennan's injury to himself—although the guy had gone through hell and high water to get right side up after the fire that ended his career and Mason's life, he was happy now. He'd even gotten engaged a few months ago. They all coped the best they knew how, even though they'd never, ever forget that horrific night they lost Mason.

Cole took a breath. *Focus.* "That apartment fire was one of the worst I've ever seen. Calls like that are one of the big reasons why the most important house rule is to always have each other's backs. No matter what."

Savannah's eyes went wide in sudden recognition. "That's why you said I had the most important job at that warehouse fire last week, isn't it? Because we were standing by in case anyone got jammed up and needed help."

"Did you think I was bullshitting you?" He knew he'd been irritated with her, but he wasn't exactly a cryptic messages kind of guy.

"No, I . . ." She paused, biting her lip hard enough to mark her skin with two half moon–shaped indentations.

"I felt like I hadn't carried my weight, and I thought you were making fun of me."

His palms turned slick at the same time his mouth went dry as dust, but neither stopped him from pinning her with a stare and saying, "Listen, Nelson. I promised to make you a great firefighter. That doesn't mean I'm not going to be hard on you, and it doesn't mean you're not going to hate me for it from time to time. But I won't ever jerk you around. I say what I mean and I mean what I say. You copy?"

Savannah nodded. "Yeah, Everett. I copy."

But rather than get all awkward, she simply went back to work with the tire. "So you're training me in order to land a spot on squad, huh?"

Cole tried—and failed—to keep his jaw from unhinging. "Who told you that?"

"Nothing's sacred around here, remember?" A flicker of a smile crossed her lips, prompting one of his own. Fucking Donovan. He might talk a tough game, but man, the guy put out more gossip than a tabloid.

"Yes," Cole said, because A) it wasn't a secret, and B) Savannah clearly knew the score. "Once your orientation is done, I'm moving to squad. But that's not really why I'm training you."

"Okay." She drew the word out, pulling it into a question. "Then what? You just ended up with the short straw and got the rookie?"

"Oh, don't get me wrong. We need a strong candidate on engine before I can move to squad, so I'm not without motivation to get you trained. But Westin asked me to put you on my hip, and I'm not about to leave Crews and Donovan and Jones short-handed just so I can be promoted."

She gave a slow nod. "The squad stuff is pretty cool. Lots of search and rescue, right?"

"Lots of everything," he said. But when he'd chosen the calling that had been in his heart nine years ago rather than the one that had been laid out for him like a suit on Sunday, he hadn't intended to go halfway. Becoming a firefighter had cost Cole all he'd known—the farm where he'd grown up, the family ties he'd stupidly believed were unbreakable. For a price that steep, he wasn't going to stop until he'd earned a spot with the best of the best.

"And you're really jonesing to be on squad with Oz as your LT?" Savannah asked, her mouth pulling as if the words had left a bitter aftertaste on their way out.

Cole straightened. This bullshit between her and Oz needed to be put to bed, once and for all. "Oz is a damned good firefighter, and he's got more tenure here than anyone," he said, his gut forming a knot. "It's not smart to piss the guy off."

Savannah swung at the tire with a solid *thwack*. "Oh, but it's just fine for him to piss me off and boss me around the kitchen as much as he pleases? Look"—she lowered her sledgehammer, folding her arms over the chest of her sweat-dampened T-shirt—"If he was giving me shit over something I'd screwed up, I wouldn't be happy about it, but I'd take it. But he's giving me shit because I'm a woman. He's not even giving me a chance to prove I can handle the job."

The conversation he'd had with the lieutenant last week rattled through his brain, but Cole dismissed it with a decisive shake of his head. Oz might not be the most PC guy on the planet, but he was one of the best firefighters Cole had ever known. Once Savannah earned his respect, he'd come around.

"Oz is giving you a hard time because this is a hard fucking job, Nelson." Cole held up a hand to fend off the argument brewing in her expression, and miracle of miracles, she let him continue. "I'm not going to lie and tell you there aren't firefighters who think women don't belong on the job. But Oz is just looking out for everyone in this house."

"Except for me. If I'm the one who knows the least, then shouldn't he be in my corner if what he really wants is for me to learn to have everyone's back?" she asked, and hell if the words didn't jab him right in the chest.

"You know what, you're right."

Savannah pulled up halfway through her swing. "What?"

Under different circumstances, Cole might be amused at having shocked her so thoroughly. But working as part of the team was the most important thing he could teach her, and if he wanted Savannah to learn to have everyone else's back, then he damn well needed to lead by example.

"You're right," Cole repeated, stepping in close to look her right in the eye. "I'm not saying I support your getting into it with Oz, or anyone else here at Eight for that matter. But you're part of the house, even if you're a rookie. From now on, I promise to have your back just like everyone else's."

As if fate had decided there was no time like the present to put his affirmation to the test, the all-call sounded from the speakers in the engine bay.

"Squad Eight, Engine Eight, Ambulance Eight. Motor vehicle accident. Highway Twenty-Nine, mile marker Ninety-Two. Requesting immediate response."

Chapter Nine

Savannah sat in the back step of Engine Eight, trying like hell to convince herself to breathe. The lurching motion of the vehicle matched the churn in her stomach, and even though she'd never been troubled by motion sickness, she found herself biting down on her tongue in order to take a swipe at her nausea.

"Okay, boys and girls," came Crews's tinny voice through the headset, and he didn't sound happy. "Dispatch has at least three vehicles in what looks like a doozy. One of them is reportedly a tractor trailer, and another looks to have hit the Jersey wall pretty good. They anticipate multiple injuries and we're closest to the scene, so let's gear the fuck up."

Savannah registered Donovan's nudge to her knee on a five-second delay. Shit, how had he already gotten his coat on *and* zipped?

"You okay, rookie?" he asked as soon as she'd whipped the headset from over her ears.

"Uh-huh." She punctuated the less-than-convincing grunt with a nod in an effort to convince them both, stabbing her arms through the sleeves of her coat and tugging the zipper up to her chin.

"On big MVA calls like this, we usually back up both

ambo and squad, depending on how many injuries and extractions we've got. Westin will give you an assignment, just like at a fire." Donovan kept his voice nice and easy and his focus on his gloves, palming his helmet with a business-as-usual grab.

Okay. She could do this. She *could*. "Copy that."

"Just stay on Everett's heel and keep your eyes wide open. You'll be fine, Tough Stuff."

Savannah barked out an unexpected laugh, and it scattered her nerves. Emulating Donovan's composure, she made a list in her head, starting with the rest of her gear and ending with all the protocol she could remember from the academy regarding trauma scenarios. Having something specific to focus on helped calm her further, her breath flowing in and out a little easier.

Until the engine squealed to a stop and her boots hit the pavement, and oh God, oh *God*, bad couldn't touch this with an eight-foot New York hook.

Two cars and an eighteen-wheeler sat at various angles across the four-lane expanse of asphalt making up Highway Twenty-Nine, which was Fairview's main in-and-out to neighboring cities. Aside from some seemingly minor damage to the rear driver's side corner, the semi looked fairly intact where it stood about sixty yards away. The other two vehicles made up for it in spades, though, both of them smashed from multiple points of severe impact and neither facing anywhere near the proper direction on the highway.

Nothing about this would end well.

"All right, people." Captain Westin's voice interrupted the panic crowding Savannah's chest, and she latched on to the smooth, controlled cadence with all her might. "Let's assess injuries and get this scene secure. Oz, you and Andersen take the red station wagon, Crews and Jones, you take the semi. Everett, you and Nelson are on that gray sedan. Donovan, radio in another ambo to back up O'Keefe and Harrison. I want trauma assessments right now. Go."

Everett looked at her, and Savannah realized with a start that he'd been standing at her side since they'd disembarked from Engine Eight.

"You practiced trauma assessments at the academy," he said, falling into motion as he spoke. Her legs autopiloted the rest of her alongside him, although she couldn't for the life of her remember her brain issuing the command to do so.

"I, uh. Yeah. On dummies." They approached the sedan, and a quick burst of adrenaline had Savannah's pulse working even harder. The entire front end of the vehicle—which was facing them even though traffic had been moving in the opposite direction—had buckled like a giant steel-and-glass accordion, with one of the tires bent at enough of an unnatural tilt to make her sweat run cold between her shoulder blades.

Everett, however, seemed as calm as a summer sunrise. "Good. Take the passenger side. Just follow my lead and tell me what you see."

Savannah forced her feet to the car's passenger side. Bits of broken safety glass crunched under her boots, and the smashed window gave her a clear line of vision to the two teenage girls in the front seat.

Oh God. Blood. There was so much blood.

Everett leaned into the space where the driver's side window used to be, his eyes moving in a critical sweep. "Hi there. My name is Cole, and I'm here to help you. Can you tell me if you're hurt?"

"Y-yes," the driver stammered, her voice carrying the high-pitched strains of both panic and pain. "My . . . my neck. And my leg. Oh God, my leg hurts so bad, but I can't open the door. It's stuck. Please, get us out of here!"

Savannah's stomach pitched at the sight of the driver's leg, clearly broken and pinned in beneath the crumple of the dashboard. The girl in the passenger seat let out a whimper, and Jesus, the jagged gash running from the bottom of her neck down to her chest had to be seven inches long.

Still, Everett's calm didn't waver. "Okay, sweetheart. I know it hurts, but you've got to stay calm for me, all right? Breathe all the way in. We're going to get you out of here as fast as we can so we can take care of your leg, but until that happens, I need to stabilize your neck to keep you safe. Nelson, what've you got?"

"I . . . I . . ." Her mind tripped backward, dragging her focus with it.

Blood spiderwebbing over the air bag in angry red starbursts, spilling over her fingers, sticky and wet . . . the dark, coppery smell filling her nostrils, clogging her senses, choking her so completely . . . and the screams . . . the screams . . .

"*Nelson.* Look at me."

She blinked back to the asphalt with a jerk, her eyes landing on Everett's.

"Hey. Just tell me what you see," he said. Whether it was the absolute composure in his stare or the urgency of the situation kicking in hard and fast, Savannah couldn't be sure. But she vaulted into motion, knocking away remnants of broken safety glass and taking a closer look at the passenger.

"Right. She's conscious, nasty laceration from the neck to the right chest. It's"—Savannah's throat worked over a tight swallow, barely keeping her gag reflex in check—"bleeding heavily."

"Get pressure on it. You're going to need to press hard," Everett said. He turned to relay their status into the radio clipped to his shoulder, then framed the driver's face with his palms to keep her neck steady, talking to her in low, smooth tones.

Do this. You have to help this girl. You have to be tough.

Savannah slid a deep breath down her windpipe and shouldered her way past the open window space. Releasing the girl's seat belt for direct access, she pressed a gloved hand over the wound, using all of her willpower not to focus on the blood steadily oozing through her fingers.

"Unnhhh. Ow." The girl moaned, her head lolling to the side as she fixed Savannah with a glassy-eyed stare. "I don't . . . my head feels . . . funny."

Shit. *Shit.* Savannah did another quick visual. There wasn't any evidence of head or facial trauma, and her skin was clammy and pale. "Can you, ah, tell me your name?" Savannah asked.

"Re . . . Rebecca."

"Do you know if you hit your head in the accident, Rebecca?" Those air bags hurt like a bitch.

"No. Not that," she slurred. "I feel . . . sleepy."

Savannah's heart slammed even faster under the thick layer of her coat. This girl was bleeding out, and fast.

"Please. Help me," Rebecca gasped, tears wobbling off her lashes. "I don't . . . I don't want to die."

Dark crimson blood pulsed over Savannah's glove. She slapped her other hand over the first, and Rebecca's chest gave far too easily beneath the pressure. More blood started to seep between the fingers on Savannah's top hand, and oh God, she couldn't make it *stop*.

"Everett! A little help here!" She darted a glance across the front seat, fear sinking into her like claws. Panic climbed the back of her throat. Where the hell were Rachel and O'Keefe?

"I'm right here, and you and Rebecca are doing just fine," Everett said, meeting her desperate stare with nothing but certainty, as if he did this sort of thing all day, every day, no big deal. "I'm keeping Melody's neck nice and steady until O'Keefe gets here with a C-collar, and then he's going to help Rebecca out with that lac."

"But she's—"

"O'Keefe knows, Nelson." Everett flicked a glance at Savannah's blood-soaked hands, and even though the gesture lasted for less than a second, it spoke volumes. "He's coming as fast as he can, and then we'll be all set."

The words somehow managed to penetrate the panic buzzing through her, knocking it down a peg. Savannah turned her face toward Rebecca's, blocking her bloody gloves from view. "Hear that, Rebecca? Help is on the way."

"But it hurts," she said, her chest heaving as she let out a guttural sob. "I'm going to die."

"No." Savannah's argument springboarded right out of her, but oh God, she had no right to say it. She scrabbled for something—*anything*—to get them both to focus. "Look, you're breathing, see? All the way in." Savannah took an exaggerated inhale, which Rebecca shakily mimicked. "Good. Okay. Just . . . let's keep doing that."

After the fourth round of in and out, O'Keefe arrived over Everett's shoulder like a miracle. "What've we got?"

"The driver has an injury to the right leg and is complaining of neck pain," he said, perfectly calm even though his arms had to be screaming with fatigue. "She's pinned in pretty good. Passenger's got a bad chest lac."

"Got it. Oz is on his way with the Jaws, and dispatch just rolled another two ambos in our direction. Let's get these two stable for extraction." O'Keefe handed the C-collar in his grasp over to Everett before moving to the passenger side of the vehicle. "Nelson, I need to get a HemCon patch on that wound to control the bleeding, but you're going to have to help me, okay?"

Savannah forced herself to nod. O'Keefe dropped his jump bag to the pavement and removed a medical packet that looked like a supersized Band-Aid. "Hey, kiddo," he said to Rebecca through the sliver of window space over Savannah's shoulder. "My name's Tom, and I'm going to put this cool bandage on your cut. It's really sticky, so it'll help you stop bleeding. Then we'll get you out of here and take you to the hospital, okay?"

Rebecca murmured a thready "okay," her chest shuddering beneath Savannah's gloves. O'Keefe dropped his voice a register, placing his next words directly into Savannah's ear.

"When I tell you, I need you to release the pressure and get her shirt off the wound. If you can't rip the buttons, I'll give you shears, but you're going to have to move fast because she's lost a lot of blood. As soon as the fabric is clear, slide out and I'll get the patch in place. You copy?"

Savannah's "no" was locked and loaded on her tongue. She wasn't a paramedic, for Chrissake. How was she supposed to do this?

"Please," Rebecca whispered, tears tracking down her face, and Savannah turned her chin to look at O'Keefe.

"Copy. Now?"

He nodded. "The sooner, the better."

Savannah scraped for a deep breath. She released the pressure on Rebecca's chest, pulling her hands back to grip the edges where the girl's shirt came together. She meant to tear the thing in a decisive yank and be done, but blood spurted from the wound, splashing onto Savannah's shoulder and hacking at her resolve.

"As fast as you can, Nelson," O'Keefe said from beside her, and she didn't think, just tugged with all her might. Once, twice, again . . .

The fabric parted down the center with a loud *rip*.

"Got it." Relief rushed through her, hard enough to

threaten her vision. She moved Rebecca's shirt aside with a wet, sickening sound, and the sight of the gaping wound sent her knees immediately off-kilter. The cut ran down to the bone, exposing muscles and all sorts of other things that were never meant to see daylight.

Oh God. Savannah's body seized right alongside her mind. She jerked upward, banging the back brim of her helmet on the window frame as she stumbled from the passenger side to make room for O'Keefe.

"Jesus Christ," rasped an all-too-familiar, all-too-condescending voice from a few steps away on the pavement. Oz stood on the driver's side of the sedan, the Jaws of Life balanced between his hands and a massive frown marking his face. "It took you long enough, Nelson."

Her adrenaline broke like a huge wave smashing into a shoreline, fear and anger surging through her veins with enough power to make her truly dizzy. Savannah's stomach twisted and clenched, her breath sticking to her lungs as it crushed her chest, and the harder she tried to slow it down, the more futile the attempts became.

"Whoa, Nelson. You solid?" The voice belonged to Donovan, but he sounded really far away.

She nodded anyway, her head feeling inordinately heavy. "Mmm-hmm."

She forced herself to focus on the car, on O'Keefe's quick movements to stabilize Rebecca and cover both her and her friend with blankets to keep them safe from debris as Everett fell in to help Oz with the extraction. But all she could see was the blood, thick on her hands, soaking her gloves and the ends of her ponytail and invading her nostrils with that deep, dirty-copper scent . . .

Savannah barely made it to the guardrail before emptying the contents of her stomach.

* * *

Cole backed Engine Eight into the middle garage bay, his muscles pounding along with his head. His adrenaline had tapped out about three seconds after he and Oz had gotten the roof off that sedan, and he'd been slowly managing his return to normal vitals ever since Westin had called the scene and ordered them back to the house.

Which was more than he could say for Savannah. He should've known from the minute he'd seen her face through that passenger window that the call would rattle her cage— shit, the way her jaw had gone rock solid every time car wrecks entered the conversation had practically been a blinking neon sign. But calls like this, grim as they had the potential to be, were part of the deal. In fact, both engine and squad handled a lot more traumas than fires in any given month.

Although Cole had to admit, she'd had one hell of an initiation with that chest wound.

He jumped down from the operator's seat, jamming a hand through his hair. To his left, Donovan's boots found the engine bay floor with a *thump*, Savannah's following suit two seconds later. She hiked her chin to an upward tilt despite the fact that everyone in the house had seen her lose her lunch over that guardrail. Even though they clearly had some work to do getting her comfortable in trauma situations, Cole couldn't help but respect her toughness after the fact.

Ordinary fear didn't stick to this woman. Whatever had prompted her response today wasn't small potatoes, and chances were, it was fucking with her head something fierce.

"Nelson."

Speaking of fierce. She stopped halfway between the engine and the door to the house, pivoting slowly. "Before you say anything, I'd like to apologize. I totally screwed up on that call, and it affected my ability to do my job. It won't happen again."

As soon as his shock had worn off—and admittedly, it took a minute—Cole said, "Apology noted and accepted. But that's not why I stopped you."

Her dark brows lifted in question. "It's not?"

"No." It might be his job to train her, and they'd drill trauma protocol until she got it right. But it was also his job to help her adjust, which included her head space. "That was a really rough call. You okay?"

"Yup," she said, the answer coming too fast not to be manufactured. "Absolutely."

"Look, Nelson—"

"If it's okay with you, I'd like to rotate in for the showers right now."

Cole paused. He was tempted to press his luck—Savannah did it all the time, it wasn't as if pushback was foreign territory for her. Plus, the sooner they dealt with whatever had sent her into that tailspin, the better trained she'd be.

But then he saw the dried blood matting the ends of the ponytail over her shoulder, the breaking point clear in her pretty brown eyes, and he didn't think. Just spoke.

"Sure. Just keep your ears on for the all-call."

"Copy that," Savannah said, but she was already in motion by the time the words left her mouth.

Cole blew out a breath and turned back toward the engine. He hadn't gotten five minutes into fixing the loose storage compartment door in the back step when Oz appeared in the open door frame.

"Everett." He sank his thumbs beneath the suspenders holding his bunker pants over his rangy frame, looking for all the world like he'd been born that way. "Nice work with the Jaws. You been practicing?"

"Thanks. Yeah, I hooked up with a couple of the guys on

Squad Four a few weeks ago, and they let me tag along on their drill day."

"Ambitious of you," Oz said, although he made it impossible for Cole to read his tone. "Anyway, Cap wants you in his office. Now."

Now *that*, Cole read loud and freaking clear. He followed Oz through the engine bay and all the way down the long hall leading to Westin's office, a thread of surprise uncurling in his chest as Oz followed him in and shut the door.

"Everett." Captain Westin steepled his fingers over the stack of file folders on his desk. "Lieutenant Osborne has raised some concerns about Nelson's response to today's trauma call. I wanted to get your take on what happened."

Cole felt both the captain's eyes on his and Oz's stare on the back of his neck, and he chose his answer with extreme care. "It was her first big trauma call, and the wreck wasn't pretty. She had some jitters, but I think she'll be able to shake them out."

"Jitters?" Oz uttered a rude noise and a swear to match. "She could barely get out of her own way, much less O'Keefe's, and she puked over the goddamn guardrail, right in front of God and everybody. I'm telling you, Cap. She's soft. She doesn't belong here."

"She did have a lot of trouble today," Westin agreed, exhaling slowly. "Her file has a lot to recommend her, but this job can knock down even the best of candidates. Maybe bringing her on was a mistake on my part."

"No." Cole heard the tenacity of his answer only after he'd let it fly. But if Captain Westin cut Savannah loose, Cole would be back in the endless queue for available squad assignments, and even then, landing one here at Eight would be as impossible as moving the moon.

Plus, despite her shaky response to today's trauma call,

Savannah wasn't a bad firefighter. She deserved a second chance to prove herself.

And it was up to him to make sure she got one.

Cole cleared his throat and tried again. "I mean, ah, respectfully, Captain, I disagree. While I can't argue that Nelson had a hard time today, she's a rookie. She's supposed to make rookie mistakes."

"Mistakes get people hurt. Or worse," Oz argued. "What if one of us gets injured on a call and she goes soft because she can't handle a little blood? Then what?"

Cole examined the situation in front of him, grabbing his best plan of action with both hands. "She's on my hip, and I promised to train her. Just give me another week. If she screws up again, it's on me."

The room went quiet, to the point that Cole could hear the clock on the wall, ticking steadily behind him. Finally, Westin slid his stare from Cole to Oz.

"Lieutenant. Can you give me a minute with Everett?"

Although the deep lines of Oz's frown said he wanted to argue, he responded with a gruff "copy that" before turning to walk out the door. Damn it, Cole was going to have to earn his way back into the guy's good graces. But strategically speaking, that would be a hell of a lot easier than finding a new spot on squad.

Not that his current one wasn't swinging in the breeze.

Captain Westin sat back in his desk chair. "I'll be honest, Everett. For the most part, I agree with you. Today's trauma call was a nasty one, and I think Nelson's just having growing pains like any other rookie."

"Yes sir," Cole said, unable to keep the relief from flooding into the words.

"However," Westin continued, his raised blond-gray brows and the flat line of his mouth permitting zero argument, "Lieutenant Osborne is right. There's damn little room for error on this job. If she can't handle her responsibilities here at Eight, especially when it comes to backing up her fellow firefighters, I won't have any problem ending her candidacy."

Cole's mouth went as dry as a dirt road in August. "Understood."

"I hope so. Because as of right now, your ass is on the line right next to hers."

Chapter Ten

Savannah pulled her messenger bag from the front seat of her Ford Escape, the black leather strap creaking in her palm from the weight of the bag's contents. But ever since yesterday's mortifying trip on the vomit comet, she'd been hard-boiled and hell-bent not to repeat her mistake, vowing to be 100 percent prepared when the next trauma call came in.

Since her shift had ended eleven hours ago without a chance to redeem herself and she couldn't incite a giant wreck in the name of practice, studying response protocols was the next best thing in her arsenal.

With her textbook-filled bag firmly in place on her shoulder, Savannah crossed the sidewalk leading up to the Fairview Library. The building dated back to the late 1800s, according to the plaque she'd just passed, and if the four-story solid stone construction was anything to go by, the place was as sturdy as it was old. Between the library proper and the offices and archive buildings surrounding it, the place took up nearly an entire city block. There were even private gardens alongside the parking lot in the back.

And one very serious-looking, undeniably sexy fire-fighter in front.

"Oh. You're early," Savannah blurted, heat creeping up the back of her neck.

Everett, however, didn't seem to notice. "So are you," he pointed out with a half smile. "It's barely six twenty."

Something about him looked the slightest bit different from usual, and she realized with a start that she'd never seen him in anything other than his FFD uniform. The snug gray T-shirt, well-worn jeans, and even better worn black work boots he had on now weren't out of the ordinary, but something about his body beneath them seemed looser, more fluid somehow. With his sand-colored lashes framing the glint in his eyes and the slight smile he still hadn't let go of, he looked almost . . . relaxed.

Not to mention as gorgeous as ever.

Savannah squeezed her muscles to douse the warmth growing between her thighs. Everett's leanly sculpted biceps and his smoldering dark green stare might check every box on her sexy ticket, but lusting after him was still an epically bad idea. While her brother had admitted that interhouse relationships did sometimes happen despite being highly frowned upon by the department, risking censure—not to mention her already rocky reputation at Eight—wasn't on her agenda. No matter how damp her panties had suddenly gotten at the sight of Everett standing there.

Time to get to work. Now would be good. Five minutes ago?

Even better.

"So, uh, thanks for agreeing to help me study," she said, turning toward the intricate glass-and-mahogany double doors of the library's main entrance. "I know it's not the most thrilling thing you could be doing on a Friday night."

"I don't mind," he said, and strangely enough, he looked like he really meant it. He reached out to palm the heavy brass door handle, ushering Savannah inside before following her over the threshold.

"Whoa." She blinked up at the two-story main lobby, all marble tiles and heavy wood and beautiful, timeless architecture. God, this place was *gorgeous*.

"Yeah, it's cool, isn't it?" Everett answered, making her realize she'd spoken her last thought out loud. "It's one of the oldest buildings in the city. Even though the place has been renovated a couple of times to modernize things like the wiring and the heating system, they've kept as much of the original construction as possible."

"You know an awful lot about the buildings around here." Savannah's curiosity hit a full simmer, but Everett waved the compliment off.

"I've been with the FFD for eight years. We go all over the city on calls, and it's smart to know about the architecture in these older places. Not that it's a hardship to check out a building like this one."

He gestured to the columns flanking the entrance to the lobby, but the main information desk was what took Savannah's breath away. The ornately carved waist-high counter formed a large square around a smaller cluster of mahogany desks, each of them looking antique and original to the library itself.

Just like the tiny, birdlike woman manning the counter.

"Hey, Mrs. Norcross," Everett said, greeting the librarian with a polite smile. The woman looked up at him, her eyes appearing huge behind the thick lenses of her reading glasses.

"Oh my! Cole Everett, is that you? What brings you out to the library tonight? There's not trouble with the carbon monoxide detector again, is there? Oh, I have such a hard time seeing that darned monitor sometimes."

"No, ma'am, no trouble at all. I'm actually here to study this evening. You wouldn't happen to have an open room upstairs, would you?"

"Of course." Mrs. Norcross reached out to pat his hand,

and Lord, the woman had to be eighty if she was a day. "You go on up to the third floor. I bet you'll have the place all to yourself."

"Thanks. I appreciate it," he said, smiling one more time before turning to head toward the large staircase behind the desk.

"Wow." The background noise from the lobby faded as they climbed the first flight of stairs, and Savannah dropped her voice to one grade above a whisper. "You know the librarian by name?"

"Yeah. The city did a huge renovation on the top floor last year, and the air-conditioning units really screwed with their carbon monoxide detectors. We came out six times in one day. By the third round, Mrs. Norcross was offering us tea and cookies. She's a nice woman."

"I'm impressed," Savannah said. "Charming little old ladies seems more Donovan's speed."

The corners of Everett's mouth ticked upward. "Charming everybody is Donovan's speed."

"Hmm. I think I missed that day at finishing school."

"Too busy bucking authority?" he asked, and she barely bit back her laugh before it interrupted everyone on the second floor.

"I'll have you know I'm a model student." Well, she had been at the academy, anyway. All that MBA stuff her mother had tried to force on her before that had been a waste of time.

Everett crossed the third-floor landing; the floor-to-ceiling bookshelves and individual study carrels made the space both hushed and private. Not that there was anyone up here with them.

"Let's see how far that gets you tonight. We've got a lot to cover."

He led the way down the far row of books, stopping outside the windowless study room at the very end. The space was nothing more than a ten-by-ten square, with two small desks pushed together in the center and four ladder-backed chairs all the way around. The wood paneling and the soft overhead lights made Savannah think of her father's study back home, and wasn't that all the reminder she needed of the truckload of worth she had to prove.

Everett shut the door behind them and hooked a hand beneath the back of one chair, eyeing the pile of books she'd started stacking in the center of her desk. "You know, studying trauma protocol will help you with the facts, and that's not a bad thing. But if you've got a different kind of hurdle jamming you up, then all the books in the world aren't going to help you clear it."

Savannah tugged at the hem of her light blue T-shirt, testing the limits of the cotton before sitting down in the chair across from him. *Stay tough.* "I just need to review the procedures," she said, although the look on Everett's face said they both knew it was a lie.

"You're afraid of blood, Nelson."

Her pulse stuttered, her defenses kicking her default response right off her tongue. "I'm not afraid of anything."

"I am."

The answer was so far outside the realm of anything she'd been expecting that Savannah bit without thinking. "Really? And what are you afraid of?"

He paused, as if his own admission had just caught up with him. "Heights. I can't stand 'em."

"You're acrophobic?" Bombshell, meet lap. Of all the things he could be afraid of, heights seemed so . . . normal.

One light brown brow arched up. "What, you were expecting the boogeyman? Armageddon, maybe? Or killer bees?"

Savannah's laugh knocked the tension right out of her chest. "No, I just . . . I'm surprised."

"That I have a fear of heights?"

"That you have a fear of anything."

"Everyone's afraid of something," he said. "It's how you manage the fear that makes or breaks you."

Everett looked at her from across the table, his green eyes flashing nearly hazel in the soft gold light spilling down from overhead. She knew she should feel vulnerable—he'd pegged her one debilitating fear from forty paces away, and that fear had made her weak. But something about his unvarnished honesty over being vulnerable, too, made Savannah open her mouth to let her words tumble right out.

"When I was a senior in high school, I was a passenger in a car accident. The guy I was dating was driving too fast and acting like an idiot. Typical teenage boy stuff." God, she could still feel the drop of her stomach, the way her adrenaline had sent a hard shot of foreboding under her skin at every backroad turn. She'd told him to knock it off, but of course, that had only made him go faster. "We crashed into another car on the way to a football game. Hard enough for the impact to send it into a hundred-year-old oak tree."

The smooth line of Everett's jaw ticked. "Were you hurt?"

"No," she said, then qualified with, "Not really, I guess. The air bag left me a little banged up, and I had some cuts from the glass. My boyfriend was okay, too, other than a really nasty bruise from his seat belt."

Everett nodded, and even though there was clearly more to the memory, he simply waited for her to share it.

"The other car was a . . . different story. There were three girls inside. We went to school with them. The two on the driver's side had only minor injuries like me and Justin, but the girl in the passenger seat was hurt really badly."

Savannah pressed her palms into the desk in front of her, the wood cool against her damp skin. Mary Anne Marbury. She'd been a year behind Savannah at the time. They'd barely known each other. Which made the fact that Savannah had seen the girl's humerus and more than half the blood in her body up close and personal seem all the more terrible.

Sweet Jesus, there had been so much blood.

"Her arm had gotten crushed in the impact, and she had a pretty bad head injury, too. She wasn't conscious at first. Everyone else was freaking out, thinking she was dead." In truth, for one gut-clenching minute, Savannah had thought so, too. Not that it had stopped her from trying to help. "I tried to get her out of the car, but her arm was pinned in, her brachial artery completely severed along with more than half of the limb. You could smell the blood from a couple feet away. It was . . ." *Gruesome. Nightmarish. Terrifying.* "Pretty awful."

"Sounds like it," Everett said. His hands lay calmly in front of him on his side of the desk, separated from Savannah's shaking fingers by only a few inches. He had nice hands—long fingers, callused and capable, strong yet not terribly work-scarred. It was a strange thing to notice, considering the gravity of the topic.

But not nearly as strange as how badly she wanted him to reach out and wrap those fingers around hers.

"When she—Mary Anne"—Savannah corrected herself, because not saying the girl's name felt somehow disrespectful—"came to, she panicked and started thrashing around, but of course that only made things worse. I swear to God, I'll never forget the sound of her screams. I did my best to help her, but she was bleeding so much, and I couldn't make it stop. The blood just kept coming, until finally, she passed out again, and after that, she didn't . . ."

Savannah broke off, forcing herself to inhale. The climate-controlled air smelled faintly of wood polish and old books, not the sharp, dark scent that clogged her memory, and she ran both hands over her hair, pressing her fingers to her scalp to ground herself. "Anyway, I guess all of that came back into my mind yesterday when we were at the scene of that wreck, and I froze. But I really meant it when I said it won't happen again."

"You should've told me."

The words arrived without accusation, but still, she huffed out a humorless laugh. "Come on, Everett. I—"

"Cole," he interrupted, prompting her brows into a one-way climb.

"What?"

"I get that we work together, but we're not at Eight right now. We're sitting here, having a conversation, just me and you." He paused, gesturing to the center of his gray T-shirt with one index finger. "You can call me Cole if you want."

"Cole," she repeated, the tension in her rib cage loosening by a fraction. "Maybe I should've realized calls like yesterday's were going to shake me up. But I couldn't just come out and say I'm scared of blood. I don't need another reason for everyone in the house to think I'm weak."

He leaned forward, his chair scraping softly against the floor. "I know you want to stay tough and prove yourself, but every last one of those guys has a trigger and gets scared on calls."

She couldn't help it. She snorted. "Are you seriously trying to tell me there's something out there that scares Oz?"

"Okay, he might not be the best example," Cole admitted, but still, he didn't let up. "Being scared *is* part of the job, though. I don't expect you to be fearless, Savannah. But I do expect you to be straight with me so I can help you deal with what scares you and get you trained."

"I just . . ." Savannah's defenses made her trip over the words, but Cole was right. Hiding her feelings wasn't going to teach her how to get past her fear so she could help people, and she sure as hell wouldn't prove her worth as a firefighter if she couldn't carry her weight. "I don't know how to lose that bad head space when it comes to car wrecks."

"Will it help you to know that both Melody and Rebecca are okay?"

Her shoulders hit the back of her chair with a graceless bump. "They are?"

Cole nodded, the small smile on his lips turning his trademark seriousness into simple honesty. "Rebecca had to have surgery to repair the damage to her chest, but as it turns out, she's a fighter. Prognosis for both girls is a full recovery."

Savannah blinked in an effort to keep all the *no way* in her brain from taking over her expression. "And how exactly did you come across that information?"

"Well, it took a little doing, but let's just say my list of contacts isn't limited to nice old ladies at the library."

Cole lifted his brows up and down just enough to make her laugh inevitable. The corners of his eyes crinkled as his laughter blended in with hers, sending a shot of sweet surprise all the way up her spine.

"Hey. You know how to smile." Without thinking, she nudged his hand with the back of her knuckles, the warmth of the contact multiplying tenfold as he nudged her in return.

"Yeah. So do you."

A minute passed before Savannah said, "Thanks. I mean, not for the smiling thing." Her blush heated a path to her temples, and God, could she be any worse at this expressing-your-softer-side stuff? "But, you know, for, um, letting me know about Melody and Rebecca. And for helping me study."

"Thanks for being straight with me about why you had trouble yesterday." For a long second, Cole looked at her, no pretenses, no pressure, just the two of them sitting there. Savannah's heart sped up, but the feeling pulsing through her was different from the unease she'd felt before.

She trusted him. And it felt frighteningly good.

Cole cleared his throat, scooping a textbook from the top of the stack and parting the pages with a *creak*. "So, ah, why don't we start with some of these protocols since that's where you seem most comfortable? Once you've got the responses down, then we can figure out the best way for you to handle the rest. Sound like a plan?"

Between Cole's low-pressure suggestion and the calm composure returning to his eyes, Savannah's answer sprang right out. "Okay, yeah. What've you got?"

She leaned over the desk, listening intently as he outlined scenario after scenario. Some of them were easy enough, and even the tricky ones became more manageable as Cole peppered in suggestions based on his experience and expertise. He seemed to have seen just about everything, from near drownings to electrocutions to one really gruesome call involving a man getting his arm caught in a residential wood chipper. But every incident had a string of responses, ordered steps to bring things closer to right side up, and the more they went over each one, the more intuitive the possible solutions became in Savannah's head. Their study session got a little dicey when Cole used his phone to pull up a few YouTube videos of actual accident footage, but the way he paused each one to matter-of-factly explain each scenario and the best ways to fix it kept her anchored and focused.

"Jeez," she said, finally pushing back in her chair. "You really weren't kidding when you said this job will show you all sorts of things that should never be seen." Putting out fires kind of seemed the least of it.

"Unfortunately, I wasn't. Lucky for us, the upside gets you through the bad days." Cole gestured to the books in front of them, and wow, they really had covered a lot of ground. "Anyway. I know this was just a start, and we'll keep working on trauma responses at the house. Finding your comfort zone will mostly be a matter of practice. But I hope tonight helped a little."

"Actually, it helped a lot. Thanks."

"No problem." He unfolded his arms into a stretch, and Savannah turned toward the door leading out to the rest of the library. They hadn't seen or heard a single person since they'd made their way upstairs—although on a Friday night, that couldn't be terribly unusual. Still, the snapshot of hallway visible beyond the glass set in their study room door looked awfully shadowed. And wait . . . were those the emergency lights illuminating the exit signs?

"Cole," Savannah said, her heart picking up its pace in her chest. "What time is it?"

"It's . . ." He palmed his phone, his brows snapping together. "Wait. This can't be right. It's ten forty-five."

"I thought the library closes at nine." She'd seen the hours printed in thick gold lettering right on the massive front doors when they'd arrived.

The same front doors that looked as sturdy and impenetrable as Fort freaking Knox.

"It does," Cole said, helping her shove her books into her messenger bag. They double-timed it to the stairwell, which was as sparsely lit as the rest of the stacks. Their footsteps cut through the otherwise eerie silence, coming to a screeching halt at the bottom of the stairs on the ground floor.

The entire library was as dark as it was empty.

Chapter Eleven

"It looks like we're locked in."

Cole shook his head, as if the movement would somehow alter the reality of the words Savannah had just said.

Nope. Nada. She simply stood in front of him, her hands on the hips of her low-slung jeans and a bold, what-now expression covering her pretty face, and he had to admit it. Of all the scenarios he'd ever strategized, breaking out of one of Fairview's oldest landmarks on a Friday night might just be the weirdest.

"The library staff usually does a sweep at closing time, but Mrs. Norcross must've missed us somehow." Not too unfathomable, since he and Savannah had been in the very last study room, and the librarian had to be pushing octogenarian status. Still, Cole was never unaware of his surroundings, and definitely not for hours. How had he lost track of that much time?

Hell if the answer to that question wasn't standing right in front of him in all her long-legged, leanly curved, everything-on-the-table glory.

Going straight up with Savannah at the beginning of their study session had been a gamble, he knew, but the best blueprint to get her to overcome her fear was for her to face it, and that meant earning her trust enough to get her to air it out.

He just hadn't realized how much going one-on-one with her would sucker punch his emotions. Savannah's hands had been right there on the desk as she'd unraveled the story of her accident, so close that Cole had been able to feel them trembling as she spoke. Her rare lack of toughness had arrowed through him with palpable force, hard enough that he'd wanted to lay waste to every logical reason not to pull her straight into his arms and kiss her until they both ran out of breath. It had taken every last ounce of his composure to focus on the task that had brought them here.

But then Savannah had balanced out her vulnerability with a double dose of determination and intelligence, making him want to do a hell of a lot more than kiss her.

And now they were stuck in the library. Together. In the dark. Alone.

This was the worst tactical plan *ever*.

Cole reached out to test the heavy double doors, but they gave the same unyielding rattle as when Savannah had tried them twenty seconds earlier. "Okay," he said, raking a hand through his hair as he started formulating a Plan B that didn't involve his dick. "There's an emergency exit over by the periodicals, and there's got to be access in the back for employees."

"I saw the emergency exit when we came in," Savannah said, her hair swishing over one shoulder as she turned toward the right-hand wall. "Why don't I check it out while you look for an employee entrance and we can meet back here in five?"

Five minutes later, their options still amounted to Cole's new best friend, Jack Shit.

"The emergency exit is a no-go," Savannah said, her voice echoing through the hushed quiet of the library even though she spoke only one notch above a whisper. "It's dead-bolted from the outside just like the front doors. This library might be as old as the hills, but it was built like a bomb shelter. Even money says that emergency exit door is four inches thick. Breaching it without a crowbar or a Halligan looks damn near impossible."

"Yeah, the employees' entrance in the back is the same." Cole flipped his cell phone into his palm. "I guess we could call the police and get a squad car out here."

Savannah reached out, her hand curling over his forearm to halt his finger over the *emergency* icon. "That still won't help unless they have the key. Plus, we're six blocks from the station, Cole. Do you really want to risk dispatch putting out a person in distress call and sending B-shift over here? We'd never hear the end of this."

Fuck. *Fuck*, she was right. "Okay, but unless you've got a Halligan in your pocket or a thing for sleeping in the stacks, we still need a way out of here."

"We have one. We just have to go outside the box to get it." Savannah's gaze drifted upward, a smile breaking over her face, but oh no. She couldn't possibly mean . . .

"There's a fire escape on the third floor outside the main window facing the gardens. Doesn't that fall under the umbrella of our expertise?"

Cole's gut bottomed out at his boots as he tried desperately to spin up a Plan C. Preferably one that had less risk of him hurtling thirty feet to a rather rude meet-and-greet with the library pavement. "Well, yeah, but we don't have any gear."

"We don't need it," Savannah pointed out, already halfway up the first-floor staircase. "All we have to do is make sure we hold on and don't fall. We can scale down as far as the fire escape will let us and then jump the last eight feet, no harm, no foul, no vandalism. Piece of cake."

His pulse tapped out *oh, is that all* in rapid-fire Morse code, but he bit back the argument welling up from his chest. Letting his emotions dictate his actions, or worse yet, turn them into *non*-actions, wasn't going to get him out of this mess. And just because he wasn't wild about heights didn't mean he hadn't hauled his bacon up ladders twice as high as the library's fire escape whenever the job dictated.

Never mind that he'd hated it with the fiery passion of a thousand white hot suns every damned time.

"Fine. Let's go." Cole made his way up the second staircase, following Savannah past the third-floor study carrels and through the shadow-lined stacks. Their feet came to a muffled halt in front of the window at the end of the middle row, and Cole had to hand it to her. At least she'd been paying attention to her exit paths.

"Okay," she said, the thick fringe of her lashes sweeping downward as she squinted through the glass. "Fire escapes are pretty standard, right? This shouldn't be too complicated."

Before he could point out that dangling themselves three stories over the ground had the potential to get *very* complicated, Savannah had thrown open the window and shimmied onto the narrow platform of the fire escape.

"Jesus Christ, Nelson." His heart jerked against his sternum, and he had one leg over the window ledge before his brain caught up with the rest of him. "Are you crazy?"

"Of course not. I'm doing exactly what we just planned." Savannah took a step toward the dropdown ladder, but then she froze, mid-move. "Oh my God, Cole. Look. Have you ever seen so many stars?"

She lowered her messenger bag and slid to the corner of the fire escape, curling her fingers around the black metal bar that served as a railing. The damned thing was flimsy on its best day, which by Cole's estimation had to have been thirty years ago. Unfortunately for him, the fire escape's lack of structural integrity didn't seem to bother Savannah a bit.

"I haven't seen the sky this clear since I was back home

in Texas." Pressing up to her toes, she tipped her face to the wide-open expanse over their heads, the mahogany waves of her hair spilling down her back as she scanned the night sky.

"Savannah." Her name scraped past his lips on a warning, but he couldn't help it. She was leaning halfway over Fairview, for fuck's sake. Her brazenness was going to be the end of her.

And with the way her eyes glittered, dark brown and dangerous in the moonlight, it might just be the end of him, too.

"I mean it," she said, the bars of the fire escape letting out a rusty *squeak* as she tilted forward just a fraction more. "It's just—"

Before he could fully register the command pumping down from the primal part of his brain, Cole's boots hit the landing, one arm snaking around Savannah's waist while the other guided her shoulders firmly against the stone exterior next to the open window.

"Beautiful," she finished on a whisper. Her chest thrummed against his, although he knew his had to be rising and falling just as fast in return.

"You're three stories above the ground." The stone was rough on his forearm where it wrapped around the back of Savannah's ribs, and good, yeah. There was something to focus on. Something solid. Something right in front of him.

He should let go of her, focus be damned. She felt too good, warm and sweet and strong with their bodies matched from shoulder to thigh.

Savannah's fingers found his hip just below the belt loop on his jeans, and Cole held her even tighter.

"The fire escape is perfectly sturdy, see?" She lowered her gaze to the platform, just for a second before latching back on to his stare. "It's holding us both up just fine."

"You still shouldn't tempt fate."

Her laugh coasted past his cheek on little more than a breathy sigh. "In case you haven't noticed, I'm not really a play-it-safe kind of girl. I'm fearless, remember? I think fate shouldn't tempt me."

Oh, to hell with fate. Cole was going to tempt her, long and hard and right goddamn now.

He slanted his mouth over hers, kissing her in one seamless stroke. Her lips were so much softer than he'd expected, so sweet and seductive at the same time that they were almost like a puzzle he was dying to figure out. Cole uncurled his fingers from their grip at Savannah's shoulder, sliding his palm under the curve of her jaw to cup her chin. Holding her in place, he coaxed her mouth open with a brush of his tongue. But rather than submissively giving in to the kiss, she returned every movement, sweeping her tongue from the hot confines of her own mouth to boldly kiss him back.

"Cole." Her fingers dug into the denim on his hip, his cock going instantly hard as her lips parted in a grin. Cole kissed her again just to taste her smile, and Christ, he didn't want to stop at her mouth.

So he didn't.

"Come here." Without waiting for her to respond, he tilted her head to one side, sliding his tongue down the line of her neck until he reached the deep V of her T-shirt. The swell of her breasts rose as she moaned, her nipples pearling against the cotton even through her bra. Savannah arched up, her spine bowing into his touch, and Cole returned to her mouth, pressing himself over every available inch of her.

She pressed back with just as much intention. Hooking her fingers through his belt loops, Savannah thrust the cradle of her hips against his, the friction sending a raw bolt of pleasure-pain from his belly to his balls. She combined the motion of her hand with her leverage on the wall, using both to rock their lower bodies in time with the rhythm of the kiss. *Fuck*, she felt so much hotter and sexier and sweeter than he'd imagined the other morning in the shower, and he wanted to let loose all of his raw, right-now emotions, to drive her as crazy as she was driving him.

He didn't just want to hear her sigh. He wanted to go the distance.

He wanted to know what she sounded like when she came.

Cole tugged his arm from behind Savannah's body, pushing her flush against the cool stone behind her. With both hands, he lifted the hem of her T-shirt over the lean muscles of her torso. But he didn't stop there. Pushing the garment to her shoulders, Cole revealed a plain white cotton bra, the hard peaks of her nipples clearly visible beneath the thin barrier of the fabric.

His groan was a foregone conclusion. "So hot," he murmured. Forget all that lacy stuff. He'd always been a fool for unadorned, no-frills cotton, especially when it covered something sinfully sweet.

Savannah's throaty laugh hinted at disbelief. She looked down at his hands, her hair tumbling forward to frame her face and cover the tops of his fingers.

"You don't believe me?" He slid a thumb over one tightly drawn nipple, feeling her shudder all the way in the base of his own spine. But the doubt on her face lingered, and oh, he was going to enjoy proving her wrong.

"Keep your eyes wide open, Savannah. Because I'm going to show you exactly how hot you are. Right. Now."

A quick slide of the thin straps at her shoulders freed both of Savannah's breasts from the cotton. For a second, Cole's pulse went haywire at the sight of her tawny-colored nipples and the perfect fit of her breasts to his palms.

He curved his fingers. Breathed in.

She watched his every movement.

Cole ran the pad of his thumb over Savannah's bare skin,

unable to keep from watching along with her. She sighed in the back of her throat, bowing her shoulders to meet more of his touch as he stroked faster, with more purpose. Although he'd thought it impossible, her nipple grew even harder under his fingers, and he sent his other hand into play along with his first.

"Oh God." She thrust her hips, but still didn't break her stare on his hands.

Despite the dark, impulsive burn pushing through his veins, he didn't scale back. "See?" Cole cupped her breast with one hand, rolling her nipple between his opposite thumb and forefinger. "You're so fucking sexy."

Savannah watched, her breath coming in short, hot bursts. He answered each one, his eyes locked on her face as hers locked on his hands. With every pass of his fingers, her gaze shuttered further, her hips pumping with growing urgency, and Cole had never wanted to make someone come so bad in his life. He dropped his mouth to the spot where her neck gave way to her shoulder, marveling at the softness of Savannah's skin. The more he tasted, the more he wanted to let loose and let go, and he trailed his mouth lower in order to fill the need burning in his chest.

Instinct combined with impulse, both screaming at him to take, to give, to lose every inhibition he had. *Yes. Fuck, yes.* His cock pulsed against the soft seam of her body, her thrusts driving him even harder as he closed his mouth over her nipple. He reached for the button on her jeans, fully intent on not stopping until he was buried inside her and they were both naked and hot and screaming in release—

"You! On the fire escape. Stop where you are. Fairview Police!"

For a split second, the haze in Cole's brain kept him from reconciling the command with reality. But then he registered Savannah's panicked stare in the moonlight, the flurry of her movements as she replaced her clothes with two blessedly well-timed tugs, and he turned just as the harsh glare of a spotlight appeared on the wall beside them.

Holy Christ. He'd just been completely, irrevocably, *painfully* cock-blocked by the Fairview Police Department.

"I think there's been a misunderstanding," he started, but the voice cut him off before he could edge in another word.

"Security alarms are pretty straightforward. Especially the silent kind, like the one on that window next to you. Now keep your hands on the railing where I can see them. Your partner, too."

Cole squinted past the spotlight. His pulse kicked at the sight of the blue flashing strobe light beyond. He needed to fix this before it fixed him *and* Savannah.

Savannah, who was standing statue-still next to him. Savannah, who had made him feel every emotion in the book, good, bad, and forbidden.

Savannah, who would very likely be unraveling under his mouth right now if they hadn't inadvertently tripped the library's security alarm.

Had he lost his goddamn *mind*?

Cole snapped his composure back into place, straightening his spine to its full height.

"My name is Cole Everett, and I'm a firefighter at Station Eight. We're not trying to break into the library. In fact, we were trying to break out."

"Everett?" The spotlight swung slightly to the side, sparing Cole's retinas at least momentarily. "It's Brett O'Halloran. What the hell are you doing up there?"

He placed the name and the voice together in a *whoosh* of relief, thanking every deity he could think of for the city-wide softball tournament that gave him connections in the FPD. Not to mention that said connection seemed none the wiser about what he'd really interrupted. "We were doing some work in the library and lost track of time. The librarian missed us before she locked up for the night, and we were just trying to get out without busting the place up."

"Good freaking luck," O'Halloran said with a scoff. "The doors on this building are one step past ridiculous. You good to get down on your own?"

"Yeah, we're both firefighters." The reminder jabbed at Cole's conscience. He turned to look at Savannah, who—other than her flushed face and kiss-swollen lips—appeared as tough as ever.

"Are you okay?" he asked quietly. He knew the question was a stupid one as soon as he let it fly, and the arch of her brow confirmed it.

"Of course." She stepped toward the building, lowering the window back into place before scooping up her bag. "Do you want to take point, or should I?"

"Go ahead."

Cole fixed his focus on the metal rungs in front of him, keeping his peripheral vision open to the narrowly set railings on either side as they descended the fire escape with an economy of movement. Savannah passed her bag off to O'Halloran's partner before smoothly jumping to the paved path beneath the end of the ladder, and a minute later, Cole reconnected with solid ground next to her.

"I called the security company and let them know to reset the alarm," O'Halloran said, jutting his chin up at the library window. "Helluva thing to get locked in, huh?"

"I guess that was my fault. We were up to our eyes studying trauma responses." Savannah held up her bag, clearly overladen with books. "I'm new at Eight, so I wanted to get a leg up. Savannah Nelson."

"Brett O'Halloran." The officer extended his hand. "I apologize for the gruff introduction a few minutes ago. Sometimes teenagers get a little rowdy on Friday nights and break into all sorts of places to hook up. Thought maybe that's what we had out here."

A renewed shot of trepidation filled Cole's gut, but Savannah simply shook her head. "Sorry to disappoint, Officer," she said. "Just us, hitting the books."

After a few parting pleasantries, O'Halloran and his partner returned to their squad car, leaving Cole and Savannah alone once again in the moonlight.

"Listen, Savannah, about what happened up there—" He broke off, scrambling for order in his head, but she shocked the hell out of him by beating him to the punch.

"You know what, it's probably best if we just forget it." She threaded her arms over the front of her T-shirt, and although her expression was unwavering, it was also free of pretense. "We work together, and neither one of us needs the blowback. It was just a moment of weakness."

Her words made perfect sense—Cole had been primed to say the exact same thing himself, for Chrissake. But still, he should've capped off his emotions before he'd ever put his mouth on her, and for that, he owed her an apology. "I'm sorry. I didn't mean to get carried away."

A flicker of something Cole couldn't identify rippled through her stare, gone before she replaced it with a brazen smile that didn't quite reach her eyes.

"It takes two, Everett. But don't worry. From now on, we'll stick to business as usual. I promise."

Chapter Twelve

Savannah leaned against her locker, the press of the metal cool against her T-shirt even though she felt anything but. A day and a half had passed since she'd walked away from Cole and their totally ill-advised, totally steamy fire escape encounter, all no-harm-no-foul.

So how come—despite thirty-six hours, two cold showers, and one dozen reasons why hooking up with another firefighter was a continentally bad idea—she could still feel Cole's mouth on her body as if he'd kissed her barely a minute ago?

And more importantly, how was she going to purge said feeling from her system when what she really wanted was for him to kiss her again?

Harder. Faster.

Lower.

Keep your eyes wide open, Savannah. Because I'm going to show you exactly how hot you are . . .

Savannah jerked her chin upward with a curse. No, she couldn't deny that the kiss she'd shared with Cole had been pretty much the most incendiary thing on the planet. The way his voice had gone needfully rough over her plain-Jane bra and modest-at-best bust, she'd had no chance at control.

But nerves of steel were the one thing Savannah needed now more than ever. *Especially* if she was going to prove herself as a firefighter.

She pushed off from her locker, determination filling her gut. The kiss had happened, and yes, it had curled her toes along with a few other, more delicate parts of her. But they'd agreed to forget it, and if Cole's serious-as-usual expression as they'd parted ways on Friday night was any indication, the gaffe was already in his rearview. At the very least, she needed to put it in hers, too.

Savannah made her way through the locker room, her footsteps echoing off the tiled walls. The tail end of breakfast had been punctuated by a call for reported smoke, but Station Thirteen had beat them to the scene, which had turned out to be a false alarm anyway. They hadn't responded to a big, active fire call since Savannah's very first shift two weeks ago, and God, she was antsier than ever to get her hands dirty.

It would sure as hell make returning the two messages her father had left on her cell phone easier.

She pressed a smile over her face, walking a straight line to the spot where Everett stood by the doors leading out to the engine bay. "Hey. You ready to get to work?"

"Sure." He pitched his voice to a low murmur, slanting a quick glance from one end of the hallway to the other. "Listen, before we get started, I just want to make sure we're good. You know. After the other night."

Savannah's palms went damp, but still, she met his eyes. They were adults. Coworkers. No need to lose their minds over some white-hot kisses and a little dirty talk on a fire escape.

So hot . . . you're so fucking sexy . . .

No one had ever called her sexy, let alone made her feel that way.

Good Lord, how Cole had made her feel that way.

"Of course," she said, blotting out the naughty memory once and for all. "I told you, the job is what's important to me."

Everett offered a slow nod. "Yeah. Me too."

Well, then. No time like the present. "So, ah, what's on tap for today?"

"Obstacle course, if you're up for it."

Savannah opened her mouth to pop back that of course she was up for it, she was a firefighter, for the love of Pete. But then she registered the lack of disdain in his olive-green eyes along with the slight edge of teasing he'd put to the words, and wait . . . he wasn't daring her.

He was *testing* her.

"Sure. Sounds fun." She scooped her hair into a ponytail, biting back her aha smile at the surprise flickering across Everett's face. She'd pay for it, she was sure. After all, the words "obstacle course" were usually synonymous with things like "hell on earth" and "day of shopping," and that was just from her limited experience at the academy. Lord knew whatever Everett had cooked up for their real-deal drills was bound to be twice as challenging.

Which was just dandy as far as Savannah was concerned. All she needed was for someone to tell her "you can't" in order for her to answer "watch me."

"Okay then. Go ahead and gear up in your bunker pants, coat, and gloves," Everett said, and she was helpless against the motion of her lips falling open.

"You do know it's supposed to be a hundred degrees today." It felt like a solid ninety already, and they hadn't even officially crossed into mid-morning yet.

Everett just nodded, grabbing his own gear from the engine. "A hundred and two, actually. Oh, and don't forget your SCBA tank."

Great. Add another thirty pounds to the party. Still, she wasn't about to back down in the face of a little sweat . . . or in this case, a lot. Savannah kicked out of her work boots, pulled her gear into place, and followed Everett through the rear exit of the engine bay.

A blast of heat and humidity flattened her as soon as she'd crossed the threshold to the empty lot-slash-basketball court beside the firehouse.

"Whoa," Savannah said, the overheated air burning a path past her throat and into her lungs. "Now that is like walking into a dog's mouth."

Everett laughed. "I take it that's a Texas saying."

"That is a Duke Nelson original. My father is full of those little gems." She caught the interest on Everett's face just a beat too late, and damn it, nothing short of the all-call was going to snag his attention now.

No such luck on being saved by the bell. "You're a little far from home, huh? How come you picked Fairview?"

She shrugged, taking a swipe at her brow with the back of one gloved hand. Jeez, it was hot. "Brad's here."

"But the rest of your family isn't, and you were obviously raised in Texas." He stopped in front of the twenty-foot ladder leaning against the station wall, which gave her a second to formulate a response.

"Obviously how?"

"Well, you can take a woman out of the South, darlin', but it's pretty tough to take the South out of a woman." He delivered the words in a flawless Southern accent, and they shocked her laughter right past her lips.

"Well done, cowboy. But that sounds more like Tennessee than Texas." Savannah's curiosity perked.

Of course, Everett's expression made the Rock of Gibraltar look like a skipping stone. The cadence of his voice returned to neutral. "Georgia, actually, although it's been a while. So all three of your brothers are firefighters?"

"Mmm-hmm." She followed him up the ladder to the flat roofline of the engine bay, and the way he focused so intently on what was in front of him rather than below him didn't get by her unnoticed.

"That's a pretty big family legacy."

"That's a pretty big understatement."

Okay, so the quip had flown out without the consent of her common sense, but between Captain Westin and instructor Brennan, chances were Everett knew her family history by now. She'd gone out of her way to keep it under wraps at the academy, but she wasn't fool enough to think no one would ever find out. Everett seemed like a pretty fair-shakes kind of guy, and anyway, it wasn't as if he'd know who Duke Nelson actually was.

Unlike, say, every other firefighter in the great state of Texas.

"My two brothers in Texas are lieutenants on truck, and obviously Brad is doing the arson investigation thing here in Fairview. Both of my uncles are house captains, all seven of my cousins are firefighters. One of them just made squad in Dallas." Savannah paused, but better to just get this out now and be done with it. "And my father has been a battalion chief for twelve years."

"Jesus," Everett breathed. "Are you kidding me?"

She pulled back to look at him, narrowing her gaze. "You didn't know?"

"No, I didn't know." He exhaled audibly. "I take it you're the first woman."

"Try the only woman," Savannah corrected. "But this is the only thing I've ever wanted to do. I wasn't just raised in a family of firefighters. I was raised to *be* a firefighter."

Everett's shoulders hitched just slightly beneath his turnout gear. "I get it. I know all about family legacies."

"You come from a family of firefighters, too?" Not too much of a shocker there. The job ran in lots of families, and Everett wasn't exactly a run-of-the-mill sort as far as ambition went.

"No. I'm the only one. So how come you came all the way out here to Virginia to be a firefighter? You've clearly got a lot of connections in Texas."

She nearly called him out on the abrupt change in subject—turnabout was fair play in the show-and-tell department, after all. But his question begged an answer, and she couldn't exactly stuff the toothpaste back into the tube. Might as well air out everything.

"I came here *because* I have connections in Texas." Savannah scraped the toe of one boot over the rooftop before planting both feet firmly into place. "Don't get me wrong, my father supports my decision to do the job one hundred percent, and I respect the hell out of the man."

It was an understatement, and not a small one, but she left it at that and continued. "So does every firefighter in Dallas, though. My brothers and cousins all worked hard to get where they are now, but it's different when you're Duke Nelson's only daughter. The only way I could guarantee that I'd get through the academy solely on my merit was to go someplace where my last name was just that. A last name."

Realization lit Everett's stare. "So you really did come to Fairview because your brother is here."

"Yes." Her belly tightened in a homesick pang, but she forced herself to brazen it out. "The decision for me not to go through the ranks in Dallas was hard on my father, although I think he understands why I made it. My family is extremely close, Brad and I in particular. I agreed to come out here to Fairview so I wouldn't be completely alone." Plus, as much as she'd rather be skinned alive than admit it, Texas hadn't quite been the same without her oldest brother around.

"Pretty ballsy move to uproot yourself for the job," he said, and wait . . . was that understanding on his face? "No wonder you're ready to jump in and prove yourself."

"It's not just about proving myself." Savannah reached down to fiddle with the roping attached to the hundred pounds of hose hanging over the side of the roof, trying to focus on the way her muscles would burn when she hauled it upward rather than the quickening thud of her heartbeat.

But instead of clamming up, she continued. "Ever since I can remember, when anyone asked me what I wanted to be when I grew up, the answer was this. My mother worried." She broke off with an irony-laden smile, because really, it was a gigantic understatement. "So for a year after college, I pushed paper in the fire marshal's office in Dallas while my mother did her best to convince me to get an MBA, or keep my clerical job, or do anything other than apply to the academy."

A muscle ticked, just slightly in Everett's jaw. "So she didn't approve of you becoming a firefighter."

"She was concerned," Savannah corrected. For all her mother's worry, she'd still been bursting with pride when Savannah had graduated from Fairview's academy at the top of her class. "But my dad . . . I think he always got it. See, I'm not a firefighter because I've got something to prove. I'm a firefighter because I've got someone to be."

"All the more reason to put everything you've got into the job," Everett said, the look of understanding returning to his face in full force.

Savannah blew out a breath. This was going to sting like a slap on sunburn, but that didn't mean it shouldn't be said. "Yeah, but as much as I hate it, you were right. I might've learned a lot at the academy, but being on shift *is* totally different. I should probably get past the whole fear of blood, learn how to assess the scene part of being a candidate before I go kicking in any doors."

"Oh, I don't know." One corner of Everett's mouth lifted

in the suggestion of a smile. "Something tells me you'd be pretty good at kicking in doors."

Savannah eked out a laugh. Honestly, all this deep-feelings stuff was giving her the shivers. "Thanks, Everett. You're all heart."

"Tell you what," he said, jutting his chin at the obstacle course laid out on the asphalt below them. "After shift, I'm going to head over to the scene of that warehouse fire we fought a couple of weeks ago. Oz already did the official report and arson's been ruled out, but I asked Westin if I could walk through to brush up on procedure for investigations. You beat Donovan's rookie time through this thing, and I'll take you with me."

Excitement sent Savannah's heartbeat into hell-yes mode. Usually, scene reports were limited to the captain or the rescue squad, and with Oz at the helm of the latter, she'd probably never get a shot at checking one out. If she got a chance to walk through on a reconstruction, even one that had been put to bed, she'd be able to brag to her arson investigator brother for a solid month.

"Has any rookie ever beat Donovan's time through this obstacle course?" she asked, and now Everett's smile traveled from ear to ear.

"One."

But rather than back down, Savannah served up a grin that went toe-to-toe with his.

"I'll tell *you* what. When I break yours too, you're throwing in breakfast before we go."

Chapter Thirteen

Cole looked up from the last station at the self-made obstacle course, pretty much praying for death. In the spirit of solidarity, not to mention keeping his ass in shape, he'd run the course with Savannah twice.

She hadn't beaten his time—or Donovan's—but she'd put everything she had into each drill, growing stronger and more efficient with each run-through.

And hell if that didn't trip Cole's trigger. Fast *and* hard.

He tamped down the want in his gut. They'd agreed to forget about what had happened on the fire escape, and truly, it was the smart play. He needed to focus on moving to squad, no matter how sexy he found her sheer determination or how much he now understood the reasons behind it. Savannah's admission of her family's legacy—and the reasons she wanted so badly to prove herself—had tempted Cole to tell her about his own. But popping off about his father, and Harvest Moon, and all the sloppy emotions that went with his hasty departure from home would only pull a thread on a sweater he'd long since abandoned. And since he wasn't going back, revisiting—even in the abstract—was pointless.

Focus, jackass. Find your strategy.

"You ready to take a knee yet, Nelson?" Cole asked, unhooking the air tank of his SCBA and lowering the thing from his screaming shoulders as she made her way toward the finish point.

Her breath heaved in and out with audible effort, her face bright with exertion, but still she said, "Nope."

"Well, too bad for you, I am. I'm all for effort, but if something catches fire, we've both got to have something left to put on the table."

Rather than argue as he expected her to, Savannah measured him with a you-might-be-right glance. "Okay. But by the end of my orientation period, I'm going to own that record. Just you wait."

He laughed. As much as her mettle drove him bat shit crazy sometimes, it really was kind of admirable. "Fair enough."

Cole shucked his gear down to his bunker pants, exhaling an oh-yeah breath at the instant drop in his body temperature despite the stifling weather in the side lot. He'd no sooner passed Savannah a bottle of water and downed one of his own, though, before the familiar piercing alarm sounded off through the speakers in the engine bay.

"Engine Eight, Squad Eight, Ambulance Eight. Report of smoke, sixteen-twelve Martinsburg Avenue. Requesting immediate response."

Cole reshouldered his gear, grabbing up the two sledge-hammers they'd used in the tire drill part of the obstacle course before his pulse even had a chance to speed up. He turned to tell Savannah to get a move on, a ripple of shock working its way down his spine as he realized she'd been right in step with him the whole time. They made it to Engine Eight at the same moment Donovan, Crews, and Jones came busting through the door from the station. Cole paused just long enough to put the sledges back into their storage compartment, then one-handed his way up to the operator's seat to fire up the engine.

"God damn, Everett. You're a hot mess." Crews lifted a brow, although his expression wasn't unfriendly.

Cole did a two-second check of the signal and his surroundings before tugging his headset into place and pulling out of the engine bay, excitement and adrenaline notching his mood into the go zone. "This is nothing, Lieu," he said, pointing to his work-messy hair and still-damp T-shirt. "You should see the other guy."

Crews clapped his headset over his ears, swinging around to throw a stare into the back step from the officer's seat next to Cole. "I'm lookin' at her, and you know what, you're right. You two are a matched freaking set."

Savannah's laughter combined with Donovan's through the headset. "Thank you, sir," she said, sounding for all the world like she meant it.

"My pleasure, rookie." Crews shook his head, but Cole caught the tail end of his smile before the guy turned back toward the computer screen on the dash. "Okay, here we go. Sixteen-twelve Martinsburg looks like a commercial building of some sort. Ah! Dispatch is calling it a restaurant. There's a report of smoke, but that's all I've got."

Cole flicked a glance at the GPS, his blood speeding up to a full thrum. "I know the area. They just built a bunch of town houses and condos back there off the main stretch. Like a city center, in walking distance from the avenue." There were no fewer than twenty shops, eating establishments, and other various businesses lined up on the bustling thoroughfare, a good half dozen of which could qualify as a restaurant.

"Wait." Donovan's voice crackled over the headset, and Cole would bet his left arm the guy was pulling up specifics on his iPhone. "Google has the address as Campisi's Italian

Bistro. It's right in between a dog groomer and a bookstore, with what looks like a park along the back border."

Cole ticked through the internal map in his mind's eye. "I recognize the name of the restaurant, but I think the place is closed down." He double-checked the location against the brightly lit path on the GPS. "We're less than ten minutes out."

"Copy," Crews said with a tight nod. "Thirteen's not going to beat us to this one. Time to move like you stole it, everybody."

Eight minutes later, Cole swung the engine onto Martinsburg Avenue. The businesses lining either side of the street weren't terribly close together, but they weren't far enough apart to keep a nasty fire from spreading in the right conditions. A thick column of smoke chugged upward from a building on the right-hand side of the avenue, smearing a dirty gray line over the flawlessly blue sky. The bitter scent of something burning invaded Cole's nose, landing on his tongue a few breaths later, and yeah. Nobody was sitting around on this call.

"We've got a live one." Crews pulled his headset off in favor of his helmet, clambering down from the engine not even three seconds after Cole had rolled through the restaurant's parking lot and thrown the transmission into Park. Cole's feet hit the ground less than a second later, his heart pinballing against his ribs as he did a rapid-fire assessment of the scene.

Two-story brick building with a cheery red, white, and green awning over the padlocked front door. CLOSED FOR BUSINESS posters plastered over the restaurant's signage. Empty parking lot. Insidious billows of soot-filled smoke pouring out of every front-facing window on the building. Something in there was burning. *Fast.*

"Let's get this fire under control." Captain Westin stood in front of his city-issued Suburban, his gear in place along with his cucumber-cool expression. "Oz, get up on that roof for a vent. Jones, you're on water lines. Crews, I want everyone else on engine inside that building with hoses in the next thirty seconds. Go."

Cole was in motion before he could register the command from his brain to fall out. He could feel Savannah directly on his heel, with Crews and Donovan right next to him, and even though the heat grew progressively more stifling with each step closer to the restaurant, he didn't stop until they'd all reached the sturdy-looking pine front door.

"Well. That's fun," Crews said, frowning at the shiny, four-inch padlock keeping them on the wrong side of the threshold. One precise snap of the bolt cutters he'd grabbed from the engine had the lock falling to the ground with a heavy *clunk*, and he lifted a brow at Cole. "You want to breach this thing so we can get to it?"

Cole gave Savannah a split-second glance, but he didn't think twice. "Okay, Nelson. Let's see how good you are at busting down doors."

Her surprise lasted for only one blink before she stepped into the space he'd just vacated by the door handle. "Copy. One busted-down door, coming right up."

She worked the flat edge of her Halligan bar into the practically microscopic space between the door and the jamb, her face bent in concentration as she crouched down lower for leverage to see what kind of locks they were dealing with. The breach was pretty straightforward, and she hadn't been bullshitting about being able to hold her own with her irons. As soon as she'd created enough of a gap to visualize the dead bolt, Savannah tilted her Halligan bar to brace the pointed prong against the jamb, using the flat end as a lever and her shoulder for force.

The push loosened the door with a creak without knocking it inward. But rather than letting the unsuccessful attempt rock her, she channeled even more *oomph* into her second go, finally forcing the door all the way in with a splintering crack.

"Way to get it, rookie." Donovan slapped the top of her helmet, grinning as they all hustled past the front door to take in the scene. Cole's throat tightened from both the blast of ashy smoke and the widespread extent of the fire, and he reached up to yank his mask into place. The entire back wall of the restaurant was engulfed in jagged rows of bright orange flames that were spreading fast, and no way was one water line going to cut it.

"Crews, report." Captain Westin's voice crackled through the two-way, and the lieutenant wasted no time answering.

"Dining room is fully involved. Blocked access to the kitchen. We're going to have our hands full here, Cap."

"I'm sending Andersen in through the Charlie side to get eyes on the kitchen. Crews, lock this thing down from your end."

Crews pivoted to look at both him and Savannah. "Everett, you and Nelson take the Delta side wall and work your way in. Donovan and I will start on the Bravo side and meet you in the middle," Crews yelled past the hiss of his regulator, his feet already in motion.

"Copy," Cole replied, lifting his voice to a near holler over the *whoosh* of flames. He turned toward Savannah, and even though her eyes were wide as hell behind the plastic shield of her mask, her stance said she was good to go.

Good fucking thing, seeing as how this fire was already mission critical and it was only getting hotter.

"All right." He readied their line on nothing more than muscle memory, the movements so deeply ingrained that he would sooner forget how to breathe than get them done. His objectives fell into place in his head, and he concentrated on the steady thump of his heartbeat in an effort to keep his control—and the situation—on the level. "Stay on my six and advance the line. Head on a swivel, you copy?"

"On your six with my head on a swivel," Savannah repeated. She held her position just behind him, keeping up with each advance as they moved toward the right-hand side of the restaurant. Thankfully, most of the tables and chairs that would've made their path a frigging nightmare under normal circumstances had been stacked against the perimeter of the dining room, and he and Savannah slowly, steadily worked their way from the far wall toward the interior. Sweat ran in a steady stream between Cole's shoulder blades, his muscles and his lungs both burning from the exertion. But Savannah backed him up on the nozzle with efficient movements, and they worked in tandem to get the blaze under control.

Although smoke clogged the restaurant's interior, the handful of large windows that hadn't been boarded up allowed in enough daylight to keep visibility out of the *hell no* range. Cole's brain fired off command after command as his body put them into motion, and finally, they managed to get the fire in the dining room contained, then extinguished. Andersen radioed in with an all clear from the kitchen, and Donovan and Crews doused the last of the flames on the restaurant's opposite wall.

"Holy shit," Crews said, pausing to give his own all clear through the two-way. "Something in this place must have been completely FUBAR to start a fire that nasty."

Cole pulled his mask from over his face, and the acrid punch of waterlogged ashes and fizzling smoke took over his senses. He surveyed what was left of the charred walls and furnishings, puddles of thick, soot-swirled water collecting over nearly every inch of the dining room floorboards. It didn't take a rocket scientist to realize the place was a total loss.

He blew out a breath. "The houses off the avenue might be new, but some of these businesses have been here for a couple decades, I think. Maybe the weather kicked something off with the electrical system."

They saw fires from old wiring all the time. Granted, things didn't usually go pear-shaped this fast, but no one had been inside to report the smell of smoke right away. Who knew how long the fire had been building before anyone had noticed.

Crews nodded with just one dip of his helmet. "Either way, the insurance company's gonna take a crazy hit on this one. Good work, you three."

"Yeah," Donovan said, his grin flashing bright white against his soot-streaked face. "Not bad for your real first fire, huh, Tough Stuff?"

The sound of Savannah's laughter snagged Cole's attention and sent a pang through his gut. The fire had been substantial enough to redline the building from cinder blocks to shingles. Yet every time he'd issued a directive, there she'd been, backing him up on the nozzle the same way anyone else on engine would. She might not've moved as intuitively as Donovan or Crews or even Jonesey would, but he hadn't had to worry about her, or the way she got the job done either.

"Thanks, Donovan. It *is* kind of a rush."

Crews grunted out a sound that was cynical on the surface, but held just a hint of amusement underneath. "Glad you think so, candidate, because we're not done yet. Unless you want an encore here, we've got to make sure this fire stays out."

They walked through the protocol for preventing flareups, gathering their gear and reloading the hoses to the engine as they went. Savannah proved to be a quick study, watching Donovan and Crews just as carefully as she watched him until everything was done.

"Nice job," Cole said, unable to contain his smile at the sight of the grin reaching all the way up to her eyes.

"Thanks, but I can't take all the credit. The guy training me doesn't suck." She waggled her brows toward her disheveled hairline, and Donovan's laughter joined in with Cole's.

"Aw, look at you, Nelson. So full of sunshine." Donovan shouldered his Halligan bar, leading the way back out into daylight and toward the engine. Cole was tempted to point out that Savannah was full of something completely different from sunshine, but the sound of a young girl's cry froze the words and his laughter right on his tongue.

"Please! Come quick! I need help." The girl belonging to the voice, who couldn't have been any more than ten, rushed toward them, the panic-stricken look on her face blotting out all the ease that had just rebuilt in Cole's gut.

"What's the matter?" he asked, immediately scanning the area for potential danger but coming up empty. "Is someone hurt?"

The girl pointed in the opposite direction from Martinsburg Avenue, toward what looked like a tree-lined jogging path leading into a slightly more wooded area. "No, but they're stuck. They just fell right into the storm drain. Please, you have to save them."

Cole's pulse triple-timed through his veins as he turned to follow the little girl, Savannah hot on his heels. Crews and Donovan fell in behind them, hollering to the guys on squad for assistance.

But Cole was already halfway across the parking lot, his sights locked on the jogging trail.

Chapter Fourteen

Savannah got six steps down the bike path behind the restaurant before her adrenaline caught up with the rest of her. But this—*this* was what she'd signed up for when she'd started at the academy. No chance in hell was she going to tap out just because of a little fatigue.

The muscles in her legs threatened to veto her conviction, but Savannah forced them to do their job regardless of the achy burn. She could raid the icebox for frozen peas as soon as they got back to the station. Right now? They had a job to do.

"Here!" The girl stopped short in front of a metal storm grate set into the neatly paved footpath, her eyes brimming with worry and tears. "My friend and I were playing in the park but we got bored and came up the trail. They must have come up from the pond over by the playground, and they fell right in."

Savannah's gaze narrowed over the holes in the storm grate, which were four-by-four inches, if that. The story wasn't adding up in her head. "Sweetheart, did your friend fall down here?"

"No." The girl shook her head, her blond braids swaying

over her shoulders. "My friend went back to the park to get help from her mom."

"Then who's in the drain?" Everett asked, bending at the knees and bracing his forearms over the tops of his bunker pants so he could look the girl in the eye.

"The ducks."

Savannah's mouth fell open. She chanced a glance at Donovan, but her fellow firefighter's baby blues said he was flying on the same nothing she was.

Oz and Andersen came clattering to a stop as they reached the group, Oz's gaze lasered in on the storm drain. "What're we looking at?" he asked.

Everett paused, pulling off his helmet to tug one hand through his hair. Reaching into one of the deep-welled pockets in his turnout gear, he palmed a flashlight and shined it past the thick, black grate. "Four . . . make that five baby ducks. They can't be more than ten days old."

Oz's silver-shot brows flew upward. "Excuse me?"

"They followed the mama," the girl said, her voice wavering in earnest now. "The mama duck was walking on the path, and me and Jody were watching from right there." She pointed to a bench on the other side of the foot path. "But the babies were too little, and they fell through the holes. Please, if they stay down there they won't have anything to eat! Can't you get them out?"

Everett slid a glance first at Crews, then at Oz. "It's about a twelve-foot drop. There's water in the bottom, which is probably the only reason they even survived the fall. But this thing isn't really meant for access from the top side. The space is really tight. I don't even know that we could get a man down there, let alone a man on a ladder."

"For baby ducks?" Oz folded his arms over his chest, staring at the grate. "I can't risk getting a man stuck in a storm drain for something like that."

Savannah eyeballed the size of the opening. "What about a woman?"

After a drawn-out beat of silence, it was Crews who finally spoke. "You want us to drop you into that storm drain so you can rescue a bunch of baby ducks?"

"Well, I'd prefer it if you didn't *drop* me," she said, smiling to offset the fresh burst of adrenaline that accompanied the offer she'd just made. "But I'd fit better than anyone else, right? Can you lower me down?"

"No," Oz said at the same time Everett said, "Maybe," and the two men locked eyes.

Everett tilted his head. "It's too tight for us to get her in there conventionally. But we could harness her up and lower her down like we do for rope rescue." He sent his gaze back down into the storm drain, clearly thinking out a plan.

But Oz wasn't having it. "*We* do rope rescue for people. And your rookie here isn't trained on squad. She's less than a month out of the academy, for Chrissake."

Donovan slipped in to guide the little girl back to the bench down the path, and Savannah bit her lip until they were out of earshot.

"It's twelve feet into a drainpipe for a quick grab. I'm pretty sure I can handle it," she said. Hell, she was nearly six feet tall on her own, and that was half the distance to the bottom. There might not be any wiggle room in that storm drain, but how hard could it be for them to slip her in long enough to scoop up a few ducks? "Look, this thing is made for water runoff, so it's all pipes and grates. I get that they're just ducks, but we all know they won't make it out of there any other way. So what's the big deal if we give this a shot?"

"You're not trained for this, that's what." Oz jabbed a finger at the grate. "And I'm none too interested in figuring out how to haul your ass out of there when you fuck this up."

"She's not going to fuck this up." Everett's voice was

quiet, but it rattled through Savannah anyway. He stood, his expression enviably calm. "I'll talk her through the whole thing. It's a straight shot to the bottom ledge, and Nelson is right. The ducks won't fit past the drainage system, otherwise they'd have floated through already. All we have to do is lower her down for a couple of minutes and then pull her back up. She's the only one of us who will fit with any room to move, and she's also the lightest. It makes sense to lower her instead of anyone else."

Oz made a rude noise, his arms threading even tighter over his soot-stained turnout gear. "I can't believe we're even standing here having this conversation."

Donovan stepped in from the spot where he'd rejoined them, his normally easygoing smile hardening by a fraction beneath the blond stubble on his chin. "Then why don't we stop talking and start getting something done?"

For a second, Savannah thought Oz would follow up on the argument flashing in his glacial stare. But then he wrapped his work-callused fingers around the radio on his shoulder. "It's Westin's call. But for the record, this is a shit idea."

Fortunately for Savannah, Captain Westin disagreed. After a quick back-and-forth over the radio with Oz and Crews, Westin appeared on the trail, surveying the storm grate with careful attention as Donovan and Crews lifted the cover from the opening.

"All right, Nelson. Oz and Andersen are going to work the ropes topside for you while Everett and Crews assist. We're going to make this quick and easy. Is that understood?"

"Yes sir," she said, slipping out of her coat and into the harness Everett held between his fingers. She stepped into the leg openings and pulled the thick nylon straps into place before holding her arms up to let Everett repeat the process over her shoulders.

"Listen," he said, stepping in close, his hands working in a series of quick, capable tugs. "That drain is really narrow. We're going to do this as fast as we can, but once you're in there, you won't have any room at all to turn or maneuver your position." He paused his movements, his fingers on the steel harness loop resting directly over the center of her chest. "The only way this is going to work is if you go down inverted."

Savannah's mouth turned to sand. "You're going to lower me upside down?"

"I'll be on the radio with you the whole time, and like Westin said, we're doing this fast." He tested the lines clipped to her harness with a couple of decisive pulls. "So let's get it done. Okay?"

He sounded so calm that her "okay" in return just popped right out. She tightened her helmet, skimming one last glance over the storm drain opening before lying sunny-side down on the footpath beside it.

Everyone's eyes were on her. She could do this.

Nerves of steel.

Savannah looked up at Everett and gave him a nod. "Let's get it done."

Crews crouched down beside her. Wrapping his arms around her shins, he levered her legs upward while she lifted her hands over her head to literally dive into the dark, dusty space. The spotlight on her helmet provided enough illumination for her to see a few feet in front of her, but not enough to signal how close she was to the bottom of the drain. Crews's voice, which had been so clear only a minute ago, faded into a muffled murmur as he lowered her farther into the yawning darkness. She felt someone—Crews? Everett?—tap the bottom of her boot, her breath catching in a hard gasp when Crews let go of her legs to let the harness support her, her body inside the drainpipe from head to heels.

Oh God. Oh *God.*

The space was tight as hell, and twice as dark.

Savannah's heart began to pound. She sucked in a breath, struggling to find some way of getting her bearings. Her temples slammed from the pressure of being upside down, her pulse drumming against her eardrums so hard she was sure they'd burst. The air was thick with the smell of mildew and wet concrete, filling her mouth and stopping up her lungs . . .

But then Everett's voice echoed over the radio. "Hey. You're completely on the line, all systems go, so we're going to start lowering you down. You good?"

She snaked a hand close to her body, fingers shaking in her gloves as she pressed the button on her two-way. "C-copy," she managed, although it was half lie, half bravado.

As if Everett sensed the fractured truth, he said, "Okay. Take deep breaths and find a good focal point. We'll have you down there in no time."

Savannah focused on the beam of the spotlight against the curve of concrete in front of her, relief splashing through her chest as she started to move downward. Inch by inch, she regained her composure, until finally, she heard the soft *whoosh* of water and spotted a flash of movement at the edge of the light's reach.

"Hold."

The line jerked to a stop, and Everett's voice followed barely a second later. "Are you at the bottom of the drain?"

Savannah tilted her head to shine her spotlight over the small, crumbling ledge by the bottom of the storm drain, a bubble of laughter welling all the way up from her belly. "Copy, but you might want to work on your math, Everett. I've got *six* baby ducks down here."

"Well," he said, his smile carrying through in his tone. "Since you're going to have your hands more full than

anticipated, I guess you'd better start grabbing them up so
we can get this show on the road."

Sure. Of all the times he could go all smartass on her, he
just had to choose the moment when she was dangling
sunny-side down in a drainpipe. "Copy that."

Savannah shook out the small nylon bag she'd tucked
into her harness, grinning at the fuzzy mob in front of her.
"I know, guys. Not ideal, but it's only temporary, and it's a
hell of a lot better than staying down here."

One by one, she scooped the wiggly little critters into the
bag, the ducks quacking their displeasure even though she
made sure to handle them gently. Her fingertips started to
tingle with each movement, her vision going slightly blurry
around the edges by the time the last dark gray-and-white
duckling slid in with his brethren, and she focused extra
hard on the wall in front of her as she radioed a breathless
"all clear." Everett's answer echoed back, and with each
upward tug, Savannah concentrated on the cadence of his
voice, counting slowly in her head.

Thirty-six . . . thirty-seven . . . thirty-eight . . .

Daylight hit her in a dizzying blast.

A pair of strong hands wrapped around her ankles, lifting
her out of the storm drain to right her on the footpath, and
oooookay. Turned out going teakettle over ass was about as
much fun as being knocked in the reverse.

"Nelson." Everett knelt between her knees, his olive-
green eyes pinning her with an assessing stare. "You good?"

She blinked back the bright white kaleidoscopes dancing in her peripheral vision. "Yeah. I'm fine," she said,
catching her breath as she passed off the ducks to Donovan's
waiting hands. "Piece of cake."

"Aw, look." Donovan cradled the bag in one arm, reaching in to scoop one of the ducklings into the center of his
glove. "We should call you the duck whisperer, Nelson."

"Oh! You did it. You saved them!" The girl's voice rang

out, her face lit with happiness and relief where she stood with her friend and her friend's mother. Donovan brought the ducks over to the periphery of the footpath, and Savannah pushed to her feet to join him.

"Yep, but I had a great team." She grinned and stroked the top of one of the ducklings' heads. She might not be big on cute and cuddly, but she had to admit, baby ducks kind of brought the adorable.

"Thank you! Oh, thank you." The girl broke into an ear-to-ear smile, throwing her arms around Savannah's waist.

"Whoa," she said, her face prickling with a startled flush as she laughed and hugged the girl back. "Um, sure thing."

Captain Westin appeared over Donovan's shoulder, his gray-blond brows raised along with the corners of his mouth. "Well done, candidate."

"Thank you, sir. But really, it was all of us." She nodded at Everett and Crews and Donovan, then widened her gesture to include Andersen and Oz. She might not like the guy, but that didn't mean she wouldn't put credit where it belonged.

"Well. Let's get these ducks to animal control and head back to the house."

Fifteen minutes had their gear packed up, and fifteen more had them back at Station Eight. Savannah's muscles screamed from exhaustion, the rest of her running on fumes from her spent adrenaline, and she'd never wanted a shower or a meal so badly in her twenty-six years.

But her fatigue and her filthiness both took a backseat to the pride filling every inch of her rib cage. Not only had she busted down a door in order to fight the fire in that restaurant, but she'd been an instrumental part of a rescue call. A part her team had needed in order to get the job done. A part that had mattered.

Best. Day. *Ever.*

Savannah jumped down from Engine Eight's back step

with a giant grin on her face, trying to flip the imaginary coin between a shower and sustenance. But before she could get halfway across the engine bay to grab either, Oz stepped into her path.

"You're awful proud of yourself, aren't you, Nelson?"

Savannah stiffened, but no way. No way was she going to let Dennis Freaking Osborne piss on her parade right now, when she'd finally done something of value. "Yeah, actually. I am."

"You aren't gonna be smiling so pretty when shit *really* goes tango uniform." He stabbed his boots into the time-buffed concrete, the jaw beneath his stubble set as hard and square as a brick-end.

"I held my own just fine today," she said, quietly metering the anger that begged to pump through every inch of her. Everett and Donovan made their way over to the spot where she stood, Crews and Jones falling in behind them, but not even their presence stopped Oz from answering with disdain that bordered on contempt.

"Today." He sneered. "Today was bullshit. You advanced a little line in a fire and saved a goddamn petting zoo. Big fucking deal."

Before she could fire off an answer, Donovan took a step closer, his normally twinkling blue eyes turning flat under the weight of his stare. "Jesus Christ, Oz. I get that she's a rookie, but come on. She did all right today."

"Oh, that's just priceless. Of course you girls on engine would go to bat for each other." Oz cut back the retort brewing on Donovan's face with a withering glare, which was pretty impressive considering Donovan looked as pissed as Savannah had ever seen him. "Tell me this, sweet pea. What if your lieutenant gets injured and needs to be hauled down three flights of steps?" Oz gestured to Crews, who had to have a good ninety pounds to go with the five inches he had on her. "Who's going to do it? Not you."

Impulse snapped hot and relentless in Savannah's chest, and it shoveled her words right out. "Yeah, and what if there had been a toddler in that storm drain instead of a bunch of ducks? Who's going to go down there and get him, Oz? Spoiler alert—not *you*."

"Okay." Everett stepped directly between her and the furious-faced lieutenant, holding up a palm in each direction as if he could stuff the tension back with his hands. "That's enough. We've all had a really charged-up morning."

"I'm not charged up from the work," Savannah argued, not taking her eyes off Oz's. The slam of her heartbeat warned her not to mouth off, but seriously, this sexist crap was wearing razor thin. "I can handle the job just fine, and I've never once asked for a double standard."

Oz's laugh was rough around the edges, all sandpaper and scorn. "Don't you get it, missy? You *are* a double standard."

She opened her mouth to settle the score once and for all, only Everett spoke first.

"Come on, Nelson." He turned his gaze on her, lifting his chin at the firehouse doors. "Why don't you go rotate in for the shower?"

Savannah's breath escaped in a shocked huff, her limbs stiffening with resentment and something else, something dark and deep that she didn't quite recognize. Of course Everett had backed her up in the field—it was his job. But when the rubber met the racetrack, all that talk about having her back, about her being part of the team, about *belonging*, it had been just that.

All talk.

She squared her shoulders despite the sting that had to be showing on her face. "Yes sir," she said, then turned and walked out of the engine bay.

Chapter Fifteen

Cole stuffed his toothbrush into his shaving kit and tucked the hem of his T-shirt into his jeans before clanging his locker shut with a heavy exhale. The clock on the wall read just after seven thirty, but Christ, he felt like he'd been here for a month rather than twenty-four hours.

A rock and a hard place would be an all-night beer bash compared to the shit storm he was looking at right now.

Although he'd had to run some pretty strategic interference for the remainder of their shift, Cole had managed to keep Oz and Savannah far enough away from each other to avoid another explosion. Engine had filled the afternoon with a handful of small-time calls, and squad had headed to one of the fire department's test facilities to do extraction drills. While Savannah hadn't given him any lip service after her frosty "yes sir" as she'd walked out of the engine bay, she also hadn't said a single syllable above what was necessary, and damn it, in the heat of the moment, he hadn't realized that his strategy to keep the peace would look like he was taking sides.

Specifically, Oz's. And while having a fellow fire-fighter's back was about as high on Cole's priority list as breathing and eating and taking the spot he'd earned on squad, in this case, he couldn't deny the truth.

Oz wasn't just acting like an ass. He was wrong. Rookie or not, woman or not, Savannah really *had* come through and proven herself yesterday. She had damn good reason to be proud.

Which meant that Cole had some work to do in the amends department.

He took a deep breath. "I believe I owe you breakfast, if you're still up for it."

Savannah froze to her spot four lockers away, the lean line of her shoulders stiffening beneath her pale yellow tank top. "I didn't beat Donovan's time through the obstacle course," she said, and while it wasn't a yes, it also wasn't a fuck straight off. Right about now, Cole couldn't afford to be choosy.

"Why don't we consider it an advance, then? I promised to take you to the scene of that warehouse fire, and truth be told, I'm starving."

Her chocolate-colored eyes went wide. "You still want to take me with you?"

"Sure," he said, sliding one palm beneath the strap of his duffel. "If you still want to go."

Savannah's return expression suggested he and his common sense had parted ways, and lucky for him, her ambition trumped her irritation. "Yeah, I still want to go. Just give me a sec here."

She stuffed a sweatshirt into the bag behind her on the bench, turning to close her locker before she shouldered her bag and followed him into the common room. After a few quick *see-ya-laters* to the guys on A-shift, they walked out of the station, headed toward the small parking area adjacent to the basketball court.

"It'll probably be easier if we head over to the warehouse together. I don't mind driving," Cole said, gesturing to his

Jeep. To his surprise, Savannah simply nodded, popping the trunk on the little Ford two parking spaces down to toss her bag inside. She slid into the Jeep's passenger seat, lifting a brow as she pulled the door shut and threaded her seat belt over her hips.

"This thing is clean enough to serve a four-course meal on." A smile pushed at the corners of her mouth, as if she was fighting the gesture and losing, and it made Cole smile in return.

"Guess I don't see much point in being sloppy."

"You should probably steer clear of my brother's place, then," she said, and yup. She was definitely trying—and failing—to hide a smile. "You know, for the sake of your Type-A sanity."

"Duly noted," he said. He slid the key into the ignition and pulled the Jeep onto Church Street, heading toward Scarlett's Diner. Station Eight's go-to daytime hangout was only a handful of blocks away, and they made it from doorstep to doorstep in about as many minutes.

"Oh, I've heard about this place." Savannah paused on the sidewalk. She looked up at the bright red sign boasting FAIRVIEW'S BEST BREAKFAST, MORNING, NOON AND MIDNIGHT, absently rubbing a palm over her stomach.

"It's not just hype." Cole nodded up at the sign, pulling the door open to usher Savannah through before following.

"Thanks," she said, making her way to a booth by the back of the L-shaped dining room. The Monday-morning breakfast crowd had dwindled down to a few stragglers now that the workday was starting for most people, so the place was comfortably quiet and equally empty. Savannah slid one of the laminated menus from the metal holder at the end of the table, but Cole's hand hesitated just shy of its twin. He knew the thing by heart, and anyway, he owed Savannah both an apology and an explanation. There was no reason to wait to deliver.

"Listen, before we go any further, I want to clear the air about yesterday."

"There's nothing to clear, really. I'm the candidate. You're training me, and you're about to move to squad, where Oz will be your commanding officer. I shouldn't have been surprised you dismissed me."

On the surface, he might've bought her no-big-deal expression and the equally noncommittal tone with which she'd paired it. But he'd been trained to see everything, and the way her shoulders had tightened ever so slightly against the red leather banquette, coupled with the press of her mouth into a thin, white line, told Cole everything Savannah hadn't.

She tacked a polite smile to her face as a waitress came by to fill their coffee cups and take their order, doubling Cole's request for Scarlett's supreme breakfast special. He spent two seconds being impressed that Savannah could put away such a high-magnitude breakfast, then a full minute carefully constructing his reply.

"I wasn't dismissing you," he said, his pulse tapping harder in his veins at the thought. "I realize in hindsight that my delivery could use a little polish, but I was actually trying to save your ass."

Savannah's lips parted, her tough façade suddenly lost. "I'm sorry. You . . . what?"

"Look, for whatever reason, Oz has a chip on his shoulder over you being in-house. I'm not saying it's right," Cole added quickly, first to head off the protest flashing in her eyes, but also because it was the truth. "But it's pretty hard to deny. You throw down against him, and he's going to win. It has nothing to do with your gender or your determination. He's been a firefighter for nearly as long as you've been alive, Savannah, and he didn't earn his tenure by selling Girl Scout cookies."

"Great. This again. So just because he's the grand pooh-bah of the Old Boys' Club and I happen to have a uterus, I'm supposed to take his shit?"

"Of course not. But you can't let him bait you, either. All Oz wants is one good reason to drag you into Westin's office. All *you* need to do is not give it to him. You came to Fairview to be a great firefighter, right?"

Savannah hesitated, finally saying, "Yeah."

Cole reached across the table, closing his fingers over the warmth of her wrist before his ironclad impulse control could kill the move. "So do it. You kicked ass yesterday on both of those calls. Even Westin saw how well you handled yourself. Just keep proving Oz wrong with your actions, and he won't have any choice but to shut up and come around."

The guy might be acting like a jackass, especially lately, but Cole had shared a house with him for eight years. When he'd told Savannah Oz was a damned good firefighter, it hadn't been for shits and giggles. Oz might be notoriously hard on rookies, Savannah in particular, but the guy damn sure knew good firefighting. Between her determination and Cole's guidance, they'd get him to see the truth so he'd back off.

They had to.

Savannah's wide-eyed blink brought Cole back to the diner, her expression a mismatch for her usual brash exterior. "You think I did a good job yesterday?"

The question was so devoid of drama or pretense, her voice so straight-up honest, that he answered in the exact same manner. "I think you did a great job yesterday."

Unable to help it, he stroked his thumb over her skin, just above the junction where her pulse point met her arm. He knew damn well that putting his hands on her now was as bad an idea as it had been a few nights ago, but there was just one small problem.

The smile on her face as he touched her was so slow and so sweet, Cole didn't want to stop.

"You're pretty good at keeping the peace, huh?" she asked, looking down at the spot where he touched her before lifting her gaze from his fingers back to his eyes. "Staying calm. Making the smart call."

Caution pinched at his throat, but he swallowed the feeling down. "Everybody's good at something."

"Have you always played it safe? Or is the Switzerland thing a new development for you?"

Although the question was as loaded as a two-dollar pistol, Cole answered it anyway. "I'm not completely non-confrontational. Every once in a while, you've got to fight a good fight."

Her brows lifted in genuine surprise. "You don't even yell at me when I screw up in training, and you don't lose your cool in car wrecks or fires or . . . hell, ever. When was the last time you got good and spitting mad?"

Damn it, he was skirting dangerous territory—especially since right now, talking to Savannah felt about as easy as touching her. And the more he talked, the more he was tempted to keep talking. Keep feeling.

You walk offa this land, you ain't my son. You'll be dead to me, y'hear?

Cole froze, his breath a forty-pound weight in his lungs. No. *No.* Dredging up his past wouldn't change anything, no matter how much that last fight had ripped at his gut.

What had happened with his old man was over. Done. Buried. And it needed to stay that way.

"It's been a while," he said, letting go of her to slide his hand back over to his side of the table. "Playing it safe is almost always the smartest move. Getting emotional only makes you sloppy."

Savannah laughed, the throaty sound hitting him point-blank in the chest. "You and your strategies. I get the idea to a point, and I even hear what you're saying about Oz, although I'm certainly not making any guarantees. But come on. You said yourself you're only human. Doesn't *anything* rile you up?" She shifted in the private confines of the high-backed banquette, leaning in closer across the expanse of Formica between them. "Piss you off? Get your blood boiling?"

"Nothing other than you, Nelson."

The answer was out before he could grab it back, but rather than taking offense, she just smiled, brazen as ever.

"Good to know, Everett. Good to know." Savannah sat back, turning her gaze around the dining room. She took in the long, chrome-lined counter and the waitress and the cook behind it, both of whom Cole had greeted by name as they'd passed by on their way to the booth. "You really do know Fairview up and down, don't you?" she asked. "Good places to eat, all the city landmarks. The people who work in them."

"I've lived here for nine years, plus I operate a fire engine. It's not so strange to have the lay of the land after that long, especially with a job that requires me to know where I'm going along with the best way to get there."

Anyone else would've taken the information at face value and moved on. But of course, Savannah just had to dare to be different. "Yeah, but just because someone lives in a town and knows the streets doesn't automatically make that place home. You just . . . I don't know. You look like you belong here in Fairview, is all."

"You're awfully observant." He selected his words with care, but Savannah just shrugged, taking a long sip from the rim of her coffee cup.

"You're the one who's training me to be that way."

Okay, so she had a point, albeit a smartass one. Still, he wasn't about to pass on the opportunity to shift the subject from home and belonging places once and for all, and anyway, they did have a little groundwork to do before they hit that warehouse. "Speaking of your training, we should probably take a look at the official report for this warehouse fire so we know what to look for once we get there."

Biting hook, line, and oh-hell-yes sinker, Savannah slid her coffee over the white and gray–speckled Formica, leaning in with bright eyes even though she'd gotten the same five broken hours of sleep Cole had. "So how do these investigations normally work?"

He placed the printout of the report he'd brought inside with him over the table, pausing to smile a silent thank-you at their waitress as she slid their breakfasts in between the pages before heading back to the counter. In between bites, Cole walked Savannah through the write-up, step by step. The fire had been ruled an accident, started by a faulty air-conditioning unit in one of the warehouse's storage bays. The whole thing was pretty cut-and-dried, from the point of origin to the path of the fire to the burn patterns left behind by the blaze. Still, the way Savannah read through the report so carefully, asking for clarification on the details and furrowing her brow as she processed every last piece of information, made Cole all the more excited to go do a routine walk-through.

"So if the wiring to one of these AC units is faulty, it can burn hot enough to ignite everything behind the walls?"

"Mmm-hmm. The warehouse is . . . I guess *was* . . . an older building, too, which didn't help. Most of the storage bays were at least half-full, so there was plenty to burn. Once something like that ignites and has fuel, especially when there's no one around to notice it right away . . ." Cole trailed off.

Savannah filled in the blank. "The fire spreads fast and is tough to contain."

"You got it."

She bit her lip, shaking a generous amount of hot sauce over the last of her scrambled eggs. "Pretty lucky the place was empty. I can't imagine having to do search and rescue on a fire like that."

"It makes fighting the fire more difficult, for sure, but you can't automatically assume that a place like that will be empty. We always have to look out for squatters, especially down in the warehouse district. Industrial Row is a notoriously tough part of Fairview," he said, reaching for the hot sauce to give his eggs the same treatment Savannah had given hers.

"I noticed it looked a lot more urban than the rest of the city, but I'll admit, I'd never been down there before last week. It's that bad, huh?"

"Sort of. There have been a couple of recent restore and rebuild projects going on down there in an effort to clean things up. As a matter of fact, Donovan's girlfriend runs one of the bigger ones—Hope House Soup Kitchen, over on Jefferson Avenue."

"Wait . . ." Savannah paused, mid-bite. "I thought Westin's daughter was in charge of Hope House."

Cole nodded. "She is. Donovan and Zoe have been a thing for about six months now."

Her fork found the edge of her plate with a clatter. "*That's* who he gets all goofy-eyed over when he's on the phone? Does he have a death wish?"

"You've met the guy, right?" he asked, half a smile twitching at his lips. They might be best friends, but Donovan wasn't exactly a paragon of impulse control. He was practically the high lord of adrenaline junkies.

It was Savannah's turn to eke out a nod. "Point taken. Still. Dating your captain's daughter is . . ."

"Risky, yeah." Cole scooped up the last strip of perfectly cooked bacon from his plate, his stomach groaning in protest but his brain too blissed out to listen, let alone care. "But the reality is, they're both adults. Risky or not, they knew what they were doing when they jumped in."

"Right. I forgot." She popped the corner of her toast past her bold grin, chewing and swallowing before she said, "You're Mr. Pragmatic over there. Just the facts, ma'am."

He laughed, but no frigging way was he going to give her the last word.

"Make fun all you want, Nelson. Facts don't lie. Now, do you want to go check out this warehouse or are you too worn out from your shift?"

Chapter Sixteen

Savannah alternated glances between the four-page report in her lap and the increasingly neglected buildings over her shoulder. Under normal circumstances, heading into a condemned warehouse in the worst part of Fairview wouldn't be at the top of her list of fun and games. But she hadn't been about to say no to tagging along on this walk-through, especially since after the fallout from yesterday's back-to-back calls, she'd thought Cole would surely blow her off.

Instead, he'd not only made good on his promise *and* kept her from hauling off and committing career hara-kiri, but for just a minute, he'd let his calm, cool exterior slip, showing Savannah that he wasn't devoid of feelings at all.

He just had a cast-iron strategy for hiding them.

Judging by the liquid-gold flash of emotion in Cole's eyes when she'd asked him about fighting a good fight, he clearly had a frickin' doozy somewhere in his past. As tempted as Savannah had been to push, she knew what it was like to want to keep your feelings close. Hell, she'd kept her family history on the down low for an entire year—mostly because she hadn't wanted special treatment at the academy, but also because facing her choice to leave home had hurt. Sometimes a lot.

What was Cole hiding that would put that kind of fire in his eyes?

"The warehouse should be coming up in a couple blocks on the right," he said, pointing to the GPS on his dashboard and yanking Savannah's thoughts back to present-day reality.

"Oh! Um, yep. Ninety-seven hundred Wabash. There's the hydrant we tapped." She gestured to the ancient fire hydrant, looking more closely at their rough-and-tumble surroundings. The streets had grown exponentially dingier the farther they'd traveled from Church Street, with the trash-strewn sidewalks cracking and fading out to match. The only other buildings on the block were a vacant warehouse boasting huge blue-and-white commercial realty signs and some sort of storage facility that looked as unattended as it was unmaintained. They might be in a less-than-savory part of the city, but chances were, she and Everett wouldn't see another soul on this little field trip.

Not that it stopped her from taking in the details. After all, a girl could never be too careful.

"Here we go," Cole said, pulling the Jeep over in front of the visibly fire-damaged warehouse, popping the car locks closed with an audible *click* as soon as they'd both set their feet on the sidewalk. "Wow. Looks just like we left it."

Savannah squinted up at the place, shielding her eyes from the sun. The heavy front door that Crews had forced open now bore a shiny steel chain with a padlock to match, and the windows on the ground level had been boarded up with plywood—although whether that was to keep squatters out or to temporarily repair damage from the fire, she couldn't really say. The windows on the second and third floors told another story, clearly having been burned out and broken during the blaze. Heavy lines of soot streaked upward over the crumbling, mud-colored bricks, and as she and Cole moved toward the threshold, the smell of stale smoke met them like the world's most bitter *un*welcome mat.

"Pretty consistent with what's here," Savannah said, holding up the pages.

Cole nodded, pulling a key ring from the back pocket of his jeans. He slid the small silver key into the padlock holding the door shut, sliding the metal bar free from its housing. "Oz did the final write-up a couple of days ago. After twenty-three years on the job, he definitely knows what he's looking at."

She bit into the smart comment daring the tip of her tongue. She might dislike Oz more than ever, but going through the report over breakfast *had* taught her some new things about reconstructing the scene of a fire.

With a swift push, the warehouse door swung on its hinges with a heavy *creak*. "Careful," Cole warned, eyeing the thing with caution. "The building is structurally stable enough for an investigation, but make no mistake. after the city inspector sees this report, he isn't going to have any choice but to condemn the place."

Savannah looked around. Most of the light spilled in from the open front door behind them since the front windows on this level had been boarded up, but in truth, the ruin appeared more minimal than she'd expected.

"The damage on the middle floors is that bad?" she asked, scanning the ash-covered but otherwise intact front room.

"Donovan said the fire was pretty tough to lock down on floors two and three. Plus the report says the entire electrical system is shot in addition to all the structural damage. But let's go see for ourselves."

Cole passed her the flashlight he'd taken from the Jeep. She clicked it on, focusing the beam on the interior door marked STAIRS as he pulled the front door shut with a bang.

In the darkness, Savannah's flashlight cast eerie shadows

over the wall. The bitter tang of smoke filled her nose, bringing her instantly back to yesterday's fire call at the restaurant. Even though the location had been a complete one-eighty from this one, all the hot, pent-up energy of the previous day roared back through her veins, reminding her of the rush of fighting a fire.

"Keep an eye on these steps. It's dark as hell in here, and the ash makes things slippery," Cole said, barely two feet behind her on the stairwell. Savannah's skin prickled with awareness as he followed her lead, gently placing his fingers over the small of her back when she faltered in the shadows.

"Sorry." Thank God he couldn't see the wash of heat that was surely covering her face from temples to chin. But who knew the endorphins from yesterday's pair of calls would have such a delayed reaction, or that something as simple and strange as the smell of smoke would set her to remembering it all so clearly?

"No worries," Cole said, and of course he was calm as ever. He followed her up the stairs, and by the time they'd reached the second-floor doorway, Savannah had wrangled her brain back from its labor strike. Mostly.

"Okay." She took a deep breath, forcing herself to scan the report in her left hand as she swung the flashlight over the second-floor space with her right. "According to this, the point of origin for the fire was the AC unit in the far right storage bay on this floor."

"2E, right?" Cole's glance darted to the door at the end of the dreary, fire-eaten hallway, and wow, what a difference one floor up made in the damage department.

"Yeah." Even though the sun filtered through the broken-out windows from the opposite side of the building, the interior of the warehouse still had an air of smoky darkness. A thick layer of ash and soot clung to everything around them, marring the few sections of drywall still standing and swirling irregular patterns over what was left of the cheap, waterlogged carpet lining the corridor.

Savannah's pulse kicked up a notch. She had surveyed a handful of scenes post-fire, but they'd all been in controlled environment drills—never the real deal, and never as extensive as this. God, how could anyone figure out what some of these twisted, charred things left behind by the fire had even been, let alone how one of them might've sparked a blaze? The fire had scorched nearly everything in its path, warping the rest.

The *clack* of her Tony Lamas echoed in the stillness. The air grew hotter as she and Cole made their way to the storage bay at the end of the row, the direct sunlight splashing in from the windows making it only marginally easier to tell what they were dealing with.

"Yeah, this definitely looks like where the fire started," Cole said, sending his stare around the room in a slow three-sixty. "See the scorch marks traveling up the wall here, next to the window where the AC unit was anchored in?"

Recognition did a slow trickle into Savannah's brain. Believing that the hunk of charred metal at her feet had once been an air-conditioning unit was nearly impossible.

"Mmm-hmm. But what about this?" she asked, pointing to an oily stain on the floor.

"Looks like a chemical of some kind. I'd guess this is residue from something that was stored here when the unit caught fire."

"Oh," Savannah said, and come to think of it, that did make sense. "So the unit was working overtime in this heat wave we've been having. The wiring shorted out and caused a spark big enough for the insulation behind the walls to catch fire."

Cole nodded. "The report does say that the AC unit was an older model. Wouldn't be the first time I've ever seen one of those dinosaurs malfunction and start a blaze. If the electrical in the building was out of date, too . . . the cause of this one is pretty much a slam dunk." He squatted down lower, bracing his forearms over the thighs of his jeans as he took a closer look at the burned-out shell of the window unit, then the torched walls and equally damaged ceiling.

"A lot of the buildings in Industrial Row are old, right?" She flipped through the pages in her hand, knowing she'd seen the information somewhere. "Ah! According to this, the warehouse was built nineteen years ago. It doesn't say if the electrical is original to the building, but . . ."

"Between an overheated AC unit and a crappy old outlet, that would be more than enough to do it."

Still, Cole's brow furrowed into a deep V, telling her in no uncertain terms that he was playing all the angles in his head even with the answers right there in front of him. Wanting to learn as much as possible from what little was left behind, Savannah wiped back a damp strand of hair that had escaped from her ponytail and rescanned the room. After three failed attempts to put a positive ID to anything that had been in the storage space, she turned her attention back to the AC unit beneath the window, turning through the pages of the report one more time to make sure it all added up in her brain.

"What?" she finally asked, unable to cage her curiosity, and Cole looked up from his spot in the center of the fire-ravaged room.

"The burn patterns on the wall are well documented in Oz's report, but there's no mention of these." He gestured to the scorch marks covering the floor. "And I can't figure them out."

Savannah knelt down next to him, listening carefully as he continued. "This warehouse leases individual storage bays, promising climate control. But it's cheaper to heat and cool each storage bay with individual window units. That way, the management company doesn't have to foot the bill for heating and cooling empty space, in case some of the storage bays go unrented."

"Pretty chintzy," she said. "But under most circumstances, it's not dangerous, is it?"

"Not in theory, no. Obviously, units can short out. Electrical fires are pretty standard fare, and with enough time and things to burn, they can get deadly fast."

Savannah held up the papers in her hand, confused. "That's exactly what this says, and the burn patterns on the walls are consistent with an electrical fire." She pointed to the thin black column seared into the wall beside the window where the air-conditioning unit had once been anchored. The scorch marks stretched all the way to the ceiling, following what she had to assume had been the path of the actual wires behind the drywall before they'd ignited and been burned beyond recognition.

Cole stood, the look on his face as serious as she'd ever seen it—and that was really saying something. "Yeah, but those aren't the burn patterns I'm talking about. Look at the damage here, in front of the window and farther inside the room."

"It's pretty extensive." Her stomach squeezed. The fire had been hot enough to burn through the linoleum tiles, warping a five-foot radius of the subfloor and torching everything that had been in its path.

"It's not extensive. It's insane," Cole corrected, not heatedly. "In order for a fire to leave damage like this, it needs to burn at both an extremely high temperature and an extremely fast rate. It's difficult to make out the pattern here because everything is so fried. But squat down and look at the floor from this angle, with the sunlight on it. See the

way the heat seems to have pushed out and up, into the center
of the room where it ignited everything in front of it?"

Shock dropped Savannah's jaw. "Almost like . . . some
sort of explosion precipitated the spread of the fire."

"Not almost." He paused to lift his gaze from the blackened floor to pin her with a stare. "Exactly."

"Okay." Her temples pounded in complaint at the
thoughts suddenly churning through her brain, and she slid
her fingers over her forehead to try to make sense of at least
one of them. "So what does that mean?"

"What it means is that Oz made a mistake."

Cole stood in the hallway outside Station Eight's common
room, taking a swipe at the same section of linoleum he'd
been mopping for the last fifteen minutes. To his left stood
the hall of pictures leading to Captain Westin's office. To the
right, the engine bay, where Oz and the rest of the guys on
squad were prepping for rescue drills. And here he was,
right smack in between.

How fucking appropriate.

Four days and one and a half shifts had passed since he'd
made the troubling discovery that Oz had misdiagnosed the
cause of that warehouse fire. Or at least, Cole *thought* he'd
misdiagnosed it. But therein lay the problem. With the
extent of the damage, diagnosing whether the electrical had
sparked first and caused the AC unit to somehow explode
or vice versa was a true case of could-be-either, and regardless, the air-conditioning unit had been the cause, hands
down. The manufacturer had been notified and was taking
all the necessary precautions. The fire was accidental either
way. No one had been hurt. The building would be torn
down and rebuilt, probably nicer and safer and better than
it had ever been.

Yet something about it sat in Cole's belly like a box full of tire irons.

Don't go trying to buy trouble. Since last week's showdown in the engine bay, things had been surprisingly low-key between Savannah and Oz. They still traded glares like baseball cards any time they shared space, but Oz had kept his distance the same way Savannah had kept to her training and assignments. She'd even learned to forgo her knee-jerk responses for smarter, more calculated moves, and Cole had to admit it.

With every passing day, she was not only proving herself as a firefighter, but becoming part of the tight-knit crew at Station Eight. Which meant that in less than three short weeks, Cole's spot on squad would be his for the taking.

Which also meant that Oz would be his LT. And there was no time like the present to clear the air with the guy once and for all.

Cole finished mopping the hallway, neatly storing the cleaning supplies before aiming his boots in the direction of the engine bay. Oz knelt down over an open nylon backpack by the squad vehicle, doing the inventory on the contents used for rope rescue.

"Hey, Lieutenant." Cole hoped to ease into the conversation and gauge Oz's mood a little, but nope. The guy barely looked up from the stainless-steel anchor plates in his hand.

"Everett."

Ten seconds passed, then twenty, and Cole sucked in a breath. Oz had never been much of a twirl-around-the-subject kind of guy. Getting right to the point was probably Cole's best strategy.

But then he caught sight of the crescent-shaped shadows under Oz's eyes, the weary lines that seemed to have intensified even more since the last time Cole had seen him, and something entirely different flew from his mouth.

"Are you okay?"

Now Oz did pause, but he didn't look happy about it. "Did you come out here to check on my feelings, Everett? See if I need some hot chocolate or a hug?"

Shit. "No, I just . . . you look tired, is all."

Okay, so it was akin to saying *hey, man, you look like crap on a cracker*, but the truth of the matter was that Oz did. Enough for Cole to risk raising the guy's ire by saying so.

"Thanks for the pep talk, but I'm solid." Oz slid his gaze back to the pulleys and carabiners in the rescue bag in front of him, and Cole knew that if he didn't speak his mind now, he wouldn't get another chance.

"Got it. Listen, I just want to make sure we're right side up with what happened in Westin's office last week. I know things got a little touchy."

Oz's hands became fists, his knuckles turning white over the nylon bag. "You should've cut Nelson loose early, like I said. I know you want that spot on squad, but she doesn't belong here."

Anger sailed through Cole's chest, hot and unexpected. "Then let her prove it. If she's not good enough, her actions will out her soon enough, just like they do with every other candidate."

"At whose expense?" Oz hissed. "Yours? Mine? That's not a risk I'm willing to take, thanks."

"Just because she's a woman?" Jesus. He was all for having Savannah prove her worth, but this guilty-before-proven-innocent stuff was just bullshit, no matter how much Oz outranked him.

"You're soft on her *because* she's a woman." Oz found his feet, his eyes flashing cold and flat. "Say what you want about treating her equal. But in the same way you think I'm being too hard on her delicate sensibilities, you ain't hard enough. Shit, Everett. She damn near cried for her mommy at that highway wreck, but did you light into her? 'Course not. You went easy on her. And from where I sit, that's goddamn dangerous."

Cole's hands turned to fists, his throat tightening enough to scrape his words. "I told you I'd train her the best I know how. That means I'm not giving her any special treatment, one way *or* the other, and she and I dealt with her response to that wreck after the fact. Look"—he paused, clinging hard to his last shred of calm despite his slamming pulse— "I get that you two aren't best friends, but this is on its way to working out just like it's supposed to. I want my spot on squad, she wants her spot on engine. I'm willing to give her a fair shake to make it happen. The only thing I'm asking is for you to do the same."

For a second, Oz looked ready to take his argument to the next level, and damn it, this was so *not* how Cole had intended the conversation to go.

But then the lieutenant took a step back. "Guess if that's the way you feel about it, I don't really have a choice, now do I?"

Cole released half of the breath he'd been gripping in his lungs. "I'm not saying she should have a double standard, Oz. But I do think she could be a damned good firefighter."

"You just keep tellin' yourself that," Oz said, keeping his icy stare fastened to Cole's for a minute longer before turning to walk toward the locker room.

"Awesome," Cole muttered under his breath even though the engine bay was now empty. "Good talk, Lieutenant."

Jamming a hand through his hair, he set his sights on the door back into the house. Rachel and O'Keefe had agreed to run through some trauma responses with him and Savannah this morning, and he wasn't about to let a craptastic morning make him pull up on work. They hadn't been called to another nasty trauma since that car wreck that had rattled Savannah, and it was only a matter of time before statistics did their thing.

You're soft on her because she's a woman . . .

Cole stopped short. He and Savannah might've been a little rough out of the gate, and even now, she still had her feisty moments that drove him bat shit crazy. But he couldn't deny finding her dedication admirable, or her determination appealing.

Or wanting her now more than ever, despite knowing that desire was a bad idea of the worst sort.

"You're not soft on her," he whispered, dismissing the notion outright. So he hadn't yelled at her when she'd screwed up—big deal. He'd never hollered at Jonesey for past mistakes, either. Recruits got plenty of that at the academy, and while it was mostly for their own good, Cole just had a different approach when it came to laying out the tough stuff.

And yelling didn't always get the desired results, anyway. He was living proof of *that*.

Cole snuffed out the feelings playing it fast and loose in his gut. He walked into the common room, where Rachel and Donovan and Savannah were all sitting around one of the tables, huddled over a pale blue piece of paper.

Rachel looked up and sent a high-level frown in his direction, and crap, that was never a good sign. "Everett! I cannot believe you didn't say one thing to Nelson about the Fireman's Ball tomorrow night."

Oh look. More crap. Although they were few and far between, the department's formal events always gave him the shakes. "To be fair, apparently neither did any of you guys. Hasn't that flyer been posted for, like, a month?"

"Really, it's fine," Savannah said at the exact same time Harrison chimed in with a snort.

"That's totally beside the point," the paramedic said, dividing a stern look between the two of them. "We spend all year wearing these totally stodgy uniforms and eating whatever meals we can in between that all-call going off."

O'Keefe chimed in from his spot on the couch. "Oh,

you're just in a pissy mood because you got barfed on at our last call."

"That is exactly my point," Rachel shot back, stabbing a finger into the air to punctuate her words. "The Fairview Hotel is one of the most upscale places in the entire city, and the FFD is going all out for this year's ball. It's our *one* night to get dressed up and have some serious fun together. And by the way, O'Keefe, you are taking our next three drunk and disorderlies. I've earned watching you get puked on for a change."

"You know, I'm not really sure my dress uniform counts as getting fancy," Savannah started, but Rachel was dialed all the way up to her pit bull setting.

"Lucky for you, the Fireman's Ball is uniform free. Formal attire for all."

Savannah's pretty face blanched. "I don't even have a dress that would—"

"I'll loan you one," Rachel said, refusing to be swayed. "Either that, or Zoe will. Right, Donovan?"

"Dude, you got puked on before I'd had my morning coffee. I know better than to fuck with you," Alex said, raising his hands in mock surrender. "Sure."

Rachel swung her stare in Cole's direction, and he resisted the urge to flinch. "You're going, too, right?"

"Um . . ." He could barely resist Savannah in her jeans and turnout gear. Put her in the right dress and his restraint would be hosed. "I don't think—"

"Fantastic," Rachel finished, breaking into a smile that would make the Cheshire cat explode with jealousy.

"Then we'll all be one big, happy, dressed-up family."

Chapter Seventeen

Savannah straightened against the driver's seat of her Escape, wishing the car's moniker could morph into reality. Even after the forty-five minutes Rachel and Alex's girlfriend Zoe had spent helping her choose a dress, then using half a roll of double-sided fashion tape to get the straps of the bra she barely needed anyway hidden in the halter-style top of said dress (who even knew there *was* such a thing!), Savannah still felt completely self-conscious. Hiding things like her bra straps was so not in her wheelhouse—not that full-length formal dresses fell in her comfort zone either. She didn't even want to get started on the three-inch heels Rachel had told her went "perfectly" with the dark green gown Zoe had plucked from her closet as a loaner. Or the fact that Cole was going to see her in this getup and probably think she was the world's worst imposter.

God, she'd bet he looked incredible in a suit. Out of one? Even better.

Her body pulsed to life beneath the swishy column of fabric draped from shoulder to ankle. Three weeks' worth of work and training had done way more than prepare Savannah to be a firefighter. The adrenaline in her system had gone from a slow build to a steady demand, to the point where if she didn't blow off at least some of this steam, she'd be in danger of spontaneous human combustion.

And with each passing minute she spent in his presence, resisting the urge to combust with Cole Everett was becoming more and more difficult.

Savannah blinked, forcing herself off Fantasy Island. All she had to do was fake her way through this party for one hour, and then she could reasonably slip back home for a double date with her sweatpants and a pint of good old Häagen-Dazs.

And if the ice cream didn't cool her off, she could always invite her vibrator and make it a threesome.

"Oh my God, knock it off." Savannah pressed her lips together, still unused to the feel of the shimmery bronze lipstick Zoe had put on her. She reached up to adjust her ponytail, her hands halting halfway when she remembered that Rachel had done some sort of updo-type thing that had required more patience and bobby pins than Savannah owned, and screw it. Even though a few strands had broken free to brush her shoulders in defiance, this was as good as it was going to get.

Curling her toes in the shoes-slash-torture devices Rachel had insisted she wear, she took a deep breath and opened her car door. Her heels clacked awkwardly over the cement in the Fairview Hotel's parking garage, but she managed to make it all the way to the bank of elevators without stumbling.

Right up until she saw the brushed silver doors starting to glide shut from fifteen paces away.

"Oh, wait! Hold the elevator," she called out, both her feet and her equilibrium reminding her in no uncertain terms that running went with heels about as well as a brushfire went with kerosene.

But then Savannah reached the door, and her world shifted on its axis for an entirely different reason.

Cole stood to one side of the elevator, his finger still in place over the softly lit button to hold the door. His stylish dark gray suit was a flawless fit, outlining his lean muscles just enough to rattle her heart in her rib cage and make her imagination work triple-time. His normally tousled hair had been combed into submission, the strong line of his jaw smooth from a fresh shave, and he looked so ridiculously handsome that Savannah's face flushed to scalding at the sight of him.

"Hey," he said, his green eyes going wide as they took a slow trip down the length of her dress and back up again. "You look—"

She lifted a hand to interrupt. "You don't have to say anything just because we're all dressed up. Really, I—"

"Gorgeous," Cole finished. "Savannah, you're gorgeous."

"Oh." The word collapsed past her lips on a whisper, and oh God, she wanted him so badly she could cry. "Well, you look, ah, nice, too."

He blinked, pulling his finger off the elevator button with a start. "Christ, I'm sorry," he said over a tiny puff of laughter, his face coloring slightly. "That probably came out sounding really inappropriate."

But the flash in his eyes lingered, matching the heat she felt as he looked at her, and all at once, Savannah was done fighting the desire rushing through her veins.

She turned toward the elevator's control panel, hitting the button to stop the movement of the car. "Is that how you meant it?"

"Savannah." Cole split her name between a warning and a plea. "Are you sure you want me to answer that question?"

One step had her close enough to touch him, although she stopped just shy of contact. She'd make her willingness clear, but if they were going to do this, the want had to be a two-way street.

Savannah tilted her head, keeping her gaze steady. "I

wouldn't have asked if I didn't, but I think we both know the score here. You can say no, in which case we'll go upstairs and walk into this party, business as usual."

He leaned forward, close enough to send the heat of his exhale over her skin. "Or?"

"Or you can say yes, in which case, we're never going to make it off this elevator."

Cole closed the slight space between them, brushing his mouth over hers in a hot, needful kiss. "Yes. *Hell* yes. You're so beautiful," he said, coaxing her lips apart just in time to capture her laugh.

"I'm not," Savannah said, darting her tongue out for a quick, impulsive taste. "It's just the dress."

She angled her head to kiss him again, but to her surprise, Cole countered. Wrapping his fingers around the curve of her jaw, he held her steady, pulling back to meet her stare.

"It's not the dress, sweetheart. It's *you*. Now shut up and let me prove you wrong."

He brought his mouth back to hers hard enough to make her lips ache, but Savannah's bottled-up need refused to stand down. She took everything Cole gave only to return it with twice the intensity, sweeping, licking, and teasing until finally, she parted from him on a gasp.

"Concede defeat?" he asked, tugging her bottom lip between his teeth. He worked the soft skin there, back and forth and back again, just hard enough for the sensation to sting.

Savannah's nipples peaked hard against the fabric of her dress, but two could play at that game.

She nipped his lip hard enough to make him groan, and dark satisfaction trilled through her belly. "Nice try. But it's going to take more than that to get me to cry uncle."

Cole's mouth tipped into a grin. "Remember, you asked for it."

Before she could move, or answer, or hell—even think, he cupped her face with one hand. Slowly, he slid his index finger over the sensitive indent of her upper lip, pausing briefly to trace the outline of her mouth before delivering a punishing kiss.

"Oh God." Savannah molded her body to his from shoulders to chest, her heart tripping against her breastbone as she parted her lips to give him better access to her mouth. And Cole took it, testing every part of her with his lips and teeth and tongue before finally pulling back with a ragged breath.

"We need to get out of here," he grated. "Right now."

"Or"—her hands grasped the lapels on his jacket, the wool sliding under her fingers as she closed the space he'd created—"we could stay here."

For a second, Cole's expression slid from dark and sexy to something a lot softer. "As much as I want you, right here, right now." He paused to kiss her, the erection pressing against her belly acting as proof positive of his words. "There are no less than two hundred firefighters upstairs, all of whom can and will 'rescue' us from this elevator in about four minutes flat if they think it's stuck. And since I plan to take all night with you . . ."

He trailed off, the green-gold glint in his stare finishing the sentence without words, and okay, yeah, they needed to go *now*.

"Excellent point," Savannah said. Cole hit the button for the garage level before releasing the hold on the elevator, sending them back into motion with a *bump*. The descent took only a minute, the doors sliding open to reveal the stone-gray interior of the parking garage, but a familiar voice interrupted their hasty exit.

"Hey, you guys!" O'Keefe grinned, jerking a thumb toward the elevator bay behind them. "Pretty sure you're going the wrong way."

Shit. Shit, shit, shitty shit! "Um . . ." Savannah sputtered, but Cole stepped in, smooth as butter on warm bread.

"Yeah, Nelson's not feeling well. I'm going to help her get home."

O'Keefe looked at her, the concern on his face obvious. "You want me to take a look? I can do a quick assessment . . ."

"Oh, that's nice of you, but no thanks." Savannah manufactured a weak smile, pressing a palm to her belly in an effort to play along. "I ate sushi for lunch, and you know how my stomach is."

Bingo. O'Keefe took a giant step backward. "Copy that. I'll tell everyone you're not feeling well. But if you can't keep anything down for more than twelve hours or you start running a fever, go to urgent care, all right?"

"You got it," she said, waiting until O'Keefe was out of earshot to add, "Well. That just solidified my reputation as a puker."

At least Cole had the good grace to put an apologetic edge to his smile. "Sorry. It was all I could think of on the fly."

"Ah, it's worth it." She pulled her keys from her tiny purse, engaging the mechanism to unlock the car doors before tossing them to Cole. "Do me a favor, would you? Drive fast."

Bless his heart, he did. Ten minutes and some extremely loose interpretation of the speed limit had them at the front door to his condo, their feet barely over the threshold before Savannah grabbed him to pull him close. Their mouths crashed together, lips parting without pleasantries, tongues tangling with hot need. The kiss sent sparks all the way to her core, and she dug her hands into Cole's hair, guiding him out of his suit jacket as she hungrily explored his mouth.

A groan slipped past his lips. "Come with me." Cupping her bare shoulders, he swung her around, but after only three paces into the shadowy foyer, he stopped.

"What are we doing?" she asked.

Cole used his grip on her shoulders to turn her halfway around. Moonlight and an ambient glow from the street lamps outside spilled in through the wall of windows in the adjacent living space, illuminating the spot where they stood just enough for Savannah to see the large, wood-framed mirror in front of her.

"I'm showing you how beautiful you are," Cole said, the hard plane of his chest pressing against her back. His gaze met hers in the reflection of the glass, and the dark, seductive promise she found there made her swallow hard.

"Cole, I—"

"Shhh." He hooked an arm around her rib cage from behind her, lifting his hand to dust the pad of one finger over her mouth. Not to be outdone—but not wanting him to let go—Savannah opened her lips, sucking his fingertip into her mouth with a swirl of her tongue.

He tensed, his breath hot on her neck. Leaving his arm in place around her, he reached down low with his other hand, gathering the green material of her dress until her thighs were exposed.

Her heart pounded. For a second, she thought to say something—surely she'd made another embarrassing error with her choice of undergarments. But Cole lifted the fabric over her hips, and the look on his face clapped her words to a stop in her throat.

"Savannah," he grated. "You're not wearing anything under here."

She closed her eyes. "Rachel said wear a thong, but . . ." Oh fuck it. Her cover was clearly blown. "I'm not girly, okay? I've never owned a thong in my life, so I figured this was the next best thing. I didn't think—"

Cole's finger was back in place over her lips in an instant. "It's sexy as hell."

"I . . . what?"

"You really do need a lesson, don't you?" His fingers

turned to a fist over the pool of fabric in his grasp, and he pulled it all the way up, exposing her bare skin from hips to ankles. Dropping the arm around her torso, he skimmed his hand down the flat of her belly, stopping just shy of her core.

"Look," he said. But the word came out reverent, far from a bossy demand, and looking away became impossible. "Look how beautiful you are."

He splayed his fingers over her sex to part her thighs. She opened readily, watching as his eyes flicked from her gaze in the reflection to a spot on the wall directly beside the mirror.

"Hold on."

Savannah took a shaky breath, angling forward to flatten her palm against the cool surface of the wall. Need pulsed through her, flaring into urgency when Cole hooked his fingers around the bend of her knee, lifting just high enough to place it over the low, slim table in front of the mirror. Oh God, with her dress rucked up around her hips and one foot off the floor, she was completely exposed, completely *vulnerable*, but in that moment, she couldn't make herself care.

Cole wasn't wrong. Tendrils of hair spiraled down around her face, framing her flushed skin and full, kiss-swollen mouth. She was dressed, but also tantalizingly naked, his fingers hovering over her in a deliciously forbidden manner to prove it. With Cole's hands on her body and his stare drilling into hers in the mirror, she looked sexier than she'd ever felt in her life.

"See? Beautiful." He parted the folds of her sex with one sinuous slide of his hand, and her moan in reply was a foregone conclusion. The muscles in her core clenched, tightening and slick in anticipation. Desperate, Savannah tipped her hips forward, her sigh turning into a scream as Cole sank a finger all the way into her heat.

"*Oh.*" Pure pleasure muffled her thoughts, sending her

hips bucking against Cole's hand. The sight of him, fingers spanning her inner thighs save the one buried inside her, sent a shot of unchecked heat sizzling under her skin. He slid out just long enough to twine two fingers together, thrusting back into her aching core, and Savannah watched his every move.

He dropped his mouth to her ear, not stopping his ministrations. "I've wanted to know what you sound like when you come since that night at the library." He crooked his fingers, tempting another moan from her throat as he discovered a hidden, sensitive spot deep between her legs. "What you look like. How tight you feel. How wet."

Savannah arched forward, meeting his movements, wordlessly begging for more. Her eyes fixed on their reflection in the mirror, on Cole's fingers pumping in and out of her sex, and the sight sent her already brazen nature into overdrive.

"Then find out. Make me come, Cole. *Please.*"

With a quick turn of his wrist, his thumb found her clit, and between the sweet circles above and the hard rhythm below, Savannah edged closer and closer to release. She widened her stance, canting her hips to increase the contact right at her center, where she needed it most. Her orgasm surged through her, bright and bold and hard enough to steal her breath, turning her fingernails into the wall in front of her and arching her back as she let loose a long, low cry.

Cole slowed the motion of his fingers even though his breath still arrived in hot bursts over her shoulder. "Jesus," he whispered, sliding his hand gently from her core and turning her to face him. "That was even hotter than I imagined."

Savannah blinked her way back down to earth, a smile curving her lips. "That was just a start." She reached up, removing his tie and freeing the buttons on his dress shirt one by one. Despite the residual traces of the climax still making her legs unsteady, she wanted Cole now more than ever.

And she meant to take him. No more waiting.

"Mmm," he murmured, raising his hands to help her. "I do like how you think."

With a few strategic tugs, he was naked from the waist up, and she paused for just a second to look her fill. Lord, the way his leanly chiseled pecs tapered into those strong, flat abs made her nearly dizzy.

And the soft dusting of honey-brown hair happy trailing its way from his navel down into his dress pants made her mouth water.

Turning toward the nearest available room—which, judging by the shadowy outline of the cabinets and the soft hum of the refrigerator, just happened to be the kitchen—Savannah beckoned for Cole to follow.

"My bedroom is just down the hall," he said, but she shook her head. Want was already rekindling between her thighs, and anyway, she'd never been much for patience or restraint.

"We'll end up there eventually. But this room has a perfectly good flat surface." She tossed a gesture at the table over her shoulder. "I say we make good use of it."

Savannah's heels clicked as she moved toward him. She lowered her hand, palming his already hard cock over his dress pants, and he hissed a breath through his teeth.

"I'm not fucking you on my kitchen table, Savannah." Still, he thrust against her fingers with a low moan, his motions picking a fight with his words. She stroked him with the clear intent to change his mind, her opposite hand making fast work of his belt buckle, then the button and zipper beneath them.

"That's fine." She looked up at him through her lashes,

her smile as wicked as she could make it. "I don't mind fucking you instead."

Cole sprang forward to clear the table in one long sweep. "You win. Kitchen table it is."

With the exception of his boxer briefs, all of his clothes hit the floor, and he reached out, sliding his hands over her dress in a frenzy.

"Where's the damned zipper on this thing?" he asked in between hard, hot kisses, and Savannah half laughed, half moaned against his mouth.

"On the side," she said, arching into Cole's touch as he stopped to skim his fingers over her nipple on his way around her rib cage. "Oh God, take it off. Take it off."

"With pleasure."

The zipper gave way with a soft rasp, but the dress didn't budge. Cole slipped his palms beneath the spaghetti-thin straps at her shoulders for another try, and damn it, she'd forgotten that Rachel had all but spackled her and her bra into the top of the dress.

"Wait, I'm kind of . . . it's a long story." She *knew* she should've just skipped the bra along with her panties in the first place. She reached behind her to unhook the clasps so the whole thing would just let go and she could be naked already, realizing a second too late that she'd put on the one and only bra she owned with a front closure.

"Savannah." Cole's eyes went as dark as his voice. "I like this dress an awful lot, but I swear on the sun, I *will* rip it off you."

"Oh, don't worry, sugar," she said, her own voice thick with need. "If I can't get it off the old-fashioned way in the next five seconds, I'm going to rip it myself."

She delved her hand beneath the now-loose bodice of the dress, relief sailing through her as her bra finally gave way with a hard twist. Without a word, she let all the fabric fall to the floor, leaving her in nothing but her heels and her very bad intentions.

Cole's hands were on her before she could move. He wrapped his arms around her waist, sliding a string of suggestive, open-mouthed kisses over her neck at the same time he lifted her feet from the floor to lay her down over the table.

A trickle of worry slid past the lusty heat building between Savannah's hips. "So, ah." The last part turned into a sigh when his tongue edged over her collarbone, and when he trailed back up to lightly bite her shoulder, she nearly lost her goddamn mind.

Nope. Not shorting out on this. "Cole. Please tell me you have condoms." Fat lot of good her stash would do from halfway across Fairview.

His soft laugh coasted over the slope of her breasts. "I do. Only I don't keep them in the kitchen, so do me a favor and hold"—he kissed the spot where her shoulders met her chest—"that"—another kiss, this one on her chin—"thought," he finished, capturing her face to lightly kiss her mouth.

He returned barely a minute later, and while the brief separation might've weakened the mood in any other situation, it only upped Savannah's urgency to have Cole inside her. She sat up, sliding her fingers under the waistband of his boxer briefs. Together, they laid waste to the one scrap of fabric between them to roll the condom into place, and Cole reached down, drawing her ass flush with the edge of the table.

"Savannah." The head of his cock slipped over her folds, pressing, insistent, and the contact sent sparks shuddering through her. Her knees fluttered apart at the same time Cole pushed, filling her slowly as she tilted forward to take him.

For just a breath, neither of them moved. Then he released a harsh exhale, gripping her hips with spread-wide fingers, and oh God, oh God, oh God, she wanted his cock buried inside her all night.

Savannah knotted her arms around Cole's shoulders, the cradle of her hips moving of its own volition. Craving even more contact, she closed the sliver of space between their upper bodies, the friction from his bare skin turning her nipples into aching, beaded points.

"God damn. You feel so good." His voice went low, tugging at her subconscious as a tiny part of her registered tinges of a familiar accent twining around his words. But then he lowered his mouth to her shoulder, finding the slim cord of muscle connecting her arm to her neck with the edge of his teeth, and Savannah forgot everything but the pleasure building deep within her.

"Cole." Pressure coiled, low and sweet in her belly, growing brighter with every thrust. Hooking her knees over the hard line of his waist, Savannah let go of his shoulders, planting her palms into the surface of the table and squeezing her inner muscles around his cock. Cole leaned forward while she angled her body back, one hand digging into her hip for leverage while the other reached around to skim the length of her lower leg. He curled his fingers around her ankle, thrusting into her harder and harder as he locked her leg all the way around his waist.

The move left no space at all where they joined. Want collided with raw pleasure in her blood, daring her to come. Cole filled her completely with every push of his hips, stretching her channel as his cock stroked her sensitive, swollen clit, and with one last thrust, she flew apart with a cry.

"That's it," Cole whispered, burying himself to the hilt while Savannah came in waves. "Ah, God. You're so tight. I can feel how hard you're coming."

His jaw clenched, the restraint on his face obvious even in the shadows, but oh no. The fact that they were even here was proof positive that holding back wasn't an option tonight.

"Cole." Savannah's voice was rough with the residual passion of her climax, and she tightened her legs around him. "I want you to come, too. Please. Come for me."

All the hesitation vanished from his face, replaced only by hot need. He rebuilt the rhythm between them, and she met every thrust, every glide and every moan. Cole's fingers bit into the flare of her hips, the sweet sting turning her on all the more as he powered into her core over and over. Finally, his body quickened, going bowstring tight against hers for just a breath before he called her name over a sharp, shuddering exhale.

For a minute, or maybe it was ten, or twenty—or God, a million—Savannah lay beneath him, too blissed out to move. Cole felt warm on top of her, his chest rising and falling with hers as their breathing slowed to normal. He drew back from her body, slipping down the hall to presumably deal with the condom, but still, she didn't move.

Savannah knew she should feel self-conscious, or concerned, or downright goddamn terrified at the repercussions of what they'd just done. But she didn't feel any of those things.

Instead, she felt safe.

"Hey." Cole appeared in the entryway to the kitchen, wearing a fresh pair of boxer briefs and a worried-as-hell expression. "I, um, brought you this."

He held up a T-shirt, and her bare feet shushed over the kitchen tiles as she crossed the floor to take it from him.

"Thanks." She shouldered her way into the soft cotton, the hem of the shirt fluttering halfway down her thighs. "There's a zero percent chance I'll ever figure out how to get back into that dress all by myself."

"Listen, Savannah—"

"Do you regret this?"

Oh, *hell*. Apparently, not even heaven and earth-moving sex could tempt her mouth out of the no-filter zone. She scrambled for a way to pretty up her point-blank question, but Cole's chin snapped up, his eyes glinting in the soft light.

"God, no." His hand moved forward, but stopped an inch shy of touching her. "I'm just . . . I didn't expect it, and I'm in unfamiliar territory here."

"Because of work."

"Of course."

Savannah didn't think, just closed the space between their hands out of pure instinct. "Lucky for us, we're not at work right now. Look, I know that will change, and it's something we'll need to deal with," she said, because as good as she felt standing there, all wrapped up in post-coital glow in Cole's kitchen, her mama also hadn't raised any dummies. "But for tonight, can't we just be me and you, like we were at the library?"

He dropped his forehead over hers, and for a second, fear pricked through her chest that he'd say no. But then he kissed her, and holy hell, being in his arms felt so far from off-limits.

"Tonight, it's me and you. Which means we'd better get moving. You promised we'd end up in my bed, but I plan to show you every room I've got along the way."

Chapter Eighteen

Cole stretched in the warmth of his bedsheets, morning sunlight slipping past the window blinds to illuminate the reality of daytime. Savannah lay on her side next to him, the steady rise and fall of her shoulders and back showing that she was still asleep even though he couldn't see her face. Cole shifted as memories of the night before slid back into focus, his muscles squeezing a slightly sore reminder of just how long it had been since he'd used them between the sheets.

And in the kitchen. And on the living room sofa.

Jesus Christ, he'd lost his *mind.* But when Savannah had rushed into that elevator last night, with her dress surrendering to all her curves and a look of sheer, uncharacteristic vulnerability covering her face, something deep in Cole's belly had snapped. He'd wanted her badly enough to break the rules, to be utterly impulsive, to act on nothing but pure, raw, reckless emotion.

And he'd loved every fucking second of it.

He let out the breath tightening his lungs. The sex had been phenomenal—of *course* he'd loved every second. That still didn't mean it had been in any way smart. But it also hadn't felt wrong, and Cole couldn't deny that he didn't want to categorize their night together as just a fling.

Mostly because, even though barely seven hours had passed since he'd last parted her legs and buried himself in the sweet, tight heat of her body until she screamed, what he wanted more than anything else was to do it again.

Holy shit. He had no plan for this.

"Wow." Savannah's throaty murmur sounded beside him. Shit. When had she rolled over and opened her eyes? "You even wake up with that serious look on your face, huh?"

"What? No, I'm good." Okay, so it might be a fractured version of the truth, but the last thing Cole wanted was for her to think he regretted sleeping with her. He might've been impulsive, but he wasn't a dick.

Savannah sighed, her lips lifting into a tiny smile before she sat up to tame her sleep-mussed hair into a knot on top of her head. "Bullshit before breakfast isn't really your style, Everett. But this conversation will probably be a lot more comfortable if we've brushed our teeth and covered our bits, so why don't we meet in the kitchen in five?"

Without waiting for a response, she pressed a lightning-fast kiss over his lips, slid out from under the covers, and scooped up the bag of clothes he'd retrieved from her car last night somewhere between rounds two and three. She didn't so much as spare a backward glance on her way out the bedroom door, and for a split second, Cole sat in his bed, completely poleaxed and more than a little enamored with her.

And how fucking dangerous was that?

After a splash of cold water and a double date with his toothbrush and a pair of basketball shorts, Cole made his way down the hall toward the kitchen. The earthy aroma of fresh coffee sent a good-morning pang through his gut, and clearly, Savannah had beat him to the caffeine punch.

"Hey. Hope you don't mind that I commandeered the

coffeepot," she said, looking cuter than anyone had a right to in her borrowed T-shirt and a pair of cutoffs that made him wish he'd thrown on a Kevlar-reinforced chastity belt instead of the thin nylon shorts that were about to publicize his brewing hard-on.

Coffee, you moron. "Nope. Not at all." He moved to the fridge, welcoming the blast of cold air as he took out the milk, then turned toward the cupboard over the coffeepot to grab two mugs. "Lucky that you had a few things in your car."

"Oh." Savannah dropped her gaze over the red cotton and faded denim, a few dark tendrils of hair breaking free to frame her face. "I got ready at Zoe's yesterday, and I always keep a bag of toiletries in my trunk for work, so . . ." Her chest lifted on a deep breath. "Anyway, do you want me to make some breakfast while we talk?"

Cole lifted a brow. "That's kind of a loaded question, given your track record at the house," he pointed out, but rather than popping off at the mouth, she just broke into a catlike smile.

"You shouldn't believe everything you see. Sometimes there's more to a story than meets the eye."

Realization gave him a hard tag in the sternum, and he lowered the coffee carafe with a *thunk*. "You can totally cook, can't you?"

Savannah buried most of her smile in her mug, but her eyes were a dead giveaway. "To be fair, my mama taught me *and* all of my brothers to cook, and I still maintain that Oz was asking for it that first day. But if you've got bread and eggs, I make a mean French toast."

Cole gestured to the stainless-steel fridge, wondering if she could be any more full of grit or surprises. "By all means. My kitchen is your kitchen."

For a couple of minutes, they moved around each other, finding a comfortable rhythm together. Savannah worked just as she did at the firehouse, with both efficient moves and 100 percent devotion to the task in front of her, making it all but impossible for Cole to feel anything but downright damned good in her presence.

"So, about last night," Savannah said, pausing to flip the piece of golden-brown French toast in the skillet in front of her. "How much trouble would we get into if anyone found out we slept together?"

Cole's muscles threatened lockdown from his spot next to her at the counter. But they couldn't just ignore their situation, and anyway, the question was valid as hell. "Neither one of us would get fired, if that's what you're asking."

"I just went through the academy. I know the rules, Cole. What I really want to know is the score."

Right. Time to bottom-line it, then. "Relationships between two people in the same house are definitely discouraged. I'm not saying they don't happen, because the truth is, they do. But that's usually between paramedics and firefighters, who don't work together as directly as you and I do."

Her knuckles pulled tight over the spatula in her grasp, but she managed a nod. "So it's different for us."

"Yes. To answer your question, if anyone found out we'd slept together, dealing with it would fall to Captain Westin." A cold sweat formed between Cole's shoulder blades despite the warmth of the kitchen. "He's a fair man, but he also runs a tight house."

"We'd both be reprimanded," Savannah said, no trace of a question in her words.

"That would probably be the least of our worries. It's hard to say because we've never had a female firefighter at Eight. But Westin's big on going by the book." The captain's integrity was one of the main reasons Cole respected the man, although not nearly the only one.

"Okay, but the only actual rule is against two people

from the same house being married," she said. "Even then, nobody gets fired."

Damn, she really *had* paid attention at the academy. "No, but in that scenario, at least one person does get transferred."

"You think Westin would boot me if he found out?" Savannah asked, clearly stunned.

"No. I don't know." The thought put a dent in Cole's already questionable composure. "I'm sure he'd argue the conflict of interest."

She slid the last piece of French toast to the serving plate at her hip, leveling him with a copper-colored stare as brazen and honest as ever. "You mean the one that doesn't exist? Come on, Cole. I get that the FFD isn't all rah-rah over things like this. But this attraction between us didn't just pop up overnight, and you've never treated me differently from Donovan or Crews or Jones. When we're at work, we work. Period."

He opened his mouth to argue—the regs weren't arbitrary, for Chrissake—but the words slammed to a stop in his throat.

Cole couldn't argue with her because she was right.

"Just because you and I know that doesn't mean Westin or anyone else in the department will agree," he said instead, and on that, she didn't fight him.

"That may be true, but they'd still have to find out." Savannah lowered her spatula, silencing the soft *whoosh* of the burner with a turn of her wrist. "Look, I'm not a big fan of secrets, but considering the circumstances, disclosure doesn't seem wise. Nobody knows what's going on between us. All we have to do is keep it that way."

"And what's going on between us?" The question was out before he could harness it, but of course, Savannah stayed true to form and met it head-on.

"Denying that I like you would make me a liar, and since

you wouldn't believe me anyway, I'm not going to insult either one of us by trying. I don't take this lightly—you know how important the job is to me." She paused, every bit of her expression punctuating the emotion behind her words. "But we're adults. What was it you said last week about Donovan and Zoe? Risky or not, they knew what they were doing when they jumped in."

Cole let out a long exhale. "I did say that." Never in a trillion years had he thought the sentiment would apply to him, but that didn't change the fact that he'd meant what he'd said.

Savannah turned, the move bringing their bodies within an inch of contact, and damn, he wanted to touch her.

She beat him to it, rising up on the balls of her bare feet to brush a kiss over his mouth. "I don't want to get married, Cole. Hell, I don't even want to get serious. But this . . ." She kissed him again. "This doesn't feel wrong to me."

"We'll have to be careful," he said, this time kissing her. "And I still won't treat you any different than I would another candidate."

"I wouldn't want you to."

Her lips slid apart, the warm heat of her body deliciously firm and strong against his, and Cole couldn't fight the truth.

Forbidden as she might be, Savannah didn't feel wrong to him, either.

Needing something to do other than focus on the knot building in his chest, Cole kissed her one more time and pulled back. He took the serving dish of French toast from the counter, moving toward the breakfast bar separating the kitchen from the living room, and Savannah grabbed the plates and silverware he'd taken from the cupboards.

"I'm not kidding when I say we'll have to be careful. Maybe we should work out some sort of plan." He gestured her onto one of the bar stools before taking a seat next to her, and it felt all too easy to kick back in his condo and share breakfast together.

"I should've known you'd formulate a strategy." Savannah laughed, splitting the thick slices of French toast between the two empty plates.

Cole's return laughter popped out without consulting his brain or better judgment. "Hey, strategies work. Anyway, Oz is on a tear lately. I'm not sure what's going on with him, but even though he's acting like an ass, he's still far from stupid."

Savannah bit her bottom lip in what he'd bet was a bid to keep a smart comment at bay. "Have you come up with anything else on that mistake he made at the warehouse fire?"

"No." Cole's shoulders tightened, but he forced them back to neutral. "I'm not even sure Oz wasn't right. That fire could've gone down exactly the way he said it did."

"But your gut is telling you something different," she said, and he noticed there was no question in her tone. Just as there was no question in his mind.

"Yeah. I think he made a mistake. Those other burn patterns are too big not to have played a factor in how the fire started."

"And?"

Damn, she was getting good at reading situations. Or maybe she was just getting good at reading him. "And Oz is too smart for a miss like that. I'm not even technically on squad yet, and I caught the discrepancy. But he didn't even mention the burn pattern in the report for the fire marshal to review. No pictures, no notation. Nothing." The guy might've worked enough double shifts to look like a shit sandwich lately, but even so, it was a weird no-call.

"Okay, so let's look at the facts," Savannah said, her forehead creasing to a *V* between her slender brows. "The warehouse is an old building that wasn't very well maintained."

Cole nodded in agreement. She'd just described pretty

much every building on Industrial Row, but . . . "Definitely accurate."

"And the air-conditioning unit in that second-floor storage bay was the cause of the fire."

"Absolutely." Between the damage and the burn patterns, the starting point was irrefutable.

Savannah continued, her seriousness and her smarts both on full display. "But even though the burn patterns on the wall show that the fire moved through the electrical system, you think the real reason it spread so quickly was because the unit somehow exploded."

"That's what the burn pattern on the floor indicates. But the thing would've had to get really hot, *really* fast. Faulty electrical wouldn't be enough to make it explode."

"No," Savannah said slowly. "But if someone tampered with the unit, it would."

Shock knifed through Cole, snapping his spine to rigid attention. "No."

"I'm not saying *Oz* tampered with it," she countered quickly. "But come on, Cole. You have to admit, some sort of foul play is at least plausible."

He turned, but none of the thoughts ricocheting around in his brain made it down the chain of command to his mouth. No way. No fucking way. Oz was a firefighter. He might be a salty son of a bitch, but the thought that he'd overlook something sketchy, either accidentally or otherwise, was asinine.

"No." Cole fought for an inhale to counter the sudden burst of emotion in his chest. *Lock it down. Focus.* "I'm not saying that unit didn't somehow burn fast enough to explode, or that Oz didn't make a mistake in not documenting the second burn pattern," he said, because the more he thought about it, the more it looked as if the guy had. "But both of those things are a far freaking cry from arson."

After a long minute, Savannah nodded. "That may be true. Either way, though, something isn't right here."

"Yeah, but unfortunately there's no way to know exactly what."

"Just because we can't find answers on this call doesn't mean we can't find answers, period," she countered without heat. "You said Oz writes up the official reports for most of the fires C-shift responds to."

Cole shifted his weight over his bar stool, his pulse evening out at the opportunity for clear, logical thought. "Reports usually fall under Westin's domain, but we've been so slammed from the redistricting over the last four months that Oz volunteered to write them up instead."

Savannah sank the side of her fork into one buttery brown corner of her French toast, although her attention was clearly still on the conversation, and the move smoothed over Cole's unease.

"That's a bit unusual for a squad lieutenant, isn't it?" she asked.

But he just shook his head. "Oz has been with the department only two years less than Westin. The same way Westin could've made battalion chief a decade ago, Oz knows enough to be a captain ten times over. He could write up these reports from a coma."

Cole paused to take a bite of his breakfast, following the mouthful with an involuntary moan. "*Damn,* Nelson. You weren't kidding." In went another bite, then another. "This French toast is like a gateway drug."

"I told you." She grinned, pointing her fork at him for emphasis before lasering back in on the topic. "Anyway, how do the write-ups work?"

"After every incident, Crews documents things from the engine side. Oz adds his notes, goes back to the scene to complete the investigation, then runs the official report up the chain of command," Cole said. "Eventually the fire marshal reviews everything and does further investigations whenever necessary. The cause of most of the fires we respond to is pretty easy to pinpoint, though."

The same way arson was nearly impossible to prove. Identical causes could be intentional or accidental, depending on what—or who—kicked them off.

"Okay. So if this warehouse thing was just an honest oversight on Oz's part, then all of his other reports should wash with their corresponding scenes, right?"

"Right," he said automatically, making the logic leap less than a second later. "So you want to go check another fire scene against Oz's report?"

"Why not?" Savannah asked, ambitious as ever. "That restaurant fire we put out last week would be the perfect place to check—you and I even saw the blaze firsthand. Comparing another report against the scene will be more experience for when you move to squad, and chances are, it'll put this whole thing to rest as a simple oversight. What've we got to lose?"

He turned the idea over in his mind, and it wasn't a half-bad strategy. "The report on that restaurant fire *is* probably done by now. I could call in a favor and have someone at the clerk's office e-mail me a copy."

No sense in bugging Westin for it when they weren't on shift, and Savannah was right. Once they made a quick run-through at the restaurant and all turned out copasetic, he'd be able to lose this weird feeling over the warehouse once and for all.

Cole looked at her, his unease finally leveling out as he dug back into his French toast. "With any luck, we'll have this thing figured out by lunch."

Chapter Nineteen

Savannah flipped her Ray-Bans into place, carefully navigating the still not-quite-familiar Fairview streets while also trying to manage all of the emotions flinging themselves around in her chest. The residual endorphins from the orgasms she'd lost count of after she and Cole had finally made it to his bedroom last night were potent enough. But adding the one-two punch of their morning-after conversation to the mix, then sticking the whole warehouse investigation mystery on top? Yeah, Savannah was pretty much as jacked up as a girl could get.

Which would be dangerous if it didn't feel so damned delicious.

"Okay." Savannah squeezed the steering wheel triple-extra tight. She needed to concentrate, stat. "So give me the highlights of the report."

Cole palmed his cell phone, flicking the screen to life with his thumb. "According to this, the fire originated in the kitchen."

"That's consistent with what we found when we got in there," she said, dialing up the fire in her mind's eye. "The whole back of the restaurant was fully involved." They hadn't even been able to get to the kitchen from their position, the flames had been so heavy.

"The damage is just as bad as the warehouse fire. Looks like something sparked the grease in the hood over the range and the fire spread through the ventilation system in the walls and ceiling. The kitchen took the brunt of it, but grease fires get out of control fast, and again, with no one to smell the smoke . . ."

"Nine-one-one doesn't get called until the fire's already rolling."

Cole nodded. He dropped his chin to scan the report silently, no doubt committing the crucial points to memory. His methodical nature might be at odds with her tendency to dive right in, but God, the way his mind seemed to work through every detail with thorough care was more than just impressive.

It was one *hell* of a turn-on.

Savannah turned onto Martinsburg Avenue, following the guidance of her GPS. She'd known suggesting they check out the scene of this fire was a slippery slope. True, they might find nothing amiss, in which case they really could just chalk up the discrepancy in the warehouse fire report to an honest mistake. But Savannah's gut thrummed with emotion, whispering hotly that there was more to this whole thing than some whoopsie-daisy oversight on Oz's part.

Enough that she'd made the bold suggestion they come looking for clues that might or might not point the finger at the superior who'd wanted to show her the door from day freaking one.

Cole's voice interrupted her thoughts with a smooth rumble. "There it is."

Savannah turned off the main thoroughfare, winding through the parking lot. She pulled around the back of the restaurant, which was heavily strung with bright yellow tape cautioning DANGER—DO NOT CROSS. "Wow. Looks like another loss."

"That's what this says." Cole lifted his phone, sliding out of the passenger seat next to her and adjusting the brim of his dark blue FFD baseball cap for a closer look at the restaurant. They approached the back of the building, and Savannah pulled up at the sight of the clearly locked employee entrance. Of course the FFD wouldn't rely on caution tape to keep people out. The scene was a massive liability for anyone not knowing how to navigate it. But Cole's movements didn't hitch as he pulled a slim leather case from the back pocket of his cargo shorts, popping the lock on the door less than a minute later.

Savannah's laugh was inescapable. "A bit off the straight and narrow, don't you think?" she asked, arching a brow at the set of lock picks just before he returned them to his pocket.

He met the look with a dark smile that made her toes curl in her cross-trainers. "I might favor a good strategy, but I never claimed to be a saint, sweetheart. Picking the locks might not be entirely on the up-and-up, but it's the path of least resistance. Anyway, we're just looking."

"Got it," she breathed. She followed him past the steel door marked EMPLOYEES ONLY, the familiar scent of bitter-burnt smoke occupying her senses enough to make her eyes water. The terra cotta–colored floor tiles bore heavy streaks of dried-up ash and soot, and the walls leading past what looked like a dry goods pantry and a storage space for cleaning supplies showed similar dirt and damage. Cole propped the back door open to let the midday summer sunlight guide their way into the kitchen, where the only other light came courtesy of the two long rectangular windows set high into the right-hand wall.

"I can't imagine the fire didn't start back here," Savannah said, swiveling her gaze around the blackened shell of the room. Two stainless-steel worktables sat crookedly on the floor tiles in the middle of the narrow galley kitchen, with a dishwashing station on the far side under the windows. The interior wall—which she assumed bordered the back wall of the dining room, judging by the damage—was burned down to the tiles spanning its entire length. A hulking six-burner range stood dead center on what was left of the wall, and once again, Savannah had no clue how she and Cole would be able to sift through this mess to uncover anything of use.

"It did." Cole clicked the button on his small Maglite, spotlighting the hood over the range. "See the burn patterns on the ceiling? With the grease that had to have been accumulating here for who knows how long, this thing would've only needed one spark to go up like a pressure cooker."

"But the restaurant was closed for business," Savannah argued. "Where's a spark going to come from if there's no one around to make one?"

His hesitation was slight, but she didn't miss it. "If the power to the building wasn't turned off, faulty electrical could've done it."

She thought back. Crews *had* said something about the electrical system, right after they'd put out the blaze. But still . . . "Is that what the report says?"

"Mmm-hmm. The wiring's definitely fried, just like at the warehouse"—Cole swung the beam of the flashlight over the drywalled section of the kitchen, which showed multiple burn patterns where the fire had scorched the wires that had once run beneath—"which backs up the report."

The *but* hung in his tone, and Savannah willed herself to wait patiently for him to voice it even though her heartbeat pounded hard and fast against her eardrums.

"But that doesn't explain these marks down here, or the debris under the grates on the cooktop."

"Oh my God." She took a step forward, then another,

until her hips pressed nearly flush with the range. The wall tiles between the cooktop and the oversized stainless-steel hood vent had been scorched by a handful of thin black lines, all of which led upward from the range's rear burners. A thick layer of ash lay piled beneath the heavy black grates, almost as if . . . "Something was set here to burn."

Cole's eyes went saucer-wide for just a split second before narrowing in concentration. "This whole place is covered in ash," he argued slowly. "If the kitchen hadn't been emptied of its inventory yet, there would've been plenty in here that could have burned after the fact."

"Yeah, but all the inventory would be over there, by the pantry. Not sitting here on the stove," Savannah pointed out, her pulse hopscotching through her veins. "And anyway, if this restaurant was out of business, nothing could've gotten caught on these burners accidentally. No one would've been here."

Which meant that whatever had caught fire on this cooktop had to have been put there on purpose.

"These burn patterns do suggest that something on this cooktop somehow caught fire and sparked upward," Cole said, quickly tacking on, "But there's no way of knowing if this was the point of origin or just another thing that got torched after the grease fire started and added to the blaze."

"*Something* had to spark this hood." No way could this just be coincidence.

The edges of Cole's mouth tightened beneath the sand-colored stubble covering his face. "Something did. It's just hard to say exactly what."

"Is any of this in Oz's report?" Savannah pointed to the ashes, nearly an inch thick over the range's three back burners.

Cole's jaw locked down to match his mouth. "No. Just the electrical and the grease fire."

A noise burst past Savannah's lips, frustration joining the

other emotions tag-teaming their way through her rib cage.
"Come on, Cole. You have to admit this doesn't add up.
There's a chance that someone started both of these fires on
purpose."

"That's a hell of a leap to make from a couple of discrepancies," he said. His face took on the same impenetrable
expression that it always did in the face of rising tension, as
if the hotter emotions ran, the calmer he'd become.

Well, fine. Savannah had enough heat for both of them.
"These aren't *discrepancies*," she started, but Cole stepped
in, curling a palm over her shoulder.

"Right now, yes, they are." The solid weight of his hand
caught her attention, his eyes serious enough to stay her
argument and make her listen. "Look, I'm not saying everything's aboveboard here. We both know it's not. But you
can't just wing accusations around about something this
major."

"My brother is on the arson investigation unit. I could
just ask—"

"No." Cole's fingers squeezed harder against the cotton
of her T-shirt. He moved closer, the intensity on his face and
the proximity of his body kicking her heat index even
higher. "You can't. Not without raising suspicion. Look"—
he broke off for a long draw of breath—"we have to be
smart about this. Accusing Oz of screwing up these reports
and calling these fires arson isn't just borrowing trouble. It's
buying it wholesale."

"Why are you so eager to defend him?" Savannah's
cheeks prickled. She and Cole had worked together for less
than a month and been sleeping together for less than a day.
Of course he wouldn't trust her enough to—

"I'm not defending Oz, Savannah. I'm trying to defend
you."

She blinked. "What?"

His chest lifted on an inhale, and following his motion,

she breathed in, too. "I get that you want to act on this," Cole said. "But you're talking about leveling some top-shelf accusations. If you do that without hard evidence and you're wrong, a quick 'sorry about that' isn't going to fix it. You'll lose your placement at Eight, and your reputation will be shot full of holes."

Damn it, he was right. "Okay, but we can't just sit on this, or worse yet, forget it."

"What we need is a plan, starting with concrete facts."

He let go of her shoulder, sending a careful gaze around the kitchen. "Arson is extremely hard to prove once, let alone twice. And while I'll admit these cases do have a few things in common, they're also equally unconnected. The locations are on opposite sides of the city, one warehouse, one restaurant, not to mention that on the off chance Oz *is* somehow involved, he's a firefighter. He's got a complete lack of motive for wanting either place to burn down."

"That we know of," Savannah countered, her instincts overflowing with things not right.

Cole stopped, just shy of the range. "Fair enough. But even though I'm willing to admit that these two reports don't pass the smell test, I'm also not ready to point the finger at Oz quite yet. He's had the back of every firefighter at Eight for the last two decades, including mine for the last eight years. You can say what you want about him person-ally, but professionally, he's still a damned good firefighter, innocent until proven otherwise."

She jammed her cross-trainers into the filthy kitchen tiles, her argument locked and loaded. But the look on Cole's face, so calm and matter-of-fact, wedged the push-back in her throat.

She'd fought for a judgment-free shot at Station Eight. If Oz was dirty, she'd prove it, the same way she'd proven herself for the last year straight.

Cole had her back. They'd get this done.

"Okay," Savannah said slowly. "So what's our first step?"

"Let me talk to him tomorrow when we're on shift so I can feel the situation out. In the meantime, we'll read through both of these reports step by step for a closer look. Then we can go from there. Just do me a favor, would you, and try to behave yourself?"

The corners of his mouth edged up in the barest sugges-tion of a smile, and despite the seriousness of the situation, Savannah found herself smiling right back.

"I make no promises to behave, Everett—at work or otherwise. Now let's go. We've got a lot on our plate today."

Savannah had no sooner pulled into the narrow parking lot adjacent to Station Eight than her cell phone started mouthing off from the side pocket of her duffel bag.

"What the hell?" At six twenty on a Thursday morning, whoever was on the other end of the line either had clumsy fingers or a death wish.

At the sight of the caller ID, Savannah's heart catapulted against her rib cage, and she pressed the phone to her ear, lickety-split. "Daddy? What's the matter?"

"Good morning to you, too, darlin'." Her father's warm baritone rumbled over the line. "Does somethin' have to be the matter for me to call my girl?"

She broke into a smile, relief spilling through her as she relaxed against the driver's seat. "Of course not. But you've got to admit, your timing is a little unconventional."

"Your brother told me you were on shift today. Said he hasn't seen hide nor hair of you for a couple'a days, and I'd been meaning to call you anyhow, so I thought I'd check in."

Ah, shit. Brad had been sawing logs by the time Savan-nah had finally dragged herself from Cole's nice, comfort-able bed (by way of his oh-so steamy shower, and then his living room one more time for good measure) last night.

She'd texted Brad twice to tell him she was fine and staying with a friend, but . . . "Yeah, I've been doing a lot of studying and stuff for work. I guess I keep missing him is all."

"And how are things going at Eight? Y'all catching any good fires down there?"

Savannah bit back the irony welling up in her mind. "A few," she said. She gave her father a quick rundown of her part in putting out last week's restaurant fire, peppering in some more details from a few of their smaller calls. When she got to the duck story, her father let out a belly laugh as rich and warm as a shot of double-barrel bourbon, and Lord above, she missed her family.

"Sounds as if you're fitting right in," her father said, his voice sobering with what came next. "I'll confess, I was a little worried. Bein' a woman in the fire department can be a hell of an uphill battle, even for someone as fearless as you."

"There are a couple of things that are harder than I thought they'd be," she admitted. Between learning how to pace herself and not chomping on the bait of Oz's rude looks and ruder under-the-breath comments, she'd had her work cut out for her these last three weeks, for sure. "But most everybody here treats me like a candidate, plain and simple."

Her father let out a soft breath. "Well, I'm glad you landed at a house where they know what you're worth, darlin'. You might be far from home, but your mama and I are still right proud."

Savannah's throat knotted, and she flattened her palm over her breastbone in an effort to soothe the ache squeezing between her ribs. "Thanks, Daddy."

The phone call ended a few minutes later, with her promising to be as careful as she was fierce, and her father telling her not to take any crap from her brother. Savannah sat in her car for a few minutes, modulating her breath and sliding her focus into place more intently than ever.

Her parents were proud of her. She didn't just have a job to do fighting fires. She had a moral obligation to get to the bottom of this thing with Oz.

Even if the man was guilty.

Savannah slid out of her SUV, slinging her duffel over one shoulder and heading through the back door to the engine bay.

"Hey, Nelson!" Donovan fell into step with her before she made it halfway across the boot-scuffed concrete, his all-American grin sending her hackles into high alert. Nobody should be so freaking happy on this side of roll call.

"What?" Savannah slung a gaze around the engine bay, but the place looked just like it always did before shift change.

For a split second, she froze. She and Cole had agreed not to tell anyone about the time they'd spent together off the clock, but he and Donovan were best friends.

Nerves of steel. Nerves of steel.

"What, what?" Donovan straightened, running a hand over the scattering of blond stubble covering his chin. "I was just saying good morning. Why, do I have something on my face?"

"Oh." Jeez, all those orgasms had scrambled her brain. "No. You just look like a mouthwash ad, that's all. How many cups of coffee have you had?"

"Me?" He pointed to himself with one hand, ushering her through the door to the house with the other. "I'm high on life, baby."

She arched a brow, totally unable to curb her laughter. "Three?"

He nodded. "Okay, yeah. I'm high on life *and* half a pot of coffee. But seriously, I just wanted to make sure you're feeling okay."

"Of course. Why wouldn't I . . . ahhhh." Cole's fib from the other night clicked into place, two seconds too late. "Right. Bad sushi. Stomach bug. It passed pretty quickly."

Which was more than she could say for the scrutiny Donovan was suddenly winging in her direction. Crap, she needed a distraction. A smart-assed comeback. Something to save her from—

"Easy for you to say. You're not the one who had to mind your shoes."

Savannah's feet clattered to a stop at the far end of the locker room. Cole stood halfway down the middle row, just as calm and cool as normal, and she launched into a wry smile that felt as natural as inhale-exhale.

"Gee, thanks, Everett. You really know how to make a girl feel special."

O'Keefe popped his head around the corner of the locker bay, serving her with a lopsided grin. "Come on, Nelson. Quit your bellyaching."

"Argh, really?" she groaned, although her laughter beat out her irritation two to one. Years' worth of familial ribbing had taught her that fighting back only made things worse, and anyway, she'd had a hunch this was coming.

Savannah walked to her locker, dropping her bag to the bench behind her and lifting up both hands. "Fine. Go ahead, you guys. Just get it over with."

"Aw, don't let them give you shit for riding the regur-gitron, Nelson," Rachel called from the opposite end of the room. "I know you're *gutsier* than these guys are giving you credit for."

"You're not nearly the first person I've seen blow their groceries over a little bad sushi," O'Keefe speculated. "Although next time, maybe a *gut* check wouldn't hurt."

"You are pretty tough, rookie," Crews added, ambling around the corner to lean on the locker a few down from hers. "I'd bet it's gonna take more than these preschoolers have got to make you go *belly* up."

Donovan waggled his blond brows, all brotherly affection. "Our candidate does have a whole lot of fire in her *belly*, doesn't she," he said, and finally, Savannah had to laugh.

"If you guys don't knock it off, I'm going to get butterflies in my *stomach*," she warned, prompting a handful of *ohs* to echo off the tiled walls.

"Coming from you, that's just dangerous," Cole said, tipping his head at the clock on the wall. "Roll call's in ten. Guess we should leave you to it."

"Thanks." Savannah turned toward her locker, a grin still on her lips. Okay, so it wasn't a great big welcome with open arms, but hell if she'd know what to do with that anyway. She'd missed her brothers and cousins for over a year now. Weird as it was, the good-natured crap made her feel like maybe—just maybe—they felt she belonged at Eight.

She popped her locker open, and no fewer than a hundred plastic emesis basins spilled out over her feet.

"What the fu . . . I am going to *murder* you guys!" Savannah's holler fell prey to deep peals of laughter, punctuated by a bright white flash from Donovan's cell phone.

"I truly think this is her best side, don't you?" he asked Cole, holding up his phone for Everett's inspection.

"Donovan, don't you dare—"

"Annnnd Facebooked," he said, tapping the screen with a flourish. He reached out, giving her head a ruffle. "Welcome to Eight, Tough Stuff."

Savannah dropped her gaze to the kidney-shaped basins littering the floor, and she couldn't help it.

She burst out laughing.

"I'm going to remember this. Jackasses," she tacked on for good measure, flashing a look at Cole. "Did you know about this?" she asked, enough under her breath that no one else heard over the laughter still floating around the locker room.

Cole lifted both hands, although his smile was a dead giveaway. "I plead the fifth."

"That's a yes." Savannah shook her head, bending down to snap up one of the light blue plastic containers. "Exactly what am I supposed to do with all of these?"

"Oh, save them for Jonesey!" Rachel said gleefully. "We're doing his locker next."

All at once, Savannah realized that the firefighter was nowhere in sight. "Hey, where is he, anyway?"

"Let's just say you're not the only one to evacuate all you ate. He spent half the Fireman's Ball doing tequila shots with the guys from Station Four. One of the paramedics over there managed to help him get home safely, but hooo. Last I saw, he was liquidly exuberant."

"Seriously?" Cole's light brown brows shot upward.

O'Keefe leaned in, his nod solemn even though his expression was not. "Three words, my brother. After-party karaoke. He texted me last night to say he'd finally made it off the ginger ale and saltines diet, and that Jose Cuervo was—and I quote—'a giant dick.'"

Donovan's bright blue eyes gleamed in the overhead fluorescents. "Holy shit, a two-fer. Rachel, quick! Go stall his ass. If we hurry up, we can get these barf bins into Jonesey's locker before roll call."

Savannah got as close to a giggle as she ever would, but the sound still emerged just shy of a snort. She started to stack the emesis basins within her reach, turning to make a comment to match her laughter, when the gruff sound of a throat being cleared stopped the words cold in her mouth.

"Fitting," Oz said, flicking a frost-encrusted glance at the basins. "You do seem to make a mess wherever you go."

"It was just a joke." She bit the inside of her cheek hard enough for it to smart. Throwing down with Oz before their day even started wouldn't land her in a happy place. No matter how badly she wanted to go tornado alley on his ass. "I'll have the mess cleaned up in a minute. Sir."

"Good. Because after that, Westin wants to see you in his office."

Chapter Twenty

Cole pushed a hand through his hair and dribbled the basketball in his grip, his nerves already half-shredded even though it was still before lunch. While Westin had ended up only needing Savannah for a quick administrative thing, Oz's intention to string her out with the ominous public delivery of the captain's request had been cool-water clear. She'd handled it like a pro, not even fidgeting through the thirty minutes of roll call and shift assignments she'd had to sit through before she could make it to Westin's office. But Oz's mind fuck had sent something slithering through Cole that he hadn't felt in years. Nine of them, to be exact.

For just a split second, he'd been tempted to say sayonara to his keep-it-cool strategy in favor of the my-fist-in-your-face plan.

"Everett." Oz stepped onto the otherwise empty basketball court, a rough, gruff embodiment of speak of the devil. "Heard you wanted a word."

Okay, so floating his request for a talk with Oz by every member of squad instead of just cutting to the chase to find the guy hadn't exactly been on Cole's original agenda. But

Oz's stunt this morning had pissed him off enough to risk a little attitude.

"Yeah." *Focus.* Chippy or not at how Oz had treated Savannah, Cole needed to get to the bottom of these wonky reports, and that meant sticking to his plan of action. "Now that we've only got about two weeks to go before I move to squad, I've been trying to brush up on a few things. I was wondering if you could help me out." He dribbled the ball a couple more times, his shoulders unusually stiff as he took a shot.

He missed by a country mile, the damned thing bouncing off the backboard with all the grace of a brick.

Oz took a few steps to retrieve the basketball, the lift of his graying brows telling Cole in no uncertain terms that the lieutenant's spider senses were tingling away. "With?"

Shit. Cole needed to dial it back. He inhaled, nice and slow. "Procedural stuff, mostly. Haven't you been writing up the incident reports for the station's fire calls for the last couple of months?"

"Ah. You mean the ones you've been reading?"

Adrenaline punched through Cole from brain to balls, but he forced himself not to react. "I'm not sure I follow."

"Of course you do. You're not a dumbass." Oz dribbled twice before sinking a perfect basket. "Westin told me you went back to the scene of that warehouse fire over on Wabash to see how investigations are done and reports are written up. Personally, I think that shit is about as exciting as wallpaper paste, but I get it. You're fresh. You want to jump into squad with both feet."

Cole swiped a forearm over his sweat-laced brow, catching the basketball as Oz passed it his way. The guy had never been a teddy bear, but right now he seemed so normal, so much like his old self, that Cole had to wonder if maybe he'd misread Oz's behavior this morning. It wasn't unlike

Oz to haze rookies a little, and hell, Cole himself had helped load both Savannah's *and* Jonesey's lockers chock-full of emesis basins not even five hours ago. Enduring a ration of mostly good-natured crap was par for the course for candidates, and he'd promised not to give Savannah any special treatment, no matter how much he liked her.

He released a breath, steady and slow. "Yeah, I'd way rather be fighting fires than reading about them, but you know the drill. The department feels like I need to know the regs inside out and backward, so I was just brushing up on investigation protocol."

"And you found something in that report you had a question about." For the briefest of moments, Oz's shoulders hitched beneath his navy-blue uniform shirt, the move sending a warning through Cole's gut. Offending the guy wouldn't get Cole anywhere he wanted to be, but laying off entirely wouldn't get him any answers, either.

He took a free throw first, then the bait. "There wasn't much left out there other than a French-fried AC unit and a hell of a lot of property damage."

"That fire had some goddamn teeth," Oz agreed slowly. He retrieved the basketball and took a shot in silence, and fuck it. Dancing around the subject wasn't going to make this a party.

"I've never seen an air-conditioning unit go up quite so hot and do that much damage," Cole said, point-blank. "You think there was something wrong with it?"

"You mean other than the shitty wiring that made it catch fire?"

Time to tread carefully. Cole cracked a smile. "Yeah. Other than that. I wasn't inside on that call, so I was just trying to get my head around how a fire that intense would start."

Oz rocked back on the heels of his boots, measuring Cole with a long look before saying, "The fire started just like I wrote it. That warehouse was your basic shithole, and the air-conditioning unit was probably old enough to have a single-digit serial number. Thing was probably working triple-time in the heat, and the wiring just couldn't handle the overload. Simple."

"Are you sure?"

The question was out before Cole's brain-to-mouth filter could kill it, and Oz's answer slipped past his clenched jaw.

"Yeah. I'm sure. If I'd seen something different, I'd have put it in my report. Why, did you have a second opinion?"

Cole's pulse flared. The only thing he had to fly on was a questionable gut feeling and some evidence that was growing more circumstantial by the second. In other words: jack shit. "No, not really. Like I said, the damage just seemed worse than a garden-variety electrical fire, so I thought I'd ask."

To Cole's surprise, Oz broke into a smile. "Fucking squad rookies. You guys think every fire is an episode of *CSI*. Sorry to disappoint, but this sure as shit ain't my first rodeo. That warehouse fire started from plain old bad electrical. Trust me."

Cole's chin snapped up at the implication. "I didn't mean any disrespect," he started, but Oz just waved him off.

"Ah. I'm not gonna fault you for taking the job seriously. Just don't go looking for glamour on squad, Everett. After twenty-three years on the job, I can promise you aren't going to find any."

"What about the restaurant fire a couple of weeks ago?"

Oz's stare snapped over Cole's like a live wire, fast and dangerous. "What about it?"

Cole willed his hands to stay steady over the basketball in his grip. But the more he'd turned over all the logical explanations for both of the fires in his mind, the hotter his instinct had flared. Something about this wasn't right.

Trouble was, Cole was going to have to push pretty hard to uncover exactly what that *something* was.

"That fire at Campisi's was just as nasty as the one at the warehouse. According to the reports, they were both caused by faulty electrical, but they seemed to spread faster than I'd expect. I'm just trying to get a handle on how that might've happened by looking at all the angles."

Fishing for information was a tactic Cole knew Oz would see through, but it was the best option he had under the circumstances. He'd already learned half of what he wanted to know from the lieutenant's reaction, anyway.

"Awfully ambitious of you to pull more than one report. And you checked out both scenes, too. Very thorough," Oz said. He gestured for the basketball, but didn't take a shot when Cole passed it over, and who was fishing for information now?

"I'm an ambitious guy," Cole said, dialing his smile up to its nice-and-easy setting. "But I think you knew that."

Oz didn't smile back. "Seems there are a few things about you I didn't know."

He passed the ball back with a whole lot more force than necessary, making Cole's adrenaline spike. But Cole needed answers, so he bit down on his tongue, giving Oz room to fill the silence.

"You never struck me as someone who had a problem with the chain of command. That mouthy candidate of yours has been rubbing off on you."

God damn it. Cole's flinch was pure reflex, but of course Oz saw it, his stare flashing for a brief second before he took a step closer.

"If you've got questions about a report, you don't go fucking around like the idiot version of Sherlock Holmes. You come to me to get answers. Nobody freelances at Eight, and they sure as shit don't *ever* do it on my rescue squad.

That's something you're gonna want to remember if you really want that spot, Everett. Do I make myself clear?"

Cole's heart ricocheted around his rib cage. His placement on squad was ultimately up to Westin, but Oz's stamp of approval went a long way to ensuring that the promotion went through. He needed to put a tourniquet on this conversation before it became a bloodbath, with his job as the casualty. This situation might not pass the smell test, but Cole wasn't ready to take the next step here. Fuck, he didn't even know what the next step *was*.

But he damned sure knew what it wasn't. He'd stuffed back every last emotion in the book for the last nine years. Flying solely on a gut feeling wasn't going to be enough. No matter how badly he wanted to fight back.

"Yes sir," Cole said. "Crystal."

"Good." Oz stared him down for another minute before turning back toward the house, and while he still looked pissed enough to spit nails, at least he seemed to take Cole at his word. Seemed like a win, considering Cole had been skating on goddamn thin ice by questioning the guy's integrity in the first place, integrity that Oz had demonstrated on the job for as long as Cole had known him. Maybe he and Savannah *had* been reading too much into those reports— after all, they were ambition personified when it came to the job.

Borrowing trouble tested your emotions, and emotions only got you burned.

But trusting the wrong person could burn just as badly. The trouble was, everywhere Cole turned, there was a fire waiting to explode.

Savannah had just drifted off to the soundtrack of Crews's snoring when the piercing sound of the all-call delivered her back to the stark reality of her darkened bunk.

"*Squad Eight, Engine Eight, Ambulance Eight. Motor vehicle accident. Forty-two hundred block of Michigan Terrace. Requesting immediate response.*"

"Nothing like a nightcap, huh, Nelson?" Donovan asked, following her toward the engine bay as she ran a hand through her hair to gather it into a ponytail.

"Mmm," she said, blinking the last of the sleep from her eyes as she worked up her focus. "I think your version of a nightcap is a little different from mine. Hopefully this is just a fender bender."

He one-handed his way into the step, already halfway out of his cross-trainers to gear up. "Doubtful. Michigan Terrace is four lanes, and people tend to drive it like NASCAR hopefuls. Even money says this one's messy."

Savannah's heart sped up at the thought, but she countered her stuttering pulse with a long, even inhale. "You're a breath of fresh air, Teflon."

Alex shot her a grin through the shadows of the step. "That's precisely why nothing ever sticks to me, Tough Stuff. I didn't get my nickname for having mad cooking skills. But even with all of this fantastic charm aside, I guarantee that I'm sure as shit right about this call."

Ten minutes later, the scene in front of them affirmed Donovan's cocky prediction with gut-clenching accuracy. There were three—no, four cars strewn over the asphalt at various angles, with twisted metal and shattered safety glass covering both lanes on the northbound side of the road.

"Okay, people. Let's get some trauma assessments." Captain Westin issued directives to kick everyone into motion, sending squad to deal with what appeared to be a gasoline spill from one vehicle's ruptured fuel line and Rachel and O'Keefe to the sporty convertible that had gotten up close and personal with a telephone pole. "Everett, you and Nelson take that black SUV. Go."

She fell into step with Cole automatically, taking in the

mangled SUV with an internal wince. While they'd handled a half dozen wrecks ranging from minor to moderate over the last few weeks, none of them had been this serious. Well, none since that first one where she'd thrown up.

"Looks like a single rider. You take the driver and I'll double-check for passengers, just to be safe," Cole said, moving around to the far side of the SUV.

Savannah resisted the urge to pull up in shock. "You want me to take point?"

He sent her a brief glance even though he didn't slow a beat. "You're good for it, right?"

She metered her breathing, running through her training in her mind. This might be the biggest wreck they'd responded to yet, but she could do this. Everyone at Eight had showed her how. "Copy. I've got the driver."

Cole's brisk nod said he believed her. They approached the SUV, and she tested the driver's side door handle, adrenaline and relief surging through her when it opened.

The relief fast-tracked to dread at the deep, jagged gash running from the driver's temples all the way up to the center of his forehead, just shy of his hairline.

"Hi there, sir. My name's Savannah, and I'm with the Fairview Fire Department. Can you tell me if you're in any pain?"

"My head," the man groaned, trying to turn toward her. Okay, good. Responsive was good. "Has there been an accident? I don't . . . I can't remember."

"I'm afraid so," she told him, her stomach pinching hard at the thick wash of blood free-flowing all the way down to the man's neck. *Nerves of steel, girl. You can help him.* She fought back the fear threatening to freeze her to the pavement. "But don't worry about a thing. We're going to take good care of you, okay?"

Savannah ran through the ABCs of trauma protocol in her mind, quickly turning the steps into action. Although his head wound was significant, it appeared to be the driver's only injury. Things got a little sketchy when he regained a little awareness and panicked, the struggle causing a blood vessel to burst in the already-deep gash, but by the time Cole had cleared the rest of the vehicle and radioed to Rachel for a C-collar and a backboard, Savannah had managed to get the man as calm and stable as possible for transport to the hospital.

"See? Told you," Donovan said, tipping his chin at her blood-soaked gloves as she shucked them into a biohazard bag.

"Yeah, remind me to take you to Vegas." She lifted a brow to highlight her sarcasm, although she couldn't help smiling. "I'm just glad that guy is headed to Fairview Hospital."

"Looks like everyone is." Donovan gestured to the two additional ambos that had rolled up while Savannah and Cole had been working the SUV. "Sure is nice to call this one a win."

They finished clearing the accident scene, letting the guys from Thirteen wait out the tow trucks and get traffic safely moving again. Savannah's watch read just after midnight when she finally climbed back into the step, and she let the rumble of the diesel engine lull her adrenaline even further off the ledge on the trip back to the house. Not even bothering to stifle her yawn, she toed out of her boots at the entryway to her bunk, her body sinking into the mattress less than two seconds after she got horizontal. The room grew quiet, save for the rustle of covers as everyone got situated . . .

And the soft buzz of her cell phone vibrating beneath her pillow.

Savannah's heart sped up in surprise as she slid her phone into her palm, tapping the screen to reveal the incoming text message.

Hey. You okay over there?

She turned toward the half wall separating her bed from Cole's, folding her smile between her lips even though no one could see the gesture.

Of course. I'm not fragile, remember? she typed, and a full minute passed before Cole replied.

I'm not asking because I think you're fragile, Nelson.

Oh, she wrote, pausing for a minute of her own before adding, Then why are you asking?

A chuff of laughter filtered over the partition, so soft that she'd have dismissed it as a sleep-laden exhale if she didn't know better, and the sound warmed her all the way to her toes.

I'm supposed to have your back, remember?

Yeah, she typed. As if he could hear the mental *but* she'd tagged to the end of the text, Cole replied.

And you're supposed to let me.

Savannah stared at her phone, her heartbeat impossibly loud against the silence in the bunks. Finally, she typed in, Okay.

Okay. Good night.

She pressed her hand to the wall between them, knowing that even if the all-call stayed silent for the rest of the night, she wouldn't sleep a wink.

Chapter Twenty-One

Savannah zipped yesterday's uniform into her duffel bag, smoothing a hand over the short-sleeved white button-down she'd replaced it with. Although last night's wreck had definitely been the biggest call of the shift, it hadn't been the last one of the night, and it also hadn't been the only one on which she'd run point. Crews had given her carte blanche on the house fire they'd responded to at 0300, and even though she'd done no more than aim a fire extinguisher at a smoldering trash can someone had used as a stunt double for an ashtray, the trust had still felt really good.

"Hey, Nelson. You heading out?"

Speaking of really good. The smooth cadence of Cole's voice interrupted her thoughts, sending a ribbon of heat uncurling between her thighs. "Oh! Ah, yep. I sure am."

"I dug up my copy of that textbook we were talking about the other day. You're welcome to borrow it if you want. It's just out in the Jeep." His words were perfectly benign, ones he could've been speaking to anyone in the house. But the glint in his olive-green eyes promised more, and God help her, more was exactly what Savannah wanted.

"That would be great. I'll walk out with you so I can grab it."

She took a deep breath, going through the motions of clanging her locker shut and taking the requisite number of footsteps through the engine bay, then the sun-drenched basketball court. Cole walked beside her, the silence between them not uncomfortable despite the sexual tension free-flowing through Savannah's body.

He opened the Jeep's passenger door, sliding a book from the seat. "Here you go. *Fire Behavior and Combustion Processes.*"

Their fingers brushed as he passed the glossy textbook over. "This says it's volume one," she said, and his fingers made a second, slower pass over her knuckles.

"Volume two is at my place. Guess you'll just have to come over to pick it up."

Her throat worked over a hard swallow. "Right now?"

"If you want."

Oh. *Oh*, did she want. "Sure. Meet you there in ten?"

Cole's smile was dark and decadent enough to eat with a spoon. "I'll be there in five."

There was something sexy as hell about a man of his word—or maybe there was just something sexy as hell about *this* man of his word. Either way, less than ten minutes later, they crossed the threshold of his condo in a hot tangle of tongues and arms and pure, uncut want, and fire behavior came in a distant second to bad behavior.

"Do you have any idea how fucking hot you look like this?" He cupped her face with both hands, holding her steady for a deep, penetrating kiss before pulling back to run his fingers over the low-slung braids brushing each of her shoulders.

Her laughter spilled into the sliver of space between them. "Cole, please. I probably smell like the firehouse."

"You smell amazing," he corrected, tipping her chin upward to brush his mouth over the sensitive skin by her ear. "And you taste even better."

As if to prove his point, Cole slowed his movements. His kisses grew intentional, full of lazy, languid sweeps of his tongue. He tightened his hand in her hair with each pass over her neck, her ear, the line of her jaw, and every kiss lit Savannah up from the inside. Her nipples pearled against the cotton of her bra, drawing a heavy exhale from Cole's throat.

"You know," he said, pausing to skim one tight bud with the pad of his thumb, and oh God, the friction of his touch through the fabric nearly made her whimper, "that does give me an idea."

Savannah lifted a brow. "What kind of idea?"

"The wet kind. Come with me."

He led her down the hall, kicking off his shoes and losing his T-shirt along the way. Her boots joined them, her jeans following suit, and by the time they got to his bathroom, Savannah wanted the rest of her clothes off, stat. She reached up, popping the button between her breasts to start freeing her shirt.

But Cole reached out, his strong, lean fingers circling her wrist. "No."

She laughed. "Forgive me if I'm wrong here, but isn't the point for us to be naked?"

"We'll be naked soon enough," he said, and the promise in his gold-green stare made her sex clench in anticipation. "But I want to undress you, and I want to take my time. I want to look at you."

Savannah's lips fell open to form a soft *O*. "What?"

Cole turned to the side, just long enough to get the water in the shower started. "I want to look at you," he said again, sliding the backs of his knuckles over her cheek as he returned to the spot where she stood. "Will you let me?"

Her heart began to race for an entirely different reason than it had when they'd come crashing into his apartment. A lust-fueled romp between the sheets, or in this case, behind the shower door, was one thing. But letting Cole look at her—really *see* her, just like this, with no barriers and no bravado—was something entirely different.

Something risky. Something vulnerable.

Something Savannah wanted.

"Yes."

Cole's eyes widened slightly before glittering with unmistakable want. He guided her back until her hips met the counter, shifting to create enough space between their bodies so that every one of his movements was clearly visible to them both. Reaching up, he tweaked the end of the braid on her right shoulder, his opposite hand finding the indent of her waistline beneath her shirt.

She flushed. Spending the morning with him hadn't been on her radar when she'd gotten dressed an hour ago in Station Eight's locker room. If it had, she'd have ditched the Pollyanna braids for something decidedly sexier. Not that she had a whole lot of hey-baby in her arsenal, but still.

As if he'd zeroed in on her thoughts, Cole said, "I like these."

"You do?"

"Mmm-hmm." The dark edges of his smile said he meant it. "This too." He slid a finger between her breasts, liberating a button on her shirt. Savannah exhaled, wanting nothing more than to rip the material wide so she could feel his hands on her.

Of course he saw her impatience, too. "The other day, we rushed. Not that I'm complaining." He capped the qualification with a smile she felt in the deepest part of her belly. "But this time, I want more."

Another turn of his wrist bared her skin down to her navel, with only the thin swath of her cotton bra covering her breasts. At least there was a tiny bit of lace on this one, although she wasn't sure it quite qualified as a bra. The salesgirl had called it a *bralette*, whatever that meant, but

Savannah had called it the perfect modesty solution for under her T-shirt when she crashed in a bunk full of fellow firefighters.

Cole's green eyes shadowed to a stormy hazel at the sight of the plain, thin straps crossing right under her sternum. He freed her last two shirt buttons, putting her hip-hugging white cotton panties on display along with her bra, and the intensity on his face knocked the breath right out of her.

"Christ." His hands moved from her waist to her shoulders, pushing her shirt to the bathroom floor. "I could look at you all day."

For a long minute, that was all Cole did. His gaze toured slowly from the crown of her head to her face, lingering briefly on her mouth before coasting lower. The steam from the shower filled the small space, sending a sheen of moisture over Savannah's skin and making the thin material of her bra and panties cling to her most sensitive spots. Cole's stare brushed across her shoulders like a touch, dipping low between the slight curve of her breasts, lower still to the juncture where her thighs came together.

Savannah's face blazed with both vulnerability and desire, but she refused to shy from either.

She trusted Cole as much as she wanted him to touch her.

Finally, he lifted his eyes, stepping forward to erase the distance between them. "I know you don't think you're beautiful, but you're wrong." He pressed two fingers over her lips, the rasp of his calluses making her pulse race. "Your smart mouth." Both fingers slid lower, down to the hollow where her collarbones joined before tracing the muscular line where her arm met her shoulder. "Your strong body." Cole skimmed back to her midline, not stopping until his hand had reached the center of her chest. "Your even stronger spirit."

He kissed her, soft but deep. "I see you, Savannah. And what I see is beautiful."

She pushed up to the balls of her feet in a rush, knotting her arms around his shoulders and crushing her mouth against his. A primal sound came from the back of Cole's throat, and he opened readily, taking just as much as he gave. The clothing left between them fell one piece at a time, and Savannah nearly argued when Cole broke the contact of their kiss.

Until he turned to lead her into the warm spray of the shower.

"You said you wanted to get clean," he said, guiding her so the steamy water spilled over both shoulders. He reached out to unwind her braids one at a time, tucking her hair behind her so it spilled down her back in soft, wet waves, then slipped a bar of soap from the ledge at his hip to lather her up from shoulders to knees.

A moan broke free from Savannah's chest. Cole's hands roamed over her skin, and even though his touches remained mostly chaste, heat bloomed in her core, aching and insistent. She let him turn her slowly around, rinsing the bubbles away before she spun back to take the soap from his hand.

"What are you doing?"

She looked up at him, meeting his molten stare through her lashes. "Returning the favor."

Savannah rolled the bar of soap between her palms until they were covered in soft, slippery bubbles, the woodsy scent she'd come to associate with Cole filling her senses and making her even hotter. Putting the soap aside, she pressed her palms to the hard plane of his chest, running them on a smooth path all the way to his hips, then down the length of his leanly muscled thighs.

His breath hitched. "I'm not sure this is a good idea."

"Why not?" The bold question flew right out, and she followed it with another pass of her hands.

Cole's cock jerked between his hips. "Because I can barely resist you as it is, sweetheart. You get to washing me, and I guarantee neither one of us will get clean."

Savannah moved one hand down the ridges of his soap-slicked abs. "You say that like it's a bad thing. But I want to touch you, Cole. I want to make you feel good." She wrapped her fingers around his cock, and even the gentle pressure of his length in her palm made her want to come.

"Savannah," he hissed, thrusting into the circle of her fingers as she moved to the side to let the water rinse him clean.

But he let her guide him back, all the way against the tiled wall. "It's okay," she said, leaning in to brush a kiss to his mouth like a promise. "If you want to lose control, I've got you."

Savannah sank to her knees in one fluid motion, too fast for Cole to protest. Her free arm slid low around the back of his hips, her opposite hand still working between his legs. The heated burst of his exhale sent desire licking through her, and Savannah pressed her lips to the crown of his cock with a smile.

Cole's exhale became a grunt, primal and full of want. "*Ah.*" He widened his stance, one palm finding her shoulder as she parted her lips and started to suck. "I'm not kidding, Savannah."

She pulled back, but only far enough to look up at him. Lord, he was gorgeous, all hard muscles and intense, pent-up need.

Need she wanted to fulfill, if only for a little while. "I'm not, either. Now shut up and let me show *you* how beautiful you are."

Flexing her grip around his body, Savannah returned her

mouth to his cock. She worked him in short, fast strokes, following the movement of her mouth with her hand, one chasing the other. Cole's grasp on her tightened. He turned his fingers in to her shoulder, the tension in his body a clear indicator of his restraint.

No. Not today. Savannah's need built right alongside his, and she deepened her movements, swirling her tongue down the seam of his cock as far as she could take him.

Cole's voice broke over a sharp curse. "So hot. God damn, your mouth feels so *hot*."

Savannah pulled back only to repeat the movement, and his muscles coiled even tighter beneath her hands and mouth. His hands cupped the back of her neck, so lightly that it seemed as if he was afraid to push her. But she wanted it, wanted to feel him on her skin and taste him in her mouth.

She wanted to see him, too.

Without slowing the rhythm of her mouth, Savannah reached back to press his hands over the back of her head, an open invitation for him to take control and lose it at the same time. Cole's fingers knotted in the wet fall of hair on her shoulders, taking everything she offered while giving her exactly what she wanted. He levered his hips, pumping against her lips with increasing urgency. Savannah slid her palm down the length of his shaft, pressing her thumb to the sweet spot at the base, and his body jerked hard under the touch.

"*Fuck*. Savannah," Cole warned, still clearly trying to fight for control even though he was losing the battle. But she'd meant it when she said she had him, and even though her body screamed with need of its own, Savannah didn't stop. His muscles pulled bowstring tight for only a split second before pulsing in climax, but still, she didn't relent. She rode Cole through every second, her name falling past his lips as she swallowed him down until there was nothing left to take. Slowly, she gentled her movements, finally parting from his body to look up at him with a smile.

But before she could say a single word, Cole hauled her off her feet and out of the shower.

Chapter Twenty-Two

Cole's legs were as unsteady as his brain, but the dark, unfettered urge to spread Savannah wide and make her scream until she ran out of breath overruled them both. Hooking his arms beneath her shoulders, he lifted her off the tile, barely thinking enough to turn the water off before he pulled her from the shower stall and led her the handful of steps to his bedroom.

"Cole, we're soaking wet," she said, blinking past her surprise. Rivulets of water beaded on her flushed skin, spiraling over her tight, tawny nipples and down the slope of her belly.

Nothing else mattered. He'd wanted Savannah ever since she'd left his place a couple of nights ago, and he wasn't going to stop until he had her. *Now.*

"That's nice." Cupping her shoulders, he walked her backward to his bed, not stopping until her thighs hit the mattress. She didn't protest as he eased her over the comforter, the shock on her pretty face turning quickly to desire as he parted her knees to situate himself between them.

Christ, but Savannah turned him on, so wet and hot and wanting. Her breasts lifted and fell in time with her quickening breath, and Cole was powerless to refuse. He leaned in, pulling one nipple past his lips, a smile parting over the hardened bud as she gasped.

"Beautiful." He wondered if he could make her come like this, was tempted for a second to try, with his mouth on her nipple, her sighs pushing him faster. But right now, in the soft morning sunlight of his bedroom with nothing between them but need, Cole didn't want fast. He didn't want to make her come just for the down and dirty of it.

He wanted to taste her.

Angling downward, he braced his hands over her waist. Her lean muscles flexed in response to his touch, and he marveled at them as he slipped even lower. Cole strung a path of open-mouthed kisses over her rib cage, tracing the rim of her navel with the tip of his tongue. Savannah shuddered, letting her knees fall even wider, and the gesture filled his senses with the heady scent of her arousal.

His moan was involuntary, and he laid her bare in one swift motion. Pressing his hands against the flat of her inner thighs, he spread her sex, tasting the seam of her body with a long, slow lick.

Holy hell, he was never going to get enough.

"Oh . . . *God.*" Savannah's mouth parted as wide as her eyes, her back bowing off the bed. Her wide-open pleasure made him repeat the ministration, once, then twice more as she trembled beneath him. Even though part of him dared the rest to go faster, to make her come as hard as she'd done him, he explored her core with soft kisses and gentle strokes, building one on top of the other until she was slick with need. His dick stirred to life again, growing harder with every one of Savannah's velvety sighs, and damn it, he needed to slow down, just like he'd needed to make her stop in the shower.

But Cole couldn't contain the pure, reflexive emotion razoring up from within him, making him crazy, reckless. Reaching low to palm the swell of her ass, he cupped her close at the same time he parted her folds with his thumbs, circling her exposed clit with a sweep of his tongue.

A guttural cry tore from Savannah's mouth, and Cole buried his tongue even deeper. Teasing her wasn't even a consideration. No, he wanted to suck that tiny, swollen bud until she broke, to penetrate her with his tongue, to taste and take and fuck her with his mouth until she flew apart beneath his touch.

Savannah began to tremble harder, her thighs quaking around his shoulders, and he realized only then that he'd done all those things without thinking. She arched upward, her spine curved tightly in release, her sex pulsing a wild beat under his tongue. A small, faraway part of him warned once again that he should wait, gather control and go slowly.

But Cole took one look at Savannah, her brown eyes glittering and her face flushed with hazy, satisfied bliss, and suddenly, his actions didn't belong to him. One brisk motion had a condom out of his bedside table drawer, another had him fully sheathed. He covered Savannah's body with his, sinking his cock between her legs in an unapologetically hard thrust.

She splayed her hands over his ass, thrusting back with equal intensity. "Cole. Oh my God, don't you dare *stop*."

Between her sexy demand and the raw pleasure rippling up his spine, he was done. He anchored his hands on her hips, pushing into her again and again. Savannah increased the pressure of her grasp, locking her arms around his lower back to hold the base of his cock flush with the top of her sex.

Her slick inner muscles squeezed, and her resulting moan dared him to pump even faster. Dark, dauntless pleasure curled up from the base of his balls to spread low through his belly, but Cole didn't stop. He pistoned into her without remorse, filling Savannah's body so many times he lost count. She came undone with a soft, keening cry, the sound triggering his own climax to break around him. Filling her core to the hilt, he erased all the space between them, covering her from mouth to shoulders to sex as he came.

Cole's awareness filtered back in increments, a sound here, a sensation there. Savannah's chest worked in rapid breaths beneath his, and he tried not to crush her with his body weight even though his deepest compulsion was to not let her go.

He wanted her close. For a lot longer than now.

Of all the emotions Cole had ever felt, this one scared him the most.

Cole sat back on the couch in his living room, surrounded by cartons of takeout Chinese food, a stack of fire and rescue manuals, and the sound of Savannah's unvarnished laughter.

"Are you seriously trying to tell me that one of instructor Brennan's very first calls as a rookie was to rescue a kitten from a tree?" Her milk chocolate stare crinkled at the edges, sending Cole even further into relaxation mode. They'd spent the day—minus three hours for a power nap midafternoon—hanging out and studying emergency response protocols, and Cole had to admit, despite the unease he'd been carrying since yesterday's conversation with Oz and his zero tolerance policy for all things impassioned, being with Savannah felt seamlessly good. After that weird intensity had crashed through him this morning post-sex, he'd waited for their emotions to finally get in the way and put a wrecking ball to what they'd started.

But instead, she'd just kissed him, rolled over to steal another one of his T-shirts, and asked if he really had the second volume of *Fire Behavior and Combustion Processes*.

With a surprised laugh, Cole had offered her a cup of coffee while he looked for the book, and the next thing he knew, the entire day had flown by in easy conversation and even easier companionship.

She nudged him with a bare foot from her adjacent spot on the couch, her sweet smile ungluing his thoughts and bringing him back to the living room.

"Yep. I swear on my eyes, one of Brennan's first calls was the proverbial cat in a tree," he said, unable to contain his grin as he maneuvered his chopsticks through his carton of crispy shredded beef. "He and Mason went rock, paper, scissors for who had to go up, and Brennan lost. The poor cat was a good twenty feet above the ground, too, in a massive oak tree. Brennan had a hell of a time trying to get it detached from the branch. Not to mention a hell of a time getting it detached from his arm after that."

It hadn't helped that Cole and Alex had been on the ground, holding the ladder steady and goading the crap out of the rookie who would end up being their best friend. God, Cole had nearly forgotten all about that day.

Savannah took a bite of her Kung Pao chicken. "Well. I guess my ducks are in good company, then. What about you? What was your first call?"

"Totally small-time, I'm afraid. My first day as a candidate ended up in back-to-back false alarms and a minor car wreck where I used my skill set to direct traffic. We did deliver a baby on the shoulder of the highway the shift after that, though, and I got to assist. So I guess that was the first call where I actually got to contribute."

"You helped deliver a baby, huh? That's pretty cool," she said, her bright eyes marking the words as genuine.

He nodded. "Probably a lot more for me than the lady having the baby, but yeah. Mom and baby did great. It *was* a pretty cool call to help out on."

"All three of my brothers had small-time calls as their

first, too. Medical assists for heart attacks and stuff like that. Of course, my father's first call was a house fire. His company ended up saving three people." Savannah laughed. "That's Duke for you, though. He had his boots on the ground and his ass in gear every chance he got, I swear. A firefighter through and through."

Something panged through Cole that he couldn't name, and so much for losing his unease. "He sounds like a good man."

Her smile didn't slip, but it did become more wistful. "He's the best. I just hope I can keep making him proud, you know?"

Yeah, he knew. "Believe me, you're doing fine," he said instead.

"Fine?" Her smile took on a sexy edge, totally at odds with the soft wisps of hair falling loose from the knot at her nape and the overly boxy T-shirt she wore over the gray boy shorts she'd pulled from her bag. She was a study in opposites, in all the things he'd never expected. Christ, even sitting here with the bitter reminder of his father barely in his rearview, Savannah still made him laugh.

"How about excellent?" Cole asked. He put his carton of Chinese food on the coffee table in favor of curling his fingers around her ankle.

"Mmm." She frowned, all show. "Keep talking."

"Determined." His fingers trailed up to the bend in her knee, pressing just hard enough to turn her exhale into a sigh.

"You have my attention," she said.

"Good, because I'm just getting started." Cole took advantage of his hold on the back of her knee, drawing her closer. "You're smart." He wrapped his hands around her waist, pulling her into his lap so they sat face-to-face. "The job is important to you. It's in your blood." He skimmed his knuckles over the blush spreading over her sun-kissed face.

"And you're passionate. You don't stop until you get what you want."

"I'd be a lot less successful if you didn't have my back."

Cole's shoulders bumped against the couch cushions in surprise. "Helping candidates become good firefighters is part of the job. Plus, in case you've forgotten, Westin needed me to make sure you were straight before I could take my spot on squad."

"Yeah, but that's not why you did it. Any one of you guys on engine could've helped me become a good firefighter. Crews, Donovan—hell, I even learn something from Jonesey on practically every shift. But you're different. You don't just want to train me. You trust me. You *see* me. Of everyone at Eight, somehow you get why I need to prove myself the most."

"I get why you need to prove yourself because I had to do the same thing. I still do, every single day," he said, and damn it, he really needed to lock up the emotion suddenly threatening its way past his throat.

The only change to Savannah's expression was the crease forming between her dark brows. "I don't understand. Everyone in the house knows how ambitious you are and how much you put into the job. Why would you need to prove yourself?"

Cole paused. It would be all too easy to give in to the defenses currently shrieking at him to shut the fuck up, and he ran through the strategies in his head that would get him there. He could distract Savannah with a quick smile and a slow kiss. He could make a sweeping generalization about how all firefighters had to prove their worth in order to make it. He could even steer the conversation back to her career instead of his to effectively snuff out the subject.

But for the first time in nine years, he didn't want to shut up. Savannah had trusted him with her family history and with all of her feelings—good, bad, and sloppy. As tough as she was, she'd trusted Cole to actually see her, not just to help her become a good firefighter, but to discover even the parts of her she didn't fully recognize.

And more than anything, Cole wanted to trust her back.

"A few weeks ago, you asked me if I was from Fairview, and I told you I'm not. I was actually born and raised on a farm in Georgia, about a hundred miles outside of Atlanta."

Savannah's body stilled over his with obvious surprise. "Your accent," she whispered.

Of course she'd picked up on that. "Yeah. It pops out every once in a while if I'm jacked up over something, but for the most part, I've lost it." Cole didn't want to add that the change had been intentional. She'd make that logic leap soon enough.

"You're awfully far from home." Her words arrived without judgment or fanfare, loosening something dark and heavy from the center of his chest.

"I might have been born and raised on that farm, but I belong in Fairview. Station Eight is my only home."

For a second, the words stuck in his throat, and Cole stopped. Yes, he trusted Savannah, but he'd never given up the true nitty-gritty of his departure from Harvest Moon to anyone, not even Alex or Brennan. He'd walked away nine years ago, vowing to forget. Maybe the past, and all the emotions that went with it, was too far gone to reveal.

But then Savannah leaned in to cup his face, her hands so strong and so sweet that Cole felt them everywhere. "Hey. Remember that night in the library?"

His heart pounded. "Yeah."

"We might work together, but we're not at Eight right now. We're just sitting here having a conversation, Cole. Me and you."

The simplicity of her expression, soft yet utterly fearless, made the words spill right out of him.

"For three generations, my family has farmed the land at Harvest Moon. My grandfather cultivated every field with his own hands. He even built the house I grew up in." Wide-planked floorboards the color of honey, the smell of fresh-baked bread floating through the windows. Funny how Cole could call it up so easily even though he'd never, ever go back. "From the time I could walk, my father started grooming me to take over the farm with my brothers."

"You have brothers?" The emotion on Savannah's face was unmistakable. Considering the affection she'd clearly shown for her family as she and Cole had swapped stories all day, it didn't shock him that she'd latch on to that.

"Two. Ben is older and Jonah's the baby." Which just went to show how much time had really passed since Cole had left the farm. Although Jonah had barely been sixteen when Cole had emptied his emotions into that screaming match with their father and then packed his bags, his brother was twenty-five now. An adult. A stranger. "We were supposed to run the farm together as a family, just like my father had with my granddad. My old man had it all planned out. It never occurred to him that one of us might not be made for it."

"When did you know you were a firefighter instead of a farmer?" Savannah asked, and the way she inherently understood that Cole had known he was a firefighter before he'd ever left Harvest Moon made it all too easy to let the rest of the story parade on out.

"When I was eighteen. A buddy of mine enrolled at the fire academy in Atlanta right after high school." Cole had spent years feeling like a square peg aiming to fit into a hole as round as a nickel, but after thirty minutes on the Atlanta Fire Department's website, he'd known exactly where he wanted to be. But sharing that little game-changer had been so much easier said than done.

"I almost left then," he continued. "But I was torn. My father might've been gruffer than most, but I had a decent life. I loved my parents and my brothers, and even though I didn't want to fulfill the family legacy, I never hated the farm. Ben had always been a natural—any idiot with two eyes and half a brain could see that he belonged there, and even though Jonas was a lot younger, he was following in my old man's footsteps, too. I felt guilty for being the odd man out and not loving the livelihood that was in my blood the way they all did, so for three years, I stayed anyway."

"That must have been tough, working on the farm even though your heart was somewhere else." Savannah brushed a hand over his forearm, and the touch grounded him as much as the simplicity of her words.

"I tried," he said, his chest squeezing under the steel band of the memory. "I really did. For those three years after high school, I threw everything I had into running Harvest Moon with my father and Ben."

Cole could still chart the calluses on his hands, still remember the way the sky looked as the sun broke over the horizon, different from how it would look as it set fourteen hours later. "But then I just couldn't take it anymore. I thought—" He broke off, hating this part of the story the most even though it burned to finally be set to words. "My father understood what it meant to love his livelihood all the way down to his bones. I knew he wouldn't be thrilled that I wanted to leave, but I was his son. I thought if I just explained to him that I wanted to be a firefighter the same way he was a farmer, he might understand."

But Samuel Everett was a tough old man who'd been raised by an even tougher old man. There'd been plenty of room for honest work and hard punishment when an Everett screwed up, but as far as Cole's father had been concerned, emotion only went in one direction. And that was if you ever let it show at all.

Cole closed his eyes. Forced in a breath. Came out with the rest. "Needless to say, my strategy to appeal to his emotions pretty much imploded. We had a huge argument, and he told me that if I left Harvest Moon to become a firefighter, I'd be dead to him. But I was twenty-one and angry and stung as hell that he'd pick that farm over me when I knew deep down that I didn't belong there. So I pulled out a map and picked the farthest place from Georgia that I could afford to get to by bus, and two days later, I enrolled at the Fairview Fire Academy."

Realization colored Savannah's eyes, sending them wide. "That's why you know the city so well. You wanted a place to belong."

Cole nodded. No point in holding the rest back now. "When I got on that bus, I vowed to leave everything in my past behind me. I dropped my accent and learned the city even better than I'd known the farm. Then I swore I'd become the best damned firefighter I possibly could, no matter what it took. When I landed at Eight after I graduated from the academy . . ." Emotion twisted, low and deep in his belly, but Savannah didn't flinch at the sight of it on his face.

"They became your family," she said. Slowly, she slid her hand from beneath his, her palm rasping over the stubble on his jaw as she moved it up to cradle his face. "I'm so sorry that what happened in your past hurt you. I can't even imagine it. But I'm not sorry that you're the man you are, Cole. You're an incredible firefighter."

"Am I?" The emotions he normally kept on lockdown combined with the frustration that had been building ever since his dicey conversation with Oz, forming a potent cocktail of nothing good in his bloodstream. "Ever since my first day on engine, all that's mattered to me is the job and my family at Eight. But for the last twenty-four hours, the only thing I can think is that one of them isn't who he seems."

Savannah shifted back over the couch cushions, her stare laced with confusion. "Did you talk to Oz about those reports yesterday while we were on shift?"

He nodded, relaying the details of the conversation he hadn't been able to share while they'd been at the firehouse for fear of being overheard. A muscle tightened in the curve of Savannah's jawline as Cole finished with Oz's threat to his spot on squad.

"What an *ass*," she hissed. "God, we have to do something."

The unease in Cole's chest bubbled. "What, exactly? While we might be able to argue that there are aspects of these fires that don't match the reports, Oz can still play the other side of the coin and say he wrote up all the pertinent facts. His time on the job speaks to his credibility, and not a little."

"Okay, but there's got to be at least enough here for arson to open a case. I could talk to my brother—"

"No." The word fired from Cole's mouth with more intensity than volume, but he still had to struggle for the inhale that came after it. "There's a chain of command in arson, just like in every firehouse. If you tell Brad you suspect someone in your house of arson—that you even have an inkling—he'll have no choice but to follow that chain. The brass over there won't hesitate to shit-can both of us if we're wrong."

"We're not wrong," she argued, and Christ, even all fired up and fighting him, she was beautiful.

"I don't think we're wrong, either," he said, even though the admission burned an exit path through his mouth. "But going off half-cocked isn't going to get us anywhere we want to be; plus, we didn't even have permission to be at that second scene after the fact. We have to be smart about this."

Savannah paused. "What's your plan?"

Cole's stomach knotted behind his FFD T-shirt. He'd struggled with the answer to that million-dollar question ever since Oz had walked away from him on the basketball court yesterday, but as much as Cole hated the betrayal of it, he couldn't turn the other cheek.

"Having each other's backs is the most important rule at Eight. It's the first thing we're taught as rookies, and it's the thing we live by above all else."

A chirp of shock fell past Savannah's lips. "You're not seriously suggesting we should have Oz's back here."

"No," Cole said. "But I am suggesting that we should trust Captain Westin to have ours. Sending this up the chain of command in our own house is the only way to deal with this, Savannah. Westin may run a tight ship, but he's a fair man." He skimmed a hand through his hair to offset the emotions threatening to steal his control. This was the right play. The *only* play. "I trust him to have my back on this."

For a long minute, Savannah said nothing. Cole knew she thought Westin was a good captain, but the truth was, she'd been on engine for a scant month, where she'd known her brother since birth. Her family ties were rooted deep. But so were Cole's, and if the two of them came in too hot on this, it was going to blow up in their faces.

"Okay."

"Okay?" He stared, unsure he'd heard her properly.

Savannah—being Savannah—met him head-on. "If you think the best strategy is to keep this in-house and go from there, then I respect that. Let's do it."

Cole released a breath, realizing only after the fact that he'd been holding the lungful nice and tight. "You can trust Westin."

"Oh, I'm not agreeing to this because I trust Westin, Cole." She looked at him, her eyes brimming with nothing but truth. "I'm doing it because I trust you. My gut is screaming that this is arson and that Oz is involved. But Station Eight's golden rule is to have each other's backs. You told me you've got mine, and I know I've got yours. We can go to Westin next shift."

In that moment, Cole knew two things. The first was that Savannah really did mean what she'd said with every ounce of her being. She trusted him to have her back, and she'd fight to have his in return, no matter what.

The second was that he was falling in love with her for it.

Chapter Twenty-Three

Savannah flipped her keys in her palm, her feet on the threshold of her brother's apartment even though her mind was a million miles away. Okay, maybe not a *million*. Maybe, more specifically, just ten miles across Fairview. At Cole's place. Where the rest of her had not only spent the last day and a half, but wanted to stay a lot longer.

And rather than scaring the hell out of her—or at the very least, motivating her to be cautious like she damn well knew it should—her desire to be with Cole only made her feel right in a way that she hadn't since she'd left Texas.

He saw her for exactly who she was, and he trusted her. He didn't just make her feel good enough.

When she was with him, she felt as if she belonged.

The story of what had happened between Cole and his father had yanked at Savannah's heartstrings yesterday, but the whole thing made so much sense. He understood her need to prove herself because his need to do the same was just as strong, his career equally important to him albeit for different reasons. She'd known in that moment exactly why his response to this whole Oz thing—hell, to *everything*—was so measured and controlled.

For nearly a decade, everyone at Eight had been his only

family. The house was the one place he belonged. Risking that, even in the face of something as major as these hinky reports, was a huge deal.

But she'd meant every ounce of what she'd said. Just as he'd trusted her with what had happened in his past, Savannah trusted Cole to make the smart move in the here and now. They both had a metric ton on the line, but she trusted him with her career.

Maybe even with her heart.

She squeezed her keys in her hand, hard enough to feel the pinch on the soft skin of her palm. "Girl. This is crazy," she whispered, her fingers shaking as she moved to unlock the door to Brad's apartment. She might've spent the last day and a half living off cold leftovers and hot sex, but things between her and Cole couldn't get serious. More serious than they were. Oh *God*, she wanted to get serious.

If they were caught together, the fallout would be epically bad.

Time to stow your endorphins, Nelson. Savannah might be wrapped up in the world's biggest afterglow, and she might care for Cole outside the bedroom more than she had any right to, but she wasn't a complete waste of space. She was tough, God damn it. She could handle whatever came her way, no matter how difficult.

Except for maybe her brother.

"I'm not gonna pretend to be your keeper, sweet pea, but you've been gone far too long for me to not break somebody's legs." Brad crossed his arms over the front of his beat-up Texas A&M T-shirt, raising a brow at her from where he stood in the kitchenette, and shit. Shit! How had she not thought her obvious absence wouldn't translate to . . . well, the obvious.

She stalled by closing the front door behind her, flipping the dead bolt with a *click*. "It's Saturday night. Shouldn't you be out . . . doing something?"

One dark brow arched. "Seems you've got that market cornered, sugar bee."

"Uh." At this point, Savannah couldn't deny that she'd been spending at least some of her downtime with a man—Brad would never buy whatever feeble excuse she could come up with on the fly, anyway. But no chance in hell was she copping to *which* man. She might be brash, but she wasn't brainless. "Okay, yeah. Maybe. It's just casual, though."

"And now I want to put Clorox to my ears and punch this guy in the face, so maybe let's not on the details, huh?" Brad held up a hand for emphasis, and she resisted the urge to sag with relief. "But you're clearly keeping company with someone. I wouldn't be doing my brotherly duties if I didn't give you a little hell and offer a blanket threat to kick the guy's ass if he steps out of line."

A tiny smile wended its way over Savannah's mouth, and she lowered her bag to the floor before joining her brother in the microscopic kitchen. "Don't you think *I'd* kick the guy's ass if he steps out of line?"

"Fair enough," Brad admitted after a minute. He leaned in to nudge her shoulder with his own, grabbing a pair of beers from the fridge and passing one over. "But grown or not, you're still my baby sister. We stick together come hell or hurricanes. It's the Nelson way."

Unease laddered down her spine despite the cool, smooth taste of the beer she'd cracked open. Yes, she'd agreed that she and Cole would talk to Captain Westin about Oz as soon as they could tomorrow, and yes, she'd trusted Cole when he'd said going up the chain of command in-house was the smartest move.

Except.

If the discrepancies in the reports weren't enough, she and Cole were risking some serious censure, not to mention his promotion to squad. They'd lock-picked their way onto that second scene, for God's sake. She had no doubt that both fires were arson and that Oz was at the very least guilty of covering them up, if not more. But she *was* starting to have doubts that she and Cole could prove it, especially to the captain who had been buddy-buddy with Oz for the past two decades.

With so much on the line, Savannah had to be sure.

"So I've been doing a lot of studying lately, trying to stay on top of things and learn as much as I can." She tried on a semi-bored expression. Brad would never swallow her complete disinterest in anything related to work, but getting overly bright-eyed would definitely catch his notice, too. "You know, procedures and fire science. Stuff like that."

Brad laughed, leaning against the counter. "Welcome to my world. Anything I can help you with?"

She forced herself not to tackle the question with too much enthusiasm, although good *Lord*, it took effort. "I don't know. Maybe. I came across a bunch of case files used as examples in a textbook. Most of them were from electrical fires."

"Oooh. Those can get crispy," her brother said, and even though she hated the deception, Savannah nodded.

"Yeah, the pictures look it. I saw an AC window unit that damn near burned a crater in the floor of a warehouse."

Brad frowned. "From faulty electrical? I guess a fire pattern like that *could* happen if the circumstances were just right, but I'm not sure it's very likely."

"You think?" She took a long sip of her beer, tasting nothing. *Nerves of steel.* "What else could've done it?"

"Well, I know I'm not the most unbiased guy on the planet when it comes to this, but I'm thinking who rather than what. Someone with less-than-honorable intentions could rig an AC unit to blow in any one of a dozen ways."

Savannah's heart thumped against her ribs. "Okay, but wouldn't they have to be there to kick it off?" She'd been wracking her brain for days now, trying to figure out how

Oz had managed to start both fires without actually being at the scene.

"Not necessarily. I know explosions seem like they'd be complicated to rig, but all you really need is heat and pressure, both of which can be triggered either remotely or on a delay. Take your AC unit, for example. For someone who knows what they're doing, removing the safety sensor and pinching off the cooling coil takes about five minutes. In an older unit, probably less."

Oh. *God*. She marshaled her voice to steadiness. "So there's your heat and your pressure. But still." She had to play devil's advocate. She had to know every angle. "Would that really be enough to spark an explosion?"

"Maybe not a huge one. But add a little creativity, and it sure would start one hell of a fire," Brad said.

"Creativity?" she asked, the tiny hairs on the back of her neck standing at complete attention.

"The heat and pressure from the bad wiring would make an AC unit burn, no doubt. But let's say someone were to add an accelerant like a flammable household cleaner to the condensation pan. Once the unit got hot enough, the thing would pump out fire instead of cold air, and then . . ." Brad put his beer on the counter at his hip, opening his fingers wide to mimic an explosion. "Your fire would go from bad to worse."

Savannah's blood turned to ice water in her veins as her mind snagged on that weird stain she'd seen on the warehouse floor. Cole had dismissed it as something that had probably been in the storage unit when the place had caught fire.

But what if it was the *reason* the warehouse had caught fire?

"That sounds major," she finally managed, but her brother just shrugged as if they were talking about the weather or what she'd had for dinner or anything else that didn't have *I work with an arsonist* written all over it.

"Like I said, it wouldn't be huge, like a bomb blast. But arson usually isn't. If an arsonist knows what he's doing, the fires can usually be blamed on other causes. It's why arson is so hard to prove." Brad shrugged. "Anyway, I know all that sounds pretty far-fetched, especially when you compare it to something as run-of-the-mill as an electrical fire. Hope it makes sense."

"Actually, it does," Savannah said.

Frighteningly, it made all the sense in the world.

After six hours of twisting and turning on her brother's couch, Savannah finally just threw in the towel and left the cushions in the past tense. A hot shower and a hotter cup of coffee got her body in gear, but her brain and her heart sat strangely unsatisfied.

She wanted Cole. Not just in the "hot sex, right now" kind of way. But in the "steal his T-shirt, curl up in his arms, trust him to have her back" kind of way.

Oh God. She really *was* in love with him.

Savannah's cell phone buzzed softly, signaling an incoming text, and her pulse jumped even faster as she slid the thing from the coffee table to her palm.

Hey. You awake?

Her smile was pure instinct. **Yeah.**

You want to meet me at Scarlett's for breakfast?

Savannah eyed the clock on the microwave, the glowing numbers cutting through the shadows. **A little early for**

breakfast, isn't it? It was barely 0520. Most normal people
still had a solid hour of REM sleep left in their cycle.

You got me, Cole answered after a minute. I don't really
care about the food. I just want you.

Savannah closed her eyes, not even trying to squash her
idiot grin.

Well. In that case, I guess I'll see you in ten.

She made it to Scarlett's in eight minutes and change, but
of course, Cole was already there. He stood out in front of
the neat brick building, looking both unassuming and utterly gorgeous as he looped an arm around her waist and
hauled her in for a kiss.

"Mmm," he murmured, running his teeth over her bottom
lip before releasing her just far enough to deliver a devastating smile. "Morning."

Savannah lost the war with her blush. "Oh. You really did
miss me," she said, pulling back to swing a glance over the
quiet, predawn hush of Church Street.

"I did. And you don't have to worry." His green-gold
stare followed hers like a heat signature. "We're blocks from
the house, and anyway, I'm always the first person in at
Eight. They're all still snoring away at home."

"Ah." She relaxed against his touch, breathing in the
clean, woodsy scent of his skin. "Well in that case, c'mere."

A minute later, Savannah reluctantly let go of Cole to let
him usher her inside the brightly lit diner. The restaurant
was sparsely populated, and they took their usual booth by
the window in the back, both ordering coffee and the breakfast special that was quickly becoming their norm. Being
around Cole sent her nerves unwinding in her belly, and
even when they briefly discussed waiting until after roll call
to go see Westin, Savannah still didn't clutch.

This was going to work out. After what Brad had told her

last night, they had more than enough for the FFD to open an investigation against Oz.

And what's more, Cole had her back.

When their breakfasts had been reduced to crumbs and smudges on their mostly empty plates, Cole ran one hand over his stomach, brushing his opposite fingers over hers.

"I guess we should head over to the house and start getting ready for roll call," he said. "You can go first if you want. I'll give you a ten-minute head start so it doesn't look like we're rolling up together."

Savannah nodded. Arriving together, especially early, might arouse suspicion, and the guys on B-shift were probably up and prepping for shift change. Still, despite the need for covert tactics, a smile tempted the corners of her mouth upward. "You go. I don't want to be responsible for you breaking your first-one-in streak."

"Careful, sweetheart." Cole slipped the check off the Formica, dishing up a mischievous smile before he unfolded himself out of their booth. "Or I'll start thinking you like me."

Savannah spent the next ten minutes corralling the butterflies taking flight against her rib cage, then another five making her way to Station Eight. She headed into the engine bay, business as usual, and jawing with Donovan and Jonesey as she changed and got ready for the impending tour calmed the nervousness skating through her. All she and Cole had to do was get through shift change and roll call. Then they'd meet in front of Westin's office and ask for a sit-down.

Nothing to it. They had each other's backs.

"Hey, Tough Stuff," Donovan said, tipping his permanently stubbled chin at the door connecting the locker room to Station Eight's interior. "You'd better hustle it. Roll call's in five."

She ran a hand over her uniform to make sure her FFD T-shirt was tucked neatly into her navy-blue uniform pants, unable to keep her sassy smile from popping out as she clanged her locker shut. "Please. Like anything has ever kept me from roll call before."

But before Donovan could work up a smartass response, the all-call echoed through the building.

Chapter Twenty-Four

"Listen up, you guys, because we're looking at a fucking barn burner," Crews barked into the headset, the tone of his voice sending Savannah's already thudding pulse into the stratosphere. "Dispatch has got multiple nine-one-one calls for a nightclub over in Cambridge Park, and the last caller reported flames already showing. The building is older than the hills, so we're gonna need to look sharp and act sharper. ETA in five."

"Copy that." Savannah hooked her headset back to its perch in the step, already starting to sweat beneath the thick cover of her turnout gear.

"Shit. I hate big calls at shift change," Jonesey muttered from beside her, yanking his hood into place. It wasn't like a firefighter to hate calls of any kind, really, and it damn sure wasn't like Donovan to tack on such a serious nod in agreement.

"We don't even have solid shift assignments, so be ready for anything, you two."

Savannah nodded, double-checking her gear and her SCBA as she focused on her inhale-exhale. A ribbon of unease curled around her chest at the thought of the thwarted trip to Westin's office, but there was nothing to be done for it now. Waiting for a few hours wouldn't change anything.

Nerves of steel, girl. Be tough.

Her boots hit the cracked pavement about five nanoseconds after Donovan's, the radio on her shoulder crackling as she cranked the volume for a good listen while she took in the scene.

The two-story nightclub had seen better days. Its worn façade and narrow windows were both difficult to clearly make out from behind the billows of dark gray smoke pouring out of the building. A sign in front proclaiming THE VAULT proved to be an accurate moniker for the place as Savannah took in the steel security gate padlocked over the front door facing the street, and damn, there were flames showing in all four of the first-floor windows.

Westin's voice grabbed Savannah's attention over the radio. "Engine, squad. We need to move fast. Oz, take the roof for a vent, and Crews, I want you and Jones on that nightmare of a front door. Everett, you and Nelson see if you can't find a point of entry in the rear. All of you, go."

Savannah gripped her Halligan bar and fell into step next to Cole. "Think there's an employee entrance back here?"

"Per code, there's got to be something other than the front door. Ah." He jerked his helmet at the rickety, sun-faded sign reading FOR DELIVERIES, PLEASE USE REAR ENTRANCE. "Looks like today's our lucky day."

The irony of Cole's words hit her in full force as they rounded the Charlie side of the nightclub. Smoke churned from the building in soot-filled streams, with thick waves of heat following closely behind. The back door was the only point of entry Savannah could see, the windowless steel slab dead-bolted in two places, but thankfully, that wasn't anything they couldn't handle with a thirty-second breach. Provided they could get past the fire threatening to swallow the place whole from the inside out.

"Everett to command, we have a secondary point of entry, first-floor door on the Charlie side. But we're showing pretty heavy smoke back here, Cap," Cole called into his radio. "We can get in, but I'd bet on the other side being pretty toasty."

Westin's voice crackled over the two-way in reply. "Command to Everett, stand by. Crews, report on the Alpha side point of entry."

"Five minutes, command," Crews clipped out. "Security door is set in goddamn cinder blocks. But we're on it."

Savannah stepped back, scanning the area behind the nightclub. She spotted a single window on the far side of the building, so small and far from the rear door that it had been easy to miss at first glance. Just a narrow stretch of smoke-smudged glass about five feet off the ground, the window was one of those horizontal affairs that served purely aesthetic purposes rather than boasting any sort of functionality. The rear lot was blessedly empty of gawkers and passersby—smoke this bitter and burnt tended to serve as a pretty good deterrent, although you never did know. But then her eyes came to a halt on a silver Mercedes tucked into an out-of-the-way parking spot by the Dumpster, and her gut iced over as the implication clicked all the way into place.

"Cole, look," Savannah said, but her feet were already in motion. With a quick grab, she snatched up one of the flimsy plastic chairs from the makeshift smoke-break area beside the door, jamming her boots onto the seat to pull herself up to the window.

Oh holy *hell*.

"Nelson to command, we've got entrapment back here, Charlie side!" Savannah's hand shook over her two-way from the bolt of sheer adrenaline coursing through her blood. "I've got eyes on an adult male in a back room." She sucked in a breath that turned to sand in her lungs. "He appears unconscious. I can see him through a window, but it's too small to breach."

"Damn it," Westin swore. "Crews, report."

"Four minutes, command."

Westin made his swear a double. "Command to Everett. Are you and Nelson a go for that back door?"

Cole looked up, meeting her eyes with a determined stare. "Affirmative, sir."

"You have ninety seconds for search and rescue. Do it."

Savannah jumped down from the chair, her brain moving at Mach 2 as they covered the ground back to the rear entrance. Cole crouched down over the threshold, angling his Halligan bar into place in the crease of the door.

"You're on my hip, Nelson, nice and easy. We're going to get this guy and get the hell out of here. You copy?"

She nodded, tugging her mask into place until it formed a snug seal around her face. "Copy," she said, although she barely heard the word over the hiss of her regulator and the absolute slam of her heartbeat in her ears. Cole wasted no time breaching the door with a splintering crack.

Despite the endorphin-laced fear threatening to take over every corner of her mind, Savannah didn't hesitate to follow him into the burning nightclub.

While Cole had known this shift would probably start with a cluster fuck of epic proportions, he hadn't realized said nightmare would actually be on fire.

That it was easily the nastiest fire he'd seen in half a year, and he and Savannah were breaching the only viable point of entry to drag an unconscious man through a ruthless maze of flames and soot and smoke?

Yeah, the two of them were going to earn every penny of this paycheck.

He swung his gaze through the rear entryway to the

building, taking in the fire-choked junction leading farther into the belly of the nightclub.

"Looks like this hallway will get us to your guy," Cole hollered through his mask, gesturing to his right. Even though the flames had rolled up the length of the corridor's interior wall, the lack of daylight and the growing abundance of smoke tag-teamed in an effort to kill his vision, and halfway down the dark, dingy hallway, he gave up trying to see. Flattening his hands against the exterior wall, he crouched down low to feel his way farther into the furnace-like space. Come on, the door to the room where this guy was trapped had to be here somewhere. It had to be—

"Got it." Deciding to forgo the pleasantries, not to mention the wasted time, of trying to find the damned doorknob in the dark, Cole barged through the door with a sharp kick. "Fire department, call out!" he bellowed through his mask, just in case there was more than one person trapped inside. But the room was small—an office of some sort, judging by the desk and file cabinet against one wall—and the daylight from the window was enough to show him that the man slumped over the threadbare carpet was definitely the only occupant.

"Sir! Sir, can you hear me?" Cole hit his knees next to the man, and Savannah whipped off her glove to press her fingers against the curve of his neck.

"He's got a pulse," she said, the relief in her voice matching the slap of emotion working through Cole's chest. He scanned the man for visible injuries, finishing just in time for the guy to let out a feeble cough.

"Where . . . what's . . . the club," the man moaned, his eyes flickering wide. "The club is on fire."

"We're with the FFD, sir. We're going to get you out of here." Savannah leaned in, her smart, capable stare flashing over the man through her mask. "Is there anyone else in the building with you?"

"No. I came—" He broke off for a sloppy inhale, sputtering the breath back with a wheezy cough, and yeah, they needed to get him the hell out of there. "I came in early to do the books. But the batteries . . . were on fire . . . by the electrical panel at the bar . . . I don't . . . I can't breathe . . ."

The man's words dissolved into a fit of coughs. Between his pastelike color and his labored breathing, there was a zero percent chance he was getting anywhere on his own steam.

Cole shook his head, just once in Savannah's direction. Smoke and heat were choking the tiny room heavily now. "We need to move."

"Copy." She pulled off her helmet, removing her mask to place it over the man's face. "Let's go."

"Nelson." Anger and sharp-edged concern crowded Cole's gut. "Put your mask back on." He knew she'd been trained to cling to the thing like it was a lifeline, mostly because it fucking was.

She replaced her helmet, tightening her chin strap with a yank. "No."

"You're breaking protocol. Put your mask back on," Cole grated. Firefighters didn't remove their masks for *anything*, and hell if he was going to let Savannah do it now. He pinned her with the most serious stare he could manage. "I don't have time to fuck around with you here."

"Then don't. This guy is barely conscious, Cole. He needs the mask more than I do, and it's a quick exit down the hallway. Now let's go."

She scrambled to her feet, and for a second, he nearly argued again. But Savannah's brand of stubborn measured in at about ninety-proof, and he hadn't been bullshitting about having zero time.

"Don't think we're done with this just because we're moving," Cole said, fully intending to chew out what was left of her ass once Westin got done with her. He worked to get the man in a fireman's carry, his muscles tightening around his bones as he shifted to lift the man and distribute the added weight across the breadth of his shoulders. All they had to do was get down the hallway, make it past that dicey junction to get to the back door, and they'd be home free.

"All right, Nelson. It's a straight shot back to the exit, and we're going to hit the bricks running. Let's do this."

She nodded, her face bent in determination despite the hard squint of her eyes against the smoke and the coughs already filtering past her lips. "Copy that."

Cole inhaled. Nailed his composure into place. Turned to step back into the hallway.

And his stomach bottomed out somewhere in the vicinity of his boots.

The fire had spread from the interior wall of the corridor, flashing over the ceiling in a foreboding orange arc. Fiery ashes rained down from the ceiling like Roman candles fizzling over a summertime sky, and the hunks of debris that followed were going to turn his straight shot down the hallway into a goddamn Hail Mary.

Cole swung around one last time to make sure Savannah was solid, but she jerked her chin down the hallway before he could even work up the words.

"I've got your back," she coughed out. "*Go.*"

He lunged down the hall. His back and shoulders burned with labor he'd surely feel later, the relentless heat turning the corridor into a pressure cooker of smoke and flames. Sweat poured from his body, adrenaline and exertion doing battle in his veins, but he tamped them both down, lasering his focus on the end of the hallway even though he could barely see four steps in front of him.

Savannah kept up with him, stride for stride. Her breaths became heavy coughs halfway through the narrow passage, and God damn it, he *knew* he should've insisted she take her mask back. But still, she stayed right on his hip.

"Whoa! Look out!" Cole's pulse spurted as a chunk of flame-engulfed drywall fell from above. He pulled up just in time, Savannah clattering to a clumsy halt behind him. She sucked in a deep breath of shock that exited in another round of raspy coughing, and the sound—hell, the entire situation—reinforced Cole's resolve with a shot of pure titanium.

They were getting out of here. Right now. He didn't give a fuck *what* he had to run through to make it happen.

He shifted to step over the burning debris, re-aiming himself at the end of the hallway. Clips of daylight slipped through the darkness from the busted back door, sending his awareness into overdrive. He pumped his legs faster, the air in his lungs feeling like the fire around him as he reached the bend in the hallway leading to the exit.

But before Cole could finish his break for the door, another piece of the Sheetrock above them collapsed, knocking Savannah to the ground with sickening force.

Savannah jerked her chin up just as a brightly burning immovable force free-fell from above, and her hand shot out in pure instinct to block it. Searing pain bolted all the way up her arm, forcing a scream from the very bottom of her chest, and her balance evaporated in a violent yank. Her senses dove into a tailspin of panic as she scrabbled wildly for purchase that didn't come, her molars slamming together in an ear-popping clack at the same time the ground rushed up to meet her. She tried to roll over, to push her way to hands and knees so she could at least try to get upright and get the hell out of here, but then her panic dug in with all its teeth.

She couldn't move.

"*Savannah!*" Cole's voice ripped through the darkness, but the burning smoke made it impossible to get a visual on anything, much less her partner. She struggled in a second, more desperate attempt to move. Burning agony took possession of her left arm, turning the call for help in her brain into another guttural scream.

"Mayday, mayday, mayday, Everett to command. Firefighter down, rear hallway, Charlie side. Partial ceiling collapse, no visual on the man down. Requesting immediate assistance. *Now.*"

Cole's radio transmission echoed in her ears. Reflexively, Savannah sucked in a breath, desperate for oxygen to relieve the steel band of pressure cranking tighter around her chest. The filthy taste of smoke invaded her mouth, scraping her already raw throat on its straight shot down her windpipe.

Her lungs constricted, rejecting all the smoke in a spasm of coughs that wracked her body, making her vision blink in and out, but no, no, *no*. She wasn't going down like this. She was going to get out of here. She was tough. She was . . .

Dizziness swam through Savannah's head as she struggled for breath, only to come up short. Panic resurfaced, cold fingers of dread slithering into her rib cage to snuff out what was left of her breath, and everything around her shrank into darkness.

Chapter Twenty-Five

Savannah . . . Jesus Christ, baby, come on. Wake up . . .

O'Keefe, get a goddamn gurney over here! You're gonna need a backboard . . .

Okay, Nelson. Hang in there. We're going to get you to Fairview Hospital. On my count, Rachel. Three, two, go . . .

Reality drifted back to Savannah in slow, sticky increments. Her head felt as if she'd been on a twenty-four-hour bender at a tequila bar, her temples throbbing and her eyes scorched dry. Her lungs weighed in at about thirty pounds apiece, and something pinched at her face—was it her mask? God, she needed to get up. She reached up to move whatever was pressing against her cheeks in order to check her surroundings.

The ripping pain in her arm made her table the recon in favor of a low groan.

"She's up!" came a familiar voice from her side, and Rachel slid into Savannah's line of sight wearing an ill-fitting smile. "Hey, girl. Welcome back. Try to be still, okay? It's me, Rachel. Can you tell me if anything hurts?"

"My arm." Whoa. Did that three-packs-a-day smoker's rasp belong to her? She blinked, her surroundings coming into focus more quickly now despite the gap in her memory of how she'd landed in the back of the ambo. "What happened?" And why was she wearing an oxygen mask?

Rachel paused. "You got a little banged up on a call, that's all. We're taking you to Fairview Hospital."

"I . . ." Savannah frowned, struggling to remember. Okay, yeah. She and Cole had gone to breakfast at Scarlett's, planning out when to go sit down with Captain Westin. But then there had been a building fire . . . a bar? No, a nightclub, with the dead-bolted rear entry and a silver sports car in the back lot . . . she and Cole had gone inside . . .

Oh my God.

Fear punched through Savannah's chest, jackknifing her off the gurney and sending the monitors behind her into a frenzy of furious beeps and blips. "Cole! Where's Everett?" she blurted, the morning's events hitting her in full force. Well, most of them, anyway. After she'd been clobbered by whatever had fallen on her in that back hallway, things were a bit blurry.

"Hold on, Nelson! He's fine." Rachel flattened her palm over the center of Savannah's T-shirt to guide her back to the gurney, and for such a petite woman, girlfriend packed some ridiculous strength. "He hauled you out of the nightclub after you were injured, but he's totally fine."

She exhaled hard enough to see stars. "What about the guy? The one we went in to rescue?"

"Stations Six and Thirteen rolled up on the scene just as Everett got you out. The paramedics from Six took your guy so we could take you, but he looked pretty stable last I saw."

"Oh. Okay." The word came out in a throaty whisper, relief making her sag against the flat mattress on the gurney. Her lungs felt as if a hippopotamus had parked itself squarely in the center of her chest for an extended vacation, and her left wrist throbbed in time with her overactive pulse. Bracing herself, Savannah worked up her focus, letting her eyes do a full body scan. Although she was still wearing her boots and bunker pants, her coat had been removed, her left arm heavily bundled in a temporary splint from just below her elbow to her fingertips.

"What happened?" she croaked, and even though Rachel's hesitation lasted for only a second, it was enough. "No bullshit, Harrison. What am I looking at here?"

Rachel bit her lip, but seemed to know better than to sweeten up the answer to Savannah's question. "Part of the ceiling collapsed in the back of the nightclub, and a pretty big piece of Sheetrock fell on you. It looks like you lifted your arm to try and shield yourself, which probably saved you from a concussion. Maybe worse. The bad news is, the impact did a number on your wrist and the debris blocked the hall. It made it a little tough to get to you right away."

"I was stuck," she said, her memory providing a brief, fuzzy snippet. "I tried to move so I could get myself out, but . . ."

"You took a feed and blacked out from the smoke inhalation," Rachel finished. "Not gonna lie, sweetie. Passing off your mask was a bonehead move. You scared the shit out of us, losing consciousness like that. I've never seen Everett move so fast."

Savannah's heart dropped. "He knows I'm okay, right? Like you said, I'm just a little"—she paused, in dire need of a breath—"Banged up."

"He knows your vitals weren't critical when we got you on board, but I'm sure as soon as the fire is under control, you can expect visitors at the hospital. It helps that you're alert now, but I'm sure the docs in the ED will run the works on your walnut, just to be sure. As for that arm . . ."

"I'll live." As if the limb in question had suddenly sprouted a will of its own, Savannah's wrist began to throb beneath the splint. "I'm sorry I scared everyone, but I really do feel okay."

Rachel smiled and rolled her pretty blue eyes. "Sell stupid someplace else, Nelson. I've seen enough people in pain to know one when I see one. Now what do you say we get your secondary assessment done so I can start a line and give you some fentanyl. Do you have any drug allergies?"

Savannah sighed, too tired and too busted to fight back. Her arm was starting to ache like a bitch. "No."

She let Rachel prod and poke—that IV freaking *hurt*—and gave her friend carte blanche permission to pass on the details of her medical condition to everyone at Eight once they got to Fairview Hospital. This day so wasn't supposed to have shaken out like this, with her getting slam-dunked by a hunk of flaming Sheetrock, Cole probably (rightfully) pissed enough to spit venom about the mask thing, and Captain Westin still unaware of Oz's involvement in the two fires that had clearly been set on purpose.

Wait . . . "Hey, Rach?" Savannah blinked, her eyelids suddenly heavy.

"Oooh, looks like that fentanyl is kicking in. You feeling okay?" Rachel asked from beside her, lifting her gaze to check Savannah's vitals on the monitor.

"Mmm-hmm." In fact, she probably felt a little *too* okay, considering the full ten-second lag of her whole thoughts-to-words ratio right now. "The fire at the nightclub. Are there any updates yet?"

Rachel chuffed out a disbelieving laugh. "Nelson, we've been in the rig for twelve minutes, and you just lost a round of full-contact dodgeball with a burning nightclub ceiling. Are you seriously asking me for an update on a scene?"

"Yeah," Savannah insisted, partly to keep her waning focus in place and partly because she needed to know. "The guy . . . in the back . . . he said something weird about batteries igniting. Does anyone know how the fire started?"

Jeez, how was she so tired all of a sudden? She had to wake up. This was important.

"Batteries? That's a new one on me." Rachel's auburn brows furrowed. "All I know is that I heard Oz say something about crappy electrical. Why?"

Savannah willed herself to stay alert, but her eyelids had other ideas.

"That's what I was afraid of," she murmured, and drifted into darkness.

All the way to Fairview Hospital, Cole saw nothing but Savannah, limp and unconscious and sprawled over the floor of that nightclub, and the image made him want to kick the shit out of something. Namely himself, for not drawing a hard line about her taking her goddamn mask back. He was pissed at her, too—Christ, it had been an epically stupid move to part with such vital equipment, even if the paramedics at Six said it had helped the nightclub guy immensely.

But now she was on a gurney, somewhere in the belly of the emergency department, and Cole was right back to square one with wanting to kick the shit out of something.

He swung Engine Eight into the hospital's side lot, reserved for emergency vehicles, right next to Station Eight's ambo. Although his instincts had screeched to find a way to ride with Savannah during transport, protocol dictated that everyone at Eight had to stay on the scene of the nightclub fire long enough to finish the call. As soon as the blaze had been under control, dispatch had taken the entire house out of service so they could drive to the hospital. O'Keefe had radioed an update that Savannah was awake and stable, and while Cole's relief had practically made him dizzy, his other emotions were pinballing through him equally hard.

Savannah had terrified the shit out of him today. She might be fearless, but she wasn't fucking bulletproof.

And he couldn't lose her.

Cole tamped down the emotions threatening to commandeer both his brain and his body. He cut a direct path through Fairview Hospital's ED with Donovan, Crews, and Jonesey right beside him, zeroing in on the spot where Rachel and O'Keefe sat in the waiting room.

"What's the update?" he managed, his pulse pumping a fresh wave of adrenaline through him at the serious looks on both paramedics' faces.

"She's stable," O'Keefe said, smart to lead off with the good. "Her vitals are decent for someone who took such a nasty feed. But with the LOC, they're going for a full workup, and her wrist injury isn't a scratch. The docs are with her right now."

"But she's alert, right? She'll be fine?" Hope swelled in Cole's chest, like a bucket being filled to critical mass.

"Yeah," Rachel said, sending his relief spilling in every direction. "I gave her some fentanyl in the rig," she added. "It made her pretty woozy at the end of the ride, but she's a fighter. She was even asking me for scene updates on the cause of the fire before the meds kicked in."

Donovan chuffed out a laugh. "That sounds like her. Little badass."

Rachel's words trickled into Cole's brain, the tiny hairs on the back of his neck beginning to stir. "What about the guy? The one we pulled out of the office at the club?"

"He's stable, although the triage nurse said he's asthmatic, so he's a little roughed up right now," O'Keefe said, nodding toward the triage desk. "I think I saw O'Halloran head back a few minutes ago to grab a statement from him, although Oz said he thought this looked like faulty electrical, so I'd bet it's just a formality."

Anger slithered down Cole's spine. *No way. Not this time.*

"Do me a favor," he said, channeling every ounce of his effort into his inhale. "Come find me if there's any word on Nelson. I've got to take care of something."

Before the others could put voice to their shocked expressions, Cole's boots were in motion on the linoleum. A ten-second Q&A with the triage nurse had him moving toward one of the curtained areas, where Brett O'Halloran stood making notes at the nurse's station.

"Hey, Everett. Looks like you guys had a helluva fire this morning. How's your candidate doing?"

"She's stable. They're still working her up." Cole's brain screamed at him to focus on anything other than the image of Savannah on that nightclub floor. "How's this guy?"

O'Halloran shifted into business mode, smoothing a hand over his FPD blues. "Grateful as hell that you and your partner showed up when you did. I guess he left early last night with a headache and came back to do the books this morning. Wasn't even supposed to be there."

Of course not. No witnesses made arson easier to cover up. "Did he say he saw anything unusual?"

"He's pretty out of it," O'Halloran admitted. "I guess he smelled the smoke from the back office and went to check it out. He said the fire spread really fast. By the time the alarms went off, his exit path was compromised. He went into the office to break the window and signal for help, but the smoke got him first."

"He didn't say anything about how he thought the fire might've started?" Cole knew he was pressing, but he was too far gone to give a shit.

This fire could've killed a civilian, not to mention any of the firefighters at Eight. If foul play was a factor, he was getting to the bottom of it. Right fucking now.

No matter *who* was involved.

"That's kind of more your department than mine," O'Halloran said, his brows-up expression indicating he'd noticed Cole's interest, loud and clear. "Why, you got a hunch here?"

Cole tugged a hand through his sweat-damp hair in an effort to buy both time and composure. "He just mentioned something about batteries when we were dragging him out. It seemed a little weird, that's all."

"Funny, he said that to me, too," O'Halloran said, flipping through his notebook. "Yeah. Said he thought he saw a pile of nine-volt batteries by one of the electrical panels in the club, burning like crazy. I guess the bouncers and managers use 'em in their headsets, but apparently they went up in record time and took everything around them along for the ride."

Cole's breath jammed in his windpipe. Batteries conducted electricity, even when they weren't plugged into anything, and on nine-volts, the positive and negative posts were close enough to kiss. Add something to complete the current, like maybe a handful of steel wool, and a bunch of flammable debris—or better yet, alcohol from the bar as an accelerant to spread the flames quickly—and bam. You'd have a hell of a fire, with nothing left behind to make the blaze look suspicious.

Even if it was arson.

"Whoa. Everett, you okay? You look like you just saw a ghost."

Cole nodded, already pivoting back toward the waiting room.

"Yeah, O'Halloran. I'm solid. I just need to find my squad lieutenant. Right now."

Chapter Twenty-Six

By the time Cole reached the waiting room, his anger was a living, breathing thing, taking over his body and torching his composure down to the bricks. He bypassed the furrowed brows and confused expressions of his station-mates—all present save Captain Westin—zeroing in on Oz's flinty gray stare.

"A word, Lieutenant," he hissed past his teeth, not stopping to see the guy's response as he continued out to the ambulance bay. As furious as he was, Cole's sewn-in instinct to keep dirty laundry in-house still ran strong, and he didn't stop until he was sure they were in a spot where no one could overhear them without being seen.

Oz crossed his arms over his sweat-stained T-shirt, a scissor-sharp frown covering his face beneath a layer of soot and stubble. "You may be jacked up from this fire, Everett, but you'd better step careful when you're talking to me."

Just like that, the tight knot of emotion in Cole's belly snapped. "And you'd better step careful, period. Are you covering up arson, Lieutenant?"

"Are you fucking your candidate?"

The words knocked into Cole unexpectedly, rendering him too shocked to move, let alone scrape up any words to speak, and Oz took full tactical advantage of Cole's surprise. He covered the pavement between them in only four steps, nailing Cole with a stare that never considered being anything less than hateful.

"What's the matter? Cat got your tongue?" Oz waved a hand, his expression sliding into a humorless smile. "I suppose it doesn't matter, since we both know the answer."

Cole grasped at his wits, although his slamming heartbeat made it a hell of a tough go. "You don't know shit," he said. Calling Oz's bluff was his best strategy, the only way to regain the upper hand.

Not that Oz was going to let that happen. "Please. Unlike you, I know enough to have real evidence when I start slinging accusations around." He whipped his cell phone from the pocket of his bunker pants, tapping the screen to life. "You and Nelson should be more discreet when you get handsy in the parking lot after shift. Oh, and when you meet up at Scarlett's. Anyone happening by could take a picture of the two of you kissing. Although gosh, you lovebirds looked sweet this morning."

Cole's blood turned subarctic in his veins. "You *followed* us?"

"I just happened to be in the right place at the right time. I can't say I blame you for balling her, really. Nelson might be a righteous pain in the ass, but she's not hard on the eyes. Bet she's a goddamn hellcat in the sack, too. But inter-house relations lead to all sorts of trouble. Relations with a candidate?" Oz paused to let out a low whistle. "Your careers could really hit the skids over a scandal this big."

Fear and something a whole lot darker climbed the back of Cole's throat. "Are you threatening me?"

Everything about Oz's expression said yes, from his flat, furious glare to the tight-fisted stance testing the hard limits of Cole's personal space.

But then he took a step back. "'Course not. I'm simply

reviewing house rules with you, Everett. In case you've forgotten how things go in the chain of command."

Cole's laugh was all disbelief. "You've got balls of solid rock, talking to me about house rules. You're committing *arson.*"

Oz's stare flashed over, dark and unrelenting. "And what've you got to prove such a weighty claim, hmm? A bunch of threadbare conjecture full of maybes and could-bes, that's what. The only time I've ever been to those scenes was on official FFD business, and I guarantee you can't prove otherwise because it's just not so. I've been fighting fires since before you even got your first hand job, son. My word *will* wash over yours, every single time."

"Maybe we should let the arson unit decide that, huh?" It was Cole's last-ditch attempt, but hell if it didn't bull's-eye its mark.

Oz froze, only for a second before his sneer curled into place. "The one your girl's brother works for, you mean? That's a bit of a conflict of interest. Especially since if you cast that stone, I'll have no choice but to throw back."

"And what if I'm willing to take the heat?" Cole asked.

This time, Oz didn't hesitate. "Then you'll lose your career, and so will your sweetheart. If you go pointing fingers, I'll tell Chief Williams that when I stumbled on your indiscretion, you threatened to ruin my name. Hell, everyone in that waiting room just saw you jawing off at me. By the time I'm done telling my side of this story and splashing the proof of your affair all over the FFD, no fire department in the country will see either one of your résumés without these photos stapled right to the top."

He stepped up, his stare as insidious as it was full of promise, and in that moment, Cole's strategy disintegrated.

"You've got nothing on me, Everett. No facts, no angle, no options. If you want to run your mouth anyway, go right ahead. But make no mistake. You choose that road, and I will burn your career to the fucking ground."

"I've got to be honest, Miss Nelson. With luck like yours, I'm tempted to send you to Vegas. After you take a few days to recover, of course."

After six hours' worth of CAT scans and concussion protocol, Savannah thought Vegas sounded like a damned good plan. She rubbed the little bandage over the spot where the nurse had just taken out her IV, more ready than ever to get her pink slip from the ED. "Thanks, Doc. But I told you, I'm really no worse for wear."

"I'm not so sure about that," the doctor argued, albeit gently. "While you've been cleared of a head injury and you escaped with a nasty sprain to that wrist, you're still going to need to take it easy."

He reviewed her release orders with her, mostly emphasizing that she needed to wear the splint on her wrist for a few more weeks and that she'd probably feel like she'd been suplexed by a professional wrestler tomorrow. She nodded and signed off on the electronic chart, listening as the doc finished his spiel.

"But I can go back to work next shift, right?" Honestly, despite the fanfare of the last few hours, she didn't feel all *that* horrible now. The grogginess from the pain meds had worn off and the high dose of ibuprofen the nurse had given her had kicked in nice and steady. She'd go bat shit crazy sitting in her brother's place for five whole days, and it wasn't as if she'd never worked through a few muscle aches before.

The doctor's sigh wasn't unkind. "You'll be on limited duty with that wrist injury, but as long as you're feeling up to it, I don't see any reason why not. Now go home and get some rest. I'll let your ride know you're good to go."

Savannah pulled back, confused. "But my ride is a cab."

After she'd proven to the guys on engine that she was, in fact, absolutely unscathed and they should get their asses back to work, everyone at Eight had headed out. Rachel had come back in the rig to drop off Savannah's duffel, but since her car was still at the station, she figured she'd just cab it back to Brad's.

"I'm sorry," the doctor said, seeming equally confused. "One of your fellow firefighters was quite adamant about staying to take you home. He didn't want to disturb you while you rested, but . . . well, he looks quite concerned. I thought you knew he was waiting outside in the lobby."

Savannah sent up a tiny prayer of thanks that her vitals were no longer being monitored; otherwise they'd probably never spit her out of this place.

Cole really did have her back.

She released a shaky exhale, her cheeks prickling hard enough to signal her blush. "Oh. Right. Um, I guess you can go ahead and tell him it's fine to come back, then."

Savannah waited for the doctor to depart, gingerly removing her blue-and-white hospital gown to trade it for the yoga pants and T-shirt in her bag. She was fumbling with the laces on her cross-trainers when the sound of the opening door made her pause.

"Hey," Cole said, and holy shit, he looked *awful*. "Here, let me help you."

"Oh, no, you don't need to. I'm . . ." She trailed off, her heart squeezing tight as he stepped in close to cradle her face between his palms. Worry lines tugged his sandy brows into a *V*, his green eyes dark with an emotion she couldn't name but felt deep in her belly as he looked at her.

"Cole, what's the matter?" She tried to pull back to look at him, her pulse tapping in true concern, but he dropped his forehead over hers, his expression bordering on desperate.

"Please, Savannah. This morning scared the hell out of

me, and everything else is just . . . I can't . . . I need to have you close, okay? Just me and you and nothing else right now. Please."

"Oh." The word collapsed past her lips. As much as she hadn't wanted to admit it before, the day really had taken a toll on her, too. The only place she wanted to be was wrapped up in Cole's arms, reassuring him that she really was fine. "Okay. Just me and you."

Wordlessly, they gathered her things and made their way to a waiting taxi. He ushered her into the backseat before sliding in after her, and Savannah belatedly realized that he was still in his bunker pants and T-shirt from this morning's call.

"You've been here this whole time?" she asked, her lips parting in shock.

Cole nodded. "The doctor said you fell asleep after everyone from Eight went back to the house. I didn't want to wake you, but I couldn't leave, so I took a personal day and Donovan said he'd run my Jeep back to my place after shift tomorrow."

"Cole, I promise I'm fine." She lifted his hands to her breastbone, pressing his palms over her heart as proof.

His exhale was slow and unsteady. "I know, sweetheart, but I'm not. So do me a favor and just let me hold you until I get that way, okay?"

Savannah settled in at his side, nestling against the warmth of his body as the short cab ride to his place slipped away. After they arrived in front of his building, she let him guide her all the way to his door. Gently steering her over the threshold, Cole lowered her bag to the floor in the same spot where his own bag usually went.

"Are you hungry? You probably haven't eaten all day," he said, making a move toward the kitchen. But instinct had her reaching out, capturing his wrist with her good hand.

"I don't want food, Cole."

He froze into place in the hallway, his body bowstring tight beneath her touch. "What do you want?"

"Truth?" She stepped into the circle of his arms, pressing a soft kiss to his neck just above his thrumming pulse point. "I want a shower."

"That's not what I meant when I said I wanted you close," he grated, although his heated exhale betrayed the words. "You're supposed to be taking it easy, Savannah."

"But we've already established that I'm fine. And anyway, I'm not kidding. Between the fire and the hospital, I really just want to get this day off me."

"Okay," he agreed slowly. "But a shower is probably a bad plan with that splint. Why don't I start a bath?"

Savannah's first compulsion was to laugh—after all, she was about as far from the bubble-bath type as it got. But Cole looked so serious, so dead set on taking care of her, that she just nodded. "That sounds good."

She followed him to the master bathroom, watching as he turned on both faucets at the foot of the oval-shaped soaking tub along the far wall. He pulled off his turnout gear, keeping his T-shirt and uniform pants in place, then crossed the bathroom tiles to skim his hands over her shoulders. Cheeks burning from the sheer intensity on his face, Savannah reached down to fumble her way out of her clothes.

Cole's fingers tightened on her shoulders, just enough to stay her movements. "Stop."

She opened her mouth to argue, but that needful expression he'd worn at the hospital was back, only now it was magnified.

"I know you're tough, Savannah. But please let me do this. Let me take care of you."

With the gentlest of motions, he lifted her T-shirt over her head, letting it flutter to the floor. The rest of her clothes quickly followed, her heart beating faster as Cole led her over to the bathtub and helped her in. Getting situated with the splint was a little awkward, but once she propped it over a rolled-up towel on the ledge of the tile surround by the wall, she was able to slide all the way into the warm water.

"Ohhh." Okay, so maybe she needed to relax a little more than she'd thought. The steamy water sent her muscles into an instant unwind, and when Cole's hands followed over her skin, she sighed again in pure pleasure.

"Good?" he asked, reaching for the soap he'd grabbed from the adjacent shower.

"Yes, but . . ." Savannah stopped, biting her bottom lip. Clearly, today had rattled him pretty hard. Letting someone take care of her wasn't necessarily in her wheelhouse, but if that was what Cole needed, she could do it.

She trusted him. She needed him.

She loved him.

"Yes," she said, melting into his touch. He ran his fingers over her neck, washing her shoulders, her uninjured arm, and her back with care. His palms slid around to her rib cage, skimming the part of her torso above the now-soapy water, and her breath hitched in her throat.

"You're getting soaked," Savannah pointed out. Water stained the side of both his T-shirt and his pants, but Cole dismissed it with a shake of his head.

"I don't care." He reached for her shoulder, but the heat blooming between her thighs from his closeness, from the intimacy of his touch even though it hadn't been overtly sexual, made her catch his wrist.

"Get in the tub with me."

"I—" Cole broke off. "You're supposed to be resting."

"I am resting," she said, gesturing down at her very naked body stretched out along the porcelain. "But I'd rather be resting with you."

"Savannah." His eyes glittered so dark, they turned

evergreen. "If I get into that bathtub with you, resting will be the furthest thing from what we end up doing."

Her body clenched at the thought, right along with her heart. "I know. Now are you getting in, or am I coming out to get you?"

Cole stood, a groan rumbling in the back of his throat and his clothes finding the floor by way of a few economical lifts and tugs. With her heart beating a rapid tattoo of anticipation against her breastbone, Savannah slid forward, allowing him enough room to lower himself into the bathtub behind her. Cole's right arm slipped around her body, his left gently securing hers out of reach of the water. A hard breath burst through her lungs, leaving her lips on a moan, and oh God, she'd never felt so hot or right or cared for in her whole life.

"Savannah." Cole's whisper coasted past her ear on a warm exhale, and she heard the unspoken question in his ragged tone.

She lifted her chin to brush a kiss over his jaw. "Yes, Cole. I'm sure. Take care of me. *Please.*"

His right arm tightened around her body, his fingers sweeping up. The ridge of his cock pressed hard against her lower back, and even though he was obviously as aroused as she was, he didn't rush. Keeping his easy grip on her left side to anchor her, Cole cupped her breast from behind with his right hand, skimming his thumb over the tight peak of her nipple.

"Oh God," she whispered, arching her spine to maximize the contact.

But Cole lightened his touch. "Easy, baby. I promise I've got you."

Savannah stilled. He returned his thumb to her nipple, letting his forefinger join in a slow, seductive roll. Her breathing quickened in time with her pulse, but she forced herself to simply slow down and let him explore her. She dropped her chin, watching as his fingers circled and slid, first over one aching nipple, then the other. His touches were both sexy and reverent, his breath strong and steady over her shoulder, and she let herself drown in the feel of each one.

"Cole." She lifted her right arm, linking it around his neck to keep him close. Their bodies fused together, his chest to her back, and when his clever fingers moved all the way under the water, Savannah's knees fell open in invitation.

Cole didn't refuse. Keeping his movements soft and slow, his hand traveled over the flat of her belly. She bit down on the urge to cant her hips upward, to thrust wildly against his touch, to drag him out of the bathtub so she could skip everything else and have him inside her right this second. He moved his fingers lower, until finally, mercifully, he reached the apex of her thighs beneath the warmth of the bathwater.

"Savannah." Her name crossed his lips with pure intensity, and he slid one finger down the length of her sex.

"*Ah.*" Savannah's voice formed more of a raspy, needful sound than an actual word. "Please. I want—"

"I know. Just stay with me. Right here," Cole said, letting his finger follow the same path again on a slow, sinuous circuit. Over and over, he teased and traced, her clit throbbing harder with each pass over the rest of her.

Savannah's knees parted as wide as the tub would allow, her pulse pounding in desire that bordered on despair. She pressed back into Cole's chest, letting him bear the weight of her upper body, another thick moan escaping from her as he parted her folds to touch her where she needed it most.

"That's it," he whispered, working the swollen bud in tight strokes. "You can let go, Savannah. I've got you. Come for me."

He increased the pressure between her legs, sending a tremor from the depth of her belly. Dropping his left hand into the water, Cole pushed into her sex with one smooth thrust of his fingers, and the sensation combined with his words sent her over the edge.

She climaxed on a gasp, her body vibrating in waves of release so bright, she trembled. Cole scaled back on his touch, holding her close as she came back to her body. But as intense as her orgasm had been, still, she wanted more.

Savannah wanted *him*. Pure and simple.

Indefinitely.

"Cole," she whispered, tilting her head to look at him. "I want to have you, too. Please. Take me to bed."

Chapter Twenty-Seven

Cole lifted Savannah out of the bathtub with every intention of giving her exactly what she'd asked for even though he knew damn well he had no business touching her. But after the train wreck of emotions that had been crashing through him ever since he'd crossed the threshold of that nightclub fire, the only thing he'd been able to think of was having her close. All the anger, all the despair and the outright fear—none of it threatened to bury him alive as long as Savannah was close.

He might have no control otherwise, but he could take care of her, just in this moment. Just him and her.

Although he'd needed Savannah in his arms so badly it knocked the breath from his lungs, he hadn't planned on having her in his bed right now, too, especially after this morning. But Cole's composure didn't stand a chance against her seductive request, and he couldn't deny how deeply he wanted her.

Savannah was the only thing keeping his emotions from unraveling at the seams. She was his calm. His control. His center.

She was his everything.

He lowered her feet to the bath mat, making sure she had

her balance before reaching for a towel. He dried her off
with a quick pass of the cotton, then guided her down the
hallway to his bedroom. Early evening light slanted through
the blinds, illuminating the space around them in soft,
golden tones that played on Savannah's tawny skin, and
Christ above, Cole had never seen anything so beautiful in
his entire life.

"Come here," she said, leaning back over the bed. The
sheets were rumpled from the night before, and Savannah
nestled beneath them, beckoning.

Need surged through him, reckless and hot. Her nipples
beaded into hard peaks, her sex swollen and slick with
arousal, and his cock jerked almost painfully against his
belly. Cole wanted to take it slow, to maintain the last shreds
of the control that had been slipping from his tenuous grasp
all day—hell, ever since he'd laid eyes on Savannah five
weeks ago.

But one "please" from her perfect, heart-shaped mouth
was all it took. Cole's last thread of control shattered in the
face of his need to have her, and he whipped his nightstand
drawer open, rolling a condom over his erection in record
time. Parting her legs with both palms, he sank into her to
the hilt, barely stopping to revel in the squeeze of her tight
inner muscles around his cock before starting to thrust.

Savannah threw her head back, moaning her approval.
"Oh God. Oh *God,* don't stop." She knotted her legs around
his waist. Canting her hips to meet the rhythm of his thrusts,
she rocked against him, and he met every move with nothing but wild need. She was so gorgeous, so strong and
fearless yet with her own brand of sweetness beneath, that
Cole was lost. He filled her again and again, drawing her to
the edge of pleasure just so he could push her over, and
when she came on a scream, his own climax razored up
from the base of his spine. He pushed into her one last time,
the wet heat of her core still gripping his cock with the

waves of her release as he called out her name and free-fell
into his own.

A few minutes passed in the hush of slower movements
and softening breath. Cole pulled back, but only far enough
to angle his shoulders against the mattress, tucking Savannah close to his side. Her breathing grew deeper, and even
though he'd tested her strength way more than he'd intended
to today, he wrapped his arms around her even tighter.

As much as Cole knew he needed to, he simply couldn't
bring himself to let her go.

. . . Mayday, mayday, mayday! Firefighter down . . .
. . . I will burn your fucking career to the ground . . .
. . . Cole, I'm sure . . . take care of me, please . . .

Cole's eyes flew open, air expanding his lungs on a sharp
inhale. The final scraps of daylight cast deepening shadows
over his bedroom, and the last twelve hours rolled through
his brain in a slideshow of emotions he tried desperately to
keep in check.

Oz was deliberately setting fires, or at the very least, covering them up. And not only was there nothing Cole could
do about it, but his career—not to mention Savannah's—sat
in the center of the dirty lieutenant's palm, just waiting for
Oz to crush it if Cole so much looked at him sideways.

No strategy in the fucking universe could make this right
without destroying them both in the process.

"Mmm . . . oh, ow." Savannah stirred, her forehead creasing in obvious discomfort as she rolled beneath the covers
and opened her eyes in a series of slow blinks.

The unease in Cole's gut tangled worse. Christ, he was
such a shit for letting his emotions lead him into bringing
her back here instead of taking her home so she could rest.
"Take it easy. Here."

He hooked an arm around her rib cage, guiding her slowly upright. Her bare body was warm against his, and despite his edginess, it took all of his willpower to make himself pull back to look for his clothes.

"I'm okay," she said, her voice thick with sleep and raspy from inhaling all that smoke. "Just a little sore."

Cole slid a pair of jeans over his hips and shouldered his way into a clean T-shirt. "I'll grab your bag. You should probably take a few more of those high-grade ibuprofen and put something in your stomach." Their breakfast at Scarlett's felt like eons ago rather than a little more than twelve hours.

The same breakfast where Oz had captured those damning pictures of him and Savannah kissing. They'd been in public, for fuck's sake, and Cole *knew* better. How could he have been careless enough to let go of his common sense so completely?

The answer was sitting right in front of him, in all her sweet and sexy glory.

Cole took a deep breath, although his lungs made him earn every last molecule. "Be right back."

The quick round trip between his bedroom and his kitchen did little to alleviate his growing dread, and he capped it off with another tour down the hall to throw some sandwiches together while Savannah got dressed. A few minutes later, she padded into the kitchen, wearing yet another of his T-shirts over her low-slung jeans.

"That's the best-looking ham and cheese sandwich I've ever seen," she said, smiling even though her body language radiated full caution.

Sure. He was plenty observant *now*. "Here. Go ahead and get started, and I'll grab some water so you can take that pill. Now that we're up, we need to talk."

Cole forced his feet toward the fridge, but three quick steps had Savannah blocking his path.

"Look, you might as well just jump right in and say it. I know you're mad at me for the stunt I pulled with my mask this morning, and I know I really scared you. I'm so sorry, Cole. I wasn't thinking, and—"

"I'm not upset about the mask." The words burned with the metallic aftertaste of a lie, and he inhaled, trying to tamp down his welling emotions. "I mean, I'm upset about that, too, but . . . Savannah, Oz knows."

Her lashes fanned all the way up in shock. "He knows we're onto him?"

"He knows we're sleeping together."

"He . . . what?" Savannah whispered, frozen to her spot on the kitchen floor. "How could he know that? We never told anybody."

"He doesn't just know. He's got pictures. He must have gotten suspicious that I knew something was off about the fires after I asked him all those questions last week, and I guess he started following me. Probably to keep tabs on whether I went back to any of the scenes again, but . . ."

It had taken all of half a day for Oz to catch him in the parking lot with Savannah, exchanging that textbook and a bunch of innuendo-laden stares before they'd impulsively driven off to his place.

"Oz isn't an idiot," Cole said, biting down on the thought that at least that made one of them. "He put two and two together and started snapping pictures, the latest of them from this morning."

Savannah's pretty face turned pale. "In front of Scarlett's?"

He nodded. "Oz is threatening to tell Chief Williams about our relationship if I say anything about the suspected arsons. He'll use it as leverage to get me kicked out of the

FFD, claiming that I threatened to ruin his career if he blew the whistle on us being together."

A flicker of anger sparked in Savannah's shell-shocked expression. "But that's bullshit! He's setting *fires*, Cole. Indiscretion is a whole lot different from fucking arson!"

"And how do we really know he's committing arson?" Cole shot back.

"You've got to be kidding me." Savannah took a step back to stare at him. "You can't possibly doubt that Oz is involved in setting these fires after he just threatened to blackmail you."

"It has nothing to do with what I believe, Savannah," he said, his frustration climbing. "Other than the fact that he did both scene investigations, we still can't connect Oz to these fires in any way. There's no clear motive and he has a stellar record with the FFD, and the causes of both fires can be plausibly explained by something other than foul play. The only thing that matters here is what we can prove in black-and-white, and right now, that's nothing."

"That's not what Brad said," she insisted, and shock sent Cole's pulse into a spiral.

"You went to your brother with this?"

His composure slipped another notch. Getting her brother involved jumped the chain of command, not to mention betraying the hell out of her word. If the FFD brass opened a formal investigation on these fires now, Oz wouldn't hesitate to jam a high-res picture of Cole and Savannah's intimate lip-lock into every in-box in the chief's office, and both of their spots at Station Eight would go into the toilet at the same time.

Savannah winced, clearly hearing her words on a five-second emotion delay. "Sort of. I didn't say anything specific about Oz. I just asked Brad what might make an AC unit burn up like the one at the warehouse, but I told him it was a textbook scenario for an electrical fire."

"And he told you he thought it could be arson." Her brother couldn't be an idiot. Textbook cases were supposed to be just that. Textbook. The guy's red flags were probably waving like mad.

"Isn't that all the more reason to say something?"

Cole's irritation snapped, hot and low in his gut. "It's all the more reason we should be watching our asses. We had a plan, and it didn't include going to your brother for a reason."

She hiked her chin. "I know, but our jobs are on the line. Yours *and* mine. I needed to be sure."

"You said you were sure when we agreed to stick to the chain of command and tell Westin," he said, unable to keep his frustration from seeping into his tone. This whole scenario was spinning out of control, and fast. "You can't just lead the way with your emotions all the time and do whatever you please."

"I'm not stupid. I was careful when I talked to Brad." Savannah moved to jam her hands into her hips, yelping in pain as her splinted hand made contact with her body, and the reminder of her injury twisted something dark and deep in Cole's rib cage.

"Right. Like you were careful yesterday? Jesus, Savannah, breaking protocol and taking off your mask could've killed you, but still, you jumped right in without thinking. Our careers are *absolutely* on the line here. We can't afford to make knee-jerk decisions without thinking."

"Wait . . ." She paused, her eyes narrowing for just a second before going round with realization. "Are you saying you don't even want to go to Westin now? You just want to sit on these fires and pretend nothing's going on?"

Another thread of his already questionable composure frayed, the slam of his heartbeat warning him that he was dangerously close to redlining. But losing his grip now would spell certain disaster, and he dug up the defenses that had kept him on the straight and narrow for the last nine years.

"We can't prove that *anything's* going on. If we say something right now, to Westin—to anybody—we'll be committing career suicide for nothing. Oz can counter every accusation we'd make on those fires, and he's got hard proof we're involved with each other. Even if he's guilty, he'll walk, and he'll ruin us for our trouble. We can't win."

"Of course." Savannah laughed, although there was no humor in it. "It all comes down to strategy. God, Cole. We can't just put this under your emotionless microscope and wait for the perfect plan to come sliding into place, all nice and neat and feeling-free."

As if they'd heard the challenge crossing her lips, every last one of the emotions Cole had been trying to control bubbled up, edging toward the surface. "So it's better to just say screw the odds and the consequences, even though Oz has us by the short hairs? If we had proof, this would be different. Of course I'd fucking say something—I'd howl it at the goddamn moon. But I can't recklessly piss everything away when there's no chance he'll go down for these fires. It's not just my job on the line. It's who I am. It's all I know."

"Believe me, I get it—"

"No." The word shot from his mouth, shattering another layer of his composure. "You don't. You've been on the job for less than eight weeks. I've been a firefighter for eight *years*. I left my family, my home, every single thing I ever knew so I could throw all I had into being here. Doing this. I don't have anything else."

Savannah's spine went rigid. "And you think I do?"

"You have options," Cole said. All the fear and anger and despair he'd been trying so hard to control rushed at him now, pouring out in his words. "You have a family who loves you. Your father is a battalion chief, for Chrissake. You can go back to Texas, join the Dallas Fire Department, and not have this mess between us follow you there."

She flinched. "So my job isn't as important as yours. You're so certain you've got more to lose."

He rammed a hand through his hair, and God help him, despite the look of sheer hurt on Savannah's face, he couldn't fight the bulletproof defenses screaming at him to buckle down and kill all the emotions threatening to end his career.

He had to cram this back and focus, not feel. If he let his emotions rule his actions, he'd never survive.

"I don't just have more to lose. You and I might have made some impulsive decisions together, but it's my name Oz is out to ruin. If I go spouting off at the mouth about a twenty-two-year rescue squad veteran without proof, no matter how guilty he is, I will lose *everything*. My firehouse, my livelihood. My life. And I'll never get it back."

Savannah stood completely still on the kitchen tiles, her eyes betraying the depth of her hurt for just a split second before her brass-knuckle demeanor roared back to life.

"Well," she said, turning on her heel toward the hallway. "At least you won't have to worry about any further repercussions from our impulsive *mess* of a relationship."

"Savannah—" he started, but she whirled back to nail him with a fiery stare.

"Do yourself a favor, Cole, and stop talking, since it seems to be what you want to do anyway. I may be brash and I may not always make the smartest calls, but I always had your back, just like you taught me. And even though it makes me a fool, I actually believed you had mine."

Her voice wavered, rasping over the last word to make it softer than the rest, but she squared her shoulders and continued, undaunted. "I might have a lot to learn as a firefighter. But there's one thing I do know. For all the mistakes I'll make being too headstrong or too bold, at least I'll never be a coward."

With that, Savannah picked up her bag and walked out the door.

Chapter Twenty-Eight

Savannah got to the lobby of Cole's building before she realized that she had no shoes on, no way to get home, and no reservations about crying in public. She had to be the biggest moron on the Eastern Seaboard. She hadn't even cried when she'd broken her ankle a couple of years ago—in three places, thank you very much—and now she was going to fall apart over a stupid broken heart?

Be tough, girl. Be . . .

Okay, nope. She wasn't tough. She wasn't tough at all.

She was a fucking sucker who'd trusted her heart to yet another person who didn't think she measured up.

Savannah needed to get out of there.

Gathering her wits even though her wrist was starting to hurt as much as her pride, she pulled her cross-trainers and her cell phone out of her duffel. Fumbling with one while dialing the other, she pulled up Brad's number and hit Send.

"Girl. Things must be at an all-time low if you're calling me from your shift." The sound of her brother's slow Texas drawl sent a potshot to Savannah's sternum, and really, what was with the waterworks?

"Actually, I'm not on shift," she managed, clearing her throat and steadying her voice with all her power. "It's kind of a long story. But can you do me a favor? Can you come get me and not ask any questions? Please?"

Brad's concern was an instant, palpable thing over the phone line. "Just tell me you're safe and not hurt."

"I'm okay." She bit her lip at the not hurt part, but Brad was going to see her splint soon enough anyway. Plus, at least *that* would heal.

How could she have believed that Cole had her back, that she belonged with him and at Station Eight, when all it had ever been was a lie?

"I'm okay," Savannah said again, forcing herself to believe it, if only for a minute.

"Just tell me where you are. I'm already on my way downstairs."

When Brad pulled his Ford F-150 up to the curb fifteen minutes later, Savannah had squashed her tears—thank God—but she was no closer to wrestling her way through the ten-car pileup of issues in front of her. Luckily, her arson investigator of a brother was too fixated on her heavily bandaged arm to notice the circles under her eyes or the bone-deep sadness that had to be showing on her face.

"Start talkin', sweet pea," he said, getting out of the truck and moving toward the passenger side.

Savannah couldn't help but let out a microscopic smile, although she couldn't back it up with any joy. "It's just a scratch. Looks worse than it is, but I got the rest of my shift off as a precaution," she answered, reaching for the handle of the F-150.

But her brother reached her first. "I know you're tough, but Duke would whip my ass from now 'til Sunday if I didn't open the door for a lady. Sadly for you, badass baby sisters do qualify."

She gave in and let her brother fuss over her—Brad had to know she'd cave at the first mention of their father, and anyway, she'd be just as concerned if her brother turned up with a splint on his wrist. Savannah got situated in the front of the truck while Brad got back behind the wheel and pulled away from the building. The sun had fully set, although she couldn't be quite sure when, and all of a sudden, the utter exhaustion she'd been holding at bay hit her like a six-ton wrecking ball. Savannah gave her brother the short and not-so-sweet (it was her, after all) version of how she'd been injured on this morning's call. Brad's jaw went granite-wall solid when she got to the part about passing off her mask, but at least he let her slide with a you're-lucky-you're-fine-but-don't-you-*ever*-do-that-again instead of the full riot act, which she was sure to get from Captain Westin anyway.

Provided she still had a house to go back to once she figured out how she was going to get out of this mess with Oz.

Brad pulled up to a stoplight, cutting her a look through the soft glow in the front of the truck. "Someone clearly picked you up from the ED, and just as clearly pissed you off good enough to call your old brother for a ride. I know you said no questions, and normally, I ain't one to pry, but . . . you want to talk about the rest of this?" he asked, hitching a thumb at the duffel between her feet.

For just a second, the whole story burned bright on Savannah's tongue. The truth needed to be told, and confessing all to Brad would definitely fast-track an investigation into Oz's wrongdoing.

So it was really a surprise when her instincts made her shake her head and say, "Not really, no."

"Okay," her brother said. "Let me know if you change your mind."

Savannah knew she needed to find a way to bring the facts to light. She was certain Oz was involved in this string of arsons, even if she couldn't prove it, and a man had nearly been killed this morning. But no matter how much her blowout with Cole stung, she couldn't deny that he'd been right about one thing.

Telling anyone what they'd uncovered was a massive risk, with life-altering stakes. And Savannah couldn't act on boldness alone. She was going to have to think long and hard to figure out how to proceed without destroying her career or Cole's. With no one at her back but me, myself, and I.

This time, she made it all the way to the bathroom in Brad's postage stamp of an apartment before the tears started to fall.

Cole rolled over and blinked the sleep from his eyes for a full ten seconds before he realized he'd never actually gone to bed. Technically, after about five hours of relentlessly searching for answers that he was fairly certain didn't exist, he'd tried to get some shut-eye. But Savannah's fresh-laundry scent had lingered all around him, and even after he'd changed every stitch of bedding including the comforter, he hadn't been able to loosen the thought of her from his mind long enough to actually drift off.

Forget a strategy. Cole was going to need a full-blown miracle to forget about this woman. Not to mention the fact that the lieutenant on the rescue squad he'd desperately wanted to be a part of was covering up arson, and there *still* wasn't a damn thing he could do about it that would stick.

Happy fucking Monday.

Cole's cell phone buzzed with an incoming text, and for a stupid, impulsive second, hope swelled in his chest. But he'd forgotten that Donovan had promised to return his Jeep today. At least the heads-up "I'm on my way" text would give Cole some time to slap together a pot of coffee and do a little damage control on his probably haggard appearance.

From the look on his best friend's face when Cole opened

the door ten minutes later, one out of two was going to have
to cut it.

"Damn, brother." Alex handed the keys to the Jeep over
with his blond brows notched sky-high. "You look like
pulverized shit."

"Thanks," Cole said, putting the keys on the small table
in the entryway. "Is Zoe downstairs waiting to give you a
ride home?"

Donovan shook his head, and not even the sight of his
buddy's loopy grin could kick Cole's mood out of the base-
ment. "Nah. She's on breakfast service at the soup kitchen,
so I'm going to run back to the firehouse from here to get
my bike. It's only six miles."

Leave it to Donovan to go big or go home. Or in this
case, go big while he was going home. "You want some
coffee before you hit the bricks?"

"Is that even a question?" Donovan asked, following
Cole into his kitchen. "Listen, all kidding about your appearance aside . . . I know yesterday's call kind of rattled
your cage. We were all a little off after what happened to
Nelson, but I didn't realize you were this jacked up."

"It was just a long day. I'll be good by next shift." Cole
reached for a pair of mugs from the cabinet, stamping out
the ache behind his breastbone and reaching for his focus.
But in his bid to get his shit together once and for all this
morning, he overcompensated with the coffee carafe, and
most of the splash meant for his cup ended up on the hem
of his T-shirt.

"Ah, shit." Cole slid the carafe back over the burner,
grabbing a dish towel to soak up the mess.

"Whoa, look out. You okay?" Donovan asked.

"Yeah, I just . . ." Cole tried to make his mouth form the
rest of his sentence, to tell Alex that he just needed to grab
another T-shirt and he'd be set, no harm, no foul.

But he'd snagged the very last one out of his drawer this morning. All of the others were MIA. Stolen by a determined, beautiful Southern woman who had snuck up on him and done the same thing to his heart.

And Cole had pushed her away—fuck, he'd completely shut down, just as he had nine years ago when he'd left Harvest Moon—because he'd been too damned scared to let himself take the risk and really feel.

Not anymore.

"No." The single syllable was all it took, and Cole's emotions rushed up after it like water flowing through a three-inch attack hose. "I'm actually not okay. I'm not even in the same universe as okay. I've been seeing Savannah for a couple of weeks now, and I'm pretty sure I'm in love with her, except Oz found out, and I think he's involved in arson. Only I can't prove it and I'm pretty sure he's going to destroy my career and now Savannah hates my guts and I don't really blame her."

Donovan's jaw unhinged. After a long second, he popped open the cabinet over the sink, grabbing two glasses and a bottle of Jameson from the shelf.

"It's eight o'clock in the morning," Cole pointed out, and it was kind of dumb that he'd blurt out his most intimate secrets in one ridiculous, rambling go, then be all rational in the next.

Guess old habits were gonna die hard.

"Yeah." Donovan didn't let that stop him from cracking the bottle open and pouring a few inches of whiskey into each glass. "But you've had the whole calm, cool, and collected thing going on ever since I met you nine years ago. Since it looks like you're going to kick that shit to the curb today . . . I figure we might as well drink while you tell me what the hell is going on."

Fair enough. It wasn't as if a little early-morning Jameson was going to elbow out all the other things threatening to level him. "It's kind of a long story."

"Oh, I got that," Donovan said, handing over one of the glasses as he parked himself at Cole's kitchen table. "You should probably take it from the top."

Cole paused, waiting for the instincts that had kept his feelings on lockdown for the last nine years to grind his feelings into dust.

Only instead, he started talking, and he didn't stop until both glasses of whiskey had been drained twice over, and all the details of the last five weeks—along with the story of his emotional departure from Harvest Moon nine years ago—had spilled out from the bottom of his chest.

"Jesus Christ, Everett." Donovan sat back in his chair, rubbing the back of his neck with one palm. "I don't even know where to start. You and Nelson have had a thing since the Fireman's Ball?"

A pang worked its way past the whiskey, and Cole nodded. "We didn't intend for it to happen. I swear I never treated her any differently at the house than I would've any other rookie."

"Oh, I know. I was right there with you two the whole time and I never had a freaking clue anything was going between you," Donovan said.

Cole's stomach clenched around all the Jameson and the dread filling it up. "Well, I don't think it's going to be an issue from here on in, since she'll probably never speak to me again unless she absolutely has to. Not that it's going to matter to Oz or anyone else who sees those pictures."

Donovan traced the rim of his empty glass with one finger, the suddenly serious expression on his face warning Cole that nothing good was on the way. "Yeah. Oz having proof of your relationship definitely jams you up, and not a little. Tell me something. You really think he's involved in these fires?"

Cole's frustration flared, and he crossed his arms over the front of his coffee-stained T-shirt. "It doesn't matter if I can't prove anything."

One corner of Donovan's mouth ticked upward, but he still didn't relent. "Would you stop being a Mr. Spock pain in the ass for one second and just answer the question?"

"Fine. Yes. I absolutely think these fires are arson, and that Oz is covering them up."

"Okay, then. That's really all you need."

He stared at his best friend, certain the guy had lost his fucking faculties. "Are you insane? Oz is going to bury me *and* Savannah if I say one word about this to anyone."

Donovan's blue eyes turned glacial. "I'm sure he'll try. Look—" He broke off to take a long breath in, his expression softening a few degrees. "I know the job is more than just a job for you, and I hear that. I really do."

Of everyone Cole knew, Alex was probably the best equipped to understand. The men and women at Station Eight were the only family either of them had, although for very different reasons.

Donovan continued. "The fact that you'd do nearly anything to defend your career makes sense. But for all that strategizing you've been doing over there, you're forgetting your two biggest cardinal rules."

"Which are?"

"Your gut is the most important tool you've got, my brother. And if it is telling you something this loud and this strong, you can trust everyone at Eight to have your back enough to at least hear both sides of the story."

Cole's shoulders hit the back of his chair with a graceless *thump*, realization pumping through his brain. Savannah could've been killed yesterday—hell, any of them could've. Defenses or no defenses, emotions or no emotions, photos or no photos, he had to go to Captain Westin. The beating his career would take was going to hurt, maybe permanently, but if Oz was guilty, he needed to go down for this. Period.

Cole needed to take the bold risk. No matter how high the stakes.

"I'm going to need one hell of a blueprint for how to do this just right," Cole said, and Donovan clapped him on the shoulder, his grin spanning from ear to ear.

"There's a shock. Let's trade in this Jameson for coffee and see what we can come up with."

Chapter Twenty-Nine

Cole sat back against the red leather banquette at Scarlett's, his body perfectly still even though his pulse was clocking in at conservatively Mach 2. Dark gray clouds darkened the stretches of sky visible through the large picture windows along the diner's perimeter, promising a late-afternoon thunderstorm that looked like it would have as much bite as bark.

Talk about going out with a bang.

The front door at Scarlett's opened with a jingle, and Captain Westin stepped inside. Cole had seen him from a half a block away, having scanned every bit of his surroundings on a continuous loop for the last twenty minutes. If Oz was still taking the scenic route through Cole's off-time, he was either doing it with a high-powered telephoto lens or an invisibility cloak. Not that it would change Cole's plan if the lieutenant was still keeping tabs on him.

Oz would find out about this conversation soon enough anyway.

"Captain Westin," Cole said, standing as the man approached the booth where he'd been waiting. "Thanks for agreeing to meet me on your day off, and in such crappy weather."

Westin shook his head, sliding across from Cole to get comfortable on his side of the booth. "No problem at all. You had a hell of a day yesterday with that nightclub fire. You feeling all right?"

Westin's light brown eyes creased at the edges in genuine concern, but Cole nodded to set his mind at ease.

"I'm fine." *Now or never, and never isn't an option.* "I do have something that I need to discuss with you, though, and it couldn't wait until next shift."

"Sounds serious," Westin said, putting a hold on saying anything further while a waitress came by to fill both coffee mugs on the table, then leave the carafe at the captain's request.

Cole took a deep breath, but he didn't hesitate. "It's a bit of a long story, but it's one you need to hear, and it's one I need to share, regardless of the consequences."

Point by point, he told Westin everything he'd discovered in the last five weeks, outlining the details from first the warehouse fire, then the blaze at the restaurant, complete with what he'd uncovered at both scenes. The story grew decidedly more difficult to tell when he admitted his relationship with Savannah, then more challenging still as he revealed Oz's threat along with the details of their heated argument at the hospital yesterday. Westin listened carefully, not interrupting even though his facial expressions very clearly ran the gamut from shock to anger to disbelief. Finally, when the whole story was nearly out, Cole pressed his palms into the Formica in front of him, his throat knotting up with emotion as he put the last piece of the truth into place.

"I know that Oz has been a firefighter for a damn long time, and that his side of the story is going to contradict mine. I also know that he's going to raise some pretty serious counterclaims, some of which are true. In fact, I know it so well, I damn near didn't have this conversation with you at all. But I was trained to trust the chain of command and do what's right above all else. So even if it costs me my job, I'd like to respectfully request that the FFD be called in to conduct a formal investigation on these fires and on Lieutenant Osborne's involvement in them."

For a minute, then two, Captain Westin remained quiet. When the two minutes doubled yet again, Cole began to silently panic. Westin had always been a fair man, one Cole had respected since he'd met him on Day One. But Oz's Day One had preceded Cole's by an entire generation, and Oz had proof of his allegations where Cole had squat in black-and-white.

"Those are some extremely grave allegations, Everett. Are you sure you're prepared to act on them?"

This is it. But even with the dread pumping full-bore in his bloodstream, Cole refused to say anything other than the truth. "Yes sir. I am."

"I see. Then I suppose our next step is to get your statement and have the arson investigation team open a case to examine the evidence more closely."

Cole shook his head, certain he'd misheard the captain. "You believe me?"

Westin's gray-blond brows lifted slightly, as if their surprise was mutual. "I believe both sides of the story are plausible, and the only way to find out where the truth lies is to uncover it impartially. You just said you're prepared to act, and if everything else you've told me is true, an investigation does seem necessary in this case."

Cole's heart picked up speed in his chest. "I would never make any of this up or threaten or discredit another firefighter the way Oz is claiming."

"You've been one of my best and brightest for eight years, Everett. I don't believe that you would, but remember, Oz hasn't made claims about anything yet. No matter what he's done or not done, he's due a fair investigation."

"Okay," Cole said slowly. "So what happens from here?"

"After you give your statement, Oz will be contacted for an interview. In the meantime, arson will roll up their sleeves and get to work on new reports and scene investigations." Westin paused, his gaze hardening. "If Oz had a hand in any wrongdoing, I feel confident the investigation will show that. But if he didn't . . ."

"I understand, Cap." Cole didn't hesitate. This was the right thing to do. The *only* thing. "I know the risks, and I'm willing to take them."

Westin nodded in acknowledgment. "I see that. You had everything to lose by bringing this to my attention, and yet you did it anyway, despite knowing you'd have to reveal personal information that would put your own position in jeopardy. Speaking of which"—his mouth bent into a definite frown—"let's address the issue of you and Ms. Nelson."

The reference to Cole's relationship with Savannah made his gut twist and drop, but he held his gaze steady on Westin's. "With respect, sir. There's no issue to address. I mean, there was an issue, obviously." He broke off, and Christ, was his chest going to feel like someone had used it for batting practice every time someone mentioned her name? "But there isn't now."

"So you and Nelson are no longer involved?"

Affirmative on the batting practice thing. Not that he didn't deserve it 100 percent after everything he'd said to her. "No sir. We're not."

"I see." One look at the captain's face told Cole that he understood the situation, plain as daylight. "Well, then, I suppose that saves me from having to remind you that the rules at Station Eight are in place for a reason, and they are not optional. I expect you to follow them, to the letter."

Cole sat up as tall as his spine would allow. "Copy that, sir. I understand."

"Good, because I'm not interested in repeating myself. Since there's no longer a conflict of interest here, I don't think we'll need to make any changes to C-shift's personnel. Provided the two of you can still maintain a strong professional relationship, that is."

"Of course," Cole said. Yes, being around Savannah was going to sting like a son of a bitch, but they were adults. She took the job seriously, and so did he.

Fuck, he missed her.

Westin cleared his throat, although his expression wasn't unkind. "I know I don't need to remind you that being a firefighter isn't like most other jobs. I'm not just asking if you can work with her, Everett. I need to know if you two can have each other's backs."

Cole didn't hesitate, just answered. "Yes. I give you my word that I will have Savannah's back, no matter what."

Even if she never knew it.

Savannah walked into Station Eight's engine bay with her medical clearance in her hand and her heart in her throat. She'd had to miss roll call—the orthopedist's office didn't open until eight, and even though the doc had snuck her in a half an hour before they officially opened up shop, she'd still needed the final okay in order to go back to work. But after a day and a half of staring at the walls in her brother's apartment while weighing every plan of action under the sun, Savannah knew what she had to do.

No matter how painful the consequences were.

"Hey! Look who's back. You're earning your nickname, Tough Stuff," Donovan called out as she made her way across the engine bay, and she noticed with relief that squad

was out on a call. She swung her gaze in a three-sixty, her
nerves thrumming in a knee-jerk shot of ridiculous anticipation as she returned the cheery greetings she got from
both Crews and Jonesey.

Cole was nowhere to be seen.

Don't be stupid. The same way this would be astronom-
ically easier without Oz on-site, having Cole off her radar
would only strengthen her focus. She needed to be tough if
she was going to make good on her plan.

And she needed to be reinforced with titanium if she was
going to get rid of the stupid ache in her heart.

"Yep," Savannah said, plastering a smile to her face that
felt about as genuine as Botox on a politician. "The orthopedist cleared me for limited duty an hour ago. All I need to
do is turn my paperwork in." It was as good a ruse as any
to get to Westin's office stat, but God, she'd waited long
enough. Even another two minutes was liable to make her
explode.

"Don't you have good timing?" Crews asked, snagging
her attention. "Cap was just out here a few minutes ago,
wondering if you'd come in yet. Said to send you back if we
saw you."

"Oh." The captain was a stickler for the rules. He probably wanted her paperwork from the doc before she even
thought about gearing up. Unless he'd already gotten her
other paperwork. "Got it. I'll go find him, then."

Savannah's work boots echoed through the empty firehouse, and she autopiloted her way past the locker room and
the common area. Her stomach jumped a little when she
reached the photo-lined hallway leading to Westin's office,
but she forced herself to laser in on the frame around the
glass inset on the door, placing her knock directly in the
center of the narrow strip of wood.

Nerves of steel. She wasn't just tough.

She was a firefighter.

"Come in." Westin's voice sounded through the glass, and Savannah gripped the door handle, her shoulders locked into place and her chin held high. But as soon as she saw Cole sitting in the chair across from Westin's desk and wearing that serious-as-hell expression she wanted to hate but couldn't, she faltered, all of her air cramming to a stop in her lungs.

"Oh. I'm sorry. I didn't mean to interrupt," she said, but Captain Westin gestured her over the threshold with a brisk wave of his fingers.

"You're not interrupting at all, Nelson. But I do think we'd all be more comfortable if you shut the door and took a seat."

Savannah did as she was told—she wasn't an idiot, after all, even if her curiosity at Cole's presence *was* starting to kill her. "Crews said you, ah, wanted to see me?"

"Actually, I got the message that you wanted to see me. You requested a meeting for first thing this shift, after your appointment with the orthopedist, didn't you?" Westin gestured to the computer monitor on his desk, and sure enough, the e-mail she'd sent him at 0600 that morning flashed front and center in his in-box.

She froze. She'd planned to honor the chain of command and tell Westin everything she knew about Oz and the fires, but she hadn't planned to do it in front of Cole. "Respectfully, sir. I was hoping we might meet in private."

Westin paused. "It's possible that the topic you wanted to discuss has already been addressed."

Her brows snapped together. "I'm sorry?"

"He knows, Savannah." Cole's voice was quiet, but it sizzled through her, bringing shock and relief and about forty other things.

She swung to face him. "Wait . . . you . . ."

"I told Captain Westin everything. Oz. The fires. The threats he made to both of our careers. All of it."

"When?" she whispered, her brain racing to try to catch up to her heart.

"Yesterday," Cole said and okay, yeah. She was going to need a minute.

Which turned out okay, because it gave Cole a chance to continue. "I made a formal statement yesterday down at Chief Williams's office, and the complaint went up the chain of command to arson investigation."

Captain Westin leaned in, looking at Savannah over the thin gold rims of his reading glasses. "I received an update this morning and relayed the news to everyone at roll call. After a preliminary look at both crime scenes, the arson investigation team felt there was enough evidence to temporarily suspend Oz pending further investigation."

Holy. *Shit.* "They're bringing him up on charges?"

"There will be a fair and thorough investigation before any charges are brought," Captain Westin said. "But as it stands, it does look as though there will be enough evidence for Oz to face formal charges for covering up these fires."

Savannah's mouth went dry, but she pushed her question past her lips anyway. She needed to know. "What about the pictures?"

A muscle clenched in Cole's jaw, but it was Captain Westin who answered. "Oz was quite vocal about the pictures of you and Everett."

She might be heartsore, not to mention pissed as hell at Cole for what he'd said, but that didn't mean he deserved to lose his career, especially over a pack of lies. "Everett never threatened to ruin Oz's name if he shared those pictures."

To her surprise, Westin nodded in agreement. "That became fairly clear once the evidence of possible foul play began rolling in from those fire scenes. Nonetheless, the department has been made aware of your relationship."

Savannah's breath wedged in her throat. But she'd been

prepared to confess the relationship to Westin anyway, and her contingency plan ensured the fallout would be as minimal as possible under the circumstances. "I understand."

"I see from this transfer request that you do," Westin said, and Cole wheeled around to pin her with a wide-eyed stare.

"What transfer request?" he demanded. But she'd never been a pushover, and she wasn't about to start now, even if she *was* sitting there in front of her captain.

"I put in a request to be transferred yesterday. The placement officer at the chief's office told me there are a few candidates who might be willing to switch houses with me so you'd still have someone to take your position on engine when you're promoted to squad. But I'd planned to tell Captain Westin the same thing you did, so I knew he'd need to transfer one of us, and . . ." Savannah paused. "I thought it should be me."

"No," Cole said, and even though it drew brows-up stares from both her and Westin, that didn't stop him from saying it again, louder. "*No*. If anyone's getting transferred over this, it's me."

Her jaw dropped open. The last eight years, his spot on squad, the house he loved—all of it would be gone if Cole transferred. "Are you out of your mind?"

"Yeah, actually, I am. But I nearly let my fear of losing control blind me to the fact that sometimes, you've got to be brash to do the right thing. You are an incredible firefighter. You're brave and you're smart and you're strong. You've earned the spot you have here, and you deserve to keep it. If one of us has to be transferred for breaking the rules, it should be me."

"You're not transferring from Eight," Savannah said, emotion welling around her words. This was insane. He was putting his livelihood on the line.

For hers.

"Oh, yes I am." Cole rushed to his feet, his hands clenched into fists at his sides. "Captain Westin, I'd like to formally request a transfer out of Station Eight, effective immediately."

"No!" She stood just as fast. "I put my transfer order in first. You're too late. He's too late, right?"

"I've got seniority," Cole argued. "I'm not—"

"That's enough!" Captain Westin's voice boomed through the office, slamming both of their arguments to an abrupt halt. He ran a hand over his tidy crew cut and let out a slow exhale. "Both of you, sit down. I'm not asking," he added, cutting off Savannah's inclination to argue.

They both sat.

"Everett, your request for a transfer is denied. You are an eight-year veteran in this house with an excellent record. I'm not about to let you leave." The captain lifted a hand, effectively cutting Cole's argument down before he could launch it, and before Savannah could even fully register both her relief and her sadness, Westin continued. "Nelson, your request for a transfer has also been denied."

"What?" she blurted inelegantly, but Westin just smiled.

"I'm a fire captain, not a matchmaker, but let me say this. While I run a tight house with even tighter rules, some of those rules are in fact left up to my discretion. Your involvement with each other isn't something I'm happy about, but it's also something I never would have suspected if the two of you hadn't come forward. It's clear to me that you can work together effectively, and even more clear that you have each other's backs. As long as you both continue to keep your personal lives outside of this firehouse, then I will continue to not ask you what you do when you're off the clock. Am I clear?"

Savannah's utterly shocked "yes sir" arrived at the same time as Cole's.

"Good. Now that we've got that squared away, I am going to leave my office for exactly ten minutes to go get a cup of coffee. You two do whatever you need to do to get right with each other. I don't care what it is as long as I never hear about it."

As soon as Westin tugged the door shut, Cole turned toward her, but where she'd expected to see his serious expression, there was nothing but pure emotion covering his face.

"Cole, I—"

"Stop." He stood, moving over to the spot where she sat poleaxed to her chair, not stopping until he'd gently guided her to her feet so he could look her in the eye. "I've stuffed my feelings down for way too long, and I can't do it anymore. First, I owe you an apology. It's not enough to make up for what I said or how I acted, I know, but"—his eyes flickered, green-gold—"I'm sorry. I'm so sorry. I was so afraid I'd lose everything just like I did nine years ago that I just clutched."

She took a shaky breath. "It didn't take you long to get your head out of your ass," she said, and *God,* would she never learn any decorum?

But Cole just laughed. "Yeah, but I never should've been so stupid in the first place. You were right. I had to learn to be a little brash in order to do the right thing."

"You were pretty brash," she admitted, but Cole just shook his head.

"No more than you. You'd planned to tell Westin what I couldn't at first, and you requested a transfer so I wouldn't lose my placement at Eight on top of it."

Her cheeks prickled. "Well, yeah, but it took me a day to realize that I couldn't just go telling anyone and everyone about Oz and these fires simply because I wanted to. I knew I needed a plan, and I trusted the chain of command."

"Looks like we switched roles a little, huh?" he asked,

stepping in closer to cup her face. "As long as I'm being fearless, I should probably tell you I'm in love with you."

Oh. God. "But I'm impetuous, and I make you crazy, and I'm not girly at all, and I steal your T-shirts, and—"

"And I love you," Cole said. "I love your passion, and you do make me crazy." His smile flashed with just a hint of wickedness. "I love your ponytail and your tough-girl attitude. And the only thing I love more than you in bunker gear is you in my T-shirts. I love you, Savannah. Whether we're at this firehouse or home in bed or on the goddamn moon, I will always have your back. Just like you'll always have my heart."

"Oh." Tears filled her eyes, but she didn't fight them. She wasn't afraid to let Cole see her, *all* of her, just as he'd let her see him. "Well, I guess that'll work out, then, because I love you, too."

And when Cole reached out to pull her close and lower his mouth to hers, Savannah realized she'd never belonged anywhere so perfectly in her life.

Epilogue

Eight weeks later

Cole stood in front of Station Eight's engine bay, a fall breeze rustling through the leaves and putting a smile on his face. He and the rest of the guys on squad had just gotten back from some badass water-rescue training, and man, the drills just never got old. His transition had been a little rocky at first, especially since it had gone down only two weeks after Oz had been suspended. But when the lieutenant had been brought up on formal charges, then quickly confessed to his part in a high-level scheme to cover up insurance fraud, everyone on squad had banded together. None of them had known about the gambling debts that had driven Oz to his actions, and Oz had chosen to jam back his problems rather than man up to reality.

Cole wasn't going to take that path. Ever.

"Hey." A familiar feminine voice pulled him from his thoughts, sending a huge smile over his face. Savannah sidled up beside him, wearing one of his FFD T-shirts along with her bunker gear, and damn, he was in love with her now more than ever. Even if he wouldn't show it or say so until 0701 tomorrow morning.

"I thought you might be out here," she said, her grin telling him his feelings were mutual. "Donovan just got to shooting his mouth off in the locker room, so all of us on engine are going to run the obstacle course. You want to keep time?"

"Sure," he said. Savannah had fit into his spot on engine perfectly when he'd moved over to squad, and now that Jonesey was officially no longer a candidate, they were running as strong as ever.

"You know"—she paused on their way through the engine bay to grab a pair of sledgehammers—"I believe a couple of months ago, you and I had a wager. If I beat your rookie record through this thing, you'd spring for breakfast. Ring any bells?"

Cole laughed. "One or two."

"Are we still on?" she asked, determination flashing in her eyes.

"I'm a man of my word, darlin'. If I make a promise, I'm good for it."

"Oh, I know," Savannah said, her ponytail swinging over her shoulder as she dished up the sassy grin that got him right in the gut every single time. "But I made a promise, too. Your record is toast."

As Cole watched her line up with Donovan and Crews and Jonesey, laughing and jawing and looking perfectly at home, he knew she'd make good on her promise.

Just like he knew he'd always love her.

Don't miss the first Rescue Squad novel,
RECKLESS,
available now!

SOMEONE'S BOUND TO GET BURNED . . .

Zoe Westin may be a fire captain's daughter, but feeding the people in her hometown of Fairview is her number one priority. Running a soup kitchen is also the perfect way to prove to her dad that helping people doesn't always mean risking life and limb. But when she's saddled with a gorgeous firefighter doing community service after yet another daredevil stunt, the kitchen has never been so hot.

Alex Donovan thrives on adrenaline, and stirring a pot of soup doesn't exactly qualify. He's not an expert at following the rules either, not even when they come from the stubborn, sexy daughter of the man who's not only his boss, but his mentor. Determined to show Zoe that not every risk ends in catastrophe, Alex challenges her both in the kitchen and out. One reckless step leads to another, but will falling for each other be a risk worth taking, or will it just get them burned?

Praise for Kimberly Kincaid and her novels

"An author on the rise."
—*RT Book Reviews*

"A sweet and sexy treat!"
—Bella Andre

"Smart, fun, and heartwarming."
—Jill Shalvis

Two things in firefighter Alex Donovan's life were dead certain. The first was where there was smoke, you could bet your lunch money there was going to be fire. The second was wherever there was fire, Alex wanted in.

No contest. No question.

"Okay, listen up, boys, 'cause it looks like we've got a live one," Alex's lieutenant, Ian Gamble, hollered over the headset from the officer's seat in the front of Engine Eight, scrolling through the confetti-colored display from dispatch with a series of clacks. "Dispatch is reporting a business fire with smoke issuing from the windows at a warehouse for a chemical supply company on Roosevelt Avenue. Looks like the place has been abandoned since the company went under last year."

"Is that down in the industrial park by the docks?" His best friend Cole Everett's tried-and-true smile disappeared as he reached down from the seat next to Alex to yank his turnout gear over his navy-blue uniform pants, and yeah. This wasn't going to be your average cat stuck in a tree scenario.

"Yup. Nearest cross street is Euclid, which puts it four blocks up from the water and smack in the middle of

Industrial Row." Gamble looked over his shoulder and into the back step of the engine, jerking his chin at the two of them in an unspoken *get your asses in gear*, and hell if Alex needed the message twice.

"Pretty shitty part of town," he said, his pulse jacking up a notch even though he reached for the SCOTT pack in the storage compartment behind his seat with ease that bordered on ho-hum. Not that his adrenaline wasn't doing the hey-now all the way through his system, because it sure as shit was. But getting torqued over a promissory note from dispatch without seeing the reality of flames only wasted precious energy. He'd learned that well enough as a candidate eight years ago.

Plus, there would be plenty of time to go yippy-ki-yay once shit started burning down.

"Does it matter that we're headed into Fairview's projects?" Luke Slater asked from Alex's other side, yanking his coat closed over his turnout gear with more attitude than anyone with three weeks' experience had a right to.

Hello. The candidate has a sore spot. Not that it would change Alex's response, or his delivery. Sugarcoating things was for ass-kissers and candy store owners, and neither title was ever going to go on his résumé.

He fixed Slater with a hard stare. "It does when there are probably squatters inside the building, Einstein. How do you think a fire starts in an abandoned warehouse anyway?" Even money said the place hadn't seen running electricity in a dog's age. With the city still in the hard grip of winter, there was zero percent chance this call site had nobody home.

"Oh." Luke dropped his chin for just a split second before picking up the slack with the rest of his gear. "Guess I wasn't thinking of it like that."

But Alex just shrugged. He'd never been one for getting

his boxers in a wad, let alone keeping 'em that way. Especially over the small stuff.

After all, life was too short. And hell if he didn't know *that*, up close and personal.

"Gotta use it for more than a hat rack, rookie." Alex tossed back the emotion in his chest like a double shot of Crown Royal, and it burned just the same as he slapped the kid's helmet with a gloved hand. "You'll learn."

Gamble eighty-sixed his smile just a second too late for Alex to miss it, the wail of the overhead sirens competing with the lieutenant's voice over the headset as he blanked the momentary blip of amusement from his face. "There's no reported entrapment, but Teflon's right. An abandoned warehouse in a neighborhood like this is ripe for squatters, even in the daytime. Plus—" Gamble broke off, the seriousness in his voice going full-on grim. "We don't know what kind of chemicals might've been left in the place. We need to go by the book on this one. Thirteen's already on-scene."

"Outstanding," Cole muttered, tacking on a few choice words to the contrary about their rival house, and Alex's gut nose-dived in agreement.

"Those guys are a bag full of dicks." Not to mention their captain was a douchebag of unrivaled proportions. Alex might not stay mad at most people for long, but he sure as hell knew a jackass when he laid eyes on one.

"I mean it, Teflon." Gamble's warning went from dark to dangerous in the span of half a breath. "I don't like those ass-clowns at Thirteen any more than you do, but a call's a call. Head up, eyes forward."

"Yeah, yeah. Copy that." Alex took off his headset, his mutter falling prey to the combination of Engine Eight's growl and the rush of noise that accompanied the final prep for a real-deal call. He went the inhale-exhale route as he triple-checked his gear, monitoring his breath along with his time as they approached the edge of town leading into Fairview's shabbier waterside neighborhoods.

"So, um, how come your nickname is Teflon?" Slater shifted against the SCOTT pack already strapped to his back, the heel of one boot doing a steady bounce against the scuffed black floor of the engine.

Alex's laugh welled up from behind his sternum, and what the hell. The rookie might be ten pounds of nerves stuffed into a five-pound bag, but at least he was curious, too. "I guess you could say it's because I've got special talents."

Slater's head jerked back. "You cook?"

Cole flipped the mouthpiece of his headset upward, tugging the thing off one ear to interject. "Hell no," he said, although his tone coupled with his laugh to cancel out any heat from the words. "Clearly you didn't partake in dinner last week when he was on KP."

"Hey," Alex argued, although he had a whole lot of nothing to back it up. He was a single guy who'd lived all by his lonesome for twelve years. Sue him for not being a gourmet chef. "Dinner wasn't that bad."

"Dude. You fucked up spaghetti."

"Italian cuisine can be extremely tricky." He tried on his very best cocky smile, the one that got him out of speeding tickets and into the panties of every pretty woman he set his sights on, but of course, Mr. Calm, Cool, and Buzzkill just snorted.

"The directions are on the freaking box." Cole lifted a hand to stop Alex from going for round two, turning his attention back to Slater. "To answer your question, Donovan here got his nickname for exactly what you just witnessed."

The candidate's dark brows lifted upward, nearly disappearing beneath the still-shiny visor on his helmet. "Which is . . . ?"

"He's slick enough to sell a cape to Superman. No matter what he gets himself into—and believe me, I've seen him get into some high-level shit—he talks his way right out of it. Trouble always slides right off him."

"Ah." Understanding dawned on Slater's face, and he swung his gaze from Cole to Alex. "Nothing ever sticks to Teflon."

"Nope," Alex said with a grin. Going through life on a bunch of should-haves and maybes was about as appealing as a prostate exam with a root canal chaser. If he wanted something, he did it without hesitation. Dealing with consequences was for after the fact, and despite Cole's smart-ass delivery, he wasn't wrong. Alex could handle anything that came his way, no matter how big, how bad, or how dangerous.

And he tempted all three on a regular basis.

Connect with Us

Visit us online at
KensingtonBooks.com
to read more from your favorite authors, see books
by series, view reading group guides, and more.

Join us on social media

for sneak peeks, chances to win books and prize packs,
and to share your thoughts with other readers.

facebook.com/kensingtonpublishing
twitter.com/kensingtonbooks

Tell us what you think!

To share your thoughts, submit a review,
or sign up for our eNewsletters, please visit:
KensingtonBooks.com/TellUs.